WHY KINGS CONFESS

WHY KINGS CONFESS

A Sebastian St. Cyr Mystery

C. S. HARRIS

AN OBSIDIAN MYSTERY

OBSIDIAN
Published by the Penguin Group
Penguin Group (USA) LLC, 375 Hudson Street,
New York, New York 10014

USA | Canada | UK | Ireland | Australia | New Zealand | India | South Africa | China
penguin.com
A Penguin Random House Company

First published by Obsidian, an imprint of New American Library,
a division of Penguin Group (USA) LLC

First Printing, March 2014

LIBRARY OF CONGRESS CATALOGING-IN-PUBLICATION DATA:

Harris, C. S.
Why kings confess: a Sebastian St. Cyr mystery/C. S. Harris.
pages cm
"An Obsidian mystery."
ISBN 978-0-451-41755-8
1. Saint Cyr, Sebastian (Fictitious character)—Fiction. 2. Private investigators—England—
London—Fiction. 3. Nobility—England—Fiction. 4. Physicians—Crimes against—Fiction. 5.
Great Britain—History—George III, 1760–1820—Fiction. 6. France—History—1789–1815—
Fiction. I. Title.
PS3566.R5877W4787 2014
813'.54—dc23   2013033807

Printed in the United States of America
1   3   5   7   9   10   8   6   4   2

Set in Weiss
Designed by Elke Sigal

For Ellen Edwards

He that covereth his sins shall not prosper;
but whoso confesseth and foresaketh them shall have mercy.

—PROVERBS 28:13

French Royal Family

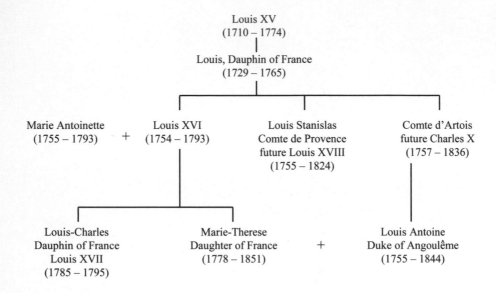

Louis XV
(1710 – 1774)

Louis, Dauphin of France
(1729 – 1765)

Marie Antoinette
(1755 – 1793)   +   Louis XVI
(1754 – 1793)

Louis Stanislas
Comte de Provence
future Louis XVIII
(1755 – 1824)

Comte d'Artois
future Charles X
(1757 – 1836)

Louis-Charles
Dauphin of France
Louis XVII
(1785 – 1795)

Marie-Therese
Daughter of France
(1778 – 1851)   +   Louis Antoine
Duke of Angoulême
(1755 – 1844)

Please note: members of the French royal family not mentioned in the book are omitted for the sake of clarity.

WHY KINGS CONFESS

Chapter 1

*P*aul Gibson lurched down the dark, narrow lane, his face raw from the cold, his fingers numb. There were times when he wandered these alleyways lost in brightly hued reveries of opium-induced euphoria. But not tonight. Tonight, Gibson clenched his jaw and tried to focus on the tap-tap of his wooden leg on the icy cobbles, the reedy wail of a babe carried on the night wind—anything that might distract his mind from the restless, hungering need that drenched his thin frame with sweat and tormented him with ghosts of what could be.

When he first noticed the woman, he thought her an apparition, a mirage of gray wool and velvet lying crumpled beside the entrance to a fetid passageway. But as he drew nearer, he saw pale flesh and the gleaming dark wetness of blood and knew she was only too real.

He drew up sharply, the dank, briny air of the nearby Thames rasping in his throat. Cat's Hole, they called this narrow lane, a refuge for thieves, prostitutes, and all the desperate dispossessed of England and beyond. He could feel his heart pounding; the stars glittered like shards of broken glass in the thin slice of cold black sky visible between the looming rooftops above. He hesitated perhaps longer than he should have. But he was a surgeon, his life dedicated to the care of others.

He pushed himself forward again.

She lay curled half on her side, one hand flung out palm up, eyes closed. He hunkered down awkwardly beside her, fingertips searching for a pulse in her slim neck. Her face was delicately boned and framed by a riot of long, flame red hair, her lashes dark and thick against the pale flesh of her smooth cheeks, her lips purple-blue with cold. Or death.

But at his touch, her eyelids fluttered open, her chest jerking on a sob and a broken, whispered prayer. *"Sainte Marie, Mère de Dieu, priez pour nous pauvres pécheurs . . ."*

"It's all right; I'm here to help you," he said gently, wondering whether she could even understand him. "Where are you hurt?"

The entire side of her head, he now saw, was matted with blood. Wide-eyed and frightened, she fixed her gaze on him. Then her focus shifted to where the black mouth of the passage yawned beside them. "Damion . . ." Her hand jerked up to clutch his sleeve. "Is he all right?"

Gibson followed her gaze. The man's body was more difficult to discern, a dark, motionless mass deep in the shadows. Gibson shook his head. "I don't know."

Her grip on his arm twisted convulsively. "Go to him. Please."

Nodding, Gibson surged upright, staggering slightly as his wooden peg took his weight and the phantom pains of a long-gone limb ripped through him.

The passage reeked of rot and excrement and the familiar coppery stench of spilled blood. The man lay sprawled on his back beside a pile of broken hogsheads and crates. It was with difficulty that Gibson picked out the once snowy white folds of a cravat, the silken sheen of what had been a fine waistcoat but was now a blood-soaked mess, horribly ripped.

"Tell me," said the woman. "Tell me he lives."

But Gibson could only stare at the body before him. The man's eyes were wide and sightless, his handsome young face pallid, his outflung arms stiffening in the cold. Someone had hacked open the corpse's chest with a ruthless savagery that spoke of rage tinged with madness. And where the heart should have been gaped only an open cavity.

Bloody and empty.

Chapter 2

*T*he dream began as it often did, with the sun shining golden warm and the laughter of children at play floating on an orange blossom–scented breeze.

Sebastian St. Cyr, Viscount Devlin, moved restlessly in his sleep, for he knew only too well what was to come. The thunder of galloping horses. A shouted order. The hiss of sabers drawn with deadly purpose from well-oiled scabbards. He gave a low moan.

"Devlin?"

Laughter turned to screams of terror. His vision filled with slashing hooves and bare steel stained dark with innocent blood.

"Devlin."

He opened his eyes, his chest heaving as he sucked in a deep, ragged breath. He felt his wife's gentle fingertips touch his lips. Her face rose above him in the darkness, her features pale in the glow of the fire that still burned warm on the bedroom hearth. "It's a dream," she whispered, although he saw the worry that drew together her dark brows. "Just a dream."

For a moment he could only stare at her, lost in the past. Then he folded his arms around Hero and drew her close, so that she could no longer see his face. It was a dream, yes. But it was also a memory, one he had never shared with anyone.

"Did I wake you?" he asked, his voice a hoarse rasp. "I'm sorry."

She shook her head, her weight shifting as she sought in vain for a comfortable position, for she was nearly nine months heavy with his child. "Your son keeps kicking me."

Smiling, he placed his hand on the taut mound of her belly and felt a strong heel grind against his palm. "Shockingly ill-mannered of her."

"I think he's beginning to find it a wee bit crowded in there."

"There is a solution."

She laughed, a low, husky sound that caught without warning at his heart, then twisted. As much as he yearned to hold this child in his arms, thoughts of the looming birth inevitably brought a sense of disquiet that came perilously close to fear. He'd read once that more than one in ten women died in childbirth. Hero's own mother had lost babe after babe—before nearly dying herself.

Yet he heard no echo of his own terror in Hero's calm voice when she said, "Not long now."

He felt the babe kick one last time, then settle as Hero snuggled beside him. He brushed his lips against her temple and murmured, "Try to sleep."

"You sleep," she said, still smiling.

He watched her eyelids drift closed, her breathing slow. Yet the tension that thrummed within him remained, and he found himself wondering if it was the coming babe that had sent his unconscious thoughts drifting back to a time he wished so desperately to forget. A cold wind stirred the heavy velvet drapes at the windows and banged an unlatched shutter somewhere in the darkness. There were nights when the high, arid mountains and ancient, stone-walled villages of

Spain and Portugal seemed a lifetime away from the London town house sleeping around him. Yet he knew they were not.

He was still awake when an urgent message arrived in Brook Street from Paul Gibson, asking for Sebastian's help.

The woman lay in a narrow bed in the front chamber of Gibson's Tower Hill surgery. The room was small and plain and lit only by a single candlestick and the enormous fire that roared on the hearth. Piles of blankets covered her thin frame, yet still she shivered. Between the blankets and the thick bandage that swathed the side of her head, Sebastian could see little of her face. But what he could see looked ominously pale and bloodless.

"Will she live?" he asked quietly, pausing in the chamber's doorway.

Gibson stood beside the bed, his gaze, like Sebastian's, on the unconscious woman before him. "Difficult to say at this point. There could be bleeding in the brain. If so . . ." He let his voice trail away.

Sebastian shifted his gaze to his friend's gaunt face. He was looking unusually haggard, even for Gibson, his cheeks hollow and unshaven, his green eyes sunken and bloodshot, his wiry frame close to emaciated. He was only in his early thirties, yet streaks of gray already showed at the temples of his dark hair.

The two men came from different worlds, one the son of a poor Irish Catholic, the other heir to the powerful Earl of Hendon. But they were old friends. Once, they'd both worn the King's colors, fighting from the mountains of Italy to the fever-racked swamps of the West Indies and the stony uplands of Iberia. As a regimental surgeon, Gibson had learned the secrets of life and death with an intimate familiarity rarely matched by his civilian peers. When a French cannonball tore off the lower part of one of his legs and left him bedeviled by chronic pain, he had come here, to London, to share his knowledge of anatomy at the teaching hospitals of St. Thomas's and

St. Bartholomew's, and to open this small surgery in the shadow of the Tower of London.

"And if there is bleeding in the brain?" Sebastian asked.

"Then she'll die."

"How can you know?"

"Only time will tell. And then there's the risk of pneumonia . . ." Gibson shook his head. "Her body temperature was dangerously low when I found her. I've packed flannel-wrapped hot bricks around her, but there's not much else I can do at this point."

"What was she able to tell you about the attack?"

"Nothing, I'm afraid. She lost consciousness when she learned of her companion's death, and she's yet to come around again. I don't even know her name."

Sebastian glanced at the bloodstained gray wool walking dress and velvet-trimmed spencer tossed over a nearby chair back. Both were worn but, other than for the new stains, clean and respectable. This was no common woman of the streets.

"And the dead man? What do you know of him?"

"He's a French physician named Dr. Damion Pelletan."

"A Frenchman?"

Gibson nodded. "According to his papers, he registered as an alien just three weeks ago." He raked his disheveled hair back from his face with splayed fingers. "The fools who pass for the authorities in St. Katharine's are convinced the attack was the work of footpads."

"St. Katharine's is a dangerous place," said Sebastian. "Especially at night. What the devil were you doing there?"

Gibson's gaze drifted away. "I . . . I sometimes feel the need to walk, of an evening."

Sebastian studied his friend's flushed, half-averted face and wondered what the hell would drive a one-legged Irish surgeon to wander the back alleys of St. Katharine's on one of the coldest nights of the year. "You're lucky you didn't fall victim to these footpads yourselves."

"Footpads had nothing to do with this."

Sebastian raised one eyebrow. "So certain?"

Gibson nodded to the middle-aged matron who dozed in a slat-backed wooden chair beside the fire. "Keep an eye on the woman," he told her. "I won't be long."

To Sebastian, he said, "There's something I want you to see."

Chapter 3

$\mathcal{A}$t the base of the frost-browned, unkempt yard that stretched to the rear of the surgery stood a low stone outbuilding where Gibson conducted both his official postmortems and the surreptitious, illegal dissections he performed on cadavers filched from the city's churchyards by body snatchers. Of one room only, with high windows to discourage the curious, the building had a flagged floor and was bitterly cold. At its center stood a granite slab with strategically placed drains and a channel cut into the outer edge.

The body of a man, still fully clothed, lay upon it.

"I haven't had a chance to begin with him yet," said Gibson, hooking the lantern he carried onto the chain that dangled over the slab.

It sometimes seemed to Sebastian as if every suicide, every bloated body pulled from the Thames, every decaying cadaver that passed through this building, had left a stench that seeped into its walls, their muted howls of anguish and despair echoing still.

He took a deep breath and entered the room. "If St. Katharine's authorities are convinced he was killed by common thieves, I'm surprised they agreed to an autopsy."

"They weren't exactly what you might call enthusiastic. To quote

Constable O'Keefe"—Gibson puffed out his cheeks, narrowed his eyes, and adopted a decidedly nasal accent—"'Wot ye want t' be botherin' wit' all that fer, then? Sure but any fool can see wot killed him.'" The lantern swung back and forth on its chain, casting macabre shadows across the slab and its grisly occupant. He put up a hand to still it. "I had to promise I wouldn't be charging the parish for my services. And I paid the lads who carried the body here myself."

Sebastian studied the slim, slightly built man upon the surgeon's slab. He was young yet, probably no more than twenty-six or twenty-eight, with a pleasant, even-featured face and high forehead framed by soft golden curls. His clothes were of good quality—better than the woman's and considerably newer, fashionably cut in the Parisian style and showing little wear. But what had once been a fine silk waistcoat and linen shirt were now ripped and soaked with blood, the chest beneath hacked open to reveal a gaping cavity.

"What the hell? He looks like he was attacked with an axe."

"It's worse than that," said Gibson, tucking his hands up under his armpits for warmth. "His heart has been removed."

Sebastian raised his gaze to the Irishman's solemn face. "Please tell me he was already dead when this was done to him."

"I honestly don't know yet."

Sebastian forced himself to look, again, at that ravaged torso. "Any chance this could be the work of a student of medicine?"

"Are you serious? Even a butcher would have been more delicate. Whoever did this made a right royal mess of it."

Sebastian shifted his gaze to the dead man's face. His eyes were large and widely spaced, the nose prominent, the mouth full lipped and soft, almost feminine. Even in death, there was a gentleness and kindness to his features that made what had been done to him seem somehow that much more horrible.

"You say he was a physician?"

Gibson nodded. "He was staying at the Gifford Arms, in York

Street. The constables brought round a gentleman from the hotel—a Monsieur Vaundreuil—to identify him."

"Yet he couldn't identify the woman?"

"Said he'd never seen her before. He also said he'd no notion what Pelletan might have been doing in St. Katharine's." Gibson rubbed the back of his neck. "I should mention that, along with his papers, the constables also found a purse containing both banknotes and silver."

"Yet they're convinced he fell victim to footpads?"

"The theory is that the thieves were interrupted."

"By you?"

"I certainly didn't see anyone. But then . . ."

"But then—what?" asked Sebastian.

Gibson colored. "I was rather lost in my own thoughts."

Sebastian watched his friend look pointedly away but remained silent.

Gibson said, "If he were English, the circumstances might be strange enough to prod even St. Katharine's authorities into taking action. But he's not; he's a Frenchman—a stranger—which makes it all too easy to simply dismiss the murder as the work of footpads and forget it."

Sebastian lowered his gaze to the pallid corpse on the slab between them. For some reason he could not have named, he knew a faint, unsettling echo of that night's troubled dream and all the unwanted memories it had provoked. For two years now he had dedicated himself to achieving a measure of justice for murder victims who would otherwise be forgotten. And it occurred to him, not for the first time, that those faraway events in Portugal had more to do with his preoccupation than he cared to explore.

He said, "Where exactly in Cat's Hole were they?"

"There's a small passage that opens up between a cooperage and a chandler's shop, on the river side of the lane. I suspect he was attacked in the street and then dragged back into the passage before this was done to him."

"And the woman?"

"Was lying in the lane, just before the passage."

Sebastian nodded and turned toward the door. "I'd best have a look around the area now, before the neighborhood begins stirring."

"Now? It's the middle of the bloody night."

Sebastian paused to look back at him. "You think it unwise of me to go wandering about St. Katharine's, alone, in the dark, do you?"

Gibson grunted and reached to unhook the lantern. "Here. At least take this."

"Thanks. But I don't really need it."

Gibson gave a rueful laugh, his fist tightening around the lantern's handle. Sebastian was as famous for his ability to see in the dark as for his keen hearing and sharp eyesight. "No, I don't suppose you do. But, Devlin . . . be careful. Whatever this is, it's ugly. Very ugly."

The ancient district known as St. Katharine's ran along the northern bank of the Thames, just to the east of the ancient Tower of London. A warren of crooked lanes, crowded tenements, and dark courts, it was named for the hospital of St. Katherine's that lay at its center.

Although called a "hospital," St. Katharine's was not so much a medical institution as a benevolent establishment dedicated to the care of the poor. As one of London's medieval "liberties," the area surrounding the old monastic buildings had long been a haven for foreign craftsmen seeking the protection it offered from the city's powerful guilds. But along with the Flemish coopers, French artisans, and German brewers who flocked to the area had come thieves and whores, beggars and vagabonds. It was not an area a wise man wandered after dark, and Sebastian found himself wondering, again, what the hell Paul Gibson had been doing here, alone, on such a cold winter's night.

Or what Damion Pelletan and his unidentified female companion had been doing here.

Sebastian walked up the dark, narrow lane with one hand on the double-barreled pistol in his pocket, his footsteps echoing hollowly in the icy silence, his senses alert for the slightest hint of movement or whisper of sound. The wind had died, and with the approach of false dawn a mist was beginning to creep up from the water's edge, thick and stealthy. In another hour, these streets would begin to fill with costermongers, apprentices, and dustmen. But for the moment, all was still.

He found the passage readily enough, just beyond the battered, shuttered facade of a cooperage. Like virtually all the lanes in St. Katharine's, Cat's Hole was too narrow for footpaths; the dilapidated, closely packed tenements and tumbledown shops rose directly from the worn, ice-glazed cobbles of the roadway itself.

It took Sebastian only a moment to find the smear of blood near the corner of the passage. The woman's blood? he wondered. Or Pelletan's?

Squatting beside the bloodstain, he studied the surrounding jumble of muddy footprints and crushed ice. But between Gibson, the constables, and the men who'd helped carry Pelletan and his injured companion to Gibson's surgery, any traces left by the murderer had been hopelessly trampled over and destroyed.

The sound of a soft snort brought up his head, and he found himself staring into the soft brown eyes of a half-grown pig that had been rooting through a nearby pile of garbage. "So," said Sebastian. "Did you see anything?"

The pig snorted again and trotted away.

Sebastian rose thoughtfully to his feet, his eyes narrowing against the thickening fog as he turned to consider the deserted lane. From here he could see the massive, soot-stained walls of the Tower rising at the far western end of the lane. Which direction had Pelletan and the unknown woman been traveling? he wondered. Toward the relatively open ground surrounding the old medieval fortress? Or had they been headed east, deep into St. Katharine's warren of dark, dangerous alleys and courtyards?

He turned his attention to the foul passageway beside him. Unlike the lane, the passage had never been paved. Beneath the soles of his Hessians, the thick, ice-crusted muck reeked of offal and manure and rotting fish heads. Yet despite the trampling of so many feet, Sebastian was able to find the impression left by the dead man's body in the lee of a pile of broken crates and hogsheads.

He hunkered down, his gaze carefully assessing the surrounding area. He noted the blood-splattered wood of a nearby crate, the piece of torn, bloodstained linen trampled into the mud, more footprints, hopelessly muddled. Then he widened his search, looking for something— anything—that might give a hint as to who had killed Damion Pelletan. He was also looking for the dead man's heart.

He did not find it.

Frustrated, he brought his gaze back to that blood-splattered pile of broken crates. What kind of a murderer hacks open his victim and steals his heart? Sebastian wondered. A madman? It was the obvious answer. Yet Sebastian had known British soldiers—even officers— who laughingly collected from their fallen enemies mementos ranging from severed fingers to ears. It was, after all, the British and French who had taught the American natives to collect scalps.

Was that what they were dealing with here? Some half-mad collector of war trophies? He supposed it was always possible. But a heart? Why would a murderer steal his victim's heart? The heart was a potent symbol of so many things: of love, of courage, of life itself. Was the theft of Damion Pelletan's heart symbolic? Or was it something else, something darker, something more . . .

Evil.

And he knew it again, that whisper of memory, elusive and troubling.

He pushed quickly to his feet.

He was turning to leave when he saw it: the clear imprint of a shoe left on a broken slat of wood half trampled into the mud. It wasn't an entire footprint, only the heel and part of the sole. But there was no mistaking that mingling of mud and blood. The shoe's wearer had obviously trod here after Damion Pelletan's death.

Reaching down, Sebastian freed the piece of wood from the muck, careful not to disturb the telltale outline of mud and blood it bore.

He stared at the imprint thoughtfully. It was always possible that the shoe's owner had come through the passage in the last several hours and had nothing to do with the murder. So Sebastian began, again, to study the confusion of footprints in the garbage-strewn muck.

It took some time, but he finally found a place where a similar shoe print had been clearly pierced by the imprint of a peg leg. Whoever left these footprints had been in the passage after Pelletan's death, but before Gibson.

Sebastian shifted his gaze, again, to the slat of wood in his hands. The shoe print wasn't much to go on—certainly not enough to identify the killer. But it forced Sebastian to reassess completely every assumption he'd made about that night's events, for there was no mistaking the curve of that arch or the fashionable shape of the small, narrowed heel.

It was the print of a woman's shoe.

Chapter 4

*W*hen Hero Devlin was twelve years old, she came to three life-altering conclusions: There were just as many stupid men as stupid women in the world—if not more; she would never, ever hide her own intelligence or knowledge in a craven attempt to conform to her society's expectations and prejudices; and as long as England's laws gave a husband virtually the same powers over his wife as those exercised by slave owners over slaves, Hero herself would never marry.

She had announced these convictions one evening at dinner. Her father, Charles, Lord Jarvis, simply continued eating as if she'd never spoken, while his mother snorted in derision. But Hero's own mother, the gentle, slightly addlebrained Annabelle, Lady Jarvis, had whispered softly, "Oh, *Hero.*"

Over the next several years, Hero's critical assessment of society had continued unabated. She read Mary Wollstonecraft and the Marquis de Condorcet. She refused to allow her revulsion at the excesses of the French Revolution to diminish her admiration for its fundamental principles. And she began to write, using her research skills and reasoning abilities to work to change the numerous injustices she observed around her daily.

Now in her mid-twenties, Hero's radical opinions remained intact. But her determination never to marry had fallen victim to a certain dark-haired, golden-eyed viscount with a mysterious past and a powerful passion of his own.

She felt the baby kick again, hard enough this time to take her breath, and she set aside the new article she was writing on London's working poor to go stand at the drawing room window overlooking the street below. A thin white mist drifted between the tall houses, dulling the rising sun to a glowing red ball and muffling the sounds of the waking city. It was just the kind of morning for a good gallop. Unfortunately, one did not gallop in Hyde Park—especially when one was nine months heavy with child.

She fought down an uncharacteristic upwelling of impatience and frustration. She had borne most of her pregnancy with ease, continuing her normal activities here and in the country, and sallying forth frequently to conduct interviews for her series of articles. But over the past few days the baby seemed to have settled. Even sitting was becoming difficult, sleep nearly impossible. And she found herself filled with a restlessness that was becoming increasingly difficult to stifle.

She was about to turn back to her article when she heard the front door open and Devlin's quick tread on the stairs. He drew up in the entrance to the drawing room to swing off his greatcoat and set aside the broken slat of wood he carried.

"I was hoping you'd lie in this morning," he said, coming to catch her to him and give her a long, lingering kiss that made her breath quicken—even now, big with his child. "You aren't sleeping much these days."

He smelled of wood smoke and frosty air and all the invigorating scents of early morning, and before she could stop herself, she said, "What I'd really like to do is go for a walk—a *real* walk, in the park."

He laughed, his hands tightening on hers. "Then let's go."

She shook her head. "Dr. Croft warns me that I may take a brief turn around the garden, once in the morning and again in the evening, but no more."

Richard Croft was London's most respected accoucheur, a pompous and self-important little man utterly convinced of the efficacy of what he called his Lowering System for the Treatment of Ladies Facing Confinement. He had tut-tutted in horror when Hero and Devlin finally returned to London after spending three months at Devlin's estate down in Hampshire, going for long walks in the bracing rural air and enjoying the countryside's abundant fresh foods. In Croft's professional opinion, anything more than a severely restricted diet and ladylike, restrained exercise could be disastrous for the safe outcome of a confinement.

"Is that before or after you have the bowl of thin gruel he allows you?" asked Devlin.

"Oh, definitely before. To exercise after taking sustenance can be fatal, you know—if you call walking in the garden exercise and thin bouillon sustenance."

He laughed again, his smile fading slowly as his gaze searched her face. "How are you feeling? Truly?"

"Truly? I'm hungry, uncomfortable, and beyond cranky. But never mind that. I want to hear about Gibson."

Another man might have sought to spare his pregnant wife the more macabre aspects of Damion Pelletan's murder. Devlin knew better. As she listened to him describe his search of Cat's Hole and the passageway where the body was found, she went to pick up the broken slat.

"A woman's shoe? Are you certain?"

"Have you ever seen a man's shoe with that kind of heel?"

She stared down at the clear imprint of mingled mud and blood. "No; you're right. This was definitely left by a woman's shoe." She looked up at him. "How difficult is it to remove a heart, anyway?"

"I honestly don't know. I'll need to ask Gibson."

The clang of a milkmaid's pails drew Hero's gaze, again, to the street. The fog was beginning to burn off, the white sky filling with seagulls wheeling above the rooftops, their haunting cries beckoning her like a siren's call. The urge welled within her again, to feel the cold mist on her face and let the wind catch at her hair and be done with this interminable waiting.

As if aware of the drift of her thoughts, Devlin said, "How about if I order the carriage and take my wife for an illicit early-morning walk in the park? We won't tell Dr. Croft, and between the fog and your heaviest pelisse, not even London's nosiest busybodies will be able to tell that my bride of six months is only weeks away from delivering my daughter."

She smiled. "Your son. I keep telling you it's a boy." Then she shook her head. "No. You need to visit the Gifford Arms Hotel and see what they can tell you about this Frenchman."

He came to bracket her cheeks with his palms and kiss her on the mouth, a long, slow kiss that reminded her they hadn't made love since the previous October, when the esteemed Dr. Richard Croft had sternly warned that she must carefully avoid any "animalistic appetites."

He said, "The Gifford Arms will wait an hour."

A small but eminently respectable hotel built of neatly squared sandstone blocks, the Gifford Arms lay on the south side of St. James's Park, not far from the intersection of James and York streets. Dating to late in the previous century, it had tidy rows of sashed windows flanking a central door that led to a short, flagged stairwell. As was typical of inns of that period, the coffee room opened off the passage to the right, with a dining parlor to the left. Closing the door against the damp cold, Sebastian breathed in the warm, welcoming scents of roasting lamb and beeswax and hearty ale. But both the entrance passage and the rooms opening off it were deserted.

"Hello," he called.

Silence.

Stepping into the oak-paneled coffee room, he turned a slow circle, his gaze drifting over the scattering of empty tables and chairs. "Hello?"

He heard a quick step, and a droopy-jowled, lanky man in a leather apron appeared in a far doorway. "May I help you, sir?" He had straight fair hair just beginning to turn gray and protuberant, widely set eyes that gave him somewhat the look of a startled mackerel.

"I'm here about Dr. Damion Pelletan," said Sebastian, choosing his words carefully.

The man's face puckered. "Oh, dear. Are you a friend of Dr. Pelletan's, sir?"

"Not exactly."

"Ah. Well, the thing is, you see, we've had the constables here. They're saying Dr. Pelletan is dead." The man edged closer and dropped his voice to a confidential whisper. "*Murdered.* In St. Katharine's, just last night. Footpads."

"How long had Dr. Pelletan been staying here?"

"'Bout three weeks, I'd say. Same as the rest of 'em."

"The rest of them?" prompted Sebastian.

"Aye. They rented the entire inn, you know. They're the only ones staying here now."

"No, I didn't know."

"Mmm. *Frenchmen.*" He said the word as if it were enough to explain any eccentricity. "Even brought in their own cook and servants, they did. I'm the only regular left."

"Are all their servants French as well?"

"Oh, aye. The lot of 'em."

"Émigrés, I assume?"

The man tweaked the top of one ear and screwed up his face. "We-ell, they *say* they are."

"But you doubt them?"

The man gave a quick look around and leaned closer still. "Seems a queer thing to do, don't it?" he asked, his voice sinking even lower. "To take over a whole hotel like this? I mean, why not hire a house, like proper Englishmen?"

"Perhaps they don't intend to be in London long. Or perhaps they're looking to purchase something."

"I ain't seen no sign of it. If you ask me, it's more than queer. I mean, why go to such pains to stay someplace all together? 'T'ain't as if they *like* each other, that's for certain."

"Do they quarrel?"

"All the time! Leastways, it sure looks and sounds like they're quarreling—not that I can understand what they're saying, mind you, seein' as how I don't speak the French and all."

"Families frequently do quarrel," observed Sebastian.

"Aye. But this lot ain't family—leastways, not most of 'em."

"Oh? Who is here besides Dr. Pelletan?"

"Well, let's see. . . . There's Harmond Vaundreuil; he's the one in charge—although I get the feeling that don't sit too well with the colonel."

"The colonel?"

"Aye. Colonel Foucher, he calls himself. Don't know the rest of his moniker. Then there's Vaundreuil's clerk. Bondurant is his name. A skinny rabbit of a man, he is—spends all his time with his nose stuck in some book."

"So only four, including Pelletan?"

"Five, if you count the girl."

"The girl?"

"Vaundreuil's daughter."

"Ah. And they hired the entire hotel?"

"Like I said, they're a queer bunch." His mouth hung open, allowing his jowls to sag even farther. "And up to no good, I'd say—or my name's not Mitt Peebles."

A heavy thump sounded overhead. Sebastian said, "When did you last see Dr. Pelletan?"

Mitt looked thoughtful. "Hmm . . . I suppose that would've been last night, when them two come looking for him."

"'Them two?'"

"A man and a woman. Didn't give their names."

"What time was this?"

"'Bout nine, maybe."

"What did the woman look like?"

"Couldn't rightly say. She wore a veil, you see."

"And the man?"

"'Fraid I didn't pay him much mind. Stayed in the background, he did. Don't recollect even hearing him speak."

"They met with Pelletan in the dining room?"

"Oh, no, sir; the doctor went outside and talked to them—like he didn't want none of the others to see them."

"And how long after that did Pelletan leave?"

"Not long. He come back in and went up to his room for his greatcoat; then he left."

"Walking?"

"I dunno. I didn't notice." Mitt frowned. "Why you asking all these questions, anyway?"

"I'm interested. Tell me this: Was the woman English or French?"

"Oh, she was a Frenchie—although I'll admit her English was considerably better than most of 'em's."

"How was she dressed?"

Mitt shrugged. "Respectable-like, I suppose you could say. But not in the first stare of fashion, if you know what I mean?"

"How old would you say she was?"

He gave another twitch of the shoulder. "Not old, but not real young, neither. With that veil, I couldn't tell you much else."

The description fit the unknown woman in Gibson's surgery. But it would also fit a thousand or more Frenchwomen in London. Sebastian said, "Tell me this: What manner of man was Dr. Pelletan? Would you describe him as pleasant? Or quick-tempered?"

"Pelletan?" Mitt paused to scratch the side of his face. "He weren't half-bad, for a Frenchman. There's no denying he was the nicest of the lot—him and Miss Madeline."

"Miss Madeline?"

"Vaundreuil's daughter."

"And how old is she?"

"'Bout twenty-five, I'd say. Maybe a bit less."

Sebastian, who had been picturing a child in pigtails, was forced to readjust his mental image. "Have you seen Miss Madeline this morning?"

"Oh, aye." Mitt's eyes narrowed with a sudden renewal of his earlier suspicion. "Why'd you say you was asking all these questions?"

"Just curious," said Sebastian.

Mitt Peebles fixed him with a long, hard stare. "You're a right curious fellow, ain't you?"

"I am, yes. Can you think of any—"

He broke off at the sound of heavy footsteps coming down the stairs, and a man's deep voice saying, *"À quelle heure?"*

Sebastian could see them now: two men, one middle-aged and stout, the other taller, younger, and considerably leaner, with the swooping sandy-haired mustache and unmistakable carriage of a military man. They crossed the short entry passage and left the inn without glancing toward the coffee room.

Sebastian nodded after them. "I take it that was Monsieur Vaundreuil and Colonel Foucher?"

"It was, yes."

Sebastian watched through the old-fashioned, wavy glass in the multipaned front windows as the two men hailed a hackney. The tall, rather gaunt man with the military bearing was unknown to him. But he recognized Harmond Vaundreuil immediately. He had seen the Frenchman just the week before, briefly, in Pall Mall, riding in a carriage with the King's powerful cousin, Charles, Lord Jarvis.

Ruthless, cunning, and utterly devoted to both the monarchy and Britain, Lord Jarvis controlled a personal network of spies and informers that made him virtually omnipotent. He was also Sebastian's new father-in-law.

And a dangerous, deadly enemy.

Chapter 5

Paul Gibson sat in a wooden chair drawn up to the unknown woman's bedside, his gaze on her face. She was so pale, her closed eyelids fragile and nearly translucent, the skin drawn tight over the exquisitely molded bones of her face. And if she didn't awaken soon, she probably never would.

He pushed to his feet and went to stare out the narrow window overlooking the ancient medieval street beyond. The sun was high enough to begin burning off the fog, but there was little warmth in it. Rows of icicles glistened from the eaves, and he could feel the bitter cold radiating off the glass. Turning, he went to stoop beside the hearth and throw more coal on the fire. He was about to straighten when he became aware of the sensation of being watched.

Glancing over at the bed, he found himself staring into a pair of dark brown eyes. "Good morning," he said, lurching awkwardly as he straightened.

Her tongue flicked out to wet her dry lips, her chest jerking as if with fear.

He said, "You needn't worry. I'm a friend."

"I remember you." Her voice was a hoarse whisper, her English accented but distinct. "You are the one who—" Her eyes darkened as if with a resurgence of remembered grief. "Is Damion truly dead?"

"Yes. I'm sorry."

She blinked rapidly several times and turned her face away, her glorious, flame-colored hair fanning out over the pillow.

"He was your friend?" Gibson asked quietly.

Rather than answer, she put her hand to her head, the long, fine fingers exploring the bandage she found there. "What happened to me?"

"You don't remember?"

"No."

He walked up to the side of the bed again. "It may eventually come back to you. Memory is a funny thing."

She looked at him again. "Where am I?"

"This is my surgery."

"You are a surgeon?"

"I am." He sketched an awkward bow. "Paul Gibson, late of His Majesty's Twenty-fifth Light Dragoons."

She let her gaze drift over him, making him wish he'd taken the time to wash and shave and maybe change his clothes.

She said, "You lost your leg fighting the French?"

"I did, yes."

"I am French."

He smiled. "I had noticed."

To his surprise, the flesh beside her eyes crinkled with amusement. Then the smile, faint as it was, faded. Her gaze drifted about the room, as if searching for something or someone. "I remember hearing another man's voice. Someone talking to you."

"The constables, perhaps."

"No; this was an educated voice."

"Ah. That would have been Lord Devlin."

"Devlin?"

"He's a friend of mine."

She was silent for a moment, lost in her own dark thoughts. Then she said, "You did not tell me what is wrong with my head."

"I suspect you were either hit, or you struck the side of your head when you fell."

"How badly am I injured?"

"I don't think the skull is fractured. But I'm worried about concussion."

"Are my pupils dilated?"

"No." The question revealed a depth of medical understanding he wouldn't have expected. "Was your father a doctor?"

Something flared in her eyes, only to be quickly hidden by the downward sweep of her lashes. "He is, yes. In Paris."

"Is there someone I should let know you're safe? I—" He decided the personal pronoun sounded too familiar and changed it. "*We* don't even know your name."

Again she studied his face, as if assessing him. "My name is Alexandrie Sauvage. I live alone, with only a servant. But Karmele is a good woman and is doubtless concerned about what has become of me."

"I'll see she knows you are safe."

She gave him directions to her rooms in Golden Square. Then she fell silent, her eyes drifting half-closed. But she was still alert—tense, even. And Gibson suspected her thoughts had returned to the man whose corpse lay in the outbuilding at the base of the yard.

Gibson said, "Do you remember why you were in Cat's Hole last night?"

Her gaze refocused on his face. "Yes, of course; Damion had agreed to go with me to see the child."

"Child? What child?"

"There is a Frenchwoman—Madame Claire Bisette—who lives in Hangman's Court. Her little girl, Cécile, is gravely ill."

"And did Pelletan see her?"

"He did, yes. But he was as baffled by her condition as I. I fear she is dying." Her head moved restlessly against the pillow. "I promised I would be back this morning to see her. I—"

Gibson put his hand on her shoulder, stilling her. "Don't distress yourself. I'll visit her, if you'd like."

Beneath his hand, her flesh was soft and warm. She stared up at him. "She has no money to pay you."

He shook his head. "It doesn't matter. Just tell me—"

He broke off, his gaze meeting hers, her eyes wide with a new leap of fear as loud voices sounded in the street outside and a heavy fist pounded on the front door.

Chapter 6

*I*n addition to extensive estates in the country, Charles, Lord Jarvis, owned a large town house on Berkeley Square that he shared with his invalid wife and his aged mother. Since his contempt for the former was matched only by his profound dislike of the latter, he spent as little time at home as possible. When in London, he could generally be found either at his clubs or in the chambers reserved for his use here, at Carlton House, by the Prince Regent.

For thirty years, he had served the House of Hanover, dedicating his prodigious intellect and unerring talents to the preservation and exaltation of his country and its monarchy. Acknowledged by all as the real power behind the Prince's fragile regency, he had steered Britain safely through decades of war and the perils of social unrest that could all too easily have consumed her.

Now he stood at the window overlooking Pall Mall, his attention seemingly divided between the forecourt below and the slight, freckle-faced Scotsman who lounged with his back to the fire, the tails of his exquisitely tailored coat lifted up and to the sides so as to better warm his backside.

Angus Kilmartin had a small bony face with oversized features and a halo of frizzy, copper-colored hair that combined to give him an almost comical appearance. But in the Scotsman's case, appearances were definitely deceptive. Kilmartin was shrewd and venal and utterly amoral. By heavily investing in well-selected war-related manufactories, he had risen in the space of twenty years to become one of the wealthiest men in Britain.

"The question is," said Kilmartin, "does his death mean anything?"

Jarvis reached for his snuffbox and flicked open the box's filigree and enamel lid with one agile fingertip. "It undoubtedly means something to someone. Whether it should concern us or not, however, remains to be seen."

"Does it?"

The silence in the room was suddenly, dangerously strained. "Are you questioning my analysis or my veracity?" asked Jarvis with deceptive calm.

A dull red stain tinged the other man's cheeks. "I'm . . . Surely you understand my concern?"

"Your concern is unnecessary." Jarvis lifted a pinch of snuff to one nostril and sniffed. "Was there something else?"

Kilmartin's fingers tightened around the brim of the hat he held in his hands. "No. Good day, sir."

He swept a precisely calculated bow, turned on his heel, and left.

Jarvis was still standing at the window, snuffbox in hand, when he heard an odd yelp from his clerk in the anteroom; an instant later, Viscount Devlin strode into the chamber without bothering to knock.

"Do come in," said Jarvis dryly.

A hard smile touched the younger man's lips. "Thank you."

He was thirty years old now, tall and lean, with a vaguely menacing bearing that reminded one of the time he'd spent as a cavalry officer. Two years ago, Jarvis had sought to have the man killed. Jarvis little realized at the time how much he would eventually come to regret that rare failure.

He slipped his snuffbox into his coat pocket and frowned. "How does my daughter?"

"She is well."

Jarvis grunted. His wife, Annabelle, had exhibited numerous shortcomings over the years of their marriage, but by far her most grievous failure was her inability to provide Jarvis with a healthy male heir. Despite numerous miscarriages and stillbirths, she had succeeded in presenting him with only two children: a disappointingly sickly and idealistic son named David, who'd gone to a watery grave at the bottom of the sea, and Hero.

Tall, strong, and brutally brilliant, Hero was exactly the sort of child who might have delighted Jarvis—*if* she'd been born a boy. As a daughter, however, she was far from satisfactory. Strong willed, unapologetically bookish, and dangerously radical in her thinking, she had sworn off marriage at an early age and dedicated herself to a succession of appalling projects, only to allow herself to be impregnated by this bastard. Jarvis had never understood exactly what happened, but he uncharacteristically had no desire to know more about it than he already did.

Now the two men faced each other across the width of the room, the air crackling with their mutual animosity.

Devlin said, "What can you tell me about Harmond Vaundreuil? And don't even think of trying to pretend you don't know him. I saw you together."

Jarvis went to settle comfortably in the Louis XIV–style chair behind his desk. He stretched out his legs, crossed his ankles, rested his folded hands on his rather large stomach, and heaved an exaggerated sigh. "You've involved yourself in the death of that young French doctor, have you? What was his name again?"

"Damion Pelletan."

"Mmm. Somehow, when I heard a certain Irish surgeon had been so unfortunate as to discover the body, I knew you would feel compelled to interfere."

"What has Vaundreuil to do with you?"

"Nothing that is any of your affair."

"Damion Pelletan's murder makes it my affair."

Jarvis possessed an unexpectedly winsome smile he had long used to cajole or deceive the unwary. He used it now, although he knew Devlin was neither cajoled nor deceived nor unwary. "Fortunately, Damion Pelletan's murder has been taken out of the hands of the bumbling East End authorities and turned over to Bow Street—by which I mean to the chief magistrate, Sir James—*not* to your good friend Sir Henry Lovejoy. So you see, there really is no need for you to involve yourself."

Devlin, in turn, showed his teeth in a hard, nasty smile. "Concerned, are you?"

"Hardly. Sir James understands the delicacy of the situation."

"Does he?"

"Let's say that, at least, he understands enough to do what must be done."

"Which is?"

"There will be no postmortem. The body has already been removed from Gibson's surgery and turned over to Vaundreuil for burial."

"And that's to be it?"

"I suggest you read the papers. Dr. Pelletan was brutally set upon by footpads. The Regent has expressed outrage at the growing boldness of the criminal class in the city, and an initiative will soon be launched to remove the worst of the ruffians from the streets. Those who make it a practice of attending the hangings at Newgate are in for some good sport in the months ahead."

Devlin's eyes narrowed. He had the strangest eyes Jarvis had ever seen—the tawny gold of a tiger, with an unnatural, almost feral gleam. For some reason Jarvis could not have named, he suddenly found himself hoping that his coming grandson—or granddaughter— would not inherit this man's damned yellow eyes. And he silently cursed Hero, again, for having mixed their noble blood with that of this bastard.

Devlin said, "Harmond Vaundreuil must be important."

"In and of himself? No. But what he stands for is very important indeed. Far more important than the death of some random physician. If you love your country, Devlin, you will heed me on this and leave well enough alone."

"Oh, I love my country, all right," said Devlin. "But I've found that my vision for Britain and your vision are frequently two very different things." He turned toward the door. "I'll tell Hero you were inquiring about her."

Jarvis stood abruptly. "I meant what I said. Do not involve yourself in this."

"Why?" Devlin paused to look back at him. "What are you concerned that I might find?"

But Jarvis simply shook his head, his nostrils quivering with the intensity of his dislike.

Chapter 7

A diminutive but earnest man with a bald head and an abnormally high-pitched voice, Sir Henry Lovejoy was the newest of Bow Street's three stipendiary magistrates. Sebastian had heard that, once, he'd been a moderately prosperous merchant, until the deaths of his wife and daughter had driven him to dedicate his life to something outside of himself. But he spoke little of those early years, or of the family he'd lost and the stern, somewhat controversial reformist religion that guided his life. In most ways, the two men could not have been more dissimilar. But there was no one whose integrity and honesty Sebastian trusted or admired more.

"Bow Street has received strict instructions from Carlton House that the residents of the Gifford Arms are under no circumstances to be approached," said Sir Henry as the two men walked along the terrace of Somerset Place, overlooking the Thames. A frigid wind was kicking up whitecaps on the turgid gray water and dashing the incoming tide against the embankment's walls. "Sir James is adamant that the wishes of the Palace be respected. There will be no investigation of Damion Pelletan's death—either officially or unofficially."

Sebastian looked over at the magistrate. "Ever hear of a murder victim in London having his heart cut out?"

Lovejoy pressed his lips into a tight, straight line and shook his head. "No. It's the most troublesome aspect of this killing, is it not? At least that ghastly detail has been kept out of the papers. It could cause a dangerous panic in the streets, were it to become known."

"Then let us hope it doesn't happen again."

"Merciful heavens." Sir Henry pressed the folds of his handkerchief to his mouth. "You think it might?"

"I honestly don't know." Sebastian stared off across the river, to where the jagged construction of the new bridge stood out stark against the heavy gray clouds. "How much do you know about the other residents of the Gifford Arms—specifically Colonel Foucher and the clerk, Bondurant?"

"Nothing, frankly. But I could ask one of my constables to look into them. I don't believe the Palace said anything in reference to making discreet inquiries *about* the residents of the inn."

Sebastian ducked his head to hide his smile.

The magistrate said, "And the woman I'm told Paul Gibson found at the murder scene? Is she still alive?"

"Last I heard. I'm on my way to Tower Hill now."

Sir Henry thrust his hands deeper into his pockets and hunched his shoulders against the bitter wind. "Perhaps when—if—she regains consciousness, much of the mystery surrounding what happened will be solved."

"Perhaps," said Sebastian, although he doubted it. He suspected that if the unknown woman in Gibson's surgery could identify Pelletan's killer, she'd be dead.

Returning to Tower Hill, Sebastian found Paul Gibson seated at his kitchen table and eating a plate of cold sliced mutton with boiled cabbage.

Like the surgery beside it, Gibson's house faced onto the old cob-
bled lane that curled around the rear of the Tower. The stone walls
were thick, the ceilings heavily beamed and low, the floors uneven.
Gibson employed a housekeeper named Mrs. Federico, although as
far as Sebastian could tell, she did little beyond cook Gibson's meals
and clean his kitchen. She refused to enter any room in which he kept
his "specimens." Since the surgeon had alcohol-filled jars containing
any number of body parts and assorted oddities scattered around the
house, her prejudice effectively restricted her to the passageway and
the kitchen.

But at the moment, the housekeeper was nowhere in sight.

"Bad luck, I'm afraid," said Gibson as Sebastian poured himself
some ale from the pitcher on the table and settled on the opposite
bench. "A couple of constables from Bow Street came and took Pelletan's body away with them."

"I heard. Did you get a chance to examine it at all?"

Gibson shook his head and paused to swallow a mouthful of cabbage. "Not really. Although I did discover how he died."

"Oh?"

"He was stabbed in the back with a dagger by someone who either knew what he was doing or got very lucky. The wound would
have pierced the heart."

"So he was dead before the killer hacked open his chest?"

"Yes."

"Thank God for that, at least." Sebastian took a long, slow swallow
of his ale. "Could you tell what the killer used to take out the heart?"

"Probably a big kitchen knife. Or a butcher knife."

"Interesting," said Sebastian.

Gibson looked up from cutting himself a slice of mutton. "Why's
that?"

"A dagger *and* a kitchen knife. Think about it: Who brings two
knives to a murder?"

Gibson chewed thoughtfully. "Someone who knows how to kill

with a dagger but realizes he needs a bigger knife to steal his victim's heart?"

"Exactly."

"In other words, our killer planned to take Pelletan's heart."

Sebastian nodded.

"Bloody hell," Gibson said softly. "But . . . why?"

"That I can't even begin to guess."

Gibson reached for the pitcher and poured them both more ale. "Did you go to Cat's Hole?"

"I did." He told Gibson, briefly, what he had found there.

"You didn't by chance find Pelletan's heart while you were having a look about, did you?"

"No. But there was a pig rooting in the passage when I arrived."

Gibson grimaced. "Bad luck, that." Pigs were notorious for eating anything and everything, human body parts included.

"You didn't see the heart last night?"

"No. But then, I don't have your ability to see in the dark. And I was a wee bit preoccupied with other things."

"How is your patient doing?"

"She awoke this morning long enough to tell me that her name is Alexandrie Sauvage and she has rooms in Golden Square. I've sent a message to her servant, telling the woman her mistress is alive but injured."

"Would it be possible for me to speak to her?"

Gibson shook his head. "She was restless and in pain, so I gave her a few drops of laudanum to help her sleep again. The possibility of bleeding in the brain still exists, so she needs to be kept as quiet as possible."

"Do you think she'll survive?"

Gibson looked troubled. "I don't know. It's still too early to say."

Sebastian shifted his position to stretch out his legs and cross his boots at the ankles. "I had an interesting conversation with one Mitt Peebles at the Gifford Arms in York Street. It seems Damion Pelletan was with a small group of Frenchmen who hired the entire hotel three weeks ago. They then turned off most of the hotel's staff and replaced them with their own servants—their own *French* servants."

"Why would they do that?"

"Presumably because they're worried about spies. I could be wrong, but I suspect Pelletan was here as part of an official delegation sent by Napoléon to explore the possibility of peace with England."

Gibson stared at him blankly. *"What?"*

"I recognized Monsieur Harmond Vaundreuil, the man you say came to identify Pelletan's body. I didn't know his name, but I've seen him before. With Jarvis."

"But . . . peace? Is it possible?"

"Six months ago, I would have said no. But Napoléon just lost half a million men in Russia and barely escaped with his own life. The Prussians and the Austrians are turning against him, and there've been rumors of plots in Paris. I'm not surprised to hear he's sent a small delegation to London with instructions to quietly put out peace feelers."

"And Alexandrie Sauvage?"

"I have no idea how she fits into any of this. But last night, a Frenchwoman and her male companion came to the hotel, asking to see Pelletan. He left shortly after talking to them."

"You think Alexandrie Sauvage was that woman?"

"It makes sense, doesn't it?"

"So who was her companion?"

"That I don't know."

Gibson nudged away his plate. "When she was awake, she told me why they were in St. Katharine's."

"Oh?"

"She says Pelletan had agreed to go with her to see a sick child who lives in Hangman's Court. She and Pelletan were on their way back from visiting the little girl when they were attacked." Gibson pushed up from the table. "I promised to go there this afternoon and take a look at the child. The mother's a poor widow." He looked over at Sebastian. "Care to come along?"

Chapter 8

"What's wrong with the child?" Sebastian asked as they wound through St. Katharine's tangle of mean streets and dark, tortuous lanes. The sun was a distant golden ball in a frigid blue sky, but there was no warmth in its brittle light. Ice crusted the mud and manure beneath their feet, and the lips of the grimy, ragged children playing in the gutters were blue with cold.

"It's a little girl of three. I'm told she was healthy enough until recently. She had the sniffles and a slight rash a couple of weeks ago but seemed to get over it. Then suddenly she couldn't move her legs. She's been getting progressively weaker and weaker, with the weakness slowly moving up her body, first to her back, then to her arms. Last night, she was having difficulty breathing. It sounds as if something is affecting the muscles in her body, and now it's hit the walls of her chest."

"Sounds . . . frightening," said Sebastian.

Gibson threw him a quick glance. "For a parent, it would be terrifying, yes."

They walked on in silence. This was one of the poorest sections of London, its streets crowded with low, squalid tenements built of decaying wood and mean shops that catered to the nearby docks. The wretched space known as Hangman's Court lay not far from the spires of the old medieval church. A question addressed to an aged woman selling roasted potatoes from a rusty barrow brought them to a warped door at the end of a dark, fetid corridor. From the other side of the panels came the sound of a woman weeping.

Gibson knocked quietly, almost apologetically.

The sobs ceased abruptly.

"Madame Bisette?" he called. "Alexandrie Sauvage asked me to call. I'm a surgeon."

They heard a soft, hesitant tread, then the sound of a bolt being drawn back.

The door swung inward to reveal a woman. She looked to be perhaps thirty-five or forty, although it was impossible to say with any certainty. Her face was blotched with tears, her eyes red and swollen, her lips trembling. Rail thin, she wore a rusty black, old-fashioned gown, relatively clean but hopelessly threadbare. The small room beyond her was icy cold and empty except for a rough pallet in the corner, on which lay a tiny form, ominously still.

"Madame Bisette?" asked Gibson, his hat in his hands.

"*Oui.*"

His gaze went to the child on the pallet. "How is she?"

The woman began to weep again.

Sebastian walked over to the pallet, gazed down at the dead child, and shook his head.

"I'm sorry," said Gibson.

"*My Cécile,*" wailed the woman, her arms wrapping around her waist, her body curling forward with the agony of her grief. "She was all I had left. What am I to do now? *What?*"

"Our apologies for disturbing you at such a time," said Sebastian, going to press several coins into her palm and close her fingers around them.

The woman stared dully at the coins in her hand, then lifted her gaze to his face. Her English was only lightly accented, her voice cultured and educated. She might be living in extreme poverty now, but she was obviously not born to it. She said, "Why are you here? Where is Alexi?"

Her use of a pet form of Alexandrie Sauvage's given name surprised him, hinting at an intimacy between the two women he hadn't expected. Sebastian said, "Madame Sauvage and Dr. Pelletan were attacked in Cat's Hole after they left here last night. Dr. Pelletan was killed."

Madame Bisette sucked in a quick breath. "And Alexi?"

"She was badly injured," said Gibson, "but I've hopes she'll recover." He hesitated, then added, "Do you know of any reason why someone might have wanted to kill Dr. Pelletan?"

The woman shook her head. "I never knew Damion Pelletan. The *doctoresse* asked him to look at Cécile."

Sebastian and Gibson exchanged glances. Sebastian said, "Alexandrie Sauvage is a physician?"

"She is, yes. She studied at Bologna." Medical schools were closed to women in both France and in England. But Italy had a tradition of female physicians that dated back to the Middle Ages.

"How long has she been in London?" asked Sebastian.

"A year, perhaps more. As a woman, of course, she cannot be licensed to practice medicine here and is only allowed to act as a midwife. But she is a good woman. She does what she can to help those in the French community."

Again, Sebastian's gaze met Gibson's. "I wonder how she came to know Pelletan," he said quietly.

The dead child's mother began to weep again, clutching her ragged shawl about her and rocking back and forth.

Sebastian reached out, awkwardly, to touch her thin shoulder. "Again, madam, our heartfelt condolences for your loss, and our apologies for disturbing you at such a time."

She sniffed, her spine stiffening with an echo of a pride long worn down and effaced. *"Merci, monsieur,"* she said, holding out the coins he had given her. "But I cannot accept your charity."

He made no move to take the money. "It's not mine. The *doctoresse* asked me to give it to you."

He could tell by the narrowing of her eyes that she knew it for a lie. But it was a lie she was obviously desperate enough to accept, because she swallowed hard and nodded, her gaze sliding away as she said, *"Merci."*

They were retracing their steps back down the dank, noisome corridor when they heard the door jerk open behind them again.

"Messieurs," she called out, stopping them. "You asked about Damion Pelletan?"

They turned toward her again. "Yes. Why?"

She scrubbed the heel of one thin hand over her wet cheeks. "When he and the *doctoresse* were here last night, for Cécile . . . I heard them talking. I did not pay attention to most of what was said, but one name they mentioned several times leapt out at me."

"What name is that?"

"Marie-Thérèse, the Duchesse d'Angoulême."

Gibson stared at her. "You mean the daughter of Marie Antoinette and King Louis XVI of France?"

"Yes."

Sebastian said, "What about Marie-Thérèse?"

The woman shook her head. "I did not hear most of what was said—my attention was all for Cécile. But I believe they were discussing a meeting between Damion Pelletan and the Princess. A meeting that worried Alexandrie Sauvage."

Chapter 9

"How much do you know about Marie-Thérèse?" Sebastian asked Gibson as they walked up St. Katharine's Lane toward the looming bulk of the parish's decrepit medieval church.

Gibson frowned. "Not much. I know she was thrown into the Temple Prison with her parents during the Revolution and kept there even after the King and Marie Antoinette were sent to the guillotine. But that's about it. Her brother died there, didn't he?"

"So they say. But for some reason I've never entirely understood, the revolutionaries allowed Marie-Thérèse to live. When she was seventeen, they released her to the Austrians in exchange for some French prisoner of war."

"And now she's here in England?"

Sebastian nodded. "Most of the French royal family is here—or at any rate, what's left of it. Louis XVI's youngest brother, Artois, has a house on South Audley Street. But the rest live on a small estate out in Buckinghamshire."

"What's the older brother's name—the one who's so heavy he can hardly walk?"

"That's Provence."

Although princes of the blood, the two surviving brothers of Louis XVI were both generally known by the titles given them at birth, the Comte de Provence and the Comte d'Artois. Both had fled France early in the Revolution, but whether one saw their flights as cowardly or wise tended to reflect one's politics.

As a female, Marie-Thérèse was barred by French law from inheriting her father's crown. But after her release from prison, she had married her first cousin, the Duc d'Angoulême, third in line to the French throne behind his childless uncle and his own father. Thus, as Angoulême's wife, Marie-Thérèse would someday become Queen of France—if there was a restoration.

Earnest and plodding, Angoulême was said to be not nearly as bright as his wife. The last Sebastian had heard, the young French prince was off with Wellington in Spain, while Artois was with his latest mistress up in Edinburgh. But there were more than enough Bourbons and their hangers-on around London to cause mischief.

"So what's she like, this princess?" Gibson asked.

"Very devout, like her father, Louis XVI. Arrogant and proud, like her mother, Marie Antoinette. And slightly mad, thanks to her experiences during the Revolution. She has devoted her life to the restoration of the Bourbons and the punishment of those she holds responsible for the deaths of her family. I've heard it said she's convinced it is God's will that the Bourbons will someday be restored to France."

"And the Revolution and Napoléon are—what? Just an unpleasant interlude?"

"Something like that."

They paused before the church of St. Katharine's, Sebastian tipping back his head to let his gaze drift over the west end's soaring buttresses and delicately hued stained glass windows. Time and shifting politics had not been kind to the graceful old structure. The roof beams sagged; tufts of moss and grass grew from the crumbling stone facade, and black holes showed where visages of saints had in better days smiled down upon the common people. Once, this had been the chapel of a religious community founded and patronized by the queens of England. Then had come Reformation, civil war, revolution, and neglect.

"What?" asked Gibson, watching him.

"I was thinking about revolutions and queens."

Gibson shook his head, not understanding.

"If England were to make peace with France now, then Napoléon would remain Emperor. I can't see that going down well with Louis XVI's daughter. She wants revenge on the men who murdered her mother and father, and she has ambitions of someday becoming Queen of France herself."

"So what the bloody hell was she doing meeting with a man who formed part of a French peace delegation?"

"It is curious, is it not?" Sebastian turned away from the ancient, soot-stained church. "I think I'd like to have a chat with Madame Sauvage's servant. Where did you say she lives? Golden Square?"

Gibson nodded. "You can tell her that her mistress is doing as well as can be expected."

"When will she be out of danger?"

Gibson stared out over the rows of mossy tombstones in the swollen churchyard beside them. "I wish I knew," he said, his face looking bleak and drawn. "I wish I knew."

Lying some blocks to the east of Bond Street, Golden Square had never been particularly fashionable. Built in the waning days of the Stuarts, its varied rooflines were more reminiscent of eighteenth-century Parisian hôtels or the decorative gables of Amsterdam than of London town houses. Once, it had been home to foreign ambassadors and artists. But a dull, dingy look had long ago settled over the area, with many of the seventeenth-century brick and stucco houses broken up into lodgings.

Sebastian spent some time talking to vendors and shopkeepers around the square, including a butler, an apothecary, and one stout, middle-aged woman with a gummy smile who sold eel pies from a stall. Madame Sauvage seemed to be a well-liked figure in the neighborhood, although no one knew much about her.

"She's a deep one," said the eel seller, giving Sebastian a wink. "Friendly enough, but keeps herself to herself, for all that."

The Frenchwoman's rooms lay on the attic floor of a four-story, gable-fronted house near the corner of Upper James Street. Sebastian's knock was answered by a plain, heavyset woman with iron gray hair and a knobby nose who peered at him suspiciously, her gaze traveling over him with obvious disapproval.

"Madame Sauvage is not here," she said in a heavy accent typical of the Basque region of France, and made as if to close the door.

Sebastian stopped it by resting his forearm against the panel, then softened the aggression of the move with a smile. "I know. My friend Paul Gibson is caring for her at his surgery."

The woman hesitated, her instinctive wariness at war with an obvious desire to obtain information about her mistress. Concern for her mistress won. "You know how she does?"

"The surgeon is hopeful she will recover, although she's not yet out of danger."

The woman's lips parted and she exhaled sharply, as if she'd been holding her breath. "Why has she not been brought here, to me, so that I may care for her?"

"I've no doubt you're more than capable," said Sebastian. "Unfortunately, she can't yet be moved."

The woman folded her arms beneath her massive bosom. "Well, you tell that surgeon that as soon as she's well enough, he's to send her home to Karmele."

Sebastian said, "Have you been with the *doctoresse* long?"

He saw a flicker of surprise, followed by a return of her earlier wariness. "How do you know she is a *doctoresse*?"

"Madame Bisette told me. I'm trying to find out who might have wanted to harm her or Dr. Pelletan, the man who was with her last night."

"And why should you care, a fine English gentleman such as yourself?"

"I care," he said simply.

She pursed her mouth and said nothing.

"When did you last see her?" he asked.

"Five—perhaps six o'clock last night. She left to visit some patients."

"Alone?"

"Yes, of course."

From one of the floors below came a child's shout, followed by a trill of delighted laughter. Sebastian said, "Do you know if she had any enemies? Someone with whom she might have quarreled recently?"

The woman was silent, her lips pressed tightly together, her nostrils flaring on a deeply indrawn breath.

"There is someone, isn't there? Who is it?"

Karmele cast a quick, furtive glance around the dark corridor, then beckoned Sebastian inside and quickly shut the door behind him.

"His name is Bullock." She dropped her voice as if still wary that she might somehow be overheard. "He's been watching her. Following her."

"Why?"

"He blames her for his brother's death, that's why. Said he was going to make her pay, he did."

"She treated the man's brother?"

Karmele shook her head. "Not his brother, no. His brother's wife."

"What happened to her?"

"She died."

Sebastian let his gaze roam the attic's low, sloped ceiling and dingy, papered walls. The space was fitted out as a small sitting room,

but judging from the rolled pallet in the corner and the cooking uten-
sils near the hearth, it also served as the kitchen and Karmele's bedroom. Through an open door on the far side he caught a glimpse of a
second chamber, barely large enough to hold a narrow bed and a
small chest. The few pieces of furniture in the two rooms looked old
and worn; a thin, tattered carpet covered the floor, and the walls were
bare of all decoration except for one small, cracked mirror.

As if aware of Sebastian's scrutiny, the woman said, *"C'est domage—"*
She caught herself, then carefully switched to English. "It is a pity,
what she is reduced to. She was born to better than this."

"I understand she came to London last year?" said Sebastian in
French.

The woman blinked in surprise but answered readily enough in
the same language. "October 1811, it was. She came with her husband, the English captain."

"She was married to an English officer?"

"She was, yes. Captain Miles Sauvage. Met him in Spain, she did."

"And where is Captain Sauvage now?"

"He died, not more than six weeks after we came here."

"You were with her in Spain?"

"I was, yes." Her tone was once again guarded, her jaw set hard.

Rather than press her on the point, Sebastian shifted to a different
tack. "Tell me more about this man you say has been threatening her."

"Bullock?" Her heavy brows drew together in a thoughtful frown.
"He's a tradesman—has a shop somewhere hereabouts. Big bear of a
man, he is, with curly black hair and a nasty scar running across his
cheek, like this—" She brought up her left hand to slash diagonally
from the outer edge of her eye to the corner of her mouth.

"And apart from Bullock, can you think of anyone else who might
have wished her harm?"

"No, no one. Why would anyone want to hurt her?"

"And did you know Dr. Damion Pelletan?"

She hesitated a moment, then shook her head. *"Non."*

"You're certain?"

"How would I know him?" she demanded, staring belligerently back at Sebastian.

"Do you know if Madame Sauvage had any contact with the exiled Bourbons?"

A slow tide of angry red crept up the woman's neck. "Those *puces*? What would the *doctoresse* want with them? She hates them."

"Really?" It was an unusual attitude for a French émigré.

"Well," said the woman hastily, as if regretting her harsh words, "I suppose the Comte de Provence is not so bad, when all is said and done. But Artois?" Her face contorted with the violence of her loathing. "And that Marie-Thérèse! She is not right in the head, that one. She lives still in the eighteenth century, and she wishes to drag France back to the past with her. You know what the *doctoresse* calls her?"

Sebastian shook his head.

"Madame Rancune. That's what the *doctoresse* calls her. Madame Rancune."

Rancune. It was a French word meaning grudge or rancor, and it carried with it more than a hint of vindictiveness and spite. He'd heard Marie-Thérèse called it before.

Madam Resentment.

Chapter 10

$\mathcal{B}$y the time Sebastian left Golden Square, the weak winter sun was disappearing fast behind a thick bank of clouds that bunched low over the city, stealing the light from the afternoon and sending the temperature plummeting.

He walked up Swallow Street, trying to make sense of a murder investigation that seemed to be going in three different directions at once. The next logical step would be to speak to Marie-Thérèse, the Duchesse d'Angoulême, herself. But the daughter of the last crowned King of France was currently living at Hartwell House, in Bucking-hamshire, nearly forty miles to the northwest of London. Under normal circumstances, he would have driven out there without a second thought. But a journey of that length presented logistical problems for a man whose wife was heavily pregnant with their first child.

After careful calculations, he decided that if he left London at dawn, driving his own curricle but with hired teams changed at twelve- to fourteen-mile intervals, he could make it there and back by early afternoon.

He altered his direction and turned toward the livery stables in Boyle Street.

"*Six teams?*" said the livery stable's owner, a gnarled little Irishman named O'Malley who'd made quite a name for himself as a jockey some decades before. "To go less than eighty miles? Ye don't think that might be a wee bit excessive, my lord?"

"I plan to make it there and back in six hours," said Sebastian.

O'Malley grinned. "Well, if anyone can do it, you can, my lord." He scratched the back of his neck. "I reckon I've just the team fer your first stage—real sweet goers they are, all four as creamy white and well matched as two twins' breasts. And, if ye've a mind to it, I could send one of me lads on ahead tonight to make sure ye get the best cattle at every change, there and back."

"I would appreciate that," said Sebastian, his gaze scanning the slice of street visible through the stable's open doorway.

He'd been aware of a vague, niggling sensation of unease ever since he left Golden Square. Now, as he studied the steady stream of wagons, carriages, and carts that filled the street, whips cracking, iron-rimmed wheels rattling over paving stones, he identified the source of that unease: He was being watched. He could not have said by whom, but he had no doubt that he was the object of someone's intense scrutiny.

"Them clouds might look nasty," said O'Malley, misunderstanding his concern, "but me bones say we won't be gettin' no snow fer a day or so yet."

"I hope your bones are right."

"Ach, ain't ne'er failed me yet, they haven't. Broke both me legs an' an arm back in 'eighty-seven, I did. The surgeon was all fer hackin' off the lot of 'em, but I told him I'd rather be dead. He swore I would be soon enough, but I proved him wrong. Been over twenty-five years now, and I ain't been surprised by the weather since."

Sebastian cast a last glance at the darkening, wind-scoured street, then turned away. "Let's have a look at those sweet goers of yours, shall we?"

The creamy white team proved to be every bit as impressive as O'Malley had said they would be. Sebastian settled with the stable owner, then walked out into the noisy bustle of Boyle Street. He could see an organ grinder standing at the corner; nearby, a blind beggar, aged and stooped, shook his cup plaintively at the press of tradesmen and apprentices hurrying past. A girl with a tray full of frost-nipped watercress, her face pinched with cold, called, "Ha'penny a bunch!" He studied each in turn, but he couldn't recall having seen any of them in Golden Square.

Every fiber of his being alert and tense, he turned toward home. But the unpleasant sense of being watched slowly evaporated, like the lingering memories of an unpleasant dream.

Sebastian returned to Brook Street to find Hero seated in one of the cane chairs at the drawing room's front bow window, a lighted candle on the table beside her, her head tipped to one side as she studied a sheet crowded with names and qualifications. The big, long-haired black cat who had adopted them some months before slept curled up on the hearth.

He paused in the doorway for a moment, just for the pleasure of looking at her. She was an unusually tall woman with large, clear gray eyes, an aquiline nose, and the kind of strong facial structure that was generally described as "handsome" rather than pretty. He had disliked her intensely the first time he met her. Now he wondered how he could ever live without her.

She looked up, caught him watching her, and smiled.

"What's this?" he asked, going to peer over her shoulder.

"A list of nursery maids suggested by the agency." She frowned and set the page aside. "I don't like the idea of entrusting my child to some young, ignorant country girl who's barely more than a child herself."

He went to warm his hands at the fire. The cat glanced up at him through slitted eyes, then settled back to sleep. "So tell them you want someone older. And educated."

"I intend to."

He turned to face her. "I'm planning to drive out to Buckinghamshire in the morning. If I change teams twice on the way out and three times on the return journey, I should be back in London by midafternoon at the latest. But if you feel uncomfortable about me going out of town, I won't."

She looked at him in confusion. "Why would I—" Enlightenment dawned, and she gave a startled trill of laughter. "Good heavens, Devlin, I hope you don't mean because of the babe?"

"I don't want you to be—"

"Left alone? I have a house full of servants and the best accoucheur in London ready to rush to my side at a moment's notice. I will not be alone. Apart from which, this babe is not coming anytime soon."

"So certain?"

"I have it on the authority of Richard Croft himself. And if you insist on hovering about me until it does come, you're liable to drive me mad."

He gave a rueful smile. "Well, I certainly wouldn't want to do that."

She pushed to her feet, the swelling weight of the child making the movement awkward, and went to draw the drapes against the coming night. "Where in Buckinghamshire?"

"Hartwell House."

She paused to look at him over one shoulder. "Good heavens; you think the Bourbons could somehow be involved in Damion Pelletan's death?"

"They might be."

He told her of his visit to the Gifford Arms Hotel, and the conversation Madame Bisette had overheard the night of Pelletan's murder, and his own less-than-productive confrontation with Jarvis.

"Do you know anything about a peace delegation from Paris?" he asked, watching her closely.

"No. But I'll see what I can find out."

"Jarvis won't tell you anything. Not now."

She gave him a smile that curled the edges of her lips and brought a secretive gleam to the shadowy depths of her intense gray eyes. "I don't intend to ask Jarvis."

That evening, as he was preparing to make an early start the following morning, Sebastian sent for his valet.

Jules Calhoun was a slim, elegant gentleman's gentleman in his early thirties, with straight flaxen hair and twinkling eyes. Affable and extraordinarily clever, he was a genius at repairing the ravages the pursuit of murderers could sometimes wreak on Sebastian's wardrobe. But for all his skill with boot blacking and starch, Calhoun was no ordinary valet. Born in one of the worst flash houses in London, he was familiar with parts of the city—and segments of its population—that would cause most valets to shudder with horror.

"Ever hear of a man named Bullock?" Sebastian asked. "I'm told he's a big, scar-faced tradesman with a shop somewhere in the vicinity of Golden Square."

Calhoun shook his head. "I don't believe so, my lord. I can look into him, if you wish."

Sebastian nodded. "But cautiously. I understand he has a nasty disposition."

Chapter 11

Sebastian left London before dawn, driving O'Malley's team of fast creamy whites and with his own young groom, or tiger, Tom, clinging to the perch at the rear of the curricle. The boy had been with Sebastian for two years now, ever since he'd tried to pick Sebastian's pocket in a low St. Giles tavern. Sebastian had been on the run at the time, charged with a murder he didn't commit. The young street urchin had saved Sebastian's life, although Tom always contended they were more than even.

They drove through misty flat meadows filled with frost-whitened grass, and sleepy villages with stone-walled, thatched-roof cottages and wind-ruffled millponds where ducks foraged amongst the freeze-nipped reeds that grew in the shallows. The sun rose in a muted pink haze above winter-bared stands of elm and birch, and still they pressed on, the team's galloping hooves eating up the miles, their heaving sides dark with sweat by the time Tom blew up for the change.

"We ain't never gonna make 'Artwell 'Ouse in three hours," said Tom, critically eyeing the new team as it was put to.

Sebastian snapped shut his watch and smiled. "Yes, we will."

They made it in just under two hours and fifty minutes.

An elegant small manor dating to the time of the Tudors, Hartwell House had been hired by the exiled Bourbons some four years before. Sebastian had heard that Sir George Lee, the owner, was not happy with the treatment his estate was receiving at the hands of the royals. As Sebastian drew up his curricle on the ragged gravel sweep before the manor's small porch, he thought he could understand why.

Crude new windows had been punched through the venerable old stone walls, while tattered laundry hung out to dry on the roof flapped in the cold wind. What was once a grand sweep of turf had been torn up here and there and planted with vegetables; the bleat of goats and the *cluck-clucking* of chickens filled the air.

"Looks worse'n a bleedin' back court in St. Giles," said Tom, scrambling forward to take the reins.

"Not exactly Versailles, is it?"

Tom scrunched up his sharp-boned face in puzzlement. "Ver-what?"

"Versailles. It's the grand palace that was home to the kings of France until the revolutionaries dragged the royal family into Paris in 1789."

"Oh." The tiger didn't look impressed. But then, Tom had no use for foreigners in general and the French in particular.

Sebastian dropped lightly to the ground. "Do keep your ears open around the stables, will you?"

Tom broke into a gap-toothed grin. "Of course, gov'nor!"

Still smiling faintly to himself, Sebastian turned toward the manor's small, somewhat shabby portico. Virtually anyone else driving out from London uninvited to see the daughter of the last crowned King of France would most likely have been curtly rebuffed. But not Sebastian St. Cyr, heir to the powerful Earl of Hendon, Chancellor of the Exchequer. The estrangement between the Earl and his heir might be well-known, but few understood its reasons, and no impov-

erished European royal was going to risk alienating the member of
the cabinet responsible for all economic and financial matters.

As a result, Sebastian waited in the dingy vestibule for only a few
minutes before a powdered footman in threadbare livery appeared to
escort him back outside and around the far wing of the house to
where Marie-Thérèse Charlotte, Daughter of France, waited to receive him at the entrance to a long topiary arcade that stretched toward a silver shimmer of water in the distance. She had been standing
with one of her ladies, her gaze on the canal. But at his approach she
turned and nodded her dismissal of the footman.

Sebastian had met her before, at various London balls and din-
ners. On those occasions she had always been every inch the King's
daughter, dressed in velvets and silks and dripping the diamonds
and pearls that her mother, Marie Antoinette, had managed to
smuggle out of France with friends in the early days of the Revolution. Today she wore a somewhat shabby gown of dark green wool,
made high at the neck with only a modest touch of lace at the collar
and cuffs; an unfashionable, heavy wool shawl draped her shoulders. But her carriage was eminently regal, her head held high as
she moved to greet him.

"Lord Devlin," she said, her voice oddly high-pitched and scratchy
and still noticeably inflected by her native Parisian accent. "How kind
of you to call."

He bowed low over the hand she offered. "Thank you for agreeing to see me on such short notice."

She inclined her head but did not smile. He had heard that she
never smiled.

Although she was still known in the popular imagination as "the
Orphan in the Temple," those days were long in the past. She was
thirty-four years old. As a child, she had been blond and blue-eyed,
but her hair had long since darkened to a dull brown. She had a tall,
sloping forehead, a long nose, protuberant, red-rimmed eyes, and a
somewhat receding chin. There was little of her mother's famous

beauty or vivacity about her, although Marie Antoinette's disastrous haughtiness was very much in evidence.

Turning, she indicated the woman who had until then remained quietly in the background. "This is my dear companion, Lady Giselle Edmondson."

Lady Giselle was of much the same age as the Princess, but both taller and more delicately built, with hair of the palest blond and an almost elfin face. The daughter of an English earl and his French wife, she had been born in Paris to an idyllic childhood of soft eiderdowns, lavender-scented gardens, and rose-tinged sunrises over the Seine. A devotee of the Enlightenment, the Earl had greeted the first stirrings of revolution with an enthusiasm bordering on delirium. The storming of the Bastille troubled him, but he'd scornfully refused to join the panicked stampede of his fellow aristocrats for the Channel. By the time the gutters flowed with blood and matted blond hair streamed from the heads of noblewomen carried on pikes through the streets, it was too late.

Gathering his young family, he tried to flee on a dark, windswept night. But they made it less than thirty miles before a howling mob surrounded their carriage. As thirteen-year-old Giselle watched with the faces of her younger brother and sister pressed tight against her skirts, the Earl and his wife were dragged from their carriage and torn limb from limb. Then the jeering, red-capped men and snarling women wrenched the children from her arms.

"We'll raise them as good sansculottes," they told her.

Sebastian had heard she spent the next three years searching for her little brother and sister. But she never found them. By the time she finally left France in the train of the newly freed Marie-Thérèse, she was just sixteen.

She had never married. But somehow she'd managed to come to terms with the horrors of her past and achieve an enviable measure of serenity. Unlike Marie-Thérèse, she did not clutch her sorrows to her or wear her sufferings as a badge of honor.

"We have met," she told Sebastian now with a warmth that was utterly lacking in the Princess, "but only once and very briefly, so I doubt you would remember it."

"The Duchess of Claiborne's ball, last June," he said, returning her smile.

She gave a startled peal of laughter. "Good heavens. How can you possibly recall it?"

He remembered because he'd found her life story so hauntingly tragic, and the degree to which she'd managed to overcome its worst effects inspiring. But all he said was, "Reports of my lamentable memory are greatly exaggerated."

She started to laugh again, then cast an almost apologetic glance toward the Princess and raised a hand to her lips, as if hiding her smile.

"Let us walk," said the Princess, turning their steps toward the canal in the distance. "Tell me, my lord: How does your wife?"

Sebastian was aware of Lady Giselle falling in several steps behind them. "She is well, thank you," he said.

"I hear she is with child. Congratulations."

"Thank you."

"And married such a short time! Your wife is fortunate indeed." Her hand fluttered to touch, ever so briefly, her own flat stomach, an unconscious movement that was there and then gone. She had been married something like thirteen years, yet had never conceived. He'd heard it said she remained convinced that God would some day send her a child, a child who would continue the Bourbon line. But time was running out, both for Marie-Thérèse and for her dynasty.

She said, "You do realize that I know why you are here."

"Do you?"

"You have made the investigation of murder your special interest, have you not? And a Frenchman named Pelletan was murdered on the streets of London two nights ago."

"You were acquainted with Dr. Damion Pelletan?"

"You are obviously aware of the fact that I was. Otherwise, why are you here?"

When Sebastian remained silent, she said, "He was a physician of some renown in Paris, you know."

"No, I didn't know."

She kept her gaze fixed straight ahead. "I thought it might be worth my while to consult with him."

"Somehow, I had the impression Dr. Pelletan was not a royalist."

He watched her mouth tighten. "No," she said. "He was not. But he was nevertheless an excellent physician."

Sebastian studied her fiercely proud profile. She was a woman who had been trained from infancy to dissemble, to never show her true thoughts or emotions. Yet there was no disguising the intense anger that smoldered beneath her carefully correct exterior. He said, "I wonder, do you know a man by the name of Harmond Vaundreuil?"

He expected her to deny it. Instead, she curled her lip and said, "Fortunately, I have never personally encountered the man. But I have heard of him, yes. A vulgar parvenu who believes himself the equal of his betters. There are many such in the government of France these days. But by the grace of God, all will soon be dispersed. Once the Bourbons are restored to their rightful position, Vaundreuil and his kind will be like so many roaches, fleeing before the bright light of God's divine will."

Sebastian kept his own features carefully bland. "What about a Frenchwoman, Alexandrie Sauvage? Do you know her?"

"Sauvage?" Marie-Thérèse drew up at the end of the allée and pivoted to look him full in the face. "I do not believe so, no," she said with perfect calm. "And now you must excuse me. I wish to walk on alone. Lady Giselle will accompany you back to the house." And she turned on her heel and left him there, her head held high, her spine stiff as she strode determinedly away.

"I'm sorry. She is rather . . . tense today," said Lady Giselle, coming up beside him.

In Sebastian's experience, Marie-Thérèse was always tense. But all he said was, "I suspect I'm quite capable of finding my way back to the house without assistance, if you would rather go after her."

Lady Giselle shook her head. "She meant it when she said she wishes to be alone."

They turned to walk side by side back down the allée. After a moment, Lady Giselle said, "I know many find the Princess cold and stiff, even aloof. But she truly is an admirable woman, strong and devout. Her days are spent helping her uncle, or visiting establishments for the relief of orphans and the poor."

"Is that what she did this last Thursday?"

"Last Thursday? Oh, no; Thursday was the twenty-first of January."

"The date is significant?"

She looked vaguely surprised, then let out her breath in a rush. "Ah, it is because you're not French; that is why you do not know. Marie-Thérèse's father, King Louis XVI of France, was guillotined at ten o'clock on the morning of January 21, 1793. Did you know she has the chemise he wore when he was killed? His confessor saved it for her. It is still stained dark with his blood. Every year on the anniversary of his death, she closets herself with the chemise in her room and spends the day in prayer. She does the same on the anniversary of her mother's murder, as well."

Twenty years, thought Sebastian. Her parents had been dead for twenty years, and she had yet to put those dark days behind her and learn to embrace the joys of the living. He wondered if Lady Giselle passed the anniversary of her own parents' deaths closeted in prayer with a bloody relic. Somehow, he doubted it.

Aloud, he said, "She stays in prayer all day?"

"From before dawn until midnight. She does not leave her room, not even for meals. Her uncle always has trays sent up for her, but she never touches them."

"So she spent Thursday alone?"

They had reached the long eastern facade of the house, its elegant row of recessed, arched windows forming an incongruous backdrop to the tethered goats and flocks of chickens. She pivoted to face him, her eyes narrowed, her head tilting to one side as she regarded him intently. "What precisely are you suggesting, my lord? That the daughter of the martyred King of France gave us all the slip and crept out to murder some insignificant Parisian physician in a London back alley?"

When Sebastian remained silent, she gave a humorless laugh and said, "But since you asked, I will answer your question. No, she did not spend the day alone. Every January twenty-first since her release from prison, I have been at her side, praying with her, and holding her when she weeps. No one has ever seen Marie-Thérèse weep in public, and no one ever will. Just as no one will ever know the torments she bears in private."

He became aware of the *creak-creak* of a wheeled chair carrying an enormously obese man toward them from around the side of the house. It was pushed not by a footman, but by a thin, foppishly dressed gentleman with a narrow, delicate face, a halo of chestnut-colored curls, and the steady, relentless gaze of a man who decided long ago to meet the world on his own terms and shrug off the consequences.

Lady Giselle cast a quick glance toward the wheeled chair. Then she gathered her skirts in a clenched fist. "Good day, my lord."

Sebastian stood on the ragged lawn and watched her long-legged stride scatter the bleating goats and squawking, disgruntled chickens as if she were chased by the squeak of the wheeled chair rolling ever closer.

Chapter 12

Sebastian nudged away a speckled hen that was showing rather too much interest in the shiny toe of one of his Hessians, and walked forward to meet the wheeled chair bearing the uncrowned King of France.

He'd been born Louis Stanislas, fourth in line to the French throne, and given the title Comte de Provence. No one ever expected the plump, self-indulgent Comte de Provence to someday be king. And so he was allowed to go his own way, neglecting his studies, amassing staggering debts, and growing fatter every year. His younger brother, the Comte d'Artois, was slim, dashing, and handsome. But not Provence. Even as a young man, he'd been obese. Now in his late fifties and crippled by gout, he could barely walk without assistance.

"Devlin!" he cried when he was still some feet away. "Don't run off yet! I want a word with you."

"Your Majesty," said Sebastian with an elegant bow.

The Comte de Provence laughed, his plump, rosy-cheeked face still surprisingly youthful and creased with a smile of habitual good cheer. "How very diplomatic of you, young man! And without a moment's hesitation too. Most people in your position hem and haw in painful indecision. You can almost see the agonized thoughts tumbling one after the other through their heads. *Do I address him as if he were indeed the crowned King of France, rather than an impoverished exile? Should I call him the Comte de Provence? Or I should follow Napoléon's lead and refer to him as the Comte d'Isle?*" The Bourbon's enormous, protuberant belly bounced up and down. "At least I have yet to have anyone address me the way my niece styles Napoléon, as 'the Criminal'!"

"Does she really?"

"Oh, yes; she has for years." Twisting awkwardly in his chair, he reached up with noticeable tenderness to touch the right hand of the man pushing him. "Ambrose, if you would be so kind? A walk toward the chapel might afford the most privacy, don't you agree?"

Ambrose LaChapelle glanced over at Sebastian, a faint, enigmatic smile curling his lips. "Oh, most definitely."

Sebastian had met LaChapelle before. Born into an aristocratic family in Avignon, he'd fled France as a youth to fight in the counterrevolutionary émigré army led by the Prince de Conde. When the army was disbanded, he'd joined the Comte de Provence in exile, first in Russia, then in Warsaw, where he'd risen quickly in his royal master's favor. Sebastian had heard that he owed his rapid elevation to his willingness to do anything for his uncrowned king.

Anything.

"Your father and I were good friends in our youth, you know," Provence said, his voice raised so as to be heard above the squeak of the chair's wheels and the crunch of the weed-choked gravel beneath their feet. The winter-bared oaks and elms of the neglected park closed in around them, dark and somber in the flat light.

"No, I didn't know," said Sebastian.

The Bourbon's eyes practically disappeared behind his puffy, smiling lids. "Hendon never told you about his salad days in Paris, did he?" He tried to laugh, but it quickly degenerated into a rasping cough. "Golden years, those were. Golden. Horses, jewels, châteaux, carriages, wine . . . We had it all. I once ran up a debt of a million livres, and my brother the King paid it off. Think of that! A million livres. What I wouldn't give for that kind of money now. We thought those days would never end. But they did." He cast Sebastian a quick, sideways glance. "I suppose you think we should have seen it coming, and so we should have—so we should! I tell Marie-Thérèse all the time that when two percent of a nation has all the wealth and the other ninety-eight percent of the people pay all the taxes, a blood-bath is inevitable. Inevitable!"

Sebastian had heard that an intense and at times acrimonious dis-agreement raged within the French royal family. The Comte de Provence favored a limited, parliamentary monarchy and was willing to give numerous concessions to the people of France if they would only allow him to return. But both Marie-Thérèse and Provence's own younger brother, Charles, Comte d'Artois, were ultraroyalists, stubbornly adhering to their belief in the divine right of kings and insisting upon nothing less than a reimposition of absolute monarchy.

Sebastian said, "In my experience, most people tend to believe even in the face of all evidence to the contrary that things will never change."

The Bourbon sighed. "True, true. Although I've been exiled from France for more than twenty years now. So, God willing, *this* is one state of affairs that will change, and soon. I would not like to die on foreign soil."

"The news from the Continent sounds encouraging—if you can call the slaughter of half a million men encouraging."

The Bourbon's jovial face went slack. "Ghastly, is it not? All those dead men, strewn across Russia."

The genuine depth of his grief took Sebastian by surprise. He found himself wondering if Marie-Thérèse had ever spared a mo-ment's sorrow for the war dead of the nation over which she hoped one day to reign as queen. Somehow, he doubted it. She was too busy hugging her own misery and loss to herself.

As if aware of the drift of his thoughts, Provence said, "But you did not come all the way out here to discuss either philosophy or my long-lost youth, did you?"

Sebastian smiled. "No, sir. I wonder, have you ever heard of a young French doctor named Damion Pelletan?"

"*Hah.*" Provence slapped the arm of his chair in triumph. "That's why you're here, is it? Told you so, Ambrose; didn't I?"

Sebastian glanced at the courtier, who kept his gaze trained straight ahead, his features composed in an expressionless mask. "So you did know him?"

"Me? No." Provence nodded toward a small redbrick building half-hidden by a nearby stand of oaks. "Look at that. See it? I'm told that at one time, it was a rectory. Now it is home to a duke, two counts, their wives and children, their aged mothers, and their unwed or widowed sisters and *their* children. There isn't an outbuilding on the estate that isn't overflowing—barns, stables, even an old Gothic folly in the gardens. In the main house itself, we've had to divide chambers and erect partitions in the gallery. I occupy what was once a small study off the library; Marie-Thérèse has an apartment next to the muniment room, and the exiled King of Sweden is in the chapel. More than two hundred people live here. Think about that! Aristocratic men and women raised in the finest châteaux of France, now sleeping in stalls and chicken coops. Believe me, in such conditions, very little happens at Hartwell House that is not soon known by all."

The spires of the estate's neo-Gothic chapel rose before them, delicate and somber in the cold winter light. Provence stared at it for a moment, then said, "What I'm trying to say is that even though she hugs the truth of it to herself, it's well-known that my niece sees many physicians. Even after all these years of marriage, she still hopes for a child. God knows, this family will never get any heirs from my loins, and nothing is more important to Marie-Thérèse than seeing the House of Bourbon restored to France for all eternity."

Sebastian said, "She is still relatively young."

"She is, she is. And there's no denying her mother took long enough to begin breeding."

Sebastian kept his gaze on the soaring spires of the chapel before them. It was well-known that Marie Antoinette's long delay in child-bearing was due entirely to her husband the King's failure to consummate their marriage for seven years. A number of rumors had circulated at the time, although most had eventually been laid to rest.

But the same rumors continued to swirl around the Comte de Provence's own marriage. Some said his wife repulsed him, while others claimed he preferred his mistresses. And then were those who said that Louis Stanislas's interest in women had always been tepid and had waned completely in his later years.

"Lovely, isn't it?" said the uncrowned king, his head tilting back, good-humored pleasure suffusing his plump face as his gaze moved with obvious appreciation over the delicate tracery of the chapel's arched windows.

But Sebastian was looking instead at the courtier, Ambrose LaChapelle.

The man was a bundle of contradictions. The tales of his courage as a volunteer in the Prince de Conde's army of counterrevolutionary exiles were legendary. A superb horseman, expert marksman, and skilled swordsman, he had once supported himself as a fencing master.

But there were whispers of another side to the French nobleman. Some said the courtier was known to don women's clothing and cruise the darkened arcades of Covent Garden and the Exchange, where he was known as "Serena Fox." And Sebastian found himself thinking about the mysterious, unknown man and woman who had sought out Damion Pelletan on the night of his death.

And about the bloody footprint left by a woman's shoe on a broken slat in the noisome passage where the physician had met his grisly end.

Chapter 13

"'Tain't ne'er seen nothin' like them stables," said Tom, his voice hollow with disgust. "They only got two ridin' 'orses in there. Two! An' one of 'em is reserved special fer the Princess. 'Alf the stalls 'ave been turned into rooms and 'ave people livin' in 'em. There was some old woman kept tryin' t'sell me a straw 'at she'd made, all the while claimin' she was the Comtesse de somethin'eranother."

"She probably was," said Sebastian, turning his tired team toward the nearby village of Stoke Mandeville, where he intended to make his next change.

"Huh. Queer lot, if ye ask me, even fer foreigners. Most o' them stableboys is French too. I ne'er seen such a close-mouthed set. Couldn't get no one t' give me the time o' day."

"Unfortunate, but probably predictable," said Sebastian.

He couldn't begin to understand how Marie-Thérèse's consultation with Dr. Damion Pelletan might possibly have anything to do with the physician's death. But neither could he get past the haunting coincidence that Pelletan's murder had fallen on the anniversary of the execution of the last crowned King of France.

Tom said, "I thought this Marie-Thérèse is s'posed to be a princess?"

"She is. The only surviving child of Marie Antoinette and King Louis XVI of France."

"So why's she called a duchess?"

"Because she's married to a duke, although at the moment he's off with Wellington in Spain."

"'E's a duke, even though 'e's the son of a count? And 'is da is a count, but also a prince—the son of a king?"

"I know it's rather confusing. But that's the way the French do it. They aren't quite as tidy about titles and ranks as the English."

"Makes no sense, if ye ask me," said Tom. "No wonder they can't even talk English proper-like."

The near leader stumbled, and Sebastian steadied his horses. He could see the mossy gray roof of the medieval church of Stoke Mandeville soaring above the treetops in the distance. The road was narrow here, a copse of beech undergrown with hazel closing in around them as he nursed the tired team up the slope. And he felt it again: a sensation of being watched that came on suddenly and intensely.

He swept around a sharp bend to find the roadway blocked by a fallen limb. He reined in hard, the team of grays coming to a snorting standstill. Tom was about to jump down and run to their heads when Sebastian said in a low voice, "Don't."

A man stepped from behind a thick stand of brush. He wore greasy canvas trousers and a threadbare brown corduroy coat and had an ugly horse pistol thrust into his waistband. His gaunt face was unshaven, his accent that of the streets of London as he said, "'Avin' a spot o' trouble there, yer lordship?" He reached up to grasp the leaders' reins above their bits. "'Ere, let me 'elp."

Rather than being calmed by his presence, the grays whinnied and tossed their heads, nostrils flaring.

Sebastian's hand tightened on his whip. "Stand back."

"Now, is that any way to respond to my friend's most generous offer of assistance?" asked a second man, this one mounted astride a showy chestnut that he nudged forward until he came to a halt some five or six feet from the curricle. He held a fine dueling pistol in his left hand; the gleaming wooden grip of its mate showed at his waist. Unlike his companion, this man wore buckskin breeches and an elegant riding coat, and his accent was pure Oxbridge. He had a rough wool scarf wrapped around the lower part of his face, so that all Sebastian could see was his dark eyes, their lashes as thick and long as a young girl's.

For a moment, his gaze met Sebastian's. Then the horseman blinked and extended the muzzle of his pistol toward Sebastian's face.

"*Run!*" Sebastian shouted at Tom. Surging to his feet, he sent the lash of his whip snaking out to flick the chestnut on its flanks.

The horse shied badly, its rider lurching in the saddle, the pistol exploding harmlessly into the treetops.

"You bastard," swore the horseman, dragging his mount back around as he reached for the second pistol.

This time Sebastian's lash struck the chestnut's withers. The horse reared up just as its rider squeezed the trigger.

The shot sent Sebastian's beaver hat tumbling end over end into the lane. "Bloody hell," Sebastian swore, and jerked his own small double-barreled flintlock from his coat pocket.

The horseman's eyes widened above the scarf, his hands tightening on his reins as he kicked the chestnut into a plunging gallop that carried him down the hill and around the bend, chevrons of mud flying up from the frenzied horse's hooves.

With an ugly snarl, the brown-coated ruffian stepped back from Sebastian's team and pulled the horse pistol from his waistband.

Sebastian thumbed back the hammer on his flintlock and shot him right between the eyes.

The man turned a slow, ungainly pirouette, then fell hard.

"Gor," whispered Tom, creeping from behind a nearby clump of hazel to stare down at the man's sprawled, still form. "Is he dead?"

"I told you to run," said Sebastian as the tiger leapt to calm the now frantic, plunging horses. "You all right?"

"Aye," said Tom, whispering soothing words that the grays seemed to understand. "Who ye reckon that lot were?"

"I don't know." Sebastian jumped down from the curricle's high seat to drag both the dead assailant and the downed limb from the roadway. He hesitated a moment, then yanked off the dead man's coat and threw it over his face in case someone with delicate sensibilities should happen to drive past before he made it back with the proper authorities. "But whoever sent them obviously wants me dead."

Chapter 14

That afternoon, Hero went to visit her mother, Annabelle, Lady Jarvis.

Her affection for her mother ran deep, although the two women were little alike. Whereas Hero was tall, dark haired, and determinedly frank in her manner, Annabelle had in her youth been pretty and petite, with soft golden curls and melting blue eyes and a sweetly charming smile. Hero had a dim memory of that woman, vivacious and loving and far more intelligent than she ever allowed anyone— least of all her husband—to suspect. But an endless succession of miscarriages and stillbirths had gradually drained her energy and sapped her confidence and joy. And then, one dreadful night, her last brutal labor had ended with another dead child, and Annabelle had suffered an apoplectic fit that left her weak in both mind and body.

Yet even with her nerves shattered and her memory and reason a shadow of what they'd once been, Annabelle still somehow managed to hold her own in the glittering, often cutthroat world of the haut ton. And Hero knew she grasped far more about her husband's clandestine affairs than Jarvis had ever realized.

The two women settled down for a cup of hot chocolate before a roaring fire in Annabelle's dressing room and chatted for a time about the latest cut of sleeves and the newest rosewater tonic. Then Hero looked over at her mother and said, "I hear there's a French peace delegation in town."

Annabelle's soft blue eyes clouded with wariness as she groped for her chocolate cup. "Where did you hear that, darling?"

Hero gave her mother a good-natured smile. "From Devlin."

"Oh, dear. I fear Jarvis will not be happy to learn that he knows."

"Devlin already confronted him about it. He denied it, of course."

"Yes, it's all very secretive."

Not for the first time, Hero found herself wondering if her mother listened at keyholes or if Jarvis was so convinced of his wife's idiocy that he no longer took care what he said around her.

"And it's still quite preliminary, as well," Annabelle said. "At least, that's what I heard your father saying to someone the other night."

"Yet it's encouraging that the delegation is here at all."

"It is, yes. It seems difficult these days to remember a time when we were not at war with the French."

Hero said, "But surely the British and French positions are quite far apart? I mean, I can't believe Napoléon will agree to abdicate."

"Oh, no; he's definitely not the type to slip quietly off the world stage, now, is he?"

"Would Britain agree to a peace that left Bonaparte as Emperor of France?"

"Well, *some* would be willing to see it happen."

But not others. The words, although unsaid, hung in the air.

Hero fiddled with her cup. "I would imagine the British position is somewhat conflicted, given the French royal family's presence here as the Prince Regent's personal guests. Obviously, Prinny would like to see the Bourbons restored to France—both because he feels for their situation as a fellow royal, and because deposed kings by their very existence tend to undermine the legitimacy of every royal still

stubbornly clinging to his own crown. And yet, which is more of a
threat to the English monarchy? The survival of Napoléon's empire?
Or the continuation of a long, expensive war that has lost the support
of England's hungry people and threatens to bankrupt the state?"

"Well, from what I understand, Prinny is certainly most vocal in
his determination to see the Bourbons restored to the throne of
France."

"And Papa?"

An unexpectedly wise smile curled her mother's lips. "Must you
ask? As far as your father is concerned, a compromise now would be
folly. He insists that we shall soon see Napoléon driven from Paris by
force of arms and a full restoration of the old ways."

"Yet Wellington is still many miles from France, let alone Paris."

"He is, yes."

"And I'm not convinced it would be either easy or wise to reim-
pose 'the old ways' on a people who have been rid of them for nearly
twenty-five years. The French have overthrown the Bourbons once,
which means they'll know they could do it again should they be so
inclined. Next time, they might be shrewd enough not to set up an
emperor in their king's place. And then we would once again have a
republican government right across the Channel—as opposed to far
across the Atlantic—inspiring all sorts of dangerous urgings amongst
the downtrodden masses."

Annabelle's hand fluttered up to press against her lips. "Good
heavens, Hero; don't let your father hear you talk like that! He'll take
you for a radical."

"But I am a radical," said Hero, and laughed softly at the look of
horror on her mother's face. She sipped her chocolate in silence for a
moment, then said, "So if Jarvis is convinced Napoléon can be defeated by force of arms, why entertain this peace delegation at all?"

"From what I gather, the Prime Minister and certain members of
the cabinet are more interested in the peace proposals than your father would like."

"Ah." Hero set aside her empty cup. "In that case, I should think the delegation's presence in London is causing a few nervous spasms out at Hartwell House."

"I don't believe the Bourbons have been told of the delegation. Although of course that doesn't mean they're necessarily ignorant of its presence." Lady Jarvis set aside her own cup and reached to take her daughter's hand. "Now, enough of this boring nonsense. I want to hear how you are feeling."

"I'm fine, Mama. Although I swear I am getting big enough to be carrying an elephant."

She regretted the words as soon as she saw the look of anxiety flit across her mother's face. "I'll be fine, Mama."

"I can't help but worry. You are my daughter."

Hero tightened her hold on her mother's hand. "Mama. I'm a good foot taller than you and quite sturdily built. I'll be fine."

"When do you see Richard Croft again?"

Hero pulled a face. "Tomorrow."

Annabelle's forehead puckered with new concern. "I know you don't care for the man, dear. But there's no denying he's the best accoucheur in Britain. Why, they say that the Regent has already secured Croft's promise that when Charlotte marries and is with child, he'll manage her confinement."

"Pity poor Princess Charlotte."

"Hero—"

"*Mama.*" Hero laughed again and leaned forward to kiss her mother's cheek. "I swear, you are worse than Devlin. I am not only as big as an elephant, but as healthy as one too. You must stop worrying!"

Annabelle tilted her head as she searched Hero's face. "Are you happy, darling?"

"Yes, very."

Annabelle patted her hand. "I'm so glad for you."

But the troubled frown remained.

Chapter 15

"And you simply left the body there, in the wood?" asked Sir Henry Lovejoy, his voice squeaky with shock.

The two men were walking down Bow Street toward the Brown Bear, an ancient tavern that served as a kind of extension of the legendary public office across the street.

Sebastian glanced over at him. "What would you have had me do? Drive into Stoke Mandeville with a dead man propped up on the curricle seat beside me?"

Sir Henry's eyes widened. "Goodness gracious, no. I must admit, I hadn't thought of that."

Sebastian turned his laugh into a credible cough. "I did alert the village magistrate. Unfortunately, during the time it took old Squire John to round up a couple of constables and a wagon in order to return with me to the scene, someone spirited away the corpse. I fear the worthy squire is more than half-convinced I made the whole thing up."

"For your own amusement?"

"Something like that." It had also made Sebastian damned late returning to London. He'd rushed back to Brook Street in an agony of apprehension and guilt, only to be told that Hero was spending the afternoon with her mother.

"I suppose it could have been highwaymen," said Sir Henry. "Times are hard."

Sebastian shook his head. "Aylesbury Vale isn't exactly Finchley Common. Apart from which, the gentleman on the chestnut did not exactly look like he was in severe financial straits."

The magistrate pursed his lips as he stared out over the crush of carts and wagons filling the narrow street. "The alternative possibility— that this attack is related to your involvement in the murder of Damion Pelletan—is troubling. Most troubling." He glanced over at Sebastian. "How many people knew you were planning to drive out to Hartwell House today?"

"My entire household, for starters. But I suspect it's more likely I was overheard making arrangements to hire a team from the livery stables in Boyle Street."

Sir Henry frowned. "You think someone followed you?"

"Yes."

"Dear me. I'll have one of the lads pop around there and see if anyone came in after you, asking questions."

Sebastian shook his head. "It might be better if I sent Tom. I wouldn't want you to fall afoul of the chief magistrate."

Sir Henry gave him a rare, tight smile. "My lads can be very discreet, when so inclined." He cleared his throat. "They made some inquiries into the gentlemen staying at the Gifford Arms, by the way."

"Oh?"

"The clerk is a man by the name of Camille Bondurant. He's trained in the law and is said to be a rather taciturn man who generally keeps to himself. He takes a constitutional every morning up and down the Mall, at precisely ten o'clock."

"And the colonel?"

"Colonel André Foucher. He was with Napoléon in Russia."

"Now, that's interesting."

"Mmm. I thought so, as well. I'm told he's fond of the Sultan's Rest—a coffeehouse near the Armoury." The magistrate started to turn into the Brown Bear, then paused to look back and say, "Did you know Pelletan's funeral has been scheduled for this evening?"

"So soon? Where?"

"The French chapel near Portman Square. At seven o'clock."

Sebastian found the chapel in Little George Street hung with black crepe and lit with branches of flaring beeswax candles. A row of high, plain windows showed black against the night sky, and a lingering memory of old incense mingled with the scents of hot wax and cold, dank stone.

The small Catholic church had been established late in the previous century by nonjuring priests fleeing the French Revolution. Its interior was plain to the point of being primitive, with only the Stations of the Cross and a scattering of wall-mounted tombs relieving the starkness. A prominently placed high-backed chair served as the "throne" of the uncrowned King of France whenever he chose to honor the congregation with his presence. If Damion Pelletan had indeed come to London as part of a delegation sent by Napoléon— as Hero's conversation with her mother that afternoon certainly suggested—then the choice of this chapel as the site of his funeral struck Sebastian as mildly ironic. But then, it would never do to forget that Napoléon had managed to have himself crowned emperor by Pope Pius VII.

Closing the door quietly behind him, Sebastian paused to glance down the short, central aisle to where a dark oaken casket draped in blue velvet stood open before the altar. He did not approach the coffin, but slipped sideways to stand against the rear wall, deep in the shadows thrown by the rickety wooden west gallery overhead.

A heavy, oppressive silence filled the church, punctuated by an occasional cough. There were only three mourners, scattered widely across the short rows of pews separated by a central aisle. He recognized Harmond Vaundreuil in the second row. The colonel, André Foucher, had taken a seat three rows back and far off to one side. As Sebastian watched, Foucher slipped his watch from his pocket and frowned down at the time. The third man, thin and bony faced, with a red nose and straight black hair, occupied the last row. Sebastian didn't recognize him, but he had his head bent over a book, his shoulders hunched against the cold. This, surely, was the clerk, Camille Bondurant.

The minutes ticked past. Sebastian crossed his arms at his chest and ignored the damp chill that seeped up through the soles of his boots as he watched the surviving members of the French delegation: three men who knew one another and lived together, attending the funeral of one of their own, yet all ignoring one another. Mitt Peebles obviously knew what he was talking about when he said they didn't like one another much.

The sound of the door opening drew Sebastian's attention to the entrance.

A slim, chestnut-haired, flamboyantly dressed man entered and paused just inside the door to remove his hat and dip his fingers in the holy water to make an absentminded sign of the cross. Sebastian stared at him. It was Ambrose LaChapelle.

What the devil is he doing here? thought Sebastian.

Intrigued, Sebastian watched the courtier slide into the pew opposite the clerk, slip to his knees, make the sign of the cross again, and bow his head in prayer. It occurred to Sebastian, watching him, that LaChapelle was the only man in the church praying.

The church bells of the city had long ago struck seven. Colonel Foucher frowned and once again checked his watch. Sebastian could hear whispers and a flutter of movement from the sacristy, suggesting that the priest was finally preparing to begin his solemn procession. Then the street door opened again with a noisy jerk and another man entered the chapel.

Of average height and build, he was some thirty-five years of age, with bored gray eyes and thick, honey-colored hair worn fashionably disarranged. His exquisitely cut coat came from one of London's best tailors, but his buckskin breeches were more suited to a ride in the park than to a funeral, and rather than a cravat, he wore a neckcloth knotted rakishly at his throat. He neither removed his high-crowned beaver hat nor bowed his head, but strode swiftly down the center aisle to draw up abruptly at the head of the open coffin.

Sebastian watched him with interest. The newcomer's name was Lord Peter Radcliff; he was the younger son of the late Duke of Linford and brother to the current Duke. To Sebastian's knowledge, he had no interest in either government or commerce, but devoted himself to a hedonistic lifestyle that revolved largely around the opera, the turf, and the kind of ruinous gaming hells popularized by the Prince Regent and his set.

So why was he here?

He stood beside the coffin for perhaps half a minute, his shoulders stiff, the fingers of his hands alternately opening and closing into fists at his sides as he stared at the dead man's pallid face. Then he turned and left the church, just as the door from the sacristy opened.

A bent, wizened priest dressed in a white alb and vested in a black stole embroidered with gold crosses tottered into the nave, accompanied by two altar boys and a waft of incense. With muted coughs and throat clearings, the assembled mourners rose to their feet.

Moving quietly, Sebastian slipped out the main entrance. But by the time he reached the footpath, Radcliff's barouche was already bowling away up George Street, its lanterns swinging wildly with the sway of the well-sprung carriage.

Sebastian was still staring thoughtfully after it when Harmond Vaundreuil walked out of the chapel behind him.

Chapter 16

Harmond Vaundreuil drew up in the shadow of the chapel's modest portico. He was built small and rotund, with fat fingers and a short neck swathed in a voluminous white cravat. He had full cheeks and the kind of eyes that practically disappeared into his round pink face when he smiled, so that the effect was one of cordial good cheer. It was an effect that Sebastian knew, even without being told, was deceptive. One did not achieve Vaundreuil's position without a ruthless opportunism and the kind of brutal self-interest that gave no quarter and took no prisoners.

"I know who you are," he said. "You're that earl's son—the one with a peculiar obsession with murder and justice. Devlin, isn't it? I saw you standing at the back of the church."

Sebastian turned to face him. "Decided not to stay for the funeral mass?"

The Frenchman gave a soft laugh. "I was trained for the priesthood, as a boy. Needless to say, the choice of a vocation was not mine. In my family, second sons joined the army and third sons became priests. If for no other reason, I shall forever be grateful to the

Revolution for sparing me a life of hypocrisy and unutterable ennui. Believe me, Damion Pelletan would have known better than to expect me to sit through his funeral mass."

"You knew Pelletan well?"

"He was my personal physician. I have a troublesome heart, you see."

"That doesn't exactly answer my question."

"No?" Vaundreuil slowly descended the last step, an odd, tight smile crinkling the flesh beside his eyes as he drew up on the footpath. "Be wise, my lord, and leave well enough alone, hmm? Believe me, it is better for all concerned if Damion Pelletan is thought to have been killed by footpads."

"Better for you, for me, or for Damion Pelletan?"

Vaundreuil's smile widened. "For everyone."

"Someone tried to kill me today, on the road from Hartwell House. You wouldn't know anything about that, would you?"

Vaundreuil laughed out loud with what sounded like genuine amusement. "They are a murderous lot, the Bourbons. And you have no idea what you are meddling in."

"Not exactly," agreed Sebastian. "But I have a very fertile imagination—plus a healthy appreciation for what the loss of half a million men in six months can do to popular perception of an upstart leader's legitimacy."

The Frenchman was no longer smiling.

Sebastian said, "Given that a member of your delegation has been—"

"*Delegation?* What nonsense is this?"

"—has been murdered, one might expect you to cooperate with any attempt to find his killer. Yet you appear to have no interest. Why is that?"

"But we are cooperating—with Bow Street. And Bow Street assures us that Pelletan was killed by footpads. Why try to make his death out to be something more than it was?"

"Damion Pelletan was not killed by footpads, and you know it."

"So certain, my lord?"

"What kind of footpad steals a man's heart and leaves his purse?"

Vaundreuil's face went utterly slack with what looked very much like horror. *"What did you say?"*

"You heard me." Sebastian studied the other man's pale, suddenly haggard features. "Would you have me believe you didn't know?"

The Frenchman swiped a shaky hand across his mouth. "No. I was not told the details. I mean, I saw the body at that dreadful surgery near the Tower. I knew the chest was— But . . . the heart? Taken?" He swallowed hard. "You are certain?"

"You find the knowledge unsettling. Why?"

"Good God; who would not find it unsettling? I mean . . . to steal a man's heart! It is barbaric. It is the work of madness. What a violent, dangerous place this London of yours is."

"True. Yet it's considerably more salubrious than Paris in, say, 1793. Wouldn't you agree?"

Vaundreuil's jaw hardened. "Those dark days are twenty years in our past."

"Twenty years is not so long ago."

The wind gusted up, scuttling a loose playbill down the street and bringing them the voice of the priest with sudden, unexpected clarity. *"Ambulabo coram Domino, in regione vivorum . . ."*

Sebastian said, "Who would want to put an end to the possibility of peace talks between Napoléon Bonaparte and the British government?"

"I never said—"

"Very well; in honor of your exquisite sensitivity to the finer points of language, I'll rephrase the question: *If* preliminary peace talks were to be held between Paris and London, who would have an interest in seeing them brought to an untimely end?"

"Truly, *monsieur?* The list is endless. In my experience, those for whom war is lucrative are rarely satiated. For them, war is opportunity, not hardship or sorrow. After all, it is rarely their sons who lie in unmarked graves on foreign soil."

Sebastian studied the fat, successful bureaucrat before him. Vaundreuil himself had obviously profited handsomely from the Revolution and the endless wars that followed it. But all Sebastian said was, "Do you have anyone in particular in mind?"

The Frenchman gave a tight-lipped smile. "Surely you know those in England who profit from war better than I, yes?"

"And the French?"

Vaundreuil shook his head. "In France, even those who once grew rich off the empire know that the efforts of the last two decades are no longer sustainable. I suspect you'll find that those French most fervently opposed to the idea of peace between England and Napoléon are to be found on *this* side of the Channel, not the other."

"You mean the royalists?"

"The émigrés, the royalists, the Bourbons. There are tens of thousands of my former compatriots here. Most dream of someday returning to France. And of revenge."

"Do the Bourbons know of your presence here in London?"

"Officially? No. But there are few involved in this conflict who do not have their own spies."

"Any chance the Comte de Provence could be behind Pelletan's death?"

"Provence?" Vaundreuil crinkled his nose in a way that turned down the corners of his mouth. "The soi-disant Louis XVIII is ill, childless, and old before his time. In my opinion, the one who bears watching is the younger brother, the Comte d'Artois. Artois, and his niece, the Duchesse d'Angoulême. It would be a mistake to dismiss Marie-Thérèse as half-mad. She is, after all, Marie Antoinette's daughter. I have heard Napoléon himself say that Marie-Thérèse is the only real man in her family."

"He fears her?"

"I would not go so far as to say he fears her. But he watches her, yes. He definitely watches her." Vaundreuil touched his hand to his hat and inclined his head. *"Monsieur."*

He was turning away when Sebastian asked, "Are you by chance acquainted with Lord Peter Radcliff?"

The Frenchman pivoted slowly to face him again. "I know the man well enough to have recognized him, if that's what you mean." An unexpected gleam of amusement lit Vaundreuil's small, dark eyes. "I assume you noticed that he, likewise, did not stay for Pelletan's funeral mass?"

"Why would a son of the Duke of Linford attend the funeral of a French physician who arrived in London only three weeks ago?"

"I believe Radcliff is married to a young Frenchwoman. Someone Pelletan knew in Paris many years ago."

Sebastian was familiar with the young Lady Peter, for her beauty was legendary. She had come to England nine years before, when her father—a highly respected general in the Grand Army—had a falling-out with Napoléon that forced the family to flee France. But she had not arrived in London penniless, for the general had managed to accumulate a small fortune that he kept safely abroad. And he had settled nearly half of his wealth on his beautiful daughter.

An unpleasant gleam shone in Vaundreuil's eyes. "Perhaps you seek too complicated a motive for this murder, *monsieur*. Perhaps what we are dealing with is a simple—if somewhat ghoulish—*affaire de coeur*. It would explain much, yes?"

"Was Pelletan in love with Lady Peter?"

"Once, perhaps; who knows? Damion Pelletan was my physician, not my friend or confidant." Vaundreuil bowed again. "And now you really must excuse me, my lord."

Sebastian watched him stroll away toward Portman Square, the cold wind flapping the tails of his black coat, while from inside the church came a low, mournful chant.

"Pie Jesu Domine, dona eis requiem. Amen."

Chapter 17

Lord Peter Radcliff was one of those men who wore the dignity of his exalted birth with an easy grace and a good-natured smile. Born into a life of rare wealth and privilege, he was a duke's second son, which meant that all responsibility for maintaining the family's vast estates and managing their considerable investments fell not to him but to his elder brother. To Lord Peter came a handsome allowance and the freedom to spend his days as he saw fit, lounging in the famous bow window at White's, hunting in Melton Mowbray, and surrounding himself with a circle of bon vivants known for their exquisite manners, their flawless taste, and their willingness to bet on almost anything.

Like his friends Beau Brummell and Lord Alvanley, he'd once enjoyed a brief career in a fashionable London regiment. But he soon sold out to devote himself to the less demanding activities of a man-about-town. His marriage eight years before to one of the most beautiful women in London had little altered his way of life. Which was why, rather than look for Lord Peter at his comfortable house in Half Moon Street, Sebastian spent the evening moving from one gentlemen's haunt to the next, from White's in St. James's Street to Watier's in Piccadilly, and then on to Limmer's—all without success.

He was sipping a fine French cognac in a fashionable coffeehouse near Conduit Street when Lord Peter entered the room and walked straight up to him.

"Why the devil are you looking for me?" he demanded, the fingers of one hand tapping against his hard thigh.

Sebastian leaned back in his seat. "I think you know."

Radcliff hesitated a moment, then ordered a brandy, pulled out the chair opposite, and sat. "I saw you at the French chapel."

Sebastian brought his cognac to his lips and regarded the Duke's son over the glass's rim. "You were friends with Damion Pelletan?"

"Me? No." Radcliff propped one exquisitely polished boot on the other knee. The posture was casual, relaxed. He had a reputation amongst his friends for easygoing charm and boundless generosity, although Sebastian knew there were those who had seen another side of him, a side that could be brusque and condescending and freezingly arrogant. "I went for the sake of my wife. He was a friend of hers when she was a child, in Paris."

"But you did know him?"

"I met him once or twice." He gave Sebastian a hooded, sideways glance. "To be frank, I don't quite understand why you've involved yourself in this. The papers are saying he was killed by footpads in St. Katharine's."

"He was killed in St. Katharine's, yes. But footpads had nothing to do with it."

Radcliff was silent for a moment, his gaze dropping to the glass he twirled back and forth between his hands. He was still an attractive man, with a wide, winning smile. But in repose, one could see that the years of dissipation were beginning to leave their marks in telltale ways, coarsening the texture of his flesh and loosening the muscle tone of his still trim frame.

Sebastian said, "What can you tell me about him? You say your wife knew him in Paris?"

Radcliff seemed to rouse himself from his brown study. "She did, yes. They grew up next door to each other on the Île de la Cité. His father is still a prominent physician at the Hôtel-Dieu or some such place."

"Oh?"

Radcliff frowned. "I seem to recall hearing about a dustup of some sort or another involving the father, but it was years ago. Something to do with the royal family during the Terror. I couldn't tell you exactly what."

"What do you know of Damion Pelletan's politics?"

"Politics?" Radcliff shook his head. "I had the impression Pelletan had no interest in politics. His passion was medicine."

It struck Sebastian as more than a little strange that someone with no interest in politics would join a peace delegation, even if simply in the capacity of a physician. But all he said was, "When was the last time you saw him?"

Radcliff took a slow, deliberate sip of his brandy, as if carefully considering his response. "I don't recall, precisely. A week ago, perhaps? Maybe more."

"Not last Thursday night?" asked Sebastian, thinking of the unidentified man and woman who had visited Pelletan at the Gifford Arms the night of his death.

Radcliff froze with his glass suspended just above the table. All traces of easygoing bonhomie had vanished, leaving him looking mulish and vaguely sulky. "No; *not* Thursday night. I spent Thursday night at home alone with my wife."

"All night?"

"Yes, damn you."

Sebastian thrust out his legs to cross his boots at the ankles. "You say you attended Pelletan's funeral for the sake of your wife. Is she distressed by his death?"

"Of course she is. What do you expect? They were old friends."

"Yet, having put in an appearance at her childhood friend's funeral, you didn't feel the need to return home and comfort her?"

Angry color mottled Radcliff's cheeks. "What the bloody hell do you mean to imply by that?"

"Have you by any chance heard precisely how Damion Pelletan was killed?"

A faint wariness crept over the other man's features. "I assumed he was bludgeoned to death. That's what footpads normally do, is it not?"

"Actually, he was stabbed in the back with a dagger. Then the killer—or killers— dragged his body into a noisome passage and cut out his heart."

Something flared in the other man's eyes, something quickly hidden by his lowered lids.

Sebastian watched him closely. "Do you have any idea why someone would want to do that? It seems rather symbolic, don't you think? To rip a man's heart from his chest."

For one fierce moment, Radcliff's gaze met his.

Then he slammed his unfinished brandy on the table and thrust up to stride quickly from the coffeehouse, the amber liquid in the glass sloshing violently back and forth until, at last, it stilled.

Half an hour later, Sebastian arrived at Tower Hill to find Paul Gibson seated on the wooden chair at the injured woman's bedside, his elbows propped on his splayed knees, his chin in his hands. A basin with a cloth stood on a nearby table, its surface splashed dark with spilled water. He raised his head at Sebastian's entrance but did not stand. In the bed, the woman lay terribly still, her eyes closed. Sweat glistened on her white forehead and drenched the flame red hair dark at the temples.

"How is she?" Sebastian asked quietly.

Gibson shook his head and let out a long, strained breath. "She's delirious. I'm afraid her fever is climbing."

"From the chill she took the night of the murder? Or from her injury?"

"There's no way to tell." He raked the disheveled hair from his face, then linked his fingers behind his neck to arch his back in a stretch. "I asked one of my colleagues at St. Bartholomew's—Dr. Lothan—to stop by and have a look at her. He wanted to blister her, bleed her, and purge her—the usual panoply of 'heroic' medicine."

"Did you let him?"

"No. I swear I've seen more men killed by bloodletting and purging than by cannon- and musket balls combined. I thanked him for his advice and showed him out. But ever since, I've been sitting here wondering if I shouldn't at least have let him try it. I mean, I'm just a simple surgeon. I can set your broken arm or cut off your mangled leg, and if you're game I might even undertake to cut out your kidney stones. But I'm no physician. I never went to Oxford or Cambridge; my Latin is abysmal, my Greek nonexistent, and the one time I tried to read Galen I gave it up after a few pages. Who am I to question a medical tradition that's endured for more than two thousand years?"

"I don't think you give yourself enough credit. You know more about the human body than any physician I've ever met."

Gibson gave a ragged laugh. "If you're dead." Reaching out, he squeezed the cloth over the basin and began again to bathe the woman's face.

"Has she said anything more?" Sebastian asked, going to stand at the foot of the bed.

Gibson had reduced the size of the bandage on the woman's head, so that Sebastian had his first good look at her. She was an attractive woman, in her late twenties or early thirties, with milky white skin faintly dusted with cinnamon across her high-bridged nose. Her eyes were closed, but Sebastian knew what color they would be if they were open: a deep, loamy brown.

"Nothing coherent," said Gibson. But then he must have sensed the subtle shift in Sebastian's posture, or perhaps a sudden charge in the air, because he turned to look at Sebastian. "What is it?"

Sebastian kept his gaze on the woman. "I've met her before."

"You have? Where?"

"Portugal. Her name was Alexandrie Beauclerc then. The last time I saw her, she swore that if our paths ever crossed again, she would kill me."

Chapter 18

The inrushing tide brought with it all the familiar, evocative scents of the distant sea and a cold, briny mist that wet Sebastian's cheeks and beaded like unshed tears on the ends of his lashes.

He stood on the ragged, unfinished arc of the new stone bridge that would someday span the Thames. The river was a foam-flecked turgid rush far below, the city quieting and slowly sinking into darkness around him. He found himself unconsciously rubbing his wrists, where the old scars still showed as white lines against his skin. He'd thought in his confident naïveté that he was somehow coming to terms with those events of three years ago. But he realized now that he'd simply fallen victim to a comfortable illusion wrought by the passage of time and the joy an unexpected, enduring love could bring.

He tried to focus on the swirling black waters of the river below. But what he saw instead were soul-destroying images from a different time, a different place. And as he turned toward shore, he could have sworn he caught the distant echo of children's laughter and the faint scent of orange blossoms overlain by the heavy stench of old blood.

❧

Some hours later, Hero paused in the doorway to the darkened library. The soft light from the streetlamp fell through the open curtains to show her the man who stood with his back to the room, his gaze on the empty street beyond. She could feel the intensity of the tension thrumming through him, see it in every line of his tall, lean body.

She'd moved quietly, but of course he heard her. Even after six months of living with this man, she still found the acuity of his senses disconcerting. He turned his head to look at her over his shoulder, and a humming silence stretched out between them.

She said, "I've watched you work to solve murders before. I know how personally you take what you do, how deeply troubled you can become. But there's something more going on here, isn't there, Devlin?"

He shifted his gaze, once again, to the window, so that she could see only his profile. He said, "I saw someone tonight who reminded me of an incident I've spent the last three years trying to forget."

"Someone you knew in the Peninsula?"

"Yes. The injured woman in Gibson's surgery."

She went to him then, sliding her arms around his waist and laying her cheek against his strong, taut back. He brought his hands up to lay them over hers at his waist and tipped back his head until it rested against hers. But he didn't say anything, and neither did she.

She knew something had happened to him during the war, something that had shattered the already frayed remnants of his youthful idealism and made a mockery of so much that Englishmen of his station traditionally held dear. It had driven him to resign his commission and plunged him into a downward spiral that came perilously close to destroying him.

But that was all she knew. And she feared what might happen if the toxic events swirling around Damion Pelletan's murder forced him to confront the unresolved demons of his past.

Sunday, 24 January

The next morning, Sebastian was easing his coat up over his shoulders when his valet said, "I believe I have discovered the individual in whom you expressed an interest."

Sebastian straightened his cuffs. "Oh?"

"His name is Sampson Bullock, and he's a cabinetmaker. He lives over his workshop on Tichborne Street, not far from Piccadilly. I took the liberty of making a few inquiries."

Sebastian glanced over at him. "Learn anything interesting?"

"It seems Mr. Bullock is not what you might call well liked in the area."

"I take it I am to infer that is an understatement?"

"Indeed. From the sound of things, he's a quarrelsome brute with a nasty temper. Most of his neighbors were reluctant even to speak of him. He has a reputation for being rather vindictive—lethally so."

"Hear anything about his brother?"

"Only that the two were much alike—both big, brawny, and foul tempered. The brother's name was Abel."

"Sampson and Abel? How very biblical. Did you discover what happened to the brother?"

"I did, my lord. He died two weeks ago."

"Under Alexandrie Sauvage's care?"

"No, my lord. He died of gaol fever. In Newgate."

A curving sweep of pubs, small shops, and tradesmen's establishments, Tichborne Street lay to the south of Golden Square, just off Piccadilly. It was a middling area, neither fashionable nor wretched. Sebastian found Bullock's shop near the corner. The shutters were up, yet the door opened to his touch—which was unexpected, given that it was early Sunday morning.

He entered a shadowy, cavernous space smelling pleasantly of freshly cut wood, linseed oil, and turpentine. An inquiry addressed to a half-starved, frightened-looking apprentice sweeping up a scattering of sawdust led Sebastian to a back room, where a massive man with a head of thick, curly black hair and a pronounced jaw was planing a long board. He had his head bent, his shoulders hunched, his arms moving in long, rhythmic sweeps.

"Sampson Bullock?" asked Sebastian, pausing on the far side of the board.

The cabinetmaker straightened slowly. He stood half a head taller than Sebastian and must have weighed nearly twenty stone, with a heavily muscled body and broad, solid chest. He was one of those men whose neck was so thick that it appeared even wider than his head. His dark eyes were unnaturally small and set close over a small nose, so that when one looked at him, the overall impression was of black hair, bulging muscles, and a red, weal-like scar that disfigured one cheek.

His eyes narrowed with obvious suspicion as he took in Sebastian's inimitably tailored dark blue coat, the snowy crispness of his cravat, the suppleness of his doeskin breeches. Then he returned to his work, the curls of wood shavings blooming beneath the plane. "We're closed. It's the Lord's day; didn't ye know?"

"It looks to me like you're working."

"Wot ye want from me? Yer kind don't buy furniture from the likes of me."

"I understand you know Alexandrie Sauvage."

Bullock tossed aside his plane. "That's wot ye're here for, is it? I heard wot happened to her—her and that French doctor." He raised one hand to point a meaty finger at Sebastian. "Think yer gonna lay the blame for that on me, do ye? Well, I ain't been near St. Katharine's. Nowhere near it."

"So where were you last Thursday night?"

"I was home in me bed, asleep. Where else would a good, God-fearin' workin'man be on a Thursday night?"

Sebastian studied the cabinetmaker's mulish, set features and watched his eyes slide away.

Sebastian said, "I understand you had a dispute of sorts with Madame Sauvage."

"Dispute? That wot ye want to call it? The bloody bitch killed me brother."

"How?"

"Wot do you mean, *how?*"

"Are you suggesting she poisoned him?"

"I ain't never said no such thing."

"It's my understanding he died of gaol fever, in Newgate. Was she treating him?"

"Of course she weren't physicking him! It were because o' that interfering little strumpet that Abel was in Newgate in the first place."

"Oh? What was he accused of having done?"

Bullock's small eyes grew dark and hard. "I ain't got nothing t' say t' ye," he muttered, and reached for his plane.

Sebastian said, "You do realize you've been seen hanging around Golden Square. Following her. Threatening her."

Bullock thrust out his heavy jaw, the puckered flesh of his scar darkening from red to an angry purple. "I got nothin' t' hide. I ain't denying I spoke me mind t' her—and why the hell shouldn't I? But I ain't never threatened her, and anyone tells ye I did is a bloody liar."

"You didn't threaten to make her pay?"

"Who told ye that? Her?"

"No."

Bullock curled his lip in a sneer. "Me, I think ye got the wrong idea about the bitch. T' hear people talk, she's some bloody angel of mercy or some such thing. But she's no angel, not by a long shot. She's got a temper on her, that one. Why, I've heard her threaten t' gut a man with a fish knife, I have, jist because she didn't like the way he were lookin' at his own wife."

Sebastian thought about the fiercely passionate woman he had known in Portugal and had no difficulty imagining such a scene.

"I can tell ye plenty o' things about that woman I bet ye don't know," Bullock was saying. "There's a fair number o' Frogs live about here, ye see. I've heard 'em talking about her—about how she was with Boney's army in Spain, and about how her lover was a French lieutenant. Not her lawful *husband*, mind you. Her lover."

"I know about the Peninsula," said Sebastian simply.

Bullock grunted, the sound reverberating deeply in his massive chest.

Sebastian let his gaze drift around the workshop, with its carcasses of half-finished cabinets, its piles of lumber, its rows of tools kept well oiled and carefully honed. "I'm still not exactly clear on the reason behind your animosity toward Madame Sauvage."

"I told ye! It was because o' her that me brother Abel was in Newgate."

"What had he done?"

"He didn't do a bleedin' thing."

"So what did she accuse him of doing?"

"Why don't ye ask her?" snarled Bullock. Then he turned pointedly back to his board, the muscles in his strong shoulders and arms bunching and flexing as he ran the plane over its surface, again and again.

Sebastian watched the curls of wood shavings scatter in fragrant drifts. If Alexandrie Sauvage had been found with her head brutally beaten to a pulp, Bullock would have seemed the obvious suspect. But she was not the main target of Thursday night's attack, and there was nothing to tie this brutish cabinetmaker to Damion Pelletan.

Sebastian should have been able to discount the possibility of the hulking tradesman's involvement out of hand, for he could think of no logical reason why Bullock would have allowed Alexandrie Sauvage to live, only to vent his wrath on her unknown French companion, instead.

Yet Sebastian could not discount him. There was a rank odor of malevolence about the man, an ugly gleam in his small black eyes that Sebastian recognized, for he had seen it before. Men like Sampson Bullock didn't simply exploit their extraordinary size and strength; they reveled in the fear it inspired in others, and they used that fear to bully and intimidate their way through life. And when the intimidation failed to achieve its intended result—or sometimes when they were simply feeling particularly mean—they killed.

And they enjoyed it.

Chapter 19

At five minutes after ten, Sebastian stood near the gates of the Carlton House Gardens and watched as the French clerk, Camille Bondurant, strode purposefully up the Mall, his arms swinging, his features wearing the blank expression of a man whose thoughts are far, far away. He wore a heavy, drab greatcoat with a thick scarf knit of shockingly blue wool wrapped around his throat; his exhalations left little white puffs in the cold air that drifted away into nothing.

Once a long sweep of crushed shells where the kings of England were fond of playing a French game called *palle maille*, the Mall lay to the north of St. James's Park. A broad gravel walkway planted with rows of lime and elm, it was mirrored on the far side of the park by what was known as Birdcage Walk. Due to its proximity to the Gifford Arms, Birdcage Walk would have seemed the more logical choice for a resident of the inn in search of exercise. But that walkway had a reputation that must have inspired Bondurant to avoid it.

"Bracing day for a walk," said Sebastian, falling into step beside him.

The Frenchman cast Sebastian a quick glance and kept walking.

He was a tall, cadaverously thin man with greasy black hair and a rawboned face. His eyes were nearly lashless and squinted, either from habit or in an effort to see Sebastian more clearly. "Do I know you?" he asked, his English guttural and heavily accented.

"I was at Damion Pelletan's funeral."

"I do not recall seeing you."

"Probably because you were reading," said Sebastian pleasantly.

The clerk drew up and swung to face him. "What do you want from me?"

"You do realize that Pelletan was murdered, don't you?"

"Of course I realize it! What do you take me for? A fool?"

"Do you know why he was killed?"

"Because he was unwise enough to venture into a dangerous section of an unfamiliar city at night? Because he was French? Because someone took exception to the cut of his coat? How should I know? And I fail to see how it is any of your affair anyway."

"Had he quarreled with anyone recently?"

"Pelletan? With whom would he quarrel? The man had no opinions on anything of importance that I could discern. Try to engage him in a discussion of Rousseau or Montesquieu, and all he would do is laugh and say that the philosophical speculations of dead men were of no interest to him."

"So what did interest him?"

"The sick—especially the poor ones." Bondurant's face twisted with contempt. "He could become quite maudlin."

"You're not fond of philanthropy, I take it?"

"No, I am not. The sooner the poor are allowed to die off, the better for society. Why encourage them to procreate?"

"Kings and emperors need to get their soldiers from somewhere," said Sebastian.

"True. The lower orders are at least good for cannon fodder."

"Something the Emperor Napoléon seems to go through at an astonishing rate."

Bondurant pursed his large mouth into a terse expression. "What has any of this to do with me?"

"You know of no one who would want to kill Pelletan?"

"I believe I already answered that question." He tightened his scarf around his neck. "Now you must excuse me. You have interrupted my constitutional."

And he strode off, arms swinging, head down, as if battling a strong wind or reading a book that was no longer there.

Sebastian's next stop was the Sultan's Rest, a coffeehouse on Dartmouth Street popular with the military men of the area.

He found the comfortable, oak-paneled room thick with tobacco smoke and filled with red-coated officers all talking and laughing at once.

The French colonel, Foucher, sat by himself in one corner, inconspicuous in his dark coat and modest cravat. His head was bent over a newspaper opened on the table before him; a cup of coffee rested at his elbow. But Sebastian knew by a certain subtle alertness about his person that the Frenchman's attention was focused more on the conversations swirling around him than on the page before him.

Working his way across the crowded room, Sebastian pulled out the chair opposite the colonel. "Mind if I have a seat?"

The colonel looked up, his hazel eyes blinking several times. "Would it stop you if I did?" he asked, leaning back in his own chair as Sebastian sat down.

The Frenchman was tall and well built, although illness and injury had left him thin and his face sallow. Sebastian could see scattered strands of white in his sandy hair and thick mustache; lines dug deep by weather and endured pain fanned the skin beside his eyes.

Sebastian cast a significant glance around the crowded room. "Popular place."

"It is, is it not?"

"I assume that's why you come here?"

A slow gleam of amusement warmed the other man's gaze. "I find I enjoy the company of military men, whatever their uniform."

"I hear you were in Russia."

"Yes."

"There aren't many who staggered out of that fiasco alive. With the exception of Napoléon himself, of course."

"No."

Sebastian rested his forearms on the tabletop and leaned into them. "Let's get over rough ground as quickly as possible, shall we? I know why Vaundreuil is here. What I don't know is why someone would stab Damion Pelletan in the back and cut out his heart. The most obvious reason would be to disrupt your mission. The mutilation of the corpse seems rather macabre, but it could be a subtle warning directed at Monsieur Vaundreuil, who I understand suffers from a heart condition."

The colonel took a slow sip of his coffee and said nothing.

"Then again," said Sebastian, "Pelletan could have been killed because he had in some way become a threat to the success of your mission."

"Is that why you are here? Because you consider me a reasonable suspect?"

"You don't think you should be?"

Foucher eased one thumb and forefinger down over his flaring mustache. "If he had simply been killed, I could see that, yes. But the very flamboyance of his murder tends to work against such an argument, does it not?"

"It does. Unless the killer were fueled by anger or the kind of bloodlust one sometimes sees on the battlefield." Sebastian let his gaze drift around the noisy room. "We've both known men who enjoy mutilating the bodies of their fallen enemies."

Again the colonel sipped his coffee and remained silent.

Sebastian said, "There is of course a third possibility: that Pelletan was killed for personal reasons. It's unlikely, given that he was only in London for three weeks. But it is still an option."

The French colonel reached for his cup again with a care that suggested his lingering injury might be to his right arm or shoulder. "You know about the woman, I assume?"

Sebastian watched the other man's face, but Foucher was very good at giving nothing away. "What woman?"

"The wife of some duke—or perhaps it is the son of a duke."

"You mean Lord Peter Radcliff?"

"Yes, that is it; his wife is very beautiful. So you do know her?"

"Yes."

The Frenchman drained his coffee and set it aside. "The husbands of beautiful women are frequently subject to passionate fits of jealousy; jealousy and possessiveness. If you seek a personal motive, that might be a good place to start, yes? Particularly given the removal of Pelletan's heart."

"Did you know that Pelletan was killed on the twentieth anniversary of the execution of Louis XVI?"

"No, I did not. You believe that to be significant?"

"Rather a coincidence if it is not, wouldn't you agree?"

The colonel wiped his mustache again and rose to his feet. "Life is full of coincidences."

He started to turn.

Sebastian stopped him by saying, "Why do you think Ambrose LaChapelle attended Pelletan's funeral mass?"

"Perhaps you should ask him," said the colonel.

Then he pushed his way through the laughing, jostling crowd, a tall, erect man with the bearing of a military officer surrounded by his nation's enemies.

Chapter 20

By the time Sebastian reached the Half Moon Street town house of Lord and Lady Peter Radcliff, thick white clouds were pressing down on the city, and he could smell a hint of snow in the frosty air.

He didn't expect to find Radcliff at home, and in that he was not disappointed. Lady Peter, also, was out. But a friendly conversation with a young kitchen maid scrubbing the area steps, her hands red with cold, elicited the information that the mistress had taken her small brother and a friend to Green Park. Sebastian thanked the girl and turned his steps toward the park.

He knew something of Lady Peter's story. She'd been born Julia Durant, in the dying days of the Ancien Régime. Her father, the younger son of a minor Rhône Valley nobleman, had trained as an artillery officer at the prestigious École Militaire in Paris. When the people of Paris rose up and overthrew the Bourbons, Georges Durant did not flee France. Rather than join the forces of the counterrevolutionaries, he remained loyal to the land of his birth, eventually becoming a trusted general, first under the National Convention, then under the Directory.

But General Durant never had much use for a certain cocky young Corsican named Napoléon Bonaparte. When Napoléon declared himself emperor in 1804, Georges Durant tried to stop him—and only narrowly escaped with his life.

Fortunately, he'd had the forethought to send his wife and children out of the country first. And before he died, the old French general managed to marry his beautiful daughter, Julia, to the younger son of an English duke.

When Sebastian walked up to her, Lady Peter was seated on an iron bench near the Lodge. She wore a thick dusky pink pelisse and a close bonnet trimmed with a delicate bunch of velvet and silk flowers and was smiling faintly as she watched her orphaned eight-year-old brother toss a ball to his friend. Then she saw Sebastian, and her smile faded.

"No, don't run away," he said as she surged to her feet, eyes wide, one hand clenching in the fine velvet cloth of her pelisse. "I take it you know why I wish to speak with you?"

She was nearly a decade younger than her husband, in her mid-twenties now, with luminous green eyes and rich brown hair that curled softly around a heart-shaped face. Her nose was small and delicately molded, her lips full, her bone structure as flawless as one of Fra Filippo Lippi's madonnas. But her eyes were red rimmed and swollen, and Sebastian had no doubt that she'd been crying. For Damion Pelletan? he wondered. Or for some other reason entirely?

He watched as a succession of conflicting emotions flitted across her lovely face, a lifetime of carefully inculcated good manners at war with an instinctive urge to snatch up her little brother and run.

Good manners won.

"Lord Devlin," she said, graciously inclining her head, although the agitation of her breathing was obvious in the rapid rise and fall of her shoulders.

"Walk with me a ways, Lady Peter?" Sebastian suggested.

She threw a quick, uncertain glance toward the two little boys and their attendant nursemaid.

"We won't go far. I'm told you knew Damion Pelletan as a child, in Paris."

"I did, yes." The native French inflections were still a soft purr in her gently modulated voice. "We grew up next door to each other. But . . . that was years ago. How could those days possibly have anything to do with Damion's death?"

"I don't know that they do. At the moment, I'm simply attempting to find out anything that might help explain what happened to him."

She turned to walk with him along the graveled path, the flounced hem of her walking dress brushing the clipped rosemary hedge that grew beside it. "What would you like to know?"

"When did you last see Dr. Pelletan?"

She hesitated a moment too long, and he had the distinct impression she was tempted to deny having seen Pelletan recently at all.

Sebastian said, "Your husband told me he saw Dr. Pelletan a week or so ago. I assume you did, as well?"

"Yes. As I said, we were old friends. He contacted me shortly after he arrived in London, and Lord Peter invited him to dinner one evening."

"When was this?"

"As my husband said: a week or so ago."

"And that was the only time you saw him?"

"No. He paid us several afternoon visits as well."

Sebastian noted her emphasis of the word "us" but decided not to press it. "Did he tell you why he was here, in London?"

She cast him a hooded sideways glance, obviously hesitant to betray her childhood friend's confidences, even after his death. "Do you know?" she asked.

"About the delegation? Yes."

She nodded, a soft breath of relief escaping her parted lips. "I don't want you to think Damion told me about the peace initiatives himself, because he did not. But my father knew Harmond Vaundreuil, in Paris. He has always been Bonaparte's creature. So when I heard Damion was here with Vaundreuil . . ." She shrugged. "It was supposed to be a secret, but the truth is often not difficult to guess."

"Why was Pelletan included in the delegation?"

"Vaundreuil has a delicate heart. He worries obsessively about his health, fretting over each and every lump and pain, and is in constant need of reassurance. They thought it best that he travel with his own physician. And then of course there is Vaundreuil's daughter."

"Madeline, isn't it?"

"Yes. You know about her?"

Sebastian shook his head.

"She was married to a young cavalry captain, François Quesnel. He was killed last December, in Spain, leaving her with child."

"Ah," said Sebastian.

They turned to walk back toward the Lodge, their gazes on the two boys, who had lost interest in the ball and now appeared to be vying to see who could hop the farthest on one foot, their shouts and laughter echoing across the park. Unlike his sister, Noël Durant was surprisingly fair headed. But he had his sister's heart-shaped face and large green eyes.

Sebastian said, "How old is your brother?"

She gave a soft smile. "He is eight."

"He lives with you?"

"He does, yes. Our mother died less than a year after his birth— not long before our father."

"I'm sorry. That must have been very difficult for you, to be left alone in a strange country."

"It was difficult, yes. But Lord Peter and I were married by then."

She had been married many years, yet had conceived no children of her own. And Sebastian found himself thinking of another child-less Frenchwoman, likewise living in exile in England.

He said, "I understand Damion Pelletan's father is also a physician."

"He is, yes."

"I'm told he was involved in some way with the French royal family, when they were in the Temple Prison. Do you know anything about that?"

He watched in fascination as the color drained from her cheeks, her voice ragged as she said, "You don't know?"

"Know what?"

"Damion's father—Philippe-Jean Pelletan—was asked by the National Convention to treat the young Dauphin."

"The son of Louis XVI and Marie Antoinette?"

"Yes."

"Dauphin de France" was the title traditionally given to the heir apparent to the French throne. Few people today could recall the actual name of Marie-Thérèse's tragic little brother; most remembered him simply as "the Lost Dauphin." He was called "lost" not so much because of his early death as because considerable mystery surrounded his ultimate fate. Thrown into prison in 1792 with his parents, his aunt Elisabeth, and his sister Marie-Thérèse, he was said to have died alone in a cold, dark cell. But within days of the announcement of his death, rumors were already flying—fantastic tales of substitutions and imposters and miraculous escapes.

"He was just ten years old at the time," said Lady Peter, nodding to her brother, who was now examining the gravel of the walkway with the intensity of a lapidary studying a new array of specimens. "Not much older than Noël is now."

"When was this?"

"Sometime in 1795. Late May or perhaps early June; I don't recall precisely."

"And?"

"The boy was very ill. By that time he had been in prison for more than two years, and he had been treated abominably." She shook her head, her lips pressed tightly together. "Half-starved, beaten, left to lie in his own filth in a dark cell. Damion's father did what he could, but it was too late. Just a few days later, the Prince died."

"Did the elder Dr. Pelletan see Marie-Thérèse at that time, as well?"

"I don't know. But I do know that after the Dauphin's death, Philippe-Jean Pelletan was brought back to the Temple and asked to perform an autopsy on the boy's body."

"And did he?"

"Yes."

Sebastian stared off across the park, a gust of wind sending dry leaves scuttling down the path before them. The skin of his face felt suddenly cold and uncomfortably tight.

"But surely—" She broke off, then tried again. "Surely you don't think that events from so long ago could have something to do with Damion's death?"

"Probably not," he said, to reassure her more than anything else. "When you saw Damion Pelletan last week, how did he seem?"

"What do you mean?"

"I have the impression that relations between the various members of the delegation are not exactly what you might call harmonious."

A faint gleam of amusement lit up her soft eyes. "No. But then, it's not surprising, is it? They were all chosen to spy on each other."

"Oh?"

"Harmond Vaundreuil might be Bonaparte's tool, but that does not mean the Emperor trusts him. Napoléon trusts no one, especially now. You know of the conspiracy to overthrow him, last December?"

Sebastian nodded.

"The colonel who is with them—Foucher—was the Emperor's selection, not Vaundreuil's."

"And the clerk?"

"Camille Bondurant is not nearly as meek-mannered or self-effacing as he would appear. I remember Damion saying once that if

Bondurant had been born two hundred years earlier, in Spain, he'd have enjoyed a brilliant career as a torturer for the Inquisition."

"And Damion Pelletan himself? Why was he selected?"

"Damion is the only one who was Harmond Vaundreuil's personal choice. He was here as a physician; he had no role in the negotiations."

"Yet he agreed to come. Do you know why?"

"Lord Peter asked him that. Damion only smiled and said it's not often a man is offered the opportunity to be a part of history."

A coal wagon rolled down the street, heavily laden and pulled by a team of shires leaning into their collars, their breath misting white in the cold air.

Sebastian said, "Did Damion ever serve in the French army as a doctor?"

She shook her head. "No. He suffered from an illness in his youth that left his limbs weakened. Perhaps that is why he agreed to accompany Vaundreuil. I think it bothered him, that he remained in Paris while others fought and died."

"He was a supporter of the Emperor?"

Her chin came up in an unexpected gesture of pride. "He was a supporter of France."

"And did he approve of the delegation's objective?"

"You mean, peace? After twenty years of war, who amongst us does not long for peace?"

"Even a peace that leaves Napoléon Bonaparte on the throne of France?"

"Damion was no royalist, if that is what you are suggesting."

"Yet he agreed to consult with Marie-Thérèse."

A shadow of worry passed over her features. "You know about that?"

Sebastian said, "The Princess has been childless for years. What made her think Damion Pelletan could help her?"

"One of Damion's passions was the study of ancient herbs, both those that have fallen out of favor here in Europe and those with long traditions amongst the natives of the Americas and India. He published a number of articles on the subject."

"Somehow, I find it difficult to picture Marie-Thérèse perusing complicated medical studies. So how did she come to hear of him?"

"I believe it was her uncle who recommended Damion to her."

Sebastian watched the boy, Noël, shove his playmate, the boys' angry voices mingling with the shrieks of the maid. "Which uncle?"

"Louis Stanislas. The Comte de Provence. The soi-disant Louis XVIII. However you care to style him. He saw Damion himself, you know, just a few days before the Princess."

"No; I didn't know." Somehow, Louis Stanislas had neglected to mention that little fact.

The boys were locked together now, rolling over and over in the winter-browned grass beneath a spreading elm.

"Did Damion Pelletan seem at all . . ." Sebastian paused, searching for the right word. "Troubled by his meetings with the Bourbons?"

She turned to face him. "He did, yes. He tried to laugh it off, but I was surprised he even mentioned them to me. I thought perhaps it was because of his father's brief and rather tragic interaction with the family."

"That the Bourbons consulted him? Or that he was troubled by his meeting with them?"

"I meant that his father's history with the family was the reason the meeting troubled him, of course." She looked puzzled. "Why would the Bourbons have decided to consult with Damion because of something his father did twenty years ago?"

If her imagination wasn't that active, Sebastian wasn't about to enlighten her. He said, "Can you think of anyone who might have wanted to harm him?"

"Damion? Good heavens, no. He was a good, gentle, caring man who devoted his life to helping others. He'd only been in London a few weeks. Why would anyone want to kill him?"

"How did he get along with Harmond Vaundreuil?"

"Well enough, I suppose. After all, Vaundreuil chose him to come here, did he not? Damion had a knack for humoring the man— calming his fears, rather than fanning them, the way so many physicians are wont to do in order to make themselves more necessary to their patients."

"And the others? Foucher and Bondurant? Did he have trouble with them?"

She frowned, as if considering the question. "I would say he was wary of both Colonel Foucher and the clerk, Bondurant. But I do not know if he ever quarreled with them."

"What about someone he might have met in England?"

She shook her head. "He didn't meet many people here in London. That was one of the main reasons the delegation hired that hotel in York Street, was it not? To avoid having to interact with many Englishmen?"

She paused, her lips parted as if with a sudden thought.

"What?" asked Sebastian, watching her.

"Last week—I think it was early Thursday morning—Noël and I were walking in Hyde Park. We saw Damion and another man there, near the Armoury. It was obvious their words were heated, so I stopped Noël when he would have run up to them."

"Did Damion see you?"

"He did, yes. Noël called out *'Bonjour!'* before I could hush him, so Damion glanced over at us. But I knew from the expression on his face that he wanted us to stay away."

"What sort of expression? Annoyance?"

"Not annoyance. More like an odd mixture of anger and fear."

"Do you know who the man was?"

"I don't number him amongst my acquaintances, but I doubt there is anyone in the West End of London who would fail to recognize him. It was Kilmartin. Angus Kilmartin."

Sebastian had a sudden clear recollection of having seen the small, bowlegged Scotsman descending the stairs from Jarvis's apartments. "Do you have any idea why Damion would have been meeting him?"

"No; none at all." She looked beyond him, to where the nurse-maid was now trying to separate the two squabbling boys. "Truly, *monsieur*, I must go."

He touched his hand to his hat and bowed his head. "Thank you for your assistance, Lady Peter. If you think of anything else that might be useful, you will let me know?"

"Yes, of course."

She turned away, the wind gusting hard enough to snatch at the rim of her bonnet. She put up a hand to steady it, and the movement pulled at the sleeve of her pelisse, baring her forearm between the braided cuff and her kid gloves. Against her pale flesh, a row of four livid bruises showed quite clearly.

Bruises in the exact pattern left by an angry man closing his big, strong hand around a woman's fragile wrist.

Chapter 21

*A*ngus Kilmartin was seated alone at a small table near the fire in White's somber, overheated dining room when Sebastian walked up and settled in the chair opposite.

"I don't recall issuing an invitation for you to join me," said the Scotsman, his voice pleasant, his face never losing its habitual expression of mild amusement.

"That's quite all right," said Sebastian. "I don't intend to stay long."

Kilmartin grunted and cut himself a slice of beefsteak.

Sebastian said, "I hear you've recently been awarded a new contract with the Navy."

"Yes."

"Congratulations."

Kilmartin glanced up at him. "You say that as if you disagree in some way with the procedure."

"Why would I?"

Just two decades before, Angus Kilmartin had been an obscure Glaswegian merchant. Today, there were few lucrative industries in which he was not invested. From his mills in Yorkshire rolled the cloth used to make uniforms for Britain's soldiers and sailors. His foundries supplied them with cannon and firearms, while from his shipyards came an endless supply of the frigates and gunboats that helped Britannia rule the waves. Over the course of twenty years of war, as Britain's artisans and craftsmen starved and sheep grazed amidst the ruined cottages of displaced Highland clansmen, Angus Kilmartin had prospered far beyond most men's wildest dreams.

"Why, indeed?" he said, carefully buttering a piece of bread. "Is this why you are here? To discuss my business ventures?"

"Actually, I'm curious about how you came to know a French doctor named Damion Pelletan."

Kilmartin chewed slowly and deliberately before swallowing. "You refer, I take it, to the young man recently set upon by footpads in St. Katharine's?"

"He was certainly killed in St. Katharine's, although I seriously doubt footpads had anything to do with it."

"And what makes you imagine I knew him?"

"You were seen arguing with him last Thursday morning in the park. That's the day he was killed, incidentally."

Kilmartin only smiled faintly, his chin tucked, his eyes downcast as he worked to cut himself another slice of beef.

Sebastian watched him. "So you don't deny it?"

The Scotsman paused with his fork halfway to his mouth, his eyes going wide. "Why should I? Pelletan was a physician. I consulted with him over a medical matter. I see no reason to furnish you with the particulars."

"And you would have me believe you met with him in the park to argue a *medical* matter?"

"I didn't exactly 'meet with' him. I encountered him by chance. We fell into a dispute."

"Over a medical matter."

"Yes."

"I wonder, how did you come to hear of him? He hadn't been in London long."

"Someone recommended him to me. I don't recall now precisely whom."

"One of the Bourbons, perhaps?" suggested Sebastian sardonically.

Kilmartin gave a faint, tight-lipped smile and shrugged. "Perhaps. Who can say?"

Sebastian let his gaze drift around the elegant, high-ceilinged room. "I assume you've heard the rumors?"

"London is full of rumors. Endlessly. To which do you refer?"

"To the suggestion that the fiasco in Russia has weakened Napoléon to the extent that he is now willing to explore the possibility of making peace with England."

"Never happen," said Kilmartin.

"So certain?"

"Napoléon would never agree to England's terms."

"And if he did?" Sebastian watched the other man's face. "You would stand to lose a lot of money."

Kilmartin's smile never slipped. "All good things must come to an end."

"True. But some eventualities can be postponed. Especially by those ruthless enough to use any means possible."

Kilmartin leaned forward, his grip on the knife and fork tightening. "What are you suggesting? That I had Damion Pelletan waylaid and murdered in some back alley in the hopes that it might disrupt the delegation from Paris? How absurd."

"I never suggested Pelletan was part of a delegation from Paris."

For a moment, Sebastian's words seemed to hang in the silence between them. The Scotsman froze, his narrowed gray eyes fixed on Sebastian's, a dark malevolence replacing the faint derision that had been there before.

He kept his voice low and even, his knife suspended in the air between them. "If I proposed to put an end to Boney's somewhat tentative peace feelers, I would do it by killing that fat former priest masquerading as a diplomat. Not his doctor."

Sebastian shook his head. "Too obvious. Why kill Vaundreuil when you can get rid of him in a different way? The man is morbidly obsessed with his own health. It's conceivable that without his doctor, he might decide to abandon his attempts at diplomacy and scuttle back across the Channel."

The humor was back in the other man's eyes. "Really? Then Pelletan's killer was more clever than I realized. I'd like to take credit, but I'm afraid I can't."

Sebastian watched the Scotsman set down his knife and reach for his ale.

"Why did you really meet with Pelletan in the park last Thursday morning?"

Kilmartin rolled his ale around on his tongue, his lips pursed, his eyes alive with mischief. But he only shook his head, as if hugging to himself some secret too amusing to share.

Sebastian was crossing the vestibule, headed toward the street, when he heard himself hailed by a mountain of a man being pushed in a wheeled chair by a flamboyantly dressed dandy.

"Sir," said Sebastian, changing direction to walk up to him. "I didn't expect to see you in London."

The Comte de Provence smiled, his cheeks bunching with rosy good cheer. "Marie-Thérèse wanted to come into town for a few days—go to the theater, maybe buy a new hat—that sort of thing. And then there's the Duchess of Claiborne's soiree Tuesday night." He gave Sebastian a studied look, as if trying to recall an elusive fact. "She's some relative of yours, is she not?"

"My aunt."

The small frown cleared. "Ah, thought so. Then perhaps we shall see you there."

"Perhaps."

Provence gave one of his belly-shaking laughs. "Not a fan of that sort of thing, are you?" His laugh turned into a cough. "Can't say I blame you at your age."

"Do I take it you're staying in South Audley Street?"

"Indeed, indeed. Artois is up chasing some light-skirts around Scotland, so if he doesn't like it, there's not much he can do about it, now, is there?"

Sebastian glanced over at Ambrose LaChapelle. But the courtier turned his head and looked away, as if distrusting his ability to maintain a straight face.

"I've discovered something interesting about the young French doctor who was killed," said Sebastian.

The uncrowned King of France let his eyes go wide in a clumsy pantomime of astonishment. "Oh?"

"It seems Damion Pelletan was the son of Dr. Philippe-Jean Pelletan—the same Dr. Pelletan who treated the young Dauphin in the Temple Prison."

"Indeed? What an odd . . . coincidence."

Sebastian studied the Bourbon's plump, self-indulgent face. One couldn't exactly call a monarch—even an uncrowned one—a liar. "You mean to say you didn't recognize the name?"

"Well, I recognized the *similarity* in the names, of course," blustered the Bourbon. "But I'd no notion they were . . . His son, you say? How very intriguing."

"Not to mention coincidental."

"Yes, yes; to be sure, to be sure."

"I wonder: Would you happen to know why Damion Pelletan was in London?"

The Comte de Provence fixed Sebastian with an unexpectedly

hard stare. And it occurred to Sebastian that however jovial his features or good-natured his demeanor, it would never do to forget that this man was the grandson of King Louis XV, or that he had grown to manhood surrounded by all the splendor and intrigue of the French court at Versailles. "Now, how would I know that?" he asked. "We don't all have the network of informants and spies available to someone such as, say, your own father-in-law."

Sebastian was aware of the courtier, LaChapelle, sucking the flesh of one inner cheek between his teeth. It was obvious that Ambrose LaChapelle realized, even if Provence himself did not, that he'd just inadvertently revealed he knew exactly why Damion Pelletan was in London.

Sebastian said, "Tell me about your nephew, the Dauphin."

The shift in topic seemed to confuse the aging Bourbon. "My nephew? What is there to tell? He was a sweet boy. Just seven years old and the picture of health when he was thrown into prison."

"What happened to him?

The old man sighed. "Nothing, at first. For some months after the execution of his father, the King, the boy was allowed to remain with his mother, aunt, and sister. But then one day the guards came and took him away. Seems the revolutionaries had ordered the jailors to remove all traces of what they called 'arrogance' and 'royalty' from him." A pinched look came over his features. "They treated him . . . very badly."

"When did he die?"

"The eighth of June, 1795."

"And Dr. Philippe-Jean Pelletan performed the autopsy?"

"He was one of the doctors present, yes."

"There were others?"

"Two or three, I believe. Although Pelletan may have been the only one who had actually seen the boy just a day or two before, when he was brought to the prison to treat his illness."

"Did he identify the body as belonging to the Dauphin?"

"*Mon Dieu.*" Angry, purple color suffused the normally placid royal's plump features. "I hope to God you are not suggesting that those ridiculous old whispers are true?"

"Which whispers?"

"As if you do not know! The idea that the Dauphin did not die in the Temple—that he was spirited away from prison while the body of some other poor lad was left in his place."

The persistence of the myth that the son of Louis XVI and Marie Antoinette had not actually died in prison was an obvious source of embarrassment and chagrin to the two uncles and cousin who dreamt of someday occupying the dead Dauphin's vacant throne. When Sebastian simply remained silent, Provence said, "Please to God you won't say anything of this to my niece, Marie-Thérèse. You've no notion the distress these rumors cause her—or how many charlatans have presented themselves to her over the years, claiming to be her long-lost brother. I've seen her made ill for days by one of those encounters."

Sebastian frowned. "She did not see the Dauphin's body after his death?"

"No. Nor had she seen him for nearly two years before that. The boy was torn from his mother's arms in the summer of 'ninety-three; Marie-Thérèse never saw him again."

"Seems curious that the revolutionaries didn't show the body to the boy's sister—if for no other reason than to remove all doubt as to his fate, once and for all."

"I wish they had," grumbled Provence, shifting his considerable weight in his chair. "They would have saved us all a great deal of bother."

"Are you certain the boy actually is dead?"

He expected the Bourbon to bluster and heatedly deny the very possibility of any suggestion the Dauphin might still live. Instead, he blinked, his eyes swimming with a sudden uprush of emotion, his skin looking mottled and prematurely old. "If by some miracle the boy did survive— I'm not saying I believe he did, mind you! But *if* by some miracle my poor nephew is truly alive out there, somewhere, he would not be fit to be king. What those animals did to him in that prison . . . Let's just say it would have destroyed him, both physically and mentally."

"What did they do to him?" asked Sebastian.

To his surprise, it was the courtier, Ambrose LaChapelle, who answered him. "You don't want to know," he said softly. "Believe me; you don't want to know."

Chapter 22

A sharp, bitter wind slapped into Sebastian's face as he walked up St. James's Street toward Piccadilly. Settling his hat more firmly on his head, he became aware of an elegant town carriage drawn by a beautifully matched team of dapple-grays slowing beside him. He heard the snap of the near window being let down, saw the crest of the House of Jarvis proudly emblazoned on the door panel.

He kept walking.

"I had a troubling conversation this morning with a certain over-wrought and somewhat choleric Parisian," said Charles, Lord Jarvis.

"Oh?" Sebastian turned onto Berkeley. The carriage rolled along beside him.

"You simply cannot leave well enough alone, can you?"

Sebastian gave a low, soft laugh. "No."

His father-in-law was not amused. "With any other man, I might be tempted to hint at all sorts of dire consequences to life and limb—your life and limb. But in this case, I realize such tactics would be counterproductive. Shall I appeal instead to your better nature?"

Sebastian drew up and pivoted to face him. "My better nature? Do explain."

The liveried coachman brought his horses to a standstill.

Jarvis chose his words carefully, obviously conscious of the listening servants. "I've no doubt that by now you know what's at stake here. Given your oft-stated attitudes toward this war, I should think you would be anxious not to do anything that might interfere with a process that could save lives. Millions of lives."

"Oh? And when have you ever cared about saving lives?"

Jarvis's face lit up with what looked like a genuine smile. "Seldom. However, I am well aware of which arguments are most likely to appeal to you. And what is at stake here is real."

Sebastian studied his father-in-law's arrogant, self-satisfied face, the aquiline nose and brutally intelligent gray eyes that were so much like Hero's. Sebastian knew of no one who was a more ardent supporter of the institution of hereditary monarchy than Jarvis. In Jarvis's thinking, Napoléon Bonaparte was an upstart Corsican soldier of fortune whose ambition-fueled ascension to the throne of France threatened to undermine every foundation of civilization and the social order. All of which made it exceedingly difficult for Sebastian to believe that Jarvis would countenance any peace treaty that might result in Britain's retirement from the field of battle, leaving Napoléon still enshrined as Emperor.

Sebastian said, "I fail to understand how my simple inquiries could possibly threaten even such a delicate process."

"You don't know everything."

"Oh? So enlighten me."

But Jarvis simply tightened his jaw and signaled his coachman to drive on, the horses' hooves clattering over the paving stones, the body of the carriage swaying with well-sprung delicacy as the team picked up speed.

Chapter 23

*L*ater that afternoon, when none of the older women Gibson typically hired to sit with his most critically ill patients was available for the approaching night, he had Alexandrie Sauvage wrapped in a blanket and carried next door to the inner chamber of his own house.

"You don't need to do this," she whispered hoarsely as he tucked his worn quilt around her.

"Yes, I do."

She was showing hopeful signs of improvement, but her eyes were still dull with fever, her cheeks hollow, her flesh like hot, dry parchment to the touch. She let her lids flutter closed, and he thought she slept. Then she said, "My woman, Karmele, is a good nurse. You could send for her."

"I will." He started to move away, then barely bit back a gasp when, without warning, a burning jolt of agony shot up his leg, as brutal and real as if someone had thrust a red-hot poker into the sole of his left foot.

The foot that was no longer there.

She opened her eyes and fixed her gaze on his face. "You're in pain. Why?"

He shook his head. "I'm fine." And when he knew from the incredulity of her expression that she didn't believe him, he said, "I sometimes get pains from my missing foot and leg. It will pass."

"There is a way—"

"Hush," he said, smoothing the covers over her. "Go to sleep."

He didn't expect her to listen to him, because he was learning that she was not the most cooperative of patients. But to his surprise, she did.

He went to settle in the chair beside the fire and carefully removed his peg leg. It did no good; the pain persisted, so intense now that if his left foot had still been attached to his body, he'd have been tempted to whack it off himself, just to end the agony. But you can't amputate a limb that isn't there.

He felt the sweat start on his face, and a fine trembling made his hand shake as he brought up one crooked arm to swipe his sleeve across his forehead. The urge to set his mind free from the pain, to escape into the sweetly hued dreams of laudanum, was damned near overwhelming. He had to grit his teeth, his hands clutching the arms of the chair, his gaze fixed on the fever-racked woman who lay in his bed.

And he found himself wondering if this was why he had brought her here, why he resisted sending for her woman. If he were only fooling himself, convincing himself that he was fighting to save her life when the truth was that by her very presence, she was saving him.

Chapter 24

"*T*he problem, my lady, is that your humors are out of balance."

Richard Croft, the most distinguished and respected accoucheur in Britain, stood with his back to the fire, his chin sunk deep into the folds of his snowy white cravat. In his early fifties, he was a slight man with wisps of fading pale hair that fell from a slightly receding hair-line. Like his face, his nose was long, his chin pronounced, his lips thin and drawn, as if he were constantly tightening and sucking them in disapproval.

Hero sat in a nearby chair, her hands in her lap, her maid stand-ing behind her. "I feel fine," she said.

"Ah." Croft tsked and shook his head with a deprecating smile that filled Hero with an undignified urge to box his ears. "You may *feel* fine, but unfortunately that does not mean that all is as it should be. What did you eat yesterday?"

Hero told him.

Croft fluttered his soft white hands in horror. "But that is far too much! You must take only a cup of tea for breakfast, and not before ten. Then, at two, you may have a bite of cold meat or some fruit—but not both. Your dinner must be equally sparse—a thin soup, per-haps, or some fowl with a small serving of well-cooked vegetables. Bland, of course."

"If I reduce myself to the regime you suggest, I shall soon be too weak to walk across the room."

"But that is precisely the idea, my lady!"

"I was reading an article yesterday written by a Dr. Agostina De-Fiore at the University of Padua—"

"A woman?" sputtered Croft. "An *Italian* woman?"

"—who argues that while a woman should take care not to gain too much weight, it is nevertheless important that she continue to consume a varied and adequate amount of healthy foods. To do oth-erwise not only debilitates the health of the mother, but also puts the child at risk."

"Utter nonsense, I'm afraid." He cleared his throat. "I trust you have been taking the purges I prescribed?"

"They don't agree with me."

"They are not supposed to agree with you! They are designed to bring your humors back into balance. My lady, I beg of you; you must trust me in this." He brought up his hands, palms together, as if he were praying. "Your color is too robust, and you have far too much energy. At this point, patients who follow my strictures are pale and languid, as befits a woman about to give birth. I shall have to bleed you again."

Hero watched in silence as he turned to remove a basin and lan-cet from his satchel.

"Most severely, I'm afraid," he said. "Under the circumstances, I suspect that to take any less than two pints would be folly."

"*Two pints?*"

"Yes, my lady," he said, advancing on her with his lips cinched tight and his eyes weary with benign contempt for the weaker sex, with whose folly he struggled daily.

By the time Sebastian reached Brook Street, a light snow had begun to fall, big, soft, white flakes that fluttered down to stick to the pavement and the iron railing guarding the area steps.

"Bit wet out there, my lord?" asked his majordomo, Morey, as he took Sebastian's hat, greatcoat, and gloves.

"I suspect we're in for a good deal more of this before nightfall." Sebastian's gaze fell on the modest gentleman's hat resting on a nearby chair. "I take it Richard Croft is here?"

"Yes, my lord. He—"

The majordomo broke off as a loud rattling clatter sounded from above.

A moment later, a small, slight man came charging down the stairs, the tails of his black coat billowing behind him, his satchel gripped before him in both hands. He had his head down, his lips clamped in an angry line, his prominent chin set mulishly. But at the sight of Sebastian, he drew up, nostrils flaring, his entire frame aquiver with his indignation.

"Lord Devlin," he said, taking the last step down to the entrance hall and bowing stiffly. "I am pleased to see that you are here, for it affords me the opportunity to tell you that I refuse—yes, refuse!—to act as Lady Devlin's accoucheur any longer. She is stubborn and opinionated, full of outlandish ideas gleaned from reading an assortment of ridiculous foreign publications. She ignores my advice, refuses my prescriptions, and just now she *threw my basin at me* when I attempted to insist that she allow me to bleed her."

"And how, precisely, did you 'insist'?"

Croft's thin chest jerked with the agitation of his breathing. "Sometimes with expectant mothers, the emotions run high and a touch of male firmness is required."

"You're fortunate she didn't take the lancet to you."

Croft's features darkened with a resurgence of fury. "Indeed, she threatened to do so." He tugged at the lower hem of his waistcoat, which had become rucked up in his hasty descent of the stairs. "I cannot be held responsible for the outcome of a confinement when the patient refuses to submit herself to my Lowering System. Therefore, I resign my position. Nor can I in all good conscience recommend her as a patient to any of my colleagues. To be frank, under the circumstances, I can't imagine how you will find anyone competent to agree to attempt to deliver her."

"Under what 'circumstances'?" asked Sebastian with deceptive restraint.

The esteemed Richard Croft opened his mouth, then thought better of what he'd been about to say, and closed it.

Sebastian advanced on him. "What the devil are you saying?"

Croft took a step back, his heels clattering against the riser of the first stair.

"*What circumstances,* damn you?"

The accoucheur swallowed hard. "The child . . ."

"Yes?"

He swallowed again. "The child is in the wrong position. By now, it should have shifted, so that the head is down in preparation for entering the birth passage. It has not done so. Instead, it is lying . . . crossways."

Sebastian felt as if someone had reached into his chest to twist his heart and elbow his gut, so that it was a moment before he was able to say, "What can be done?"

Croft shook his head. "Nothing."

"What do you mean, nothing?"

"The child may turn itself."

"And if it doesn't?"

The accoucheur sidled toward the door. "Some babes which present in a breech position are born successfully."

"And the mothers?"

"Some mothers survive," said Croft. "But . . ."

"But?"

Croft straightened his spine and met Sebastian's fierce gaze with a fortitude Sebastian couldn't help but admire.

"But rarely both."

Chapter 25

Sebastian found Hero standing at the window of her chamber, one hand on the panel of heavy drapes at her side, her gaze on the flurry of snow falling from the sky.

"I owe the poor man an apology," she said as Sebastian came to stand behind her.

"Did you really throw his basin at him?"

"I did. Shameful, is it not?"

He slipped his arms around her and drew her back against him. She smelled of silk and lavender and herself, and for a moment the upswelling of emotions within him was so powerful that he had to squeeze his eyes shut. "Perhaps. But nevertheless understandable. The man is a pompous, pedantic ass."

She shook her head. "Croft may be an idiot, but he means well. He truly believes in what he prescribes."

When Sebastian remained silent, she said, "I take it he told you the child will in all likelihood be breech?"

"He said it might still turn."

"It might."

He brought his hands up to rest them on the swell of her belly. He hoped she didn't notice that they weren't quite steady. He said, "We need to find a new accoucheur—preferably one who is not an idiot."

"They're all idiots." She tipped her head back against his shoulder, her lips curving into an odd smile. "If you ask me, the child's position is the real reason Croft bowed out. He's afraid."

What accoucheur in his right mind wouldn't be afraid of attending Lord Jarvis's daughter in a difficult delivery? thought Sebastian. But he didn't say it.

"What about Gibson?" she suggested.

"Gibson is a surgeon, not a physician or accoucheur," he reminded her.

"You think I care for that? You know as well as I do that he's delivered babies. Surely he could at least recommend someone."

"Unfortunately, I believe he shares your opinion of the profession. But I can ask."

He was silent for a moment, his thoughts crowded again with the memory of all the babes her mother had lost. *Why had she lost them?* he wondered. Were they breech? Or did they die for some other reason entirely? Some abnormality that had in the end come close to taking Lady Jarvis's life, as well.

"I know what you're thinking," said Hero. "But I am not my mother."

She turned in his arms, her hand coming up to cup his cheek as she kissed him on the mouth. "Everything will be fine."

He speared his fingers through her hair, cradling the back of her head and holding her close as he let his gaze drift over the familiar line of her cheeks, the soft curve of her lips. He wanted to tell her that the thought of losing her terrified him, that he could no longer even imagine a life without her in it. Yet he'd never said these things to her, never even whispered those three simple words, "I love you." To say them now would seem to suggest that he feared she might die. And so he kept silent.

She was braver than he. "I don't intend to die, Devlin."

He rested his forehead against hers. But he still said nothing, for she knew as well as he that the hour of our death is rarely of our own choosing.

By the time Sebastian reached Tower Hill, the snow was falling thick and fast, big flakes that stung his face and rapidly covered the city in a blanket of white.

"Good God, Devlin," said Gibson as Sebastian came in stomping snow off his boots. "What in the name of all that's holy are you doing out in this?"

Sebastian shrugged out of his wet greatcoat. "I need the name of a good accoucheur, Gibson."

Gibson paused in the act of leading the way to his small parlor to look back at him in surprise. "I was under the impression the esteemed Richard Croft would be attending Lady Devlin."

"He resigned. He would have me believe it is because Lady Devlin is not the most meek and cooperative patient—which I will be the first to admit she is not. But if truth be told, I think it's because he's afraid of Jarvis. The babe is lying breech, Gibson."

"I wouldn't worry too much at this point; it's early days, yet. The babe's not due until April. It will turn when it's ready."

Sebastian met his friend's gaze. "I'm afraid that's a polite fiction, told to still the tongues of Society's gossips. The child is expected in a week or two."

"Ah." The expression on the Irishman's face confirmed every one of Sebastian's worse fears, and then some. "Mother Mary," he said softly, and turned away to pour two glasses of burgundy.

"It's bad, isn't it?" said Sebastian, watching him.

Gibson held out one of the wineglasses. "Sometimes a babe will shift at the last minute."

Sebastian took his glass and drank long and deep. "The name of a good accoucheur, Gibson; I need one. Quickly."

Gibson pushed a tumbled lock of hair off his forehead. Sebastian noticed that his friend had not only shaved, but also put on a clean cravat and evidently bullied Mrs. Federico into ironing one of his shirts too. "Let me think on it a bit. I'll ask around tomorrow."

Sebastian went to sink into one of the cracked leather chairs beside the fire. It was then that he noticed someone had picked up the newspapers that normally littered the floor. He let his gaze drift over the recently dusted mantel, the fresh candles in the sconces flanking the fireplace. "How is your patient?"

"You can ask me yourself," said Alexandrie Sauvage, coming to stand in the doorway.

She looked much the same as Sebastian remembered her from three years before, her hair still the same riotous cloud of sunset-shot fire, her eyes the same unexpectedly dark brown. But away from the hot sun of Spain, her skin was paler, and she was thinner, her cheekbones more pronounced in a way that gave her an air of fragility he knew was utterly deceptive.

"Good God; what are you doing out of bed?" Gibson demanded, going to steer her wobbly steps to a nearby chair.

She wore the same faded dress he'd seen that first night, and from the looks of things, she'd just pulled it on. "I heard you talking," she said, settling with a soft, quickly suppressed sigh into the chair opposite his. He could see the tight lines bracketing her lips and knew how much it had cost her to leave her bed.

"You don't look like you should be up."

"She shouldn't be," said Gibson.

Her gaze met Sebastian's. He saw the flare of smoldering animosity in her eyes, and something else, like the wariness of a cornered fox.

He said, "What can you tell us about the night Damion Pelletan was killed?"

She put her hand to her forehead, as if the mere effort of thought brought a renewed surge of pain. "I'm afraid I don't remember much."

"Can you tell us the name of the man who went with you to the Gifford Arms?"

She frowned at him in confusion, her hand falling back to her side. "What man? What are you talking about? I went alone. That I do remember."

Gibson and Sebastian exchanged looks. Sebastian said, "According to a certain Mitt Peeples, a veiled woman and an unknown man asked to see Pelletan at about nine o'clock the night he died. He went outside to speak to them. Then he came inside for his greatcoat, and left."

She shook her head. "I don't know anything about them. Damion never mentioned them to me. When I arrived at the inn, he was standing outside, staring up at the stars. I asked what he was doing—it was so cold that night. He said he was just . . . thinking."

Sebastian studied her pale, tightly held face. But if she was lying, she was giving nothing away. "And then what?"

"I asked him to come with me to see Claire Bisette's child. He went inside for his greatcoat; then we hailed a hackney carriage. We told the jarvey where we wanted to go, only when we reached the Tower, the man refused to enter St. Katharine's and insisted on setting us down, so we had to walk the rest of the way to Hangman's Court. After that . . ." She shrugged. "I know we saw Cécile, but I barely remember it. And nothing after that."

She held Sebastian's gaze, as if defying him to disbelieve her, and he thought, *Why? Why would she be keeping back something that might lead them to the person or persons who had tried to kill her?*

She said, "I heard what you said, about your wife."

"What about my wife?"

"There is a way to turn a babe in the womb that involves manually applying pressure to the belly to externally manipulate the child. But it must be done soon. If you leave it too late, it becomes considerably more difficult."

"Sounds dangerous."

"Not if you know what you're doing."

Sebastian glanced over at Gibson. "Is it possible?"

Gibson shrugged. "I've heard tales of such a thing being done. But are they true? I don't know. I've never spoken to anyone who's attempted it."

"I have done it," said Alexandrie Sauvage, leaning forward. "It doesn't always work. But you must allow me to at least make the attempt. If the babe doesn't turn before its time comes . . ." Her voice trailed off, and Sebastian felt a renewed yawn of terror open up within him.

He said, "No."

She flopped back in the chair, her hands gripping the worn, rolled leather arms. "What do you think? That I would deliberately harm an innocent child and a woman I have never met? Simply to get back at you?"

"Yes."

She pushed to her feet, her face white, her arms trembling with the effort. "Your friend is a fool," she told Gibson, and left the room.

Gibson stared after her.

Sebastian said, "You didn't tell me she was better."

"She isn't better. Her fever has broken, but I meant it when I said she shouldn't be up." He brought his gaze back to Sebastian's face. "Care to tell me what the bloody hell that was about?"

"You mean to say she hasn't told you?"

"No."

Sebastian drained his wine and went to pour himself another glass. "You remember I said I'd seen her before, in Portugal?"

"Yes."

"I was on a mission for Colonel Sinclair Oliphant when I was taken captive by a troop of French cavalry. She was with them. Her lover was a lieutenant named Tissot. When I escaped, I killed him."

There was more to the tale—far more. But Gibson had been back in London by the time of the incident, and Sebastian had never told his friend any of the wretched details.

Gibson said, "You think she holds a grudge against you?"

Sebastian looked over at him. The wind blew the snow against the windowpane, like a soft whisper from a long-vanished past. "What do you think?"

Gibson went to throw more coal on the fire. Then he simply stood there, one hand braced against the mantel, his gaze on the fire before him.

After a moment, Sebastian said, "I've discovered something that may or may not be relevant. Damion Pelletan's father was one of the doctors who performed the autopsy on the little Dauphin when he died in the Temple. He also treated the boy before his death."

Gibson turned to stare at him. "You can't be serious."

"The Comte de Provence himself confirmed it."

Gibson shook his head. "I don't like the sound of that."

"Neither do I. Particularly when you consider that Damion Pelletan was murdered on the anniversary of Louis XVI's death."

Gibson pushed away from the fireplace. "How much do you know about the death of the last Dauphin?"

"I'm not sure how much anyone knows about those days. But there's a courtier who is close to Provence—a man by the name of Ambrose LaChapelle. I think he knows considerably more than he's letting on. About a lot of things."

"Do you think you can convince him to talk?"

Sebastian finished his wine and set the glass aside. "I don't know. But I intend to try."

Chapter 26

After Devlin left, Gibson went to stand in the doorway to the inner chamber.

Alexandrie Sauvage lay, still dressed, atop the bed. She had her head tipped back, her eyes closed. He could see what the effort of rising even for those few moments had cost her in every fragile line of her being.

He said, "That was not wise."

She turned her face to look at him. "I am getting better."

"You won't if you keep pulling stunts like this one."

A ghost of a smile touched her lips. She had a full, generous mouth, gently curved in a way that made a man long to rub the pad of his thumb along its soft lines.

She said, "He hadn't told you? About Portugal, I mean."

"No."

Her slim throat worked as she swallowed. "And does it alter your opinion of me, to know that I once took a lover?"

"Why should it? I've had a few lovers myself, you know." He'd never had a wife, though, and no woman at all since he lost his leg. But he didn't see any reason to tell her that.

"That's different."

"I don't know why it should be."

"You know why. Our society expects—no, *demands*—very different conduct from women and men."

He said, "What happened to you, after your lover was killed?"

He thought for a moment she wasn't going to answer him, and if he could have unsaid the question, he would have. It was too personal, too much a betrayal of his interest in her, and he knew by the pinched look around her eyes that those days had been bleak.

She said, "I took up with a British captain—Miles Sauvage. He— how do you English say it? Ah, yes; I remember. *He made an honest woman of me.* It's a curious expression, don't you agree? An 'honest woman' is a very different creature from an 'honest man' and has nothing to do with the truth or lack thereof. Just as a woman's honor is a very different thing from a man's. It's as if when it comes to women, all possible virtues—honesty, honor, even virtue itself—are reduced simply to whom we allow between our legs."

When he said nothing, she gave a crooked smile. "Now I have shocked you."

He shook his head. "I don't shock as easily as you may think. Although that was your intent, was it not? To shock me?"

She tilted her head, her gaze on his face. And he knew he'd read her right. But he was unprepared for her next assault.

She said, "I wonder, does your good friend Viscount Devlin know of your taste for opium?"

Gibson sucked in a quick breath. "He knows I take laudanum from time to time. He was with me when they cut off what was left of my leg—held me down while the surgeon went at me with his saw."

"How long ago now?"

"Four—five years."

In Gibson's experience, four out of five men who lost an arm or a leg—or a hand, or a foot—suffered intermittent pain that seemed to come from their missing limb. The fact that the limb was no longer there didn't make the pain any less "real"—or any less agonizing. Sometimes it felt like an intense, crippling cramp; at other times it was as sharp and stabbing as a knife blade thrust deep into long-vanished flesh. It could go on and on, then suddenly disappear—only to start up again without warning a few minutes or a few days later. For many men, the pains came less frequently with the passage of time until they eventually vanished altogether, usually after a few months.

But for some, the pains never went away. He'd known men to take their own lives, simply to get away from the pain.

He said, "The laudanum helps me focus on . . . other things."

"Yes. But it takes more and more every year, does it not?" She paused, then said gently, "You know where this will end."

"I can control it."

"How? By walking the stews of London when the urge to lose yourself entirely in a poppy-hued mist threatens to become overwhelming?"

"How did you—" He broke off.

"How did I know that's why you were in St. Katharine's the night you found me? Call it a good guess. How do I know you've taken laudanum tonight? It's quite dark in here, yet your pupils are little more than pinpricks."

"I can control it," he said again.

"If you truly believe that, you are a fool."

He felt hot color stain his cheeks, but whether it was from anger or shame he couldn't have said.

He carefully straightened his spine. "I will leave you to rest," he said and limped from the room, shutting the door carefully behind him.

At various times during the evening he was tempted to rejoin the argument. There were two small chambers at the front of his house, one leading to the other and both overlooking the street. He had given her the inner room, and he could see the glow of her candle beneath the door, hear by her occasional cough that she was still awake. But he resisted, as much because he suspected he would lose any argument on the subject as from the knowledge that the last thing she needed in her condition was a heated dispute with a delusional opium eater.

He stood in the darkened outer chamber, his gaze on the snowy street beyond the cold-frosted window. A few stray flakes still drifted down, but for now the snow appeared to have ended, leaving the street ankle deep in a soft white layer of fluff. The sky above was dark and starless, the moon hidden behind the thick clouds pressing down on the city, the roofs of the ancient stone houses of Tower Hill shrouded thick with snow and dripping icicles that glimmered in the lantern of a passing carriage.

For a brief instant, the lantern light played over the harsh features of a man who stood in the shadows of a doorway opposite. Then the carriage rattled past, and the man disappeared again into darkness.

Gibson was aware of the door opening behind him, of Alexandrie Sauvage coming to stand beside him. She wore only her shift, with a blanket wrapped around her shoulders for warmth.

She said, "I couldn't sleep. It was wrong of me to taunt you the way I did. It is difficult enough to resist the allure of opium when the pain for which it was prescribed has ended. But when the pain persists . . ."

"You weren't wrong."

She gave him a crooked smile that caught treacherously at his chest. "Not in what I said, no. But for the way in which I said it, I owe you an apology. You saved my life, and I repaid you abominably."

"Ach, many's the time I've been called a fool—and worse. It's not as if—"

He broke off as a faint red glow, like tobacco burning in the bowl of a clay pipe, showed from out of the darkness. For perhaps the thousandth time in his life, Gibson found himself wishing he possessed Devlin's unnatural ability to see in the dark.

"What is it?" she asked.

Gibson nodded to the snow-filled street before them. "There's a man in the arch of that doorway, across the lane. I noticed him a few minutes ago. He's just standing there—and he's none too anxious to be seen."

"You think he's watching the house?"

"Why else is he there? I had a quick glimpse of him when the light from a passing carriage lantern fell on him. I don't think I've ever seen him before. He's a big brute, with long, curly dark hair and a neck thick enough to rival the piers of London Bridge."

"*Bullock*," she whispered, her lips parting, the fingertips of one hand coming up to press against the frosted glass of the window.

He shifted his gaze to the woman beside him. "And who might 'Bullock' be?"

"He's a Tichborne Street cabinetmaker who blames me for his brother's death."

"What the devil would he be doing here?"

She shook her head. "I don't know how he found out where I am. But he's been watching me for weeks—following me."

"That a fact?" Gibson pushed away from the window. "Well, I think maybe I'll just go on out there and ask Mr. Bullock what the bloody hell he thinks he's doing."

She caught his arm as he headed for the door, pulling him back around with a strength that surprised him. "Are you mad? Bullock once killed an apprentice with his bare hands—caved in the poor lad's skull. Somehow he managed to convince the magistrates it was manslaughter and got off with only being burned in the hand. But it wasn't manslaughter; it was murder."

Gibson gave her a smile that showed his teeth. "That's me, all right: a one-legged mad fool."

Something leapt in her eyes. "I didn't mean—"

The rattle of a wagon trace jerked their attention again to the lane. A brewer's wagon labored through the snow, pulled by a heavy team and proceeded by a trotting linkboy. The linkboy's flaring torch played over the crumbling archway where the curly-headed man had lurked.

It was now empty.

"He's gone," she said, her hand clenching on the folds of the blanket she held tightly around her. "This is what he does. He watches me for a while, and then he goes away."

"And did it never occur to you that this Bullock could very well be the man who attacked you in Cat's Hole and ripped out Damion Pelletan's heart?"

She shook her head. "If he'd killed me, it might make sense. But why let me live and kill Damion?" An arrested expression came over her features. "Unless—"

"Unless what?" prompted Gibson when she broke off.

But she only shook her head, her face pale, her lips pressed tightly together as if she was afraid to give voice to her thoughts.

Chapter 27

That evening, as the snow continued to fall, Sebastian prowled the taverns and coffeehouses of the city.

He began in Pall Mall and Piccadilly, targeting very specific establishments, places like the White Hart and the Queen's Head that catered to a special kind of clientele. As he ventured farther east, the patrons became perceptively rougher, bricklayers and butchers now mingling with barristers, soldiers, and the occasional well-dressed dandy or Corinthian. They were a disparate lot, although all shared one dangerous secret: In an age when carnal knowledge of one's own sex was a capital offense, these men risked death to meet and mingle with one another.

Many of the men, or "mollies" as they often called themselves, adopted aliases: colorful monikers like Marigold Mistress, or Nell Gin, or St. Giles's Jan. Sebastian was looking for a certain well-known flamboyant Miss Molly known as Serena Fox.

But he was having trouble finding her.

He was standing at the counter of a tavern just off Lincoln's Inn Fields, drinking a pint of ale and watching two men—one dressed in an elegant blue velvet gown, the other a bricklayer in heavy boots—dance, when a tall, slim woman in an emerald silk gown came to lean against a nearby wall, her hands behind her back, her head tilted to one side. "I hear you're looking for Serena Fox. Rather indefatigably."

Sebastian shifted his stance and took a slow swallow of his ale. The woman was no longer young, but her softly curling chestnut hair was still vibrant, the flesh of her strong, square jaw still taut, her mouth wide and full. "Hello, LaChapelle," said Sebastian.

She pursed her lips and shook her head, her French accent a throaty purr. "Here, it is Serena. What do you want with me?"

"I need some rather delicate information. And asking questions of royals—even dethroned ones—tends to be both difficult and unproductive."

"Is there a reason why I should help you?"

Sebastian took a deep drink of his ale. "Three days ago, a man with ties to the Bourbons had his heart ripped out by an unknown killer. I should think that would be reason enough for anyone interested in the well-being of the dynasty."

Serena's features remained flawlessly composed. But Sebastian saw her nostrils flare on a quick, betraying breath. "I can tell you some things. What do you want to know?"

"Is it true that Marie-Thérèse shuts herself in her chamber every twenty-first of January and devotes the day to prayer?"

"Every January twenty-first and every October sixteenth."

"Why the sixteenth of October?"

"That is the day her mother, Marie Antoinette, was guillotined."

"What about the eighth of June?"

Serena shook her head, not understanding. "What's the significance of the eighth of June?"

"That's the date her little brother, the Dauphin, died in the Temple Prison—according to Provence."

"Ah, that's right." Serena turned to signal for a brandy.

Sebastian watched her. He said, "Marie-Thérèse doesn't believe her little brother is really dead, does she?"

Serena raked her hair back from her head in a gesture that was considerably more masculine than feminine. "I suspect it would be more accurate to say she *hopes* he is alive. But I have always suspected that in her heart of hearts she knows he is not."

"Tell me what happened to him."

Serena lowered her gaze to the amber liquid in her glass. It was a moment before she spoke. "The Dauphin was eight years old when he was taken from the room in which Marie Antoinette and Marie-Thérèse were kept, and thrust alone into a cell directly below them. When he cried for his mother, his jailors beat him. Unmercifully. His mother and sister could hear his screams, hear him begging for them to stop. But that was only the beginning." He paused.

"Go on."

"The revolutionaries—perhaps even Robespierre himself—drew up a confession they insisted he sign. When he refused, they beat him again. Day after day."

"What sort of confession?"

"In it, he claimed to have been seduced by his mother and debauched by his sister and his aunt, Elisabeth. They wanted to use it at the Queen's trial."

"Did he sign it?"

"In the end, yes."

"But surely no one believed such nonsense?"

Serena shrugged. "Far too many people will believe anything of those they hate, no matter how absurd or patently fabricated it may be. And to the revolutionaries, the Bourbons became the personification of evil."

"What happened after he did as they demanded and signed the confession?"

"I've heard his jailors had promised that if he signed, he'd be allowed to rejoin what was left of his family. But it was a promise they did not keep. His jailor was a member of the Paris Commune, a cobbler named Antoine Simon. Simon's instructions were to erase all traces of gentility and pride in the boy. On good days, Simon and his wife taught him the language of the gutters, plied him with wine, put a *bonnet rouge* on his head, and taught him to sing the *Marseillaise.* On bad days, they beat him, just for the fun of it."

Sebastian took a swallow of his ale, but it tasted bitter and flat on his tongue.

Serena said, "Yet as bad as all that was, it eventually grew worse. Simon and his wife were replaced with new jailors, who starved the boy and refused to empty his slop bucket. The window of his cell was blocked up, depriving the child of both light and air. He grew increasingly ill. With no one to care for him, he was simply left to lie in his own excrement. He eventually lost the ability either to walk or speak." Serena glanced over at Sebastian. "You're certain you want to hear this?"

"Yes."

Serena nodded. "We know these things because, after the events of Thermidor, inquiries were made. A representative of the National Convention, a man by the name of Barras, was sent to visit the children in the Temple. He found the Dauphin lying on a filthy cot in a dark, noisome room so foul no one could even enter it. His skin was gray-green, his rags and hair alive with vermin, his stomach bloated from starvation, his half-naked body covered with bruises and welts from his endless beatings."

"And his mind?"

"He was visibly terrified of anyone and everyone who came near him, and completely unable to speak."

"So what happened?"

"At Barras's insistence, the child was given a new jailor, a man named Laurent, who was ordered to see that the boy was bathed and fed, and his cell cleaned. They say that on occasion Laurent would even carry the boy up to the Tower's battlements so that he could breathe the fresh air and watch the birds flying in the sky. But it was all too late. The boy was desperately ill. He died."

"And how was Marie-Thérèse treated all this time?"

The question seemed to puzzle the courtier. "She remained in the room she had shared with her mother and aunt before their executions. It was a prison cell, yes, and somewhat shabby. But it was nothing like the hellhole in which her brother was left to rot. The walls were papered, the bed canopied, the mantel of white marble—although the hearth was often cold, and for a time she was forbidden both candles and a tinderbox."

"She was not starved or beaten?"

"She was not well fed, but she was not starved—or beaten."

Sebastian was silent, his gaze on the shadows near the stairs, where the bricklayer and his erstwhile dancing partner were locked in a passionate embrace.

After a moment, Serena said, "You think what happened nearly twenty years ago has something to do with the murder of the French physician?"

"You don't?"

Serena's tongue flicked out to touch her dry lips. "I have heard—I don't know that it is true, mind you, but . . ."

"Yes?" prompted Sebastian.

"I have heard that one of the doctors who performed the autopsy wrapped the Dauphin's heart in his handkerchief and took it away with him."

"Good God. Why?"

"It is traditional, in France, to preserve the hearts of the members of the royal family. The bodies of the kings and queens of France were buried in Saint-Denis. But their hearts and other organs were ceremoniously preserved elsewhere, most typically at Val-de-Grâce."

Sebastian studied the molly's delicate features. "What are you suggesting?"

But Serena only shook her head, her lips pressed firmly together as if some thoughts were too terrible to be spoken aloud.

Sebastian arrived back at Brook Street to find Hero in the library with a stack of books on the table beside her, the black cat curled up asleep on the hearth nearby. She looked up as he paused in the doorway, the golden light from the fire shimmering in her hair and throwing soft shadows across the calm features of her face. She looked so alive, so vibrant and healthy, that he could not believe she might be dead in a matter of days.

She said, "Stop looking at me like that."

He gave a startled huff of laughter. "Like what?"

"You know what I mean. I take it you saw Gibson?"

"I did. He says he'll make some inquiries tomorrow." He came to place his hands on her shoulders, his thumbs brushing back and forth across the nape of her neck. After a moment, he said, "The Frenchwoman—Alexandrie Sauvage—is an Italian-trained physician now practicing as a midwife. She says there is a way to turn a babe in the womb. It involves applying pressure to the belly. She claims she has done it before."

He felt Hero stiffen beneath his hands. "Does Gibson believe it's possible?"

"He doesn't know. And even the woman herself admits that it can be dangerous if not done properly."

"Do you trust her?"

"No." He dropped his hands to his sides. "I killed someone who was dear to her once."

"In Portugal?"

"Yes."

Hero closed the book she'd been reading and set it aside with the others. "Perhaps the babe will turn itself."

"Perhaps." He tilted his head to read the title of the slim volume. *"Réflexions Historiques sur Marie Antoinette.* What's all this?"

"I've been reading various accounts of what happened to the royal family during the Terror."

"And?"

"What Lady Giselle told you is true; Marie-Thérèse does indeed have the bloodstained chemise worn by her father at the guillotine. The King's confessor saved it and gave it to her."

"Seems a rather ghoulish thing to do."

"It does. Yet I gather she cherishes it. It makes you wonder, does it not, about the time-honored role of the royal confessor?"

"A delicate position requiring much tact, I should think. Not so difficult when dealing with someone like Louis XVI, who by all accounts was a devout, loving husband and father, and who tried hard to be a just and honest king. But how do you in all sincerity grant absolution to a Louis XIV—or a Richard III? Someone whose actions so obviously and repeatedly violate the dictates of his faith?"

"I don't understand how such kings can honestly think they have received absolution. Perhaps they don't actually believe in their professed religion."

"Perhaps. Although I suspect it's more likely they believe they have a special divine dispensation from above."

She looked up at him. "To sin and kill without compunction?"

"Yes."

"Then why bother to confess at all?"

"That I don't know. I suppose I could always try asking Marie-Thérèse herself."

Hero gave a soft laugh. "That would be interesting."

He went to hunker beside the cat, which raised its head and looked at Sebastian with an air of bored tolerance. The cat had been with them for four months now but still lacked a name. None of the various suggestions they'd come up with ever seemed to do justice to the cat's unique combination of arrogance and ennui.

"I just had an interesting conversation with Ambrose LaChapelle," he said.

"Oh?"

In quiet, measured tones, Sebastian repeated the French courtier's description of the treatment given the Dauphin in the Temple Prison.

"I've heard some of this before," she said when he had finished, "but not all of it. That poor child."

She watched him scratch the cat behind its ears. Then she said, "There's something about LaChapelle's tale that bothers you. What?"

Sebastian shifted his hand to stroke beneath the cat's chin, the cat lifting its head and slitting its eyes in rare contentment. "There's too much in the traditional story of the Orphans in the Temple that simply doesn't add up."

"Such as?"

"Why subject the boy to such savagely brutal treatment when his sister was allowed to live in comparative comfort in the room just above him?"

"Once Louis XVI went to the guillotine, his son became the uncrowned King Louis XVII of France—the symbol of everything the revolutionaries hated. Marie-Thérèse, on the other hand, was a girl. A daughter of the King, yes, but under Salic Law she could never inherit the throne."

"True. But Spain once observed Salic Law too, and they managed to get around it. The risk was very real that France might someday do the same. So I don't think we can say she was no threat to the revolutionaries or the Republic. Yet they let her live."

"What else?"

"I'm bothered by the shifts in the Dauphin's condition that LaChapelle described taking place. The Simons—the couple who had been the boy's first jailors—were suddenly removed and replaced with a changing succession of guards. At the same time, his cell's window was covered, leaving the boy in the dark. Why do that?"

"To be cruel."

"It's possible. But I can think of another reason."

"You mean, so that no one could get a good look at him or recognize him? Good heavens, Sebastian, surely you're not giving credence to those romantic tales about the Dauphin being spirited away from his prison, with some poor, deaf-mute child left to die in his place?"

Sebastian rose to his feet. "No; of course not. It's just . . . Why the devil did they not show the dead Dauphin's body to his sister? She was right there—not simply in the same prison, but in the same tower, in the room directly above his. Why leave her in doubt? Why allow the whispers to spread and grow? Why not put all possibility of a substitution to rest, once and for all?"

"How do you know they didn't show her the dead Dauphin?"

He shook his head. "I don't understand."

"What if they did show her the child's body, only she was so horrified by his condition that she blocked the sight from her mind?"

"I hadn't thought of that, but you might be right."

He went to pour himself a glass of brandy. "I think both the Comte de Provence and Marie-Thérèse were perfectly aware of the fact that Damion Pelletan was the son of the man who treated the Dauphin at the time of his death in the Temple."

"Surely you can't think that's the reason Pelletan was killed? Who would murder a man for something his father did nearly twenty years ago?"

"Isn't that what the revolutionaries did? They killed a ten-year-old boy for the sins of his forefathers."

"But . . . Provence is far too fat and crippled to have done something like this."

"I'm not suggesting he did it himself. But he could certainly have hired someone. Someone such as the gentleman who tried to kill me outside of Stoke Mandeville."

"I can't believe it of him."

"I notice you don't say the same thing about Marie-Thérèse."

She started to say something, then stopped and bit her lip.

"You can't, can you?" said Sebastian.

Hero shook her head. "There is much about Marie-Thérèse that I admire. She survived a terrible ordeal and suffered a brutal succession of heart-wrenching sorrows. That she came through it with anything even vaguely resembling sanity is truly remarkable. But for all that, I still cannot like her. It isn't just the haughtiness, or the rigidity, or the ostentatious, intolerant piety. Someone once described Marie-Thérèse to me as a consummate performer, and I suspect that she truly is. To my knowledge, no one has ever seen her looking happy, although you also never see her appear anything but calm in public. Yet I've been told that in reality she is anything but calm. She has hysterics. She's been known to faint at the sight of a barred window, and she trembles violently at the beat of a drum or the peal of a church bell. She has never really recovered from what was done to her. And while no one could ever in any way hold that against her, I still—"

"Don't trust her?"

"I wouldn't trust either her sincerity or her sanity."

Sebastian was silent for a moment. Then he said, "LaChapelle told me something else. He said that as part of the autopsy, the boy's heart was removed."

Hero's gaze met his. "Oh, God," she whispered. "You think *that's* why Damion's killer stole his heart? In some twisted kind of revenge?"

"I don't know. But what are the odds that Philippe-Jean Pelletan would participate in an autopsy that removed the dead Dauphin's heart, only to have the heart of his own murdered son taken some twenty years later? What are the odds?"

Chapter 28

*B*y morning, the temperature had risen a few degrees above freezing, the thaw turning the snow-filled streets of the city into thickly churned rivers of brown slush. But the wind was still icy cold, with a pervasive, bone-chilling dampness that sent market women scurrying down the footpaths with shawls drawn up over their heads and their shoulders hunched.

Sebastian turned up the collar of his greatcoat and resisted the urge to stomp his cold feet. He was standing on the pavement outside the French Catholic chapel near Portman Square. The church had no bell tower, under a decree of King George III himself; only a simple Latin cross set back into the facade helped differentiate it from the two stables flanking the plain brick building. But he could hear a rustling from within, and a moment later, as the Anglican church bells of the city began to chime the hour, a small huddle of older men and women, their bodies portly and dressed almost uniformly in black, exited the church's plain doors and drifted away.

Sebastian stood with his hands clasped behind his back and waited.

He'd heard it said that every morning of her life, Marie-Thérèse rose with the dawn, made her own bed, and swept her own room, before devoting the next hour to prayer. It was what she had done each day of the more than three years she'd spent in a lonely prison cell in Paris, and she had never lost the practice. At Hartwell House, she attended daily mass with her own chaplain. But in London she came here, to the French chapel, to pray with her fellow exiles.

There were some who found the story of a king's daughter continuing to make her own bed admirable, and in a way it was. But to Sebastian it also spoke of the kind of deep and lingering trauma only too familiar to any man who had ever been to war.

Somehow, alone in her prison cell in the tower of the Knights Templar's ancient monastery, Marie-Thérèse had convinced herself that the daily practice of this homely ritual would keep her sane. It had. And so, even though she had now been free for nearly twenty years, she'd never dared to relax her self-imposed regime. It was as if the very act of making her bed and sweeping her room still kept the demons of madness at bay. Perhaps it did.

The bells of the city had long since tolled into silence. But it was another ten minutes before Marie-Thérèse herself made an appearance, trailed by her long-suffering companion, the Lady Giselle Edmondson.

"Monsieur le Vicomte," said the King's daughter, her half boots making soft, squishy noises in the slushy footpath. "This is unexpected."

He swept a gracious bow. "Your uncle told me you had decided to spend a few days in town."

"Yes. As much as I enjoy the country, I find that I do miss the theater." She cast him a speculative sideways glance. "Although I was disappointed to hear that Kat Boleyn is not treading the boards this season. She is always such a joy to watch. Don't you agree?"

An observer might have thought the remark entirely innocent—might have believed her ignorant of the fact that the actress Kat

Boleyn had for many years been Sebastian's mistress. But he saw the spiteful gleam in her eyes, and he knew better.

The jibe was both deliberate and breathtakingly malicious.

"It is a pity, yes," he said, keeping his own voice bland with effort. "But understandable, given the circumstances of her late husband's recent death. One can surely appreciate her need to spend a few months away from the city, recovering from such a loss."

"True." She sucked in her cheeks. "You wouldn't by chance know where she has gone?"

"No," he said baldly.

He did not, in truth, know where Kat had sought refuge. But wherever it was, he hoped she was finding the peace of mind she so desperately needed.

A faint frown of disappointment pulled down the corners of the Princess's lips, then was gone. She smoothed a hand over her pelisse. "So many murders! The streets of London are very dangerous, are they not?"

"They certainly can be. I've been wondering, did you know that Dr. Damion Pelletan was the son of Philippe-Jean Pelletan, the physician who treated your brother in the Temple Prison?"

Her lips flattened, and she shook her head determinedly from side to side. "No; I did not."

For someone who had spent a lifetime dissembling, she was a terrible liar. He said, "That's not the real reason you decided to see Pelletan?"

"*You dare?*" A vicious snarl twisted her lips and quivered the tense muscles of her face. "You dare to contradict me, daughter of a king of France? Me, a descendant of the sainted Louis himself?"

Sebastian held her gaze. "Whoever killed Damion Pelletan also removed his heart. Do you have any idea why they would do that?"

The violence of her reaction both surprised and puzzled him. Her eyes widened, and she gasped, one fist coming up to press against her lips.

"Madame," said Lady Giselle, rushing forward to slip an arm around the *duchesse*'s thick waist and urge her toward the waiting carriage. "Here, let me help you." She paused only to throw a piercing, furious glare over her shoulder at Sebastian. "You are despicable."

A soft clapping of gloved hands echoed in the sudden stillness.

Sebastian turned to find Ambrose LaChapelle slowly descending the steps from the chapel, his hands raised as if he were applauding a fine performance, the crook of a furled umbrella slung over one forearm.

"Congratulations," said the courtier. "She'll never forgive you for that, you know. You have just broken one of the cardinal rules. One does not contradict a member of the French royal family, no matter how ridiculous or patently false their utterances may be. Fifteen years ago, a certain Madame Senlis ventured within Marie-Thérèse's hearing to correct the Comte de Provence's faulty memory of some trivial incident from their youth. Marie-Thérèse has still not forgiven the unfortunate woman—and she never will."

"Madame Rancune," said Sebastian, watching as, in the distance, Lady Giselle tenderly tucked a fur-lined robe around the *duchesse*.

"You have no idea."

The two men turned together to walk up the street toward Portman Square.

Sebastian said, "Why did you attend Damion Pelletan's funeral?"

"I am not sure. Out of respect, I suppose."

"Is that all?"

LaChapelle cast him a quick, sideways glance. "Eighteen years ago, the boy who was destined to be King Louis XVII of France died in a filthy prison cell at the age of ten. Yet even before his body was consigned to an anonymous grave in some forgotten churchyard, the rumors had already begun to fly. There is no denying that while the boy lived, there were several plots hatched to spirit the Dauphin away and replace him with another boy, a mute, dying of consumption. So after his death, it is inevitable that some would cling to the hope that one of those plots succeeded—that a switch was made, that the child who died in the Temple was an imposter, and that the Dauphin himself still lives."

"What does any of this have to do with Damion Pelletan?"

"Few people alive today know the truth of what happened in the Temple Prison. Dr. Philippe-Jean Pelletan may be one of them. But the senior Pelletan is in France, beyond the Bourbons' ability to question him. There was hope that Damion Pelletan, the son, might know some of the events of those dark days. But he claimed he did not."

"Did the Bourbons believe him?"

"Frankly? I doubt it."

The two men walked on in silence for a moment. Then Sebastian said, "You do realize that, depending on where the truth lies, the House of Bourbon could conceivably have had two distinct motives for killing Damion Pelletan?"

"Two?"

"The first, obviously, would be to disrupt the delegation from Paris, thus putting an end to the possibility of any peace accord that would leave Napoléon Bonaparte as Emperor of France."

"Such a peace will never come to pass, with or without Pelletan's murder."

"Perhaps. But why take the chance?"

LaChapelle snorted. "To even suggest that the French royal family would stoop to murder is absurd."

"To recover their kingdom? What is one more man's death when millions have already died?"

The Frenchman's jaw tightened. "And your second so-called motive?"

"Revenge."

"Seriously? For what?"

"Damion Pelletan's father was brought to the Temple to treat the critically ill Dauphin. But the boy died anyway. One could conceivably fault the physician for his death."

"One would need to be brutal and cruel beyond measure to kill an innocent young man simply to avenge oneself on the man's father."

"And to cut out his heart?" said Sebastian.

They drew up at the edge of the square and Sebastian turned to face the courtier. But the Frenchman simply shook his head and shifted his gaze to the elliptical gardens at the center of the square, where children laughed and frolicked in the snow.

Sebastian said, "What are the chances that a substitution was made in the prison? That the son of Louis XVI and Marie Antoinette lives?"

Ambrose LaChapelle shook his head. "There is no Lost Dauphin. I told you this tale to explain the interest of Provence and Marie-Thérèse in Dr. Pelletan. But there is no doubt in my mind that the son of Louis XVI and Marie Antoinette is dead. He died eighteen years ago in prison and lies buried in a pauper's grave in the churchyard of Ste. Marguerite. Believe me, *monsieur*: If you seek Damion Pelletan's murderer, there is no need to delve so deeply into the events of the dark and distant past. There are plenty of motives to be found in the life the man was living here and now."

"Oh? Such as?"

"You have heard, I assume, of the fighting within the delegation from Paris?"

"Yes."

"Have you never wondered why Damion Pelletan agreed to come to London as Harmond Vaundreuil's personal physician? I have heard it was for love."

"For love?" repeated Sebastian.

"Mmm. Vaundreuil's daughter, Madame Madeline Quesnel, is a very attractive woman."

"She is with child. By her dead husband."

"She is, yes. But some women are never more beautiful than when they are with child. And she is, as you say, a widow."

"What precisely are you suggesting? That Pelletan was murdered by a rival for Madame Quesnel's affections?"

"You suggest that Damion Pelletan's heart was removed because his father may once have removed the heart of the dead Dauphin. I find it more likely that he fell victim to a rival in an *affaire de coeur.*"

Sebastian studied the courtier's long, delicate face. The faint traces of last night's rouge were still visible in the pores of his skin. "Why should I believe you?"

LaChapelle shrugged, as if whether Sebastian believed him or not was a matter of supreme indifference to him. "Look into it. I think you might be surprised by what you learn."

Then he turned and walked away, his furled umbrella twirling around and around as he softly hummed a familiar tune. It took Sebastian a moment to place the song.

It was the *Marseillaise.*

Chapter 29

*M*itt Peebles was sweeping the melting snow from the footpath before the Gifford Arms when Sebastian walked up to him.

"You again," said Mitt, wagging a finger at Sebastian. "I know who you are now. And I know why you was asking me all them questions."

"Oh? Who told you?"

"Nobody told me!" He tapped his finger against his forehead, his head cocked sideways as if pondering a great philosophical problem. "Done figured it out all by meself, I did."

"Impressive." Sebastian lifted his gaze to the inn's symmetrical facade.

"If you're looking for Harmond Vaundreuil, he ain't here. Went off with the other two early this morning, he did. Most likely won't be back before midafternoon."

"What about Monsieur Vaundreuil's daughter, Madame Quesnel?"

"Oh, she's here, all right." Mitt jerked his head toward the rear of the inn. "There's a private garden out the back; gate's by the stables. That's where you can usually find her. She likes to walk more'n anybody I ever did see, and it don't matter the weather."

"Thank you," said Sebastian, passing the man a coin.

Mitt's face split into a huge grin. "Anytime, your lordship. Anytime."

Tucked away between the row houses of York Street and the Recruit House that faced onto Birdcage Walk, the garden was irregular in shape, with its western end divided into four sections by paths that met at a wooden arbor covered with the thick, bare branches of an old wisteria. He found her there, one hand resting on the weathered wood beside her as she stared off over closely planted beds still blanketed white by last night's fall of wet snow. She stood utterly still, and he had the impression her thoughts were far, far away, in both time and place.

She wore a heavy black wool cloak that swelled gently over her rounded belly, and a close bonnet with a black velvet poke shielding her face. But at the sound of his approach, she turned, her features registering surprise but not alarm.

"Madame Quesnel?" he asked, bowing. "My apologies for intruding. My name is Devlin."

She couldn't have been more than twenty-three or twenty-four, with milky white skin and pretty, even features. "I know who you are," she said in a softly lilting accent. "My father pointed you out to me the other day. He says you are looking into the death of Damion Pelletan. Is that true?"

"I am, yes."

"Good."

"Somehow I get the impression your father doesn't exactly share your sentiments."

"No; of course he does not. If anything, he is furious with Dr. Pelletan for getting himself killed—as if he did it deliberately to sabotage Father's mission."

Something of his reaction must have shown on her face, because she gave a wry smile and said, "You are surprised that I would mention Father's mission? I see no point in continuing a fiction when you already know the truth."

"Thank you for that, at least."

They turned to walk along a brick path that led toward the distant park. "How long had you known Dr. Pelletan?" Sebastian asked.

"Two—perhaps three years. Father began seeing him shortly after he developed heart problems. He credits Dr. Pelletan with keeping him alive, so he is taking this death quite personally."

"But not so personally as to try to help catch his physician's killer?"

"My father's priorities are . . . elsewhere."

Sebastian studied her half-averted profile. "What manner of man was he?"

"Damion Pelletan? I doubt you will find anyone with anything harsh to say about him. He was everything you could wish for in a physician, and more. Gentle, kind . . ."

Her words were admiring. But he could detect nothing of the attitude of the lover in her manner.

"Do you know anything of his family, in Paris?" Sebastian asked. "Does he leave a wife?"

She shook her head. "No. He never married."

"What about a fiancée? Was he betrothed?"

"No." A faint smile touched her eyes, then slowly faded, as if the memory his words had provoked was too sad to hold. "He told me once that he fell in love at the age of eleven and swore never to love another."

"As did many of us," said Sebastian. "It seldom endures."

"Perhaps. Although in Dr. Pelletan's case, he actually did remain faithful."

"What happened to the object of his love? Did she die?"

"No. Her father was forced to flee France, and she had to go with him. She swore she would wait for Damion. But she did not."

Sebastian stared out over the snow-covered garden, its careful plantings invisible beneath the anonymous hollows and bumps of the blanketing white. "I take it she married someone else?"

"Yes. Some years ago."

"And yet he loved her still?"

"He did. Always."

Sebastian kept his voice level. "Do you know the woman's name?"

"Only her first name. He called her 'Julia.'"

The gate slammed behind them, a sharp clang of metal against metal. Sebastian turned to see Harmond Vaundreuil striding toward them, his gloved hands curled into fists that swung at his sides, his feet splayed out to keep from slipping on the slushy path.

"You!" he shouted, his voice booming out when he was still some twenty or more feet away, one pointed finger coming up to punch the air between them. "What are you doing here? You stay away from my daughter, you hear? You stay away from her!"

Sebastian touched his hat and bowed to the young widow. "Thank you for your assistance."

He saw no shadow of fear in her eyes. Vaundreuil's noisy bluster obviously did not frighten her. "I'd like to help in any way I can," she said quietly. "I want Damion Pelletan's killer brought to justice."

Harmond Vaundreuil's voice cut across the snow-filled garden. "Why are you here? What do you think my daughter can tell you that could possibly be of any use to you? Pelletan was set upon by footpads; you want to find his killers, go search for them in the stews and gutters of London. Not here!"

Sebastian touched his hat again. "*Monsieur.*"

The Frenchman drew up, his puffy face red, his breath coming in wheezy gasps that billowed white around him as he glared silently back at Sebastian.

Sebastian brushed past him on his way to the gate.

"You stay away from my daughter!" Vaundreuil shouted after him. "You hear? Do you hear me?"

Sebastian pivoted to face him again. "You're afraid of something. What is it?"

But Vaundreuil only clenched his jaw, his eyes bulging like those of a man who has just seen his worst nightmare come true.

"So Lady Peter lied to you," said Hero, one hand tucked through the crook of Sebastian's arm. It was just before noon, and they had come here, to Hyde Park, for the kind of brisk walk Richard Croft frowned upon. What with the cold and the wet snow and the unfashionable hour, they essentially had the park to themselves. But the pathways were slippery enough that she was being very careful where she put her feet. "Damion Pelletan and his Julia were considerably more than mere childhood friends."

"They were indeed. Although it's always possible she didn't realize just how deeply his affections were engaged."

"She knew. She promised to wait for him."

"True. But that was long ago. She may not have known that he was still in love with her. It's been nine years since her family was forced to leave France. That's a long time."

"Not for some men," Hero said quietly, and Sebastian felt his face grow hot, for he had loved Kat Boleyn for eight long years and more, and Hero knew it.

After a moment, she said, "You think that is why Pelletan decided to come to London? To see her again?"

"I'd say it's a strong possibility. Although it doesn't reflect well on him, given that she's been happily married for some years now."

"You don't know that she's happily married."

Sebastian thought about the bruises he'd seen on her arm, the black and blue imprints of an angry man's punishing fingers. "You're right; I don't know. In fact, given what I know of Lord Peter Radcliff, I suspect she's been *unhappily* married for most of those years."

Hero looked over at him. "I wonder if Damion Pelletan knew that?"

Sebastian met her gaze. "That's a question I intend to ask her."

Lady Peter Radcliff was in Clifford's Lending Library in the Strand, reaching to put a slim blue volume back up on a high shelf, when Sebastian took it from her and slipped it into place.

"Allow me," he said.

"Thank you." She twisted her gloved hands around the strings of her reticule, her lovely eyes darting this way and that, as if in fear that they might be observed.

Today she wore an elegant walking dress of jaconet muslin, with three piped flounces and a purple velvet spencer. But the gown was not quite in the latest style, and it occurred to Sebastian, looking at her, that Lord Peter's finances might not be in the best of order.

He said quietly, "I've discovered you haven't been truthful with me, Lady Peter."

Her lips parted with a quickly indrawn breath. "I don't know what you could possibly mean."

"Damion Pelletan wasn't simply your childhood friend. He was once in love with you, as you were with him. When you left Paris, you promised to wait for him. Forever."

He expected her to deny it. Instead, she dropped her gaze to her hands and sank her teeth into her lower lip. "Forever is a long time," she said in a voice that was little more than a whisper. "Especially for a woman."

"Did you know he was still in love with you?"

She shook her head slowly back and forth. But he saw the telltale flush deepening in her cheeks and knew it for a lie.

He said, "I'm told Damion Pelletan came to London because of a woman. It was you, wasn't it?"

"No! Please," she said hoarsely, her gaze lifting to his, pleading. "If my husband hears I've been seen talking to you, he'll—"

"Beat you?"

All color drained from her face. "No!"

"Damion Pelletan came to London to see a woman. If not you, then who was it?" he pressed.

She backed away from him, her head still shaking from side to side. "His sister," she whispered. "He came here to see his sister."

"His sister? What sister?"

She stared at him as if his lack of knowledge took her by surprise. "Alexi."

Sebastian could feel his pulse pounding in his throat. "Are you telling me that Alexandrie Sauvage is Damion Pelletan's *sister?*"

"Didn't you know?"

"No. No, I did not."

Chapter 30

Sebastian's loud knock at the surgery on Tower Hill was met with silence.

Smothering an oath, he pounded on the house next door, expecting Gibson's housekeeper, Mrs. Federico, to answer. Instead, Gibson's door was opened by Alexi Sauvage herself.

She stood with one hand on the latch, her face set in hostile lines, so that he thought for a moment that she might slam the door in his face.

He said, "Where is Gibson?"

"At St. Bartholomew's."

He let his gaze rove over her. She wore the same worn gray walking dress from the night of her attack, although someone had obviously made an effort to clean the stains from its cloth. "You appear to be much better."

"I am. I told Gibson this morning that I am well enough to go home."

"Yet you're still here," he said, pushing past her into the passageway.

She closed the door with a snap and swung to face him. "He disagrees."

Sebastian searched her face, the delicate, cinnamon-dusted nose, the dark brown eyes, the high cheekbones, looking for some resemblance to the man he'd seen so briefly on Gibson's slab.

He couldn't find it.

She put one hand on her hip, "I understand you consider Paul Gibson your friend."

"He is my friend, yes. Why?"

"Do you know your friend is an opium eater?"

This was not the conversation Sebastian had come here intending to have. "I know he takes laudanum from time to time."

"He has moved far beyond that."

When Sebastian remained silent, she said, "You knew, yet you've done nothing?"

"What would you have me do? He's in pain—severe, soul-corroding pain. As a physician, you of all people should understand that. Opium is how he deals with it."

"It's killing him."

"The pain would kill him."

"There are things that can be done to help."

"With the pain, or with his opium ad—" He started to say "addiction" and changed it to "—problem."

"Both."

"I didn't come here to talk about Gibson. I want to know why the bloody hell you didn't tell us that Damion Pelletan was your brother."

She held herself painfully straight. "How did you find out?"

"Does it matter?"

"I suppose not." She gave a small, peculiar shrug. "I recognized your voice that first night. I didn't tell you any more than I had to because I don't trust you."

"Because of Portugal?"

"Of course; does that seem so difficult to believe?"

He studied the signs of strain around her nostrils, the dark shadows in her eyes. But whether they were because of her recent illness or because of the bitter memories his presence aroused, he could not have said. "Have you remembered anything more about what happened in Cat's Hole?"

"Some—but not all." She swallowed. "I remember leaving Madame Bisette's room and walking back up the lane, toward the Tower; we were hoping to find a hackney there. It was so cold and dark, and Damion was . . . nervous."

"Nervous? Why?"

"From the time he was a little boy, Damion always hated the dark."

"So what happened?"

"I thought I heard footsteps behind us. At first they were some distance away, but they kept getting closer. I turned to see who it was and—" She broke off and shook her head. "That's the last thing I remember."

He said, "Tell me about Sampson Bullock."

Her eyes widened in surprise, then narrowed. "How do you know of him?"

"I know he threatened to kill you. Why the hell didn't you think to mention him?"

"But I did—at least to Gibson. Bullock threatened *me*, not Damion. How could he possibly have anything to do with what happened?"

"He holds you responsible for the death of his brother. And now I discover that Damion was *your* brother. We're talking about a man who grew up in the kind of family that names its children Sampson and Abel. I can see him harboring some rather nasty, biblical attitudes toward revenge."

"An eye for an eye and a brother for a brother? Is that what you're suggesting?" She tipped her head to one side as if considering it. "But . . . Bullock had no way of knowing that Damion was my brother. No one knows."

"I know. So does the person who told me. Bullock could have found out."

She shook her head. "No. Damion was killed because of his association with the delegation from Paris."

"The number of people who knew about the peace negotiations is small."

"Then that should make it easier to find those responsible."

He searched her thin, pale face. He could see the lines left there by the harsh life she'd lived, by her recent injury and the lingering fever she was still fighting. They had not moved from the passageway, but simply stood beside the door, old adversaries facing each other in the narrow, confined space. She leaned back against the wall. And though she would never admit it, he knew that simply being on her feet this long had tired her.

She said, "Damion told me he was approached by a man who tried to bribe him."

"Bribe him? To what end?"

"Something to do with the delegation. He was frightened by the encounter—he feared both what the man might do to him for refusing, as well as what might happen if the others found out he'd been approached."

"Why didn't you tell me this before?"

When she simply stared back at him, he said, "Your brother refused to cooperate?"

A fierce light flared in the dark depths of her eyes. "*Mon Dieu;* of course he refused! What sort of man do you think he was?"

"Who tried to bribe him?"

She frowned. "I can't recall his name precisely. I believe he was Scottish. Something like Kilmer, or Kilminster, or—"

"Kilmartin?"

"Yes, that was it," said Damion Pelletan's sister. "Kilmartin."

Chapter 31

*N*o man was a more reliable presence at the various soirees, balls, and breakfasts given by London's fashionable hostesses than Angus Kilmartin. Sebastian suspected Kilmartin worked such gatherings in much the same spirit as a pickpocket worked the crowds at a hanging, ever on the lookout for a new connection or a stray tidbit of information he could use to increase his personal wealth. Or perhaps he was simply driven by the need to show the world that a humble Glaswegian merchant's son was now wealthy and powerful enough to be invited almost anywhere.

That afternoon's most fashionable, must-attend event was a lavish winter wonderland–themed breakfast given by the Countess of Morley at her vast Grosvenor Square town house. Society "breakfasts," like "morning visits," were actually afternoon affairs, due to the fact that very few residents of Mayfair rolled out of bed before noon.

When Sebastian walked up to him, Angus Kilmartin was contemplating the exquisite ice sculptures decorating Lady Morley's long buffet table. The Scotsman threw Sebastian a brief glance, then turned his attention to the array of delicacies spread out before him.

"Didn't expect to see you here," said Kilmartin, helping himself to foie gras and toast.

Sebastian lifted a glass of champagne from the tray of a passing waiter. "Oh? Why's that?"

"You aren't exactly known for your fondness for social gatherings."

"I do occasionally put in an appearance."

"But not, I suspect, without an ulterior motive. Am I to infer that I am your purpose?"

Sebastian took a slow sip of his champagne. "As a matter of fact, you are. You lied to me."

To call a gentleman a liar was the supreme affront to his honor, an insult that was traditionally met with a challenge to a duel. But Kilmartin merely let his gaze drift over the assembled throng, a bland smile on his comical, freckled face. "I lie all the time. I've never subscribed to the pathetic belief that we owe our fellow men the truth."

"An interesting philosophy."

"At least I'm honest about it."

Sebastian gave a soft laugh. "True. I'm curious: What was Damion Pelletan's reaction when you tried to bribe him?"

Kilmartin brought his gaze back to Sebastian's face. His smile never slipped. "Heard about that, did you? Well, if you must know, he leapt at my offer. What did you think? That he became righteously indignant and threatened to expose me, so that I saw no option but to creep up behind him in a darkened alley and cut out his heart? Not his tongue, mind you—surely a more fitting punishment for one with a tendency to talk too much—but his heart? Please; spare me this drivel."

Sebastian took another sip of his champagne and somehow resisted the impulse to dash the contents of his glass into the man's self-satisfied face. "What, precisely, did you want Pelletan to do for you? He wasn't formally a part of the delegation; he was simply a physician."

Kilmartin rolled his eyes. "You don't have much of an imagination, do you?"

Sebastian studied the Scotsman's bland smile. He could think of two services Pelletan might have provided Kilmartin, one considerably nastier than the other. Kilmartin could have paid the physician to eavesdrop on the various members of the delegation and report their conversations back to him.

Or he could have pressured Pelletan to poison his own patient.

"And did he perform as well as you anticipated?" Sebastian asked.

Kilmartin heaved a heavy sigh. "Unfortunately, no. Someone else obviously got to him first."

"A statement meant to implicate—whom? Harmond Vaundreuil himself?"

Kilmartin's smile spread into something wide and toothy. "Far be it for me to encroach on your self-appointed avocation as a crusader for justice, but you do seem to require a helpful nudge in the right direction."

"Your generosity overwhelms me."

Kilmartin splayed one hand over his chest and gave a mocking bow. "I must confess, that's not something I hear every day."

"Philanthropy, like honesty, not being a belief to which you subscribe?"

"Exactly." Kilmartin's pale eyes glinted with malice masquerading as amusement. "But I seem to be feeling unusually generous today, so I'll give you another little hint to the wise: Don't make the mistake of giving too much credence to Pelletan's sister; she has her own secrets she's most anxious to hide."

"How do you know Damion Pelletan had a sister?"

Kilmartin laughed. "Information is a valuable commodity. And I like to trade in valuable commodities."

"Information can also be quite dangerous."

For one intense moment, the Scotsman's smile slipped. Then he pressed his lips together, the ends of his mouth curling up, his chin dimpling as he pulled it back in a grimace. "Only to those without the resources to use it correctly." He gave a low, mocking bow and said, "My lord."

Sebastian was watching Kilmartin weave his way through the crowd when he became aware of a stout, gray-haired, fierce-eyed dowager bearing down upon him.

She was the Dowager Duchess of Claiborne, born Lady Henrietta St. Cyr, sister to the current Earl of Hendon and, as far as the world knew, Sebastian's aunt. Now older than seventy, Henrietta had never been a beauty. But she had a regal presence, a brutal will, and a tenacious memory that made her a force to be reckoned with in Society. By far her most attractive feature was the startlingly vivid eyes that were the hallmark of her family—the blue St. Cyr eyes so noticeably lacking in Sebastian.

"Aunt," said Sebastian, stooping to brush her cheek with a kiss. She was wearing a puce satin gown trimmed in pale pink, with an extraordinarily hideous headpiece of towering striped satin ornamented with a bouquet of pink and puce-colored feathers. He stepped back, eyes widening as if in rapt admiration. "What a particularly fetching turban. You're one of the few women I know who can carry off the color puce. And with pink, no less."

She swatted at him. "Huh. Think to turn me up sweet, do you? Well, let me tell you right now, it won't work. I know why you're here."

"You do?"

"I do. Hendon told me you've involved yourself in this dreadful new murder."

Sebastian held himself very still. "What does Hendon know of it?"

"More than you might think," she said vaguely.

"What does that mean?"

She worked her lips back and forth in a way that reminded him of her brother. "He's worried about you, Devlin."

"I see no reason why he should be."

"He heard about the attack near Stoke Mandeville."

"Oh? And then he saw fit to edify you with the tale?"

"No; that was Claiborne." Claiborne was Henrietta's long-suffering son and the current Duke of Claiborne.

"How very busy of him."

"Claiborne has always been very busy. It's a tendency he inherited from his father."

Sebastian laughed out loud, for he'd known few men more taciturn than Henrietta's late husband, the Third Duke of Claiborne. Henrietta, on the other hand, rivaled Jarvis in her ability to ferret out the secrets and scandals of the various members of the haut ton— although unlike Jarvis, she was driven solely by a boundless curiosity about her fellow beings.

She fixed him with a level stare. "I take it you're not coming to my soiree on Tuesday night. As usual."

"No."

She sniffed. "How does your wife?"

"She is well, thank you. Quite well."

"I chanced to see her in Berkeley Square a few days ago. Any possibility she might be carrying twins?"

Sebastian gave a laugh that sounded hollow even to his own ears. "No; no chance of that."

"No? That explains a few things," she said cryptically, then deliberately moved away before he could challenge her on the statement.

Chapter 32

*P*aul Gibson trudged up the hill toward home, his gaze on the somber bulk of the Tower looming before him. The light was fading rapidly from the sky, leaving the ancient battlements silhouetted against the darkening clouds. He could feel the temperature dropping with each step, the icy wind chafing his cheeks and freezing his nostrils as he sucked in air. But that didn't stop a thin layer of sweat from forming on his forehead. The sense of unease that had dogged him for blocks was growing ever-more oppressive with each step. It was as if he could *feel* someone behind him, their eyes boring into his back.

Finally, when he could bear it no longer, he whipped around. "Who's there?" he cried to the nearly empty street, only to feel more than a wee bit foolish as he looked into the beady eyes of a dirty white hen that stopped midpeck to raise her head and stare at him.

Straightening his shoulders, he self-consciously adjusted the set of his coat and continued up the hill, his peg leg *tap-tapping* hollowly with each step. He tried to tell himself he was tired, worn down by the events of the last several days, and bedeviled by the wispy remnants of last night's laudanum.

Yet the feeling of being watched remained.

It was with a sigh of relief that he saw the golden glow of candle-light shining through the front windows of his house. He pushed open his front door and breathed in the rich aroma of a hearty stew. Leaning back against the closed door, he squeezed his eyes shut and tried to still the heavy pounding of his heart. Alexi Sauvage was right, he thought; those damned poppies were going to kill him at the rate he was going. Kill him, or steal what was left of his mind.

The sound of a soft step on the worn flagging of the passage made him open his eyes. She stood before him, a slim, fiery-haired woman dressed in a gown of mossy green he'd never seen before.

"You should be resting," he said.

She shook her head. "I am tired of resting. I'm better. Truly, I am. Besides, someone needed to fix your supper."

"My supper?" He frowned. "Where the d—" He started to say "devil" but caught himself just in time. "—dickens is Mrs. Federico?"

"I am afraid your housekeeper has a rather low opinion of the French."

"She what?"

"She promised to return tomorrow, after I am gone."

He became aware of the bundle of her things resting just inside the door, and its significance hit him so hard it nearly took his breath. "You're leaving?"

"I sent for Karmele. She's gone to fetch us a hackney. But I wanted to stay long enough to tell you good-bye."

She took the two steps necessary to close the distance between them. For one glorious moment he thought she meant to kiss him, and he told himself he was six kinds of an Irish fool. She rested her palms on the front of his coat. He could feel the heat of her hands against his chest, feel his heart pounding against his ribs. Then she tipped her head to brush her lips against his ever so softly before taking a step back again.

Her hands fell to her sides. "There simply are no words adequate for the task of thanking someone who has saved your life," she said. "But I don't know what else to say except . . . *merci.*"

Somehow, he found enough breath to answer her. "You don't need to be going yet."

"Yes, I do." Her gaze met his. "And you know why as well as I do."

A long silence drew out between them, filled with their measured breathing and words best left unspoken.

He said, "What about that man—the one who was watching you last night—"

"Bullock?" She shrugged. "I can handle Bullock."

She was so bloody brave and stubborn she frightened him. "And Damion Pelletan's killer?" he asked, his voice rough with the force of his emotions. "Can you 'handle' him too?"

She lifted her chin in that way she had. "I refuse to live my life in fear. But . . . I will be careful. I promise."

The rattle of a trace chain and the clatter of hooves on the cobbles outside announced the arrival of her hackney. She stooped to catch up her bundle and reached for the latch. Then she paused to look back at him. "I meant what I said last night. You don't need to live with the pain from your missing leg. I can help you. There's a trick that uses a box and mirrors to fool the mind into—"

He shook his head. "No."

"And you call me stubborn." She jerked open the door.

The hackney was old and broken-down and smelled of moldy hay and spilled ale. Gibson was conscious of her woman, Karmele, scowling at him from the vehicle's interior, her arms crossed beneath her massive breasts as he handed Alexi up into the carriage. He wished he could say something—anything—to stop this moment and hold her in his life. But the jarvey was already cracking his whip. The carriage rolled forward.

He raised one hand in an awkward gesture of farewell. But she kept her gaze fixed straight ahead, her hair a bright flame lost all too soon in the gloom of the night. It wasn't until she was gone that he realized he hadn't actually called her stubborn.

He'd only thought it.

The impulse to lose himself in opium's sweet embraces was strong enough to propel Gibson away from Tower Hill that night. Resisting a secondary urge to seek a coarser type of oblivion at his local pub, he caught a hackney to Mayfair and met Devlin at a quiet coffee-house in Hanover Square.

"I can look at your face and see that you haven't brought me good news," said Devlin, ordering coffee for them both.

Gibson eased out a soft sigh as he settled in a chair near the fire, glad to get off his peg leg. "Part of the problem is Richard Croft. He's been very busy going about justifying himself to anyone and every-one who'll listen. Technically I suppose he could claim he's been dis-creet, but it's amazing how much a man can somehow manage to convey without actually saying it. Most people are wise enough to discern the truth—that Croft resigned because he feared Jarvis's wrath should something go wrong. But rather than helping matters, that's probably only made the situation worse."

"All I need is one name," said Devlin, leaning his forearms on the table between them.

Gibson wrapped his cold-numbed hands around his steaming coffee. "Well . . . My colleague Lothan has offered to consult with Lady Devlin. But to be frank, I don't think he'll find favor with her any more than Croft did—less so, in fact. If anything, he's worse than Croft when it comes to the employment of bloodletting, purges, and emetics. And he absolutely refuses under any circumstances to use forceps, which I'm afraid may become necessary in this case."

Devlin listened to him in silence, his lean, handsome face looking unnaturally bleak and hollow eyed. "So what do you suggest?"

Gibson took a sip of the coffee and burned his tongue. "There are a few men I still haven't managed to contact yet. But if worse comes to worst . . ." He paused, drew a deep breath, and said, "What about Alexandrie Sauvage? She's a physician and an accoucheur, and she—"

"No."

Gibson dropped his gaze to his steaming cup. He knew he should tell Devlin that Alexi had left his surgery and returned to Golden Square. But somehow his throat closed up at the very thought of even trying to talk about it. He said instead, "Have you learned anything more about the men who attacked you outside Stoke Mandeville?"

"No. I had a message from Sir Henry a bit ago, saying his constables came up empty-handed at the livery stables. But I'm not surprised. Whoever we're dealing with here isn't careless enough to leave a clear trail."

"Seems to me the two aren't necessarily linked—Pelletan's murder and the attack on you, I mean. It could be that you're making someone connected to either the Bourbons or the peace initiatives nervous."

"I've no doubt my questions are making a lot of people uncomfortable."

A silence fell between them, both men lost in their own thoughts. After a moment, Devlin said, "What are the chances the babe could still turn? Give me an honest answer, Gibson."

Gibson forced himself to meet his friend's gaze. "In truth, they're small. But it is possible. I've known babes to turn within hours of a confinement."

Devlin nodded silently.

But the look in his eyes was that of a man staring into the yawning abyss of hell.

Chapter 33

*T*hat night, in his dreams, Sebastian breathed again the familiar scent of orange blossoms. Except this time the laughing shouts of the children were far away, like a haunting portent of things to come. This time, he felt the sharp edge of a too-tight rope biting deep into the flesh of his wrists and a hot, sticky wetness that trickled down the side of his face from the gash near his eye.

The moonlight was the color of bleached pewter, the air frigid with the sudden chill that darkness can bring to the mountains even after a warm spring day. He sat with his legs sprawled awkwardly before him, his bound hands wrenched painfully behind his back. The ground beneath him was bare, hard-packed earth. A fitful wind bent the crooked limbs of the trees overhead and filled the night with dancing, grotesque shadows.

He could smell wood smoke and the tantalizing aroma of roasting meat, hear the murmured voices of tired soldiers. The burnt-out shell of what had once been a gracious villa sprawled nearby, its empty arched windows glowing orange from the light of scattered campfires kindled within the lee of its protective stone walls.

The woman was careful not to get too close to him. Her skin was kissed golden by the sun, her hair a halo of fire in the night. She wore the rough trousers and rugged shirt of a Spanish peasant, with a bandolier slung across the fullness of her breasts. She looked like a Spanish *guerrillero*, but she was not. She was French, like the men who had captured him.

She said, "He won't let you die easily."

Sebastian gave her a smile that was supposed to be cocky but, thanks to his split lip and swollen face, probably came out lopsided. "Is that why you're here? To spare me the delights your Major Rousseau has planned for me in the morning? Out of the goodness of your heart, I assume?"

Her eyes narrowed. "Your colonel betrayed you. You do realize that, don't you?"

He deliberately widened his smile and felt the cut at the corner of his mouth crack open and bleed again. "I don't believe you."

"Then you are a fool."

"Most men are, sooner or later."

She'd been hunkered down before him, arms draped over her knees in the posture of one who has spent many nights around a campfire. Now she pushed to her feet. "It doesn't need to end this way."

"With my death? I think that's a foregone conclusion."

"True. Yet death can come with agonizing, unbearable slowness. Or it can come quickly . . . when there is no need to prolong it."

Sebastian forced himself to hold her gaze, his voice calm, although his guts were roiling with the knowledge of the horror her words promised. "I'll think about your offer."

"Don't think too long."

She took a step back, then another and another, careful not to turn away until she was far beyond his reach, as if there weren't two guards with their muskets trained on him, as if he weren't tied up like a hog ready for slaughter.

The pounding of the blood in Sebastian's ears had grown so loud that he could no longer hear the rush of the wind through the cedars overhead or the melancholy song of a lark heralding the coming of the day. Then he opened his eyes to find a familiar room filled with the soft light of early dawn.

He turned his head to see Hero asleep beside him, her dark hair tumbled around her face, her lashes long and dark against the flesh of her cheeks. Yet the emotions from the distant past remained so intense that he had to suck in a deep, shaky breath in an attempt to ease them.

He swung his legs over the edge of the bed, his curled fists pressing into the softness at his sides. He felt Hero's splayed hand warm against the small of his bare back.

"Bad dreams again?" she asked quietly.

"Yes."

He rose to his feet.

She watched him walk across the room. "Going someplace?"

"I want to talk to Alexandrie Sauvage's woman again."

She pushed up on her elbow. "At this hour?"

"The sun's nearly up."

"Devlin—"

He turned to look back at her.

"When you knew Alexandrie Sauvage before, in Portugal . . . was she your lover?"

He went to kneel beside her on the bed, his knees denting the mattress at her hip, his gaze locked with hers. "No. I killed her lover."

"Why?"

"Because otherwise he would have killed me."

"Then she can't blame you for it."

"If she killed me—even in self-defense—would you blame her for it?"

Hero didn't even blink. "Yes. Forever."

Tuesday, 26 January

The frigid morning air smelled of coal smoke and fresh horse droppings and roasting coffee. Sebastian pushed his way through the early crush of apprentices, tradesmen, and women wrapped in their warmest shawls with the handles of market baskets looped over their arms, their breath showing white in the misty air. Heavy gray clouds pressed down on the city, obscuring the feeble light of the rising sun and promising more snow or a biting sleet. He was crossing the square toward Alexi's house when one of the women he'd spoken to before, a street vendor, called out to him from behind her stall.

"She's back, y'know."

Sebastian paused beside the stall, the warm odor of eel pies rising from the tray before him. "You mean Madame Sauvage?"

"Aye. Came back just last night, she did. Got a big gash on the side o' her head—just here." She tilted her head and put up a hand encased in a darned wool glove to touch the matted gray hair above her ear. "Says she don't know who done it, but we all know."

"Oh? Who's that?"

"That cabinetmaker, Bullock! That's who. Any fool can see that."

"You mean the man who holds her responsible for the death of his brother?"

"That's right."

"And how, precisely, does he blame her for the death of a man who succumbed to gaol fever?"

"She's the one accused Abel Bullock of murder, she did."

"Whom had he murdered?"

"His own wife, that's who. Mattie was her name. Now, I'm not sayin' she were anythin' like an angel—she had a tongue on her could blister the hide off a mule, and she was a bit too fond of the gin, if ye know what I mean? But then, what woman wouldn't be, if'n she had to put up with the likes of Abel Bullock?"

"What happened?" Sebastian asked.

"Mattie come to Madame Sauvage one night maybe three, four weeks ago. A sight she was, with both eyes black and a split lip and hurtin' so bad she could hardly walk. Madame Sauvage had delivered Mattie's last babe, ye see, so I guess Mattie figured she could trust her. Claimed she'd tumbled down the stairs, but any fool could take one look at her an' see she'd been worked over by a man's fist. Kicked her too—right in her belly. Madame Sauvage did what she could, but some things can't be fixed. Died, she did. Somethin' ruptured inside her."

"There was an inquest?"

"Aye. Problem was, the Bullock brothers, they both swore she'd fallen down them steps. And though there was plenty what heard her screaming an' Abel cursin' her and hittin' on her, folks was too scared to step forward and say it."

"Afraid of the Bullock brothers, you mean?"

The woman dropped her voice and leaned forward, her eyes opened so wide he could see the white rimming her gray irises. "Mattie weren't the first them two 'ave killed."

"So what happened?"

"Madame Sauvage come forward. Said there weren't no doubt but what Mattie'd had a beatin', and that before Mattie breathed her last, she said her husband had done it."

"And the coroner believed her?"

"She was real persuasive, she was. They committed Abel to Newgate to stand trial. Not for manslaughter, but murder."

"He died of gaol fever before he came to trial?" asked Sebastian, his head tipping back as he studied the attic windows in the Dutch-like roofline of the corner house.

"He did. And ever since, Sampson Bullock's been telling anyone who'll listen that he's gonna make her pay. He says—" She broke off, her mouth sagging open, her head turning as a low rumble reverberated across the square.

Sebastian saw a flash of light behind the windows on the fourth floor of the corner house. A concussive blast shattered the morning calm, splintering windows and sending roof tiles and singed rafters exploding upward on a massive white plume of billowing smoke.

Then a hail of gritty dust and glass and burnt debris rained down on the screaming crowd in the square.

Chapter 34

His breath coming harsh and fast, Sebastian tore up the stairs. He paused on the second landing to yank off his cravat and tie it around his mouth and nose. From above came the crackle of flames biting into dry old wood and the roar of a combustion so fierce he could feel the draft on the sweat of his forehead. Somewhere between the second and third floors he came upon a little girl in a singed pinafore, her fair curls framing a pallid, smudged face. He scooped her up, her limp hand dangling as he plunged back downstairs with her.

He was aware of grim-faced men pushing past him up the stairs, some armed with axes, others carrying flexible leather hoses clamped together with brass fittings. He stumbled out into the rubble-strewn, misty square to find it filled with screaming women and shouting men and the clanging bells of the engines, each with a pair of men frantically working the cross handles to pump water from their cisterns. He started across the pavement toward the square's central gardens, rubble and broken glass crunching beneath his feet, and heard someone scream, "Georgina!"

The child in his arms stirred, and he turned to see a woman, tears streaming down her blackened face, her muslin gown hanging in dirty tatters, stumble toward him with arms outstretched.

"Georgina! Oh, thank God!"

Surrendering the child to her mother, Sebastian pushed his way back across the street. Someone handed him a tankard of ale and he paused to gulp it down thankfully. He was giving it back to a buxom woman with a tray when his gaze fell on the body of Alexi Sauvage's Basque servant, Karmele, lying on the pavement where someone had left her, so blackened and shattered he didn't need a second look to know she was dead.

Bloody hell. Swiping his sleeve across his face, he headed back into the house just as a tall, skinny man with a nasty gash across his forehead stumbled out the door to croak, "Ain't nobody left alive in there."

Sebastian grabbed his arm as he passed. "You're certain?"

The man stared at him mutely and nodded, red-rimmed eyes pale in a black, sweat-streaked face.

Sebastian let his head fall back, his gaze raking the top of the house. Feather-light streaks of black ash were still falling from out of the misty gray sky. But the flames had subsided, leaving the air thick with the pungent stench of wet, burned wood.

He tore off the cravat he'd shoved back down around his neck and used it to wipe his face. Six years in the army had given him a painful familiarity with gunpowder explosions. He had no doubt as to what he had just witnessed, just as he had no doubt that Alexandrie Sauvage had been the intended target. The blast had been sited directly beneath her rooms.

What kind of monster could without hesitation or remorse risk killing or maiming an entire house full of innocent men, women, and children, simply to murder one woman? Who would do something like that? And why?

He glanced back at Karmele's body to see a young woman with a halo of dark red hair kneeling on the pavement beside her, one

charred hand cradled in her lap, her head bowed as if in silent prayer.
An empty market basket rested on the pavement beside her.

Sebastian walked up to her, not stopping until the toes of his
Hessians nearly touched the worn, mossy green gown puddled on
the debris-strewn pavement around her. He watched her stiffen, her
gaze lifting slowly from his boots to his face.

"I thought you were dead," he said.

She shook her head. "The cold, damp weather always makes Karmele's rheumatism act up. I offered to go buy the bread this morning."

He hunkered down beside her, his gaze hard on her face. "If you
know anything—*anything*—that might explain who is doing this, or
why, you must tell me."

Her face was ashen pale, the sprinkle of cinnamon across the high
bridge of her nose standing out stark as she lifted her gaze to the fire-
blackened bricks of the roofline above them. "What makes you think
this was directed at me? It could have been an accident."

"This was no accident. It was a small charge of gunpowder deliberately staged in the rooms directly beneath yours. What do you
know about the tenant on the floor below you?"

She shook her head. "Last I heard, the rooms were empty. There
was an old widow—a Mrs. Goodman. But she died a week or so ago."

She fell silent, her gaze coming to rest, again, on her woman.

He said softly, "Are you all right?"

She swallowed hard. "Yes." But he knew what she was thinking,
that this was all somehow, ultimately, her fault, that she had caused
Karmele's death.

He said, "How long ago did you leave the building?"

"Just minutes before the explosion. I was crossing Brewer Street
when I heard it."

"It's possible you left right after the killer set the fuse. You didn't
notice anyone strange as you were leaving?"

"No." She cast a quick, probing glance at the crowd of people mill-
ing about them. "Are you saying whoever did this could still be here?"

Sebastian let his own gaze drift around the rubble-strewn square, thronged now with gawkers. "Whoever lit that fuse would have wanted to be well away from the building itself before the powder blew. But I doubt he went far. He'd want to be here to see it—and to make certain nothing went awry."

"But something did go awry," she said, her voice a husky rasp. "I am still alive."

He brought his gaze back to her face. "Why would someone want to kill you? Not Damion Pelletan, but *you?*"

"I do not know! Mother of God, you think I would not tell you if I did?"

He held her furious gaze for one long moment. "Yes."

Jules Calhoun let out a pained sigh. "I may be able to salvage the buckskins, my lord," he said. "But the coat and waistcoat are hopelessly ruined. And the cravat."

"Sorry," said Sebastian, pulling a clean shirt over his head.

"And your boots! I fear they may never be the same again."

"If anyone can save them, you can."

Calhoun made an inelegant noise deep in his throat.

Sebastian said, "When you were asking around Tichborne Street about Bullock, did anyone mention whether or not he had a military background?"

Calhoun looked up from the boots. "I don't believe so, no. Why?"

"He has what looks like a scar from a saber slash across his cheek. I'd be interested to know if he spent some time in the army—and if so, with what sort of a unit."

"You think Bullock could have set that gunpowder to explode?"

"I'd find it difficult to believe he has the requisite knowledge—unless there's something in his background we don't know about."

Calhoun turned toward the door, the charred clothes held in one extended hand. "I'll see what I can find, my lord."

"Calhoun?"

The valet paused to look back at him.

"Be careful."

The conviction that Alexandrie Sauvage was hiding something re-mained.

And so that afternoon Sebastian went to see one of the few peo-ple he knew in London who was familiar with her—and still alive.

He'd no doubt that Claire Bisette had honestly told him all she could remember of Alexi's visit to her lodgings that night with Da-mion Pelletan. But a woman raw with grief over her child's recent death was unlikely to make a reliable witness.

He found Cat's Hole crowded with beggars and seamen and ven-dors selling everything from pickled eggs and salted herrings to cracked old shoes and mended tin pots. The air was thick with the smell of the river and overflowing bog houses and unwashed human-ity. His knock on the door at the end of the corridor off Hangman's Court went unanswered for so long he was beginning to think Claire Bisette had moved away. Then the door swung slowly inward to re-veal the sad-eyed woman he remembered from the other night.

"I'm sorry to bother you again," he said, removing his hat. "But I wonder if I might ask you a few more questions about the night Dr. Damion Pelletan was killed?"

He realized she was younger than he'd first taken her to be, prob-ably closer to thirty than forty. She had her dark blond hair pulled back into a neat bun, and the wild look of unimaginable anguish he remembered had been replaced by a quiet kind of hopeless despair that was in its own way even more heartbreaking to witness.

She nodded and stepped back to allow him to enter. *"Monsieur."*

The room was as cold and forlorn as it had been the first time Sebastian had seen it. And he knew without being told that she had spent the money he'd given her not on fuel or food for herself, but on securing a proper burial for her dead child.

As if aware of the drift of his thoughts, she squared her shoulders with a ghost of pride and said, "What was it you wished to know?"

"I realize this might be a difficult question to answer since you'd never met Damion Pelletan before that night, but . . . did he seem at all agitated in any way? Angry? Or perhaps even afraid for some reason?"

Her eyes narrowed. Instead of answering, she said, "How is Alexi Sauvage?" The question was not the non sequitur it might have seemed.

"She is much improved. Unfortunately, the blow to her head has affected her memory. She recalls little from that night. Which is why I was hoping you might be able to help us piece together what happened, and why."

The Frenchwoman continued to stare at him for a moment longer. But the answer seemed to satisfy her. She went to stand at a small cracked window overlooking the dark, narrow courtyard below. "I found him a most gentle, generous man, and he could not have been kinder to me. But . . ."

"But?" prompted Sebastian.

"Since your last visit, I've been trying to recall everything that was said that night. He and the *doctoresse* were arguing—and I don't mean about Cécile."

"Do you remember what about?"

"The conversation was held in undertones, but I heard enough to understand that the disagreement was over a woman. Not a patient, but someone from Dr. Pelletan's personal life."

"A woman?"

She nodded. "I had the impression the woman was someone from his past who is now wed to another. I could be wrong—it was all said in whispers, and I was so very distracted—but I had the impression he wanted this woman to leave her husband."

"And Alexandrie Sauvage thought that would be a mistake?"

"She did, yes."

"Did she say why?"

"If she did, I did not hear it. When your child is ill . . ." Her voice trailed away.

Claire Bisette was a woman whose life had been crowded with unimaginable hardships and sorrows. For the sake of her child, she had kept going, struggling every day to find food, to survive. But now, with Cécile dead, it was as if something had died within her too. And Sebastian knew it was her will to live.

He said, "When was the last time you ate?"

She shook her head. "I don't know. It does not matter."

"It does." He removed one of his cards from his pocket and held it out to her. "My wife is due to be confined shortly and is in need of a nursemaid for our first child. She would prefer to engage someone older and better educated than those typically sent by the employment agencies. I realize that such a position is far below the station to which you were once accustomed, but it is a beginning."

Rather than take the card, she shook her head, one hand running self-consciously down the side of her ragged, old-fashioned gown. "I could not possibly present myself to your wife looking like this."

"A lack of proper clothing is easily remedied, unlike deficiencies in education, experience, and character."

When she refused to take the card, he laid it on the wooden mantel of the cold hearth. "I'll tell Lady Devlin to expect you," he said, and then left before she could hand it back to him.

Sebastian tried to remember what Alexandrie Sauvage had told him about Lady Peter Radcliff. But when he thought about it, he realized he couldn't recall having discussed the beautiful, sad-eyed Frenchwoman with Damion Pelletan's sister at all. When she'd been fighting for her life in the aftereffects of concussion and possible pneumonia, he could understand the omission. But he found it difficult to believe that a woman truly interested in finding her brother's killer would fail to disclose his dangerous interest in another man's wife.

Lady Peter's reasons for failing to reveal the true extent of her involvement with the young French doctor were considerably easier to understand.

Lord Peter Radcliff's beautiful French-born wife was watching her little brother race two gaily colored wooden sailboats across the narrow strip of ornamental water in Green Park when Sebastian walked up to her. A blustery wind scuttled a tumble of gray clouds overhead, sending shifting patterns of light and shadow across the ruffled surface of the water and billowing the cloth sails of the crudely fashioned boats. "Noël," Lady Peter called, laughing. "I think the blue one is going to win." Then she froze, the merriment dying from her eyes as she turned her head to see Sebastian.

She wore a fur-trimmed pelisse of dark hunter green wool made high at the throat and long in the sleeves. And it occurred to Sebastian that even on balmy days she invariably stayed away from styles that revealed too much of her skin.

But nothing could disguise the livid bruise that rode high on her left cheekbone.

Chapter 35

*L*ady Peter stood very still, only her shoulders jerking with the agitation of her breathing as she watched Sebastian walk up to her. And he found himself wondering why she feared him so much.

She said, "Why are you here? What do you want from me?"

"Only some information about Damion Pelletan." He shifted his gaze to the mock naval race before them. "Who made the boats? Lord Peter?"

She shook her head. "Noël. He has ambitions to go to sea."

"It can be a lucrative career," said Sebastian.

"It can also be a deadly one—even when England is not at war, as it is now."

"England will always be at war with someone, somewhere."

"True." He was aware of her gaze lifting from the boats to his face. "But you didn't come here to discuss my brother's future career options, did you, Lord Devlin?"

He watched the two boats skim across the choppy surface of the water. "You told me you grew up next door to Damion Pelletan, in Paris."

"Y-yes," she said warily, obviously unsure where he was going with this.

"How well did you know his sister, Alexi?"

"Alexi?" She let out her breath in a soft sigh, as if relieved by the seemingly innocuous direction of the conversation. "Not well. She was six years older than I, and very serious. She always dreamt of becoming a physician. She had little use for dolls or needlework or silly little girls like me."

"She went to the University of Bologna to study?"

Lady Peter nodded. "She was just sixteen. Dr. Philippe had an uncle there, and she went to stay with him."

"What do you know of her first husband—Beauclerc, wasn't it?"

"Yes. He was a physician as well. I never knew him; I believe they met in Bologna. When he joined the Grand Army, Alexi went with him."

"He was killed?"

"Yes." She watched Noël run along the water's edge, shouting encouragement to first one boat, then the other. "Why are you asking me these questions about Alexi?"

"I'm wondering why she would take such care to preserve your secret."

Lady Peter turned her head to look at him, her breath leaving her body in an odd, forced laugh. "Secret? What secret?"

"Damion Pelletan didn't come to London to see his sister, did he? He came to see you. Did he come here intending to try to convince you to leave England and go back to France with him? Or was that a decision he reached only after he saw you?"

The new bruise stood out starkly against the ashen pallor of her face. "No! I've no idea what you are talking about!"

"You said Damion Pelletan came to dinner one evening and paid you a few formal calls."

"Yes."

"Then how did he come to know Noël?" Children traditionally made no appearance at formal meals or visits.

She stared at him with wide, frightened eyes. "I don't understand."

"You told me that on the morning of his death, last Thursday, you saw Pelletan in the park arguing with Kilmartin. You said Noël called out to Damion and would have run to him if you hadn't stopped him. That suggests that Noël not only knew Damion Pelletan, but that he considered him a friend. How did your little brother come to know him so well?"

Rather than answer, she looked out over the wind-wrinkled water, her throat working painfully as she swallowed.

"Did Lord Peter find out about Damion?" Sebastian asked quietly. "Is that why he hit you?"

"My husband does not beat me," she said with awful dignity.

"Where did you get the bruise on your face, Lady Peter?"

One gloved hand crept up to touch her cheek, then fluttered self-consciously away. "I . . . I tripped. It was the silliest thing. I tripped and smacked my face against the side of a bureau."

Sebastian watched Noël run around to the far bank to try to catch his boats. "Does Lord Peter know that you and Damion Pelletan were once considerably more than childhood friends?"

She shook her head.

"So he didn't realize that Pelletan was still in love with you?"

"No! He didn't know anything, I swear it." She started to touch her bruise again. Then, as if becoming aware of what she was about to do, she curled her hand into a fist and dropped it to her side.

In England, a husband was legally empowered to beat his wife. He was expected to restrain himself to "gentle chastisement," but the forces of the law usually looked the other way unless he so far forgot himself as to kill the poor, hapless woman. Even then, he could frequently plead manslaughter and get away with a simple burning on the hand.

The law was not always so tolerant of a jealous husband who killed a real or imagined rival for his wife's affections.

Lady Peter said, "There—there is something I did not tell you."

"Oh?"

She bit her lower lip, her gaze sliding away from him, as if frantically calculating how much to tell him—and how much to keep hidden. "You're right; I did see Damion more frequently than I admitted before—perhaps more than I ought to have. He reminded me so much of happier days, of springtime along the Seine, when my parents were still alive and I was young and carefree."

"And?"

"Damion would sometimes meet Noël and me here, in the park. I last spoke to him late Wednesday afternoon—the day before he died. I knew as soon as I saw him just how upset he was."

"Did he tell you why?"

"At first he tried to shrug it off, saying the constant quarreling amongst the various members of the delegation was becoming tiring. But he finally admitted he'd discovered something that troubled him—something about Vaundreuil."

"About Vaundreuil's health?"

"No. Damion told me once that Vaundreuil's heart is nowhere near as bad as Vaundreuil believes it to be—that if he would only eat sensibly and drink in moderation, he would in all likelihood live to a ripe old age." She watched Noël hunker down to retrieve his boats. "Whatever worried him involved the peace negotiations. He told me he was considering approaching Colonel Foucher with what he knew."

"Do you think he did?"

"I don't know. He may have decided instead to confront Vaundreuil directly."

Sebastian studied her flawless profile, the exquisite lines of her face marred by the ugly purple bruise. "Did Damion ever tell you someone was trying to bribe him?"

"Good heavens, no. Bribe him to do what?"

"Spy on the other members of the delegation, perhaps?"

"You mean work for the English? Damion would never have agreed to do such a thing. He was an honorable man—and fiercely loyal to France. He had no interest in money."

"There are other ways of persuading a man to do things against his will."

"By threats, you mean?" She shook her head. "Damion would never have allowed himself to be coerced into doing something dishonorable."

"Even if the threats weren't against Damion himself, but against someone he loved?"

Her gaze drifted back to her little brother, who had left his boats on the bank and was now following a waddling, complaining duck across winter-browned grass scattered with patches of melting snow. She swallowed hard, the silence filling with the rush of the wind and the slap of the water against the shore and the homely *quack-quack* of the duck.

Sebastian said, "Why did you decide to tell me about Vaundreuil now?"

She shook her head, as if unable or unwilling to put her motivation into words.

And he was not cruel enough to do it for her.

Harmond Vaundreuil was sitting at a table in the coffee room of the Gifford Arms when Sebastian walked in. An array of papers covered the surface before him; he had a quill in one hand, his head bent, a pair of gold-rimmed spectacles perched on his nose. He cast Sebastian a quick glance, then returned to his work.

"The coffee room is not open to the public," he said in his heavy Parisian accent.

Sebastian went to stand with his back to the roaring fire. "Good. Then we don't need to be worried about an interruption."

Vaundreuil grunted and dipped his pen in the small pot of ink at his elbow.

"How are the negotiations progressing?" Sebastian asked pleasantly as the Frenchman's quill scratched across his paper.

"Why don't you ask your father-in-law? Or your own father, for that matter."

Sebastian was careful to keep all sign of surprise off his face. But the truth was, he had not known until now that Hendon was also involved in the preliminary peace discussions.

When he remained silent, Vaundreuil grunted again and said, "Still determinedly chasing the illusion that Damion Pelletan was killed by someone other than a band of London's notorious footpads?"

"Something like that. Tell me: Was Pelletan an ardent supporter of the Emperor Napoléon?"

"Dr. Pelletan was a dedicated physician. To my knowledge, he wasn't an ardent supporter of anyone."

"But he favored peace?"

"He did."

"And was he pleased with the direction the negotiations were taking?"

Vaundreuil lifted his head in a way that enabled him to look at Sebastian over the upper rims of his spectacles. "Damion Pelletan had no part in the negotiations."

"But he knew how they were progressing, did he not?"

"No."

"No?"

"No." The Frenchman went back to his writing.

Sebastian said, "Did you know Damion Pelletan has a sister here in London?"

"I did, yes. Now you really must excuse me; I am very busy. Would you kindly go away and allow me to finish my work?"

"In a moment. Are you not even curious to know what happened to him?"

"I am a diplomat, not a policeman. The wrong kind of curiosity is a luxury I cannot afford. If Damion Pelletan's murderer must go free for the negotiations to continue, then so be it."

"I can understand that. But what if Pelletan was killed by someone intent on disrupting your mission? Surely it has occurred to you that the murderer might well try again—by targeting someone else in your party?"

Vaundreuil dropped his pen, a splotch of ink flowing across the paper as his head came up. His gaze met Sebastian's across the room, then jerked away as footsteps sounded on the paving outside the inn's sashed windows.

Sebastian heard a man's voice, followed by a woman's gentle laughter. It took him a moment to realize who it was. Then he saw Colonel Foucher walking side by side with Madeline Quesnel, a market basket slung over her arm.

And there was no disguising the raw fear that gusted across her father's face as he confronted a new and obviously terrifying possibility.

A smothering envelope of dense fog was descending on the city, yellow and heavy with the bitter stench of coal smoke.

Leaving the Gifford Arms, Sebastian turned toward the hackney stand at the end of York Street. It was only midafternoon, but the streets were unnaturally deserted, the pavement slick with condensation and grime, every sound magnified or distorted by the suffocating shroud of foul, heavy moisture. He could hear the rattle of a harness in the distance, the shouts of boatmen out on the river . . .

And the steady rhythm of a man's footsteps that seemed to start up out of nowhere and gained on him, fast.

Chapter 36

Sebastian walked on, his senses suddenly, intensely alert.

The shadow's footsteps kept pace with him.

He passed a gnarled old workman in a blue smock, his gray bearded face beaded with moisture, his head bent as he hurried on without a second glance. A moment later came the thump of two bodies colliding and the workman's angry, "Oy! Why don't ye watch where yer goin'?" The shadow's footsteps hesitated for an instant, then resumed and quickened.

Sebastian stepped sideways, turning so that his back was to the brick wall of the town house beside him as he stopped and listened.

Damn this fog.

A man stepped out of the swirling mist: a gentleman, clad in a fashionable greatcoat and beaver hat with a heavy scarf that obscured the lower part of his face. He held his left hand straight down at his side, the folds of his greatcoat all but obscuring the dagger clutched in his fist.

"Looking for me?" said Sebastian.

For one startled instant, the man's gaze met Sebastian's and his dark, heavily lashed eyes blinked as he realized just how radically the situation had suddenly altered. Not only had he lost the benefit of surprise, but it was considerably easier to knife a man in the back than to confront him face-to-face.

Sebastian took a step forward. "What's the matter? Can't get at my back?"

The would-be assailant turned and darted into the street.

Sebastian leapt after him.

A team of bay shires appeared out of the fog, heads bent as they leaned into their harnesses, the heavily loaded dray they pulled rattling over the uneven paving. The man drew up and spun around, his knife flashing just as Sebastian's foot slid on the wet stones. Before he could jerk out of the way, the blade slashed along Sebastian's forearm. Sebastian fought to regain his balance on the icy pavement, slipped, and went down hard.

The man whirled and ran.

"Bloody hell," swore Sebastian, scrambling to his feet, his bleeding arm held crimped to his chest. A whip cracked, the air filling with harsh shouts and the jingle of harness as a wide-eyed pair of grays reared suddenly in the gloom. Sebastian ducked out of the way of the horses' slashing hooves, then swerved to dodge a lumbering dowager's carriage.

By the time he reached the opposite footpath, the greatcoated man in the heavy scarf had disappeared.

"Your questions are obviously making someone uncomfortable," said Gibson, laying a neat row of stitches along the gash in Sebastian's arm.

Sebastian grunted. "The question is: Who?" He was seated on the table in Gibson's surgery, stripped to his waist, a glass of brandy cradled in his good, right hand.

Gibson tied off his thread. "Any chance Monsieur Harmond Vaundreuil could have had his own physician killed?"

"You mean because he discovered someone—probably Kilmartin—was trying to bribe Pelletan?" Sebastian took a slow swallow of his brandy. "It's certainly possible. It wouldn't matter whether or not Pelletan actually accepted Kilmartin's bribe, if Vaundreuil somehow came to hear of it. And there's no doubt in my mind that Vaundreuil is afraid of something. I just don't know what."

"The other members of his delegation, perhaps?"

"Perhaps." He remembered the horror Vaundreuil had shown when told the killer had removed Pelletan's heart. He still believed that horror was real. But it was always possible the Frenchman had simply been ignorant of his own henchman's viciousness.

Sebastian watched Gibson smear a foul-smelling salve over the wound. "What I find difficult to understand is why Vaundreuil or one of his associates would want to plant a charge of gunpowder in Golden Square in an effort to kill Damion Pelletan's sister. But then, that could be because Madame Sauvage is being considerably less honest with us than she could be. About a lot of things."

He was aware of Gibson stiffening. "What's that supposed to mean?"

"I've discovered that Damion Pelletan was trying to convince Lord Peter Radcliff's pretty young wife to run away with him. In fact, Pelletan and his sister were actually arguing about it just moments before he was murdered. Now, why do you suppose she neglected to tell us that?"

A woman's voice sounded from the doorway behind him. "I've told you there is much I still don't recall from that night."

Sebastian turned to look at her. She wore the same old-fashioned gown from that morning, the smudges of black at her knees still visible from where she'd knelt beside the body of her dead servant woman. And it occurred to him that everything she owned had probably been lost in the explosion and fire.

He glanced at Gibson, who was preparing to wrap a bandage around the injured arm. A faint but clearly discernable flush of color rode high on the surgeon's gaunt cheekbones. And Sebastian knew without being told that Gibson had offered the now homeless Frenchwoman a place to stay—and she had accepted.

He looked back at Madame Sauvage. "How long had you known?"

"That Damion wanted Julia to return with him to France? He only told me that night, as we were walking up Cat's Hole to see Cécile."

"Did he tell you why?"

"You mean that he had discovered Radcliff was beating her? Yes."

"And it never occurred to you that a man violent enough to use his fists on his helpless young wife might also be violent enough to kill the man proposing to steal that wife away from him?"

"I told you, I only learned what Damion intended the night of the attack. I simply did not recall it."

Sebastian let his gaze drift over the pale, fine-boned features of her face. Not only was she a habitual liar, but she wasn't particularly good at it. How the hell Gibson couldn't see that was beyond him. But all he said was, "Tell me about your father's autopsy of the Dauphin in the Temple Prison."

The sudden shift in topic seemed to confuse her. She stared at him, her eyes wide. "What?"

"Your father was one of the doctors who performed an autopsy on Marie-Thérèse's ten-year-old brother, the Dauphin of France, after his death in prison. You were—how old? Twelve? Thirteen?"

"I was fourteen."

"So you must recall something about it. I take it you were already interested in medicine at the time. Surely he discussed it with you."

"He did."

"Did he believe the dead boy he saw in the Temple was in fact the son of Louis XVI and Marie Antoinette?"

She moved to stand before the room's fireplace, her back to them, her gaze on the small blaze on the hearth. "My father saw the boy alive only once or twice, when he was called to the Temple just days before the child's death. He never had any doubt that the boy who died in prison was that same child."

"Yet that's not to say the child he treated was actually the Dauphin."

"No," she said quietly. "I have seen the autopsy report—my father kept a copy himself. It has been years since I read it, but I remember noticing that he was very careful to state that the body was identified by the jailors as belonging to the Dauphin. He himself did not make the identification."

"Did he believe the dead child actually was the Dauphin?"

"I honestly do not know. It's not something he likes to talk about. I do know he was confused because the jailors insisted to him that the child's final illness had come on suddenly. Yet the boy died of a long-standing case of tuberculosis."

"Did he? Or was that simply the story that was put out? A fiction much less damning than to admit that he died of mistreatment or neglect."

"No; my father told me the child whose body he autopsied most definitely died of tuberculosis."

Sebastian looked at Gibson, who had his head bent, his attention seemingly all for the task of tying off the bandage. In the sudden hush, the buffeting of the wind against the heavy old windows and the creak of a cart's axle in the lane outside sounded unnaturally loud.

Alexi Sauvage said, "What precisely are you suggesting? A moment ago, you would have had me believe that Lord Peter Radcliff killed my brother for coveting his wife. Now you're saying Damion's death is somehow linked to an autopsy my father performed nearly twenty years ago? Are you actually suggesting that the Dauphin somehow survived his imprisonment, and my father knew it? But . . . that's absurd!"

"Is it?"

"It is, yes. My father must have believed the Dauphin died in the Temple. Otherwise, why would he—" She broke off, her chest jerking on a suddenly indrawn breath.

"What is it?" asked Sebastian, watching her. "Otherwise why would he *what?*"

Her tongue crept out to slide across her cracked lower lip. "At the conclusion of the autopsy, my father wrapped the boy's heart in his handkerchief and smuggled it out of the prison hidden in the pocket of his coat. He soaked the heart in alcohol and has kept it preserved in a crystal vase in his office ever since."

"Are you telling me your father was the physician who removed the Dauphin's heart? *And he still has it?*"

"Yes."

"And you didn't tell us this? Why?"

Her jaw tightened, her eyes flashing with scorn. "My father has performed hundreds of autopsies over the course of his career. It is preposterous to think that Damion's murder here, in London, is somehow linked to a death that occurred in Paris decades ago. My brother was killed because he was part of a delegation seeking a peace that is anathema to powerful interests here in England, both political and economic. Powerful interests that include your own father-in-law!"

Sebastian returned her hard stare. "I might be able to accept that more easily if it weren't for one problem."

"What's that?"

"Why would Lord Jarvis—or anyone else involved in the peace negotiations, for that matter—want to steal your brother's heart?"

Chapter 37

"Do you think Gibson is in love with Alexandrie Sauvage?" Hero asked.

It was after dinner, and they were seated in their drawing room. Hero was petting the bored-looking black cat, while Sebastian—who saw no reason to follow the popular custom of drinking port in solitary splendor at his dining table when he could be enjoying the company of his wife—held a glass of burgundy. He was dressed in the silk knee breeches, white stockings, and buckled shoes that were de rigueur for a gentleman attending a formal London function. It was the night of his aunt Henrietta's musical soiree, and he had suddenly discovered a very good reason for attending.

He took a slow swallow of his wine, for Hero's question had given voice to one of his own concerns. "I'm very much afraid he might be."

"It could be good for him."

"Perhaps—if we were talking about any woman other than Alexi Sauvage."

"Maybe you're wrong about her."

Across the room, her gaze met his, then dropped to the hand she moved slowly up and down the cat's back.

"You don't need to tell me," she said quietly, her voice suddenly, oddly scratchy, so that he wondered what she had seen in his face.

He could hear the rattle of carriage wheels on the pavement outside, the whisper of ash falling on the hearth. The memory of that spring was like a frozen shiver across the skin, an incubus that stole his breath and tormented his soul. "No; I do. I should have told you before." He found he had to draw a deep breath before he could go on. "I met her three years ago, when I was serving as an observing officer for a vain, pompous, and extraordinarily vindictive colonel named Sinclair Oliphant. Wellington's forces were already beginning to push into Spain, and Oliphant was in charge of securing the mountain passes out of Portugal.

"One day, he ordered me to carry sealed dispatches to a band of partisans said to be camped in a small valley below the ancient convent of Santa Iria. Except it was all a hoax. Oliphant knew the partisans weren't there, and he'd had one of his spies tip off a French force operating in the area. They were waiting for me."

Hero stared at him. "He deliberately had you captured? But . . . why?"

"There was a large landowner in the area—Antonio Álvares Cabral—who was refusing to cooperate with Oliphant. Álvares Cabral wanted to make certain the French were gone for good before he risked throwing in his lot with the British. I didn't know it at the time, but the dispatches I carried were false; they were written specifically to fool the French into thinking the abbess of the convent of Santa Iria was in league with the partisans." Sebastian kept his gaze on his wine, glowing warm and red in the fire's light. "The abbess was Álvares Cabral's daughter."

Hero's hand had stilled its rhythmic motion. "Alexandrie Sauvage was with the French forces?"

"She was—although she was Alexi Beauclerc then. By that time,

her first husband had died, and she'd taken up with a French lieutenant named Tissot."

"So what happened?"

"After he read the dispatches I'd carried, the French major, Rousseau, rode off with some of his men. He was planning to torture me in
the morning for whatever other information I might have, then kill
me. But I managed to escape shortly before dawn—by killing Lieutenant Tissot."

"Alexi Sauvage's lover?"

"Yes."

There was more to the story, of course—much more. But he
wasn't sure he was capable of talking about it. Still.

Hero had the sensitivity not to press him. She said, "You think
Alexi Sauvage would deliberately hurt Gibson, just to get back at
you?"

"I don't know. But my distrust of her motives doesn't stem only
from what happened in Portugal. She's a beautiful young Frenchwoman who attended one of the best universities in Europe. Gibson
is a one-legged Irish opium eater who learned everything he knows
about surgery on the world's battlefields."

"He's a good man."

"He is. But I'm not convinced Alexandrie Sauvage is the kind of
woman to appreciate that. She keeps lying to us—about her father's
theft of the Dauphin's heart, about her brother's intentions with Lady
Peter, about the fact that Damion Pelletan even *was* her brother."

"Not telling you something isn't exactly the same as lying."

"It is in my book—at least when we're talking about murder."

"I can understand her lingering animosity toward you. But if she
truly loved her brother . . . why be so secretive?"

"I don't know." He glanced at the clock, set aside his wine, and
rose to his feet.

She rose with him, upsetting the disgruntled cat, who arched his
back and glared at Sebastian. "I still can't believe you're going to ask

Marie-Thérèse about her brother's heart in the middle of your aunt Henrietta's soiree."

"Not Marie-Thérèse, Lady Giselle. I have it on excellent authority that Marie-Thérèse will never condescend to speak to me again, ever since I committed the unforgivable sin of daring to contradict her royal personage. It's one of the many hazards of believing in the divine right of kings; you start equating yourself with God, which means you see your enemies as not merely annoying or unpleasant, but the literal servants of Satan."

"What do you expect Lady Giselle to tell you?"

"Nothing, actually. But I want to watch her face when I ask her whether or not Marie-Thérèse knows about the fate of the Dauphin's heart."

"Surely you don't think *Marie-Thérèse* killed Damion Pelletan?"

"Do I think she personally cut out his heart? No. She and Lady Giselle were closeted in prayer that night, remember? But I'd say she's more than capable of delegating the task to one of the hundreds of sycophants hanging around Hartwell House."

"But . . . why? Why would she want the heart of a man whose only sin was that his father performed an autopsy on a dead child?"

"Revenge? Malice? An exchange of missing body parts? I don't know. But the connection is there, somewhere. I just haven't found it yet."

London might still be thin of company, but virtually everyone who was anyone appeared to have decided to attend the Duchess of Claiborne's soiree that evening. As he pushed his way through the crowded reception rooms, Sebastian counted two royal dukes, a dozen ambassadors, and nearly enough peers to fill the House of Lords. The strains of one of Haydn's string quartets drifted through the cavernous town house. The rendition was exquisite, although no one really seemed to be listening to it.

"Good God, Devlin," exclaimed his aunt when she saw him. "What are you doing here?"

She was looking regal in purple satin and the magnificent Claiborne diamonds, her gray head crowned by a towering purple velvet turban sporting an enormous diamond and pearl brooch.

He bent to kiss her rouged and powdered cheek. "I was invited, remember?"

"And you turned me down. Twice. The only time you ever come to these things is when you want something." She regarded him through narrowed eyes. "What is it now?"

He lifted a glass of champagne from a passing waiter and smiled. "Who. In this case, it's definitely a 'who.' The Duchesse d'Angoulême and her devoted companion, Lady Giselle Edmondson. They are here, I assume? Your soiree was given as one of the reasons for their removal to London—that, and the theater. Although I'm told the latter is not such a draw now that Miss Kat Boleyn has inexplicitly chosen to absent herself this season."

"Marie-Thérèse said that to you?"

"She did."

"Nasty woman. I swear, if she ever does become Queen of France, they'll have another revolution."

"She is here, I take it?"

"She is. I saw her go down to supper just moments ago. None of the Bourbons ever miss a chance at a free meal."

He found Marie-Thérèse seated on one of the brocade-covered chairs lined up against the wall of the dining room, where a buffet of delicacies had been spread to tempt the jaded appetites of the guests. She wore an elegant gown of turquoise silk with a plunging neckline designed to show off her mother's famous drop pearl necklace; three white plumes nodded from the curls piled on her head, and she had a white ostrich-plume fan she waved languidly back and forth, although it was not hot.

He saw her stiffen, her gaze meeting his across the crowded room. Then she looked pointedly away.

Smiling faintly, he walked up to where Lady Giselle was awk-wardly endeavoring to fill two plates, one for herself and one for the Princess. "Here; allow me to help you," he said, relieving her of one of the plates.

"Thank you." She gave him a wry, almost conspiratorial smile. "I saw the look she threw you just now. You ought by rights to be dead on the floor."

"I'm told she'll never forgive me. But you have?"

"I understand what you're trying to do. I can appreciate that—even admire it—however much I might disapprove of some of your methods."

Sebastian's hand hovered over the nearest platters. "Crab and asparagus?"

"Yes, please."

He added them to the plate in his hand.

She reached for a serving of shrimp in aspic. "You've obviously sought me out for a reason; what is it?"

Sebastian studied her still faintly smiling profile. "Somehow, I suspect you're not going to approve of what I have to say."

She gave a soft laugh. "Shall I undertake not to throw this plate of food at your head?"

"That might help. You see, I've made a rather troubling discovery. It seems that not only did Damion Pelletan's father perform an autopsy on the boy identified as the Dauphin; he also removed and carried away with him the child's heart. He still has it."

She was no longer smiling. Her lips parted, two little white lines appearing at the corners of her mouth as her hand tightened so hard on the plate she held that he wondered it didn't crack. "I did not know that. Are you certain?"

If she were an actress, she was a world-class one. Sebastian said, "I'm told he keeps it in a crystal vase in his study. Why would he do that?"

She reached for a bread roll. "It has long been the practice in

France to preserve the internal organs of the royal family separately from their bodies. The burial of the royals' remains typically took place at the basilica of Saint-Denis. But their hearts and entrails were willed to various places. The previous Dauphin of France had his heart buried at Val-de-Grâce, along with those of scores of other kings and queens and princes of the blood."

Sebastian wondered if she'd heard of the fate of those hearts during the Revolution. Their precious silver and gold reliquaries torn open and sent to the mint to be melted down, the hearts were put into a wheelbarrow and burned—except for a few that were sold to painters, who liked to use the dried organs to create a special rare red-brown pigment known as "mummia."

He said, "So you're suggesting—what? That Dr. Philippe-Jean Pelletan was a royalist? That he took the Dauphin's heart so that even if his body were consigned to a common grave, his heart might at least be preserved?"

"I don't know Dr. Pelletan's politics. But he has managed to hold on to his position at the Hôtel-Dieu in Paris through the Revolution, the Directory, and now Napoléon's empire. Whatever his opinions, he is obviously most adept at keeping them to himself."

Sebastian glanced toward Marie-Thérèse, who sat rigidly staring at him with palpable dislike. He said, "Pelletan took a risk, preserving the heart of the child who died in the Temple. He obviously believed the boy was indeed the Dauphin."

"The rumors that the Dauphin somehow escaped the Temple— that the boy who died in his place was an unfortunate deaf-mute imposter—are just that: rumors. A myth. A tale told to comfort those unable to accept the harshness of reality."

"Yet the rumors persist."

"They do, yes. I will never understand why the revolutionaries failed to show Marie-Thérèse her brother's body. Perhaps after years of neglect and mistreatment, they feared she might not recognize him. Or perhaps they feared allowing her to see the state to which their cruelty had reduced him. But there is no doubt in my mind that the last son of Louis XVI and Marie Antoinette died in the Temple in 1795. To suggest otherwise is as ridiculous as to lend credence to the silly tales of the Dark Countess."

Sebastian shook his head, not understanding. "What Dark Countess?"

Lady Giselle gave a small, tight laugh that held no real humor. "Ask Ambrose LaChapelle. I've no doubt he would enjoy telling you the story." She took the second plate from Sebastian's hand. "And now you must excuse me, my lord. Thank you for your assistance."

He watched her return to the Princess's side and fuss about her with unfailing good humor. A few glances were thrown in his direction, but he had no doubt Lady Giselle was seriously editing her recital of their conversation.

He went in search of Ambrose LaChapelle. But neither the French courtier nor the Comte de Provence was in attendance that night. Sebastian was just calling for his hat and cloak when a small, lithe figure in a tiger's striped waistcoat wiggled in through the crush, deftly evading all attempts to collar him.

"Guv'nor!" cried Tom, panting as he skidded to a halt. "Come quick!"

Sebastian felt his stomach twist as he gripped the boy's slim shoulders. "What is it? Is it Lady Devlin?"

"What? Oh, Lord no. It's Sir 'Enry Lovejoy. 'E says t' tell ye that Frenchy colonel 'as been found dead, on the Old Swan Stairs. And wait till ye 'ear what the killer done t' 'im!"

Chapter 38

W hat was left of Colonel André Foucher lay sprawled on his back halfway up—or halfway down, depending on one's perspective—the ancient, slime-covered granite steps known as the Old Swan Stairs. Located at the base of Swan Lane just above London Bridge, the stairs led from the lane down to the Thames.

By day, it was a busy landing point for the wherrymen and barges that plied the river. But at this hour of the night, the river was deserted. A heavy, wet fog swirled around the body; the air was thick with the smell of the river and damp stone and death. His arms were thrown up on either side of his head, elbows slightly bent, palms toward the white sky. Sebastian took only one look at the man's face before turning away.

"Good God. What did they do to him?"

Sir Henry Lovejoy stood at the edge of the steps with his hands thrust deep into the pockets of his greatcoat. He had a scarf wrapped around his neck and held his shoulders hunched forward, although whether it was from the cold or the horror of what lay before him, Sebastian couldn't have said.

The magistrate cleared his throat. "It appears someone has gouged out his eyes."

"And his heart?"

"Oh, he still has that."

Sebastian squinted down the river, toward the bridge. But the fog was so thick he couldn't see five feet in front of his face. "How did you even find him?"

"A wherryman tripped over him."

"Has anyone spoken to Harmond Vaundreuil?"

"Not exactly. The clerk, Camille Bondurant, identified the body. According to the constable who carried the news to the Gifford Arms, Monsieur Vaundreuil took the news quite badly. He's now dosed himself with laudanum and taken to his bed." Lovejoy's disgust at this Gallic display of sensitivity flattened his face and quivered his nose, although he felt compelled to add, "I gather he has a bad heart."

"He thinks he does, at any rate."

"Having two of your party of five murdered—brutally—is enough to give anyone a bad heart."

"True."

Sebastian hunkered down beside the murdered man and forced himself to take another look. A dark stain of blood spread out from beneath the body. "How was he killed?"

"Stabbed in the back, from the looks of things. But we'll know more when Gibson's had a go at him."

"I wonder why the eyes?" Sebastian said, half to himself.

"It is rather symbolic, is it not? Rather like the theft of Pelletan's heart. Perhaps Foucher saw something he was not supposed to see."

Sebastian let out a long, troubled breath. In his arrogance, he'd thought he was narrowing in on who had killed Damion Pelletan, and why. But Foucher's death—and, more important, what had been done to him after death—suggested that the focus of Sebastian's inquiries so far had been all wrong.

He pushed to his feet. "Have you heard anything about this morning's explosion in Golden Square?"

Lovejoy nodded. "I saw a preliminary report not long ago. It seems the rooms in which the charge was set were empty; the woman who previously occupied them died last week."

"Convenient. No one saw anything?"

"Apparently not. But there's no doubt that whoever set the blast knew what he was doing. I'm told the gunpowder was contained in such a way that the full force of the blast went upward."

"Toward Alexandrie Sauvage's rooms."

"Yes."

Sebastian brought his gaze back to the French colonel's ruined face. He'd become convinced that the theft of Damion Pelletan's heart was somehow connected to the reason for his murder. But Foucher's death complicated that scenario even as it underscored his conviction that they were dealing with a killer who was either far from sane or else diabolically clever.

Or perhaps both.

The problem was, how did that morning's attempt on the life of Alexi Sauvage fit into any of it?

"Nothing symbolic about trying to blow someone up," he said aloud.

Lovejoy swallowed. "If there is, I don't see it."

Sebastian nodded and started up the stairs, the soles of his dress shoes slipping on the wet, slimy stones. Then he paused to look back as a thought occurred to him. "What was Foucher doing here, anyway?"

"That we don't know."

"Monsieur Vaundreuil picked a damned inconvenient time to dose himself with laudanum."

"Perhaps he'll have developed more of a stiff upper lip by tomorrow."

"One can only hope," said Sebastian.

Wednesday, 27 January

The next morning, Charles, Lord Jarvis, was still in his dressing room when he heard someone ringing an impertinent peal at the distant front door. He pulled on an exquisite pair of unmentionables and calmly buttoned the flap.

His valet's head jerked around, eyes widening at the sound of a shout, followed by a light, quick step on the stairs.

Jarvis said, "From the sounds of things, I shall shortly be receiving a visitor. You may leave us."

"Yes, my lord." The valet bowed and moved toward the door, just as the handle turned and Viscount Devlin walked into the room.

"Oh, good," said Devlin. "You're still here." He was dressed in doeskin breeches, tall Hessians, and a black coat, and he brought with him all the smells of a foggy London.

Jarvis wrinkled his nose and reached for a starched white cravat. "As you see."

Devlin shut the door in the interested valet's face. "I take it you've heard about Colonel Foucher?"

"I have."

He was aware of Devlin studying him, those ungodly yellow eyes glowing with a fierce passion. "Is it you? Is this all part of some diabolical scheme to frighten Harmond Vaundreuil into fleeing back across the Channel?"

"By plucking out the hearts and eyes of his underlings? How revoltingly Gothic. What do you suggest I do next? Eliminate the clerk—what's his name?"

"Bondurant."

"—by having his tongue cut out?"

"If anyone's capable of it, you are."

Jarvis laughed. "Thank you. Or was that meant as an insult?" He carefully settled the wide strip of linen around his neck. "While I've no doubt such a simple solution would appeal to you, the fact remains that it is not I. Nor do I know who is doing this. But I won't pretend to be even vaguely troubled by the turn of events. If Vaundreuil is still in London by the end of the week, I'll be very much surprised."

Devlin stood with his legs braced wide, his head thrown back, his jaw set hard. "Yet you would have had me believe you were concerned my inquiries might disrupt the progress of the negotiations."

"I was concerned." Jarvis smiled. "If not quite for the reasons I led you to believe."

"Would peace with France really be so bad?"

"As long as Napoléon still rules as Emperor? Yes."

"Who would you have in his place? The Comte de Provence?"

"For a time. He is next in line, after all, and one must at least appear to observe the traditional order of succession. Provence is a fool and ridiculously infatuated with the more extreme permutations of constitutional monarchy. But he's old before his time and hopelessly fat. He won't last long."

"And then what? His brother, Artois? The man is a dangerous reactionary as well as being foolish and vain and hopelessly profligate. The French would never put up with him for long."

"I think perhaps you underestimate Artois's enthusiasm for repression. He watched the mistakes his brother Louis XVI made back in 1789, giving in to one demand after the next, when a few well-placed whiffs of grapeshot would have scuttled the entire Revolution before it had a chance to gather momentum."

Devlin remained silent.

After a moment, Jarvis smiled. "You know, of course, that I've had men watching the French delegation since their arrival?"

"I didn't know, but I can't say that I'm exactly surprised. Would you have me believe they observed something useful?"

"As to its usefulness, that is not for me to say. But I do know they witnessed an interesting quarrel between Damion Pelletan and his sister on the night he died."

The Viscount's eyes narrowed. "You knew Alexandrie Sauvage was Pelletan's sister?"

Jarvis kept his gaze on the mirror, his fingers adjusting the folds of his cravat.

Devlin said, "Where precisely did this quarrel occur?"

"At the Gifford Arms. I'm told that a man and a woman arrived first; they spoke to Pelletan for a time, then retired. Madame Sauvage appeared just as Pelletan was about to return to the inn."

"You're not telling me anything I don't know."

"Really? How industrious of you. Only, I gather you somehow neglected to hear of the quarrel which then took place."

"And what precisely was the subject of this quarrel?"

"That, my informant was too far away to hear."

"Then how did he know it was a quarrel?"

"It was rather heated. There was no mistaking the level of passion involved."

"And the man and woman who came before? Who were they?"

"My observer was unable to make an identification."

"Indeed?"

Jarvis smiled at the Viscount's posture of stiff incredulity. "Yes, indeed."

"Why are you telling me this now?"

"Because this obsession of yours with the death of Damion Pelletan is becoming tiresome. You belong at home with your pregnant wife."

"Hero is fine. Believe me, she wouldn't thank you for encouraging me to hover anxiously about her."

Jarvis smoothed the line of his waistcoat, his gaze hard on his son-in-law's face. "If my daughter dies because of the babe you planted in her belly, I swear to God, I will kill you. Personally."

Devlin's gaze met his and held it. And Jarvis saw there a deep and quiet awareness of the looming danger to Hero that Jarvis realized matched his own.

"She's not going to die."

Chapter 39

*A*lexandrie Sauvage answered Sebastian's knock at the door of Gibson's surgery on Tower Hill.

"Gibson is in the yard, performing the autopsy on Colonel Foucher," she said.

"Good." Sebastian brushed past her when she would have shut the door again. "You're the person I wanted to see."

She stood for a moment with one hand on the latch, the fog creeping in around them. Then she closed the door and turned to face him. "What do you want?"

She wore the only dress she now possessed, although she had fastened an apron over it. The apron was liberally smudged with grime, and there was a dirty streak across one cheek. He realized she'd been scrubbing the small room to the right of the door, making it her own. He should have been relieved to discover that she was staying in the surgery rather than in Gibson's house. Only he wasn't sure it made much of a difference.

He said, "You told me that the night Damion Pelletan was killed, you went to the Gifford Arms and found him standing in front of the inn."

"Y-yes," she said slowly, as if mistrusting where his questions were leading.

"What exactly did you say to him? 'There's a sick child I'd like you to look at; please come'?"

"Something like that, yes."

"Nothing else? And then you left for St. Katharine's?"

"Yes."

"And as you walked up Cat's Hole, he told you he wanted Lady Peter to run away with him, and you quarreled?"

"Yes." She stared back at him, her brown eyes dark with suspicion and what looked very much like hate.

He said, "So what did you argue about at the Gifford Arms? Given everything I've learned about Damion Pelletan, I find it difficult to believe you had to work to convince him to come with you. So what the devil were you quarreling about?"

"Who told you we argued at the inn?"

"Damion was part of a French delegation sent to London on a delicate mission. It's hardly to be wondered at that he was being watched."

"By Jarvis, you mean?"

When Sebastian didn't say anything, she huffed a scornful, breathy laugh. "What exactly are you suggesting? That I quarreled with my brother, lured him into a dark alley, cut out his heart, and then hit myself over the head? Oh, and then blew up my servant woman when she threatened to expose my evil deeds to the world?" Bright color appeared high on her cheeks. "I am a doctor. I save lives; I do not take them."

It had, in fact, occurred to him that she might be far more involved in her own brother's death than she would like them to believe. But all he said was, "The argument at the inn: What was it about?"

She shook her head. "I can't tell you. It involves a secret that is not mine to reveal."

Sebastian stared at her. "What the devil do you think I'm going to do? Shout it from the rooftops? Take out an advertisement in the *Times*? God damn you! Three people are already dead. How many more must die before you start being honest with me? Tell me what the bloody argument was about."

She went to stand at the narrow window overlooking the lane. But the fog was so thick it was like trying to look through yellow soup.

She said, "Damion had discovered that I knew . . . something. That I had known it, for nine years. Something he believed I should have told him. I'm sorry, but more than that I cannot say."

For nine years. *Nine years . . .*

"Bloody hell," said Sebastian. He was seeing a blond, green-eyed boy sailing two painted wooden boats across the water, while his sister watched him with a mother's intense love and pride. "It's Noël Durant, isn't it? The boy isn't Lady Peter's 'brother'; he's her son. By Damion Pelletan."

She turned to stare at him, her face slack with astonishment. "You knew?"

He shook his head. "No. I'd assumed Pelletan came to London because he'd somehow learned of Lord Peter's treatment of his wife. But he came because of the boy, didn't he? How did he ever happen to learn the truth?"

"From an old priest whose deathbed he attended in Paris. The priest was delirious. At first Damion thought he was only rambling nonsense. Except the more he heard, the more the old man's words came to make sense."

"Julia Durant knew she was with child before she left Paris?"

"She did, yes."

"Then why the hell didn't she tell the man she claimed to love?"

"Because she was sixteen. Because she was afraid. Because her father had assured her the family's flight from France would be temporary. Only, it wasn't."

"And so she found herself a refugee in London," Sebastian said softly. "Unwed, and growing increasingly heavy with child. The poor girl."

Alexandrie Sauvage nodded. "Once the general and his wife realized what was happening, they kept Julia out of sight. They knew that if the truth ever became known, she would be hopelessly ruined. Madame Durant was young enough to pretend to be with child herself. I'm told she even went so far as to strap a pillow to her belly when she appeared in public. In due time, the child was born and presented as General Durant's son."

"He had no other children?"

"Two older sons. Both died fighting Napoléon."

Sebastian had always wondered why the aging French general married his only daughter to a man like Lord Peter Radcliff. Yes, Radcliff was a duke's son, handsome and brilliantly connected. But a general with Durant's experience with men must surely have seen his son-in-law for the vain, self-absorbed dissolute he was.

Now it all made sense.

Sebastian said, "Does Radcliff know?"

"About Noël, you mean? I'm not certain."

"Yet you knew."

"Julia told me before she left Paris. She told me in confidence, and I swore I'd never tell anyone."

"Did Pelletan know Radcliff beats her?"

"Before he came? No. But it didn't take him long to figure it out. That's when he tried to convince her to go back to Paris with him— for her sake, as well as for the boy's."

"How did he discover you'd been aware of the child all along?"

"Something Julia said to him. He was furious. I tried to make him understand that it was a secret told to me in confidence. How could I have betrayed it? But he wouldn't listen."

"Yet he went with you to St. Katharine's, to see the sick child?"

"Damion was a physician. He would never put his own personal emotions ahead of the well-being of a patient. He went with me. But he was in a passion. We were still arguing about it after we left Hangman's Court."

Sebastian studied her tightly held features. It explained why, if someone were following them, they hadn't heard the footsteps until it was too late. But while it might, believably, give Lord Peter Radcliff a stronger reason to kill his wife's former lover, it did nothing to explain the deaths of either Karmele or Colonel Foucher.

He said, "Do you think Lady Peter was still in love with Damion?"

"I think she was, yes."

"Yet she was reluctant to return with him to Paris?"

"She said she'd made a commitment to Lord Peter—a commitment she couldn't go back on."

"Despite the fact he beat her?"

"I've known women to make excuses for men who beat them so badly they died."

"You mean like Abel Bullock's wife?"

"Yes."

Sebastian studied her calm, proud face. She was the kind of woman who had long ago turned her back on society's expectations for one of her sex. She had studied medicine at an Italian university and joined her physician-husband in following Napoléon's Grand Army. And when he died, she'd taken a lieutenant as her lover and continued ministering to the medical needs of the soldiers. How she had then ended up with an English captain as her husband, Sebastian could only guess. But the realization that Gibson was falling daily more and more under her spell twisted at Sebastian's guts and made him want to shake some sense into his friend.

He said, "Why are you here? I mean here, at Gibson's."

He expected her to deliberately misunderstand his question, to make excuses and claim the need for a place of refuge. Instead, she said, "Someone needs to help him."

"Gibson? He's doing just fine. Or at least, he was." *Before you came into his life.*

"If you mean he was doing a fine job of killing himself, you are right. Do you have any idea what long-term use of opium does to the human body? Especially at the levels at which he has been taking it."

"He doesn't go overboard that often."

"How do you know?"

Sebastian opened his mouth, then closed it. The truth was, he'd seen little of Gibson these past four months or more.

He said, "The man is in pain. How do you expect him to live with that?"

"I can help him with the pain, if he will only let me."

"The way you helped the children and nuns of Santa Iria?"

Her head jerked back as if he'd slapped her. "I didn't know . . ."

"Yes, you did. You knew. And you let it happen."

Her voice was a harsh tear. "If the blood of those children is on my hands, it's on yours too."

"Yes. The difference between you and me is that I've never denied it."

She stared back at him, and the death-haunted memories of that long-ago Portuguese spring were like a hushed presence in the room with them.

He said, "Paul Gibson is my friend. I won't let you destroy him."

"Destroy him?" She gave a ringing laugh. "What in God's name do you think I'm going to do to him? Pluck out his heart *and* his soul?"

"How many husbands and lovers have you had? How many are still alive?"

She didn't answer, but the flesh of her face pulled taut across the bones and her eyes darkened with the power of some emotion he couldn't quite define.

He settled his hat on his head and turned toward the door.

He was about to close it behind him when she took a quick step forward, one hand fisted in her grimy apron, the other coming up to thrust back the lock of vibrant hair that had tumbled onto her forehead. "Four. I've had four. Two lovers, two husbands. And you are right; all are dead. And all but the last were killed by *Englishmen*." She practically spat the last word at him.

"What happened to the last one?" he asked. "What happened to Captain Miles Sauvage?"

But she simply wrenched the door from his grip and slammed it in his face.

Chapter 40

*G*ibson was leaning against the slab in the center of the small stone outbuilding at the base of the yard, his arms smeared with gore up to the elbows, when Sebastian came to stand in the entrance.

What was left of Colonel André Foucher lay faceup on the slab, his body naked and eviscerated, his ruined eyes hideous in the glare of the lantern Gibson had lit against the morning gloom.

"Ah, there you are," said the surgeon, laying aside his scalpel and reaching for a rag to wipe his hands. "There's something I wanted you to see. Here; help me turn him over."

Between them, they eased the French colonel over to reveal the back of his long, slim torso. The purple slit low between his shoulder blades was clearly visible.

"So he was stabbed," said Sebastian.

"He was indeed. With a dagger. And here's something interesting: Judging by the angle of the blade's entry, I'd say it's a good bet that the man who stabbed him is not right-handed. I could be wrong, mind you; it's always possible the killer was standing in such a way as to have the same effect. But it's far more likely you're looking for a left-handed murderer. I just wish I'd had Pelletan's body long enough to know if he was stabbed in the same way."

"The man who tried to kill me—twice—is left-handed." Sebastian studied the freshly healed scar running the length of the colonel's right arm. "Doesn't seem right, somehow, for him to have managed to survive Napoléon's debacle in Russia, only to be stabbed in the back in London."

"Bit ironic, that's for sure. You can bet he didn't see this as a dangerous assignment." Gibson paused. "Know if he had any family?"

Sebastian shook his head. "I never asked."

Together, they turned the corpse again, and Sebastian found he had to look away from that ravaged face. "What can you tell me about the damage to his eyes?"

"I suspect whoever knifed him in the back then took his dagger to the eyes. It's very crudely done."

"Like Pelletan's heart." Sebastian rubbed his own eyes with a splayed thumb and forefinger, then swiped his hand down over the lower part of his face.

"Any idea why he was killed?" Gibson asked.

"I have lots of ideas. The problem is figuring out which of them is right. He could have been killed by someone intent on disrupting the peace negotiations. Or he could have died because he knew something about what happened to Pelletan."

Gibson wiped his hands again and reached for his scalpel. "I'm not quite finished here, but I'll be surprised if there's anything more to be learned."

Sebastian started to turn toward the door, then paused to say, "I spoke to Alexi Sauvage just now."

"Oh?" said Gibson without looking up.

"She tells me Lady Peter's young 'brother' is actually her son—by Damion Pelletan. Did you know?"

Gibson shook his head. "No."

"She says she was told about the child in confidence and felt honor bound to keep Lady Peter's secret. But I think that's not the only thing she's still holding back from us."

"She's very frightened."

She didn't strike Sebastian as frightened, but all he said was, "I hope you know what you're doing."

Gibson looked up then, his green eyes glinting. "What the devil is that supposed to mean?"

"You know."

But Gibson only ducked his head again, a flush of anger or chagrin riding high on his gaunt cheeks.

Chapter 41

*H*ero spent much of the morning in the offices of the *Times*, talking to John Walter, the editor who was publishing her series of articles on London's working poor. She handed him her latest piece on the city's brickmakers. And then she asked him, with studied casualness, if he'd ever heard of a convent in Portugal called Santa Iria.

He stared back at her, his face unusually grim, his eyes blinking several times before he said, "I have, yes. Why do you ask?"

"I want to know what happened there in 1810."

He pushed up from his desk chair and went to stand at the somewhat grimy window overlooking the fog-choked street, the fingers of one hand worrying his watch chain. "It's not pretty," he warned her.

"Tell me."

And so he did.

She arrived back at Brook Street to see Devlin standing outside, at the edge of the rear terrace. He had his back to the house, his gaze on the fog-shrouded, winter-browned garden that stretched down to the mews. He still wore his caped driving coat, and she suspected he'd only just walked up from the stables. But there was a brittle tautness to the tilt of his head that reminded her in some indefinable way of the nights she'd awakened in the hours before dawn to find him bedeviled by dreams of a time and place he could not forget.

He turned when she let herself out of the house and walked up to him, her arms wrapped across her chest for warmth. She could see the strain of too many sleepless nights in the hollowness of his cheeks and the dark, bruiselike quality of the flesh around his strange yellow eyes.

She said, "You've been talking to Alexi Sauvage again."

A breath of amusement flickered across his features. "How did you know?"

She shook her head. "I wish to God that woman had never come back into your life."

He stared out at the thick, killing fog. "It's not her. She's simply . . . a reminder."

"I found out today what happened at Santa Iria. You went there, didn't you?" She kept her gaze on his hard profile. "After you escaped from the French camp. You went there, and you saw what the French had done."

He nodded, his jaw set hard, his gaze still fixed on the rain-trodden garden below. "I suppose I knew in my heart that I was too late, but . . . I kept hoping I might somehow be in time to warn them. To stop . . ."

She tried to say something, anything, only to find that she could not.

After a moment, he continued. "I was too late, of course. Major Rousseau and his men had already attacked the convent." He wrapped his hands around the stone balustrade before him, the wind flapping the shoulder capes of his driving coat. Hero found she could not look at his face. "Santa Iria wasn't just a convent; it was also an orphanage. The French killed everything that moved, then set fire to the buildings. There was nothing left alive. Not a goat, not a dog, not a babe in its cradle. Nothing."

From the distance came the crack of a whip, the thunder of hooves from an unseen carriage driven up the street, fast.

"And Antonio Álvares Cabral's daughter?" asked Hero. "The abbess?"

"Rousseau tried to make her talk, except . . . the poor woman knew nothing." He swallowed. "You can imagine what they did to her."

Hero suspected she probably could not imagine—did not want to imagine. The editor at the *Times* had been blessedly vague about the details. She said, "Your dreams . . . That's what you see?"

"Not always. But often. Sometimes I see them not as I found them but as they would have been . . . before."

She said, "It wasn't your fault."

"Yes, it was. I'm the one who carried those false dispatches into French hands. My ignorance in no way excuses either my gullibility or my culpability. I knew what sort of man Oliphant was."

"But—how could anyone have known what he intended? He deliberately sent the French against that convent, hoping that their brutality would drive Álvares Cabral into the arms of the British." She hesitated. "Did it work?"

Devlin shook his head. "No. When the old man saw what the French had done—to his daughter, to the children, to the other nuns—he collapsed and died."

Hero felt a deep and powerful rage building within her. "And Oliphant? What happened to him?"

"I rode straight from the blood-soaked ruins of the convent to our camp. I was going to kill him. I knew I'd hang for it, but I didn't care." Devlin huffed a soft sound devoid of any trace of humor. "He'd been recalled to headquarters. His older brother had died, and he's now Lord Oliphant. Last I heard, he's been appointed Governor of Jamaica. I've never seen him again."

"And then you sold out?"

"Yes. Although it wasn't only because of Oliphant and Santa Iria. That was simply the culmination of so much that had gone before. We like to think we're more civilized, more honorable, more righteous than our enemies, but we're not. Just ask the dead women and children of Copenhagen, of Badajoz, of Dublin, of a thousand forgotten hamlets and farms. And once you realize that, it does rather beg the question: Why am I fighting? Why am I killing?"

She rested her hand on his arm, felt the fine tremors going through him. She thought of the memories he carried with him always, the sights and smells and sounds, and the suffocating weight of guilt. "It wasn't your fault," she said again. "The deaths of those women and children are on Oliphant's head. On Oliphant, and the French major, Rousseau, and the English and French officials who put two such men in positions of power."

But he only pressed his lips into a tight, strange smile and gave a faint shake of his head.

She said, "What happened to Rousseau?"

"He's dead," said Devlin. And she knew without being told that, somehow, before Devlin left the Peninsula, he'd tracked down the French major and killed him.

"Good."

She touched her hand to his cheek, and he turned toward her, his arms coming around her to draw her close, his cheek pressed to the side of her hair. She felt his chest lift against hers as he drew in a ragged breath and held her tight. And then he said the words she'd long thought she'd never hear.

"God, how I love you, Hero. So much. So much . . ."

Chapter 42

*P*aul Gibson spent the afternoon explaining the functions and structure of the human kidney to a full theater at St. Thomas's Hospital. Normally, he would good-naturedly rap the knuckles of any dozing audience member with a boiled fibula and patiently field questions that showed a decided lack of attention on the part of confused students. But not today. Today, every sleepy student, every ridiculous question, filled him with an unholy rage. It took a while, but he finally admitted to himself the origins of his uncharacteristic irritation.

He wanted to get back to Tower Hill. To Alexi.

Sure, then, but you're six kinds of a bloody fool, he told himself in disgust. What are you thinking? That a fine young woman such as her might be interested in you? That she might see you as a man—a real man, with all of a man's needs and desires and dreams?

Laughing at himself, he determinedly refocused his attention on the task at hand and resolved to think no more about her.

Then he let his audience go half an hour early.

He hurried back across London Bridge to the city, the crutch he used when he had to cover great distances swinging with a rhythmic *tap, tap.* The fog was so thick it could strangle a man if he made the mistake of breathing too deeply, and Gibson could feel the beads of moisture-encrusted grit reddening his eyes, until between the fog and his own watering vision he was nearly blind.

And still he hurried on.

He'd just passed the Monument when he knew, again, that he was being followed.

He whirled around, stumbling awkwardly as he almost lost his balance. "Who is it?" he called, his voice echoing hollowly back at him from out of the impenetrable murky gloom. "Why are you following me?"

For a long, dreadful moment, he heard only the drip of moisture and the splash of a wherryman's oars out on the river. But he knew this time that it wasn't his imagination. Someone was following him. Someone had been following him, off and on, for days. And rather than feel foolish for believing it, he suddenly felt foolish for ever having doubted it. For doubting himself. For having kept his fears and suspicions quiet.

For not having hailed a bloody hackney when he left the hospital.

"What do you want from me?" he cried, his hand tightening around the cross brace of his crutch.

The shape of a man materialized out of the fog. Massive shoulders. Broad barrel chest. Long, heavily muscled arms. At first, the features were indistinct. Then Gibson saw the overly long, curly black hair and knew he was looking at Sampson Bullock.

"What do you want?" asked Gibson again.

Bullock drew up, an insolent smile slitting his beard-stubbled face. "What makes ye think I want anything with ye?"

"I know who you are. You're Bullock."

The smile broadened. "Told ye 'bout me, did she? Did she tell ye 'bout how she killed me baby brother?"

"She told me he beat his wife so badly she died."

The smile was gone. "Never did. The bloody bitch fell down the stairs."

"Don't you mean he kicked her down the stairs?"

As soon as the words were said, Gibson wondered what kind of crazy, foolhardy courage had moved him to utter them. Once, he'd been a scrappy fellow, more than able to hold his own in a brawl and not above fighting a bit dirty when the occasion warranted it. But those days were far behind him, whereas Sampson Bullock looked like the kind of man who could wring the neck of an ox with his bare hands.

Gibson watched the big tradesman's upper lip curl, his nose wrinkling as he gritted his teeth together as if in a snarl. Then a strange light of amusement flooded into his face, and he laughed.

"She's stayin' wit' ye again, ain't she? Like ye can protect her." The tradesman's small black eyes swept him scornfully. "A one-legged Irish surgeon? Think yer up to it, do ye?"

One of his big hands swept out to close around Gibson's neck, the fingers digging deep into flesh and sinew. Still smiling, Bullock swung Gibson up and around to slam his back against the brick wall of the shop beside them. He was dimly aware of his crutch falling to the pavement with a clatter. All his being was focused on the viselike grip squeezing his throat, choking off his air.

"What's the matter, Irishman? Can't breathe?"

Gibson clawed frantically at the massive hand clamped around his throat. He heard a roaring in his ears. His vision dimmed, took on a strange, bloodred hue. He felt rather than saw Bullock thrust his face so close that his rough beard scraped Gibson's cheek and a foul odor of rotten teeth washed over him.

"Ye tell her. Tell that bitch fer me. Tell her I'm gonna get her when I'm good an' ready. But I'm gonna make her pay a bit more first."

Still smiling, Bullock moved his outstretched arm back and forth, grinding the back of Gibson's head against the rough brick wall behind him.

Then he took a step back and let Gibson go.

Gibson lost his balance, falling to his good knee, his peg leg sprawled out to one side as he struggled to keep from collapsing. He cradled his burning throat in his hands, sought to draw air deep into his lungs. He smelled his own fear in the sweat that slicked his body, felt the fog damp against his face.

When he looked up, the man was gone.

Gibson was bent over a basin, trying to pour water over the back of his head, when Alexi came to take the pitcher out of his hand.

"Here; let me do that for you."

She took the cloth from his other hand and worked to gently clean the blood and bits of grit left by the bricks. "What happened to you?"

"Sampson Bullock evidently believes that the best way to ensure that his messages are delivered is to grind the messenger's head into the nearest wall."

Her hands stilled at their task. "Bullock did this?"

"It's nothing."

"What did he say?"

Gibson straightened slowly. He was painfully conscious of having stripped off his coat, so that he stood before her in shirtsleeves and waistcoat.

"What did he say?" she asked again when he didn't answer.

He reached for a towel to dry his face and the back of his neck. Water dripped from his hair to run down his cheek, and he swiped at it.

She said, "I take it he threatened me?" She set aside the cloth she still held and turned toward the door. "I think I'll go tell Mr. Sampson Bullock that if, in the future, he has anything to say to me, he needs to learn to say it to my face."

"No."

He snagged her arm, hauling her back around to look at him. Her color was high, her fine brown eyes snapping with anger. He said,

"What happened today wasn't about threatening you. It was about demeaning me, about making me feel his power and emphasizing my own weakness. If you go see him now, you'll be helping him to shame me. It'd be like saying I can't even take care of myself, let alone you."

She drew in a quick breath that parted her lips and jerked her chest. "You saved my life. I never meant to bring you danger. But that's what I have done."

He gave her what he hoped came off as a cocky smile. "I'm not as helpless as you and Sampson Bullock seem inclined to believe."

"I know you're not helpless."

Their gazes met, held. She was still so close to him. And somewhere along the line, without him quite noticing it, the conversation had subtly shifted. Perhaps not so much in words, but in focus. He realized he was still holding the towel and awkwardly set it aside, suddenly at a loss for what to do with his hands.

He was painfully attuned to the subtle charge of raw awareness in the room, conscious of each breath he drew, of the rhythm of his blood pumping through every part of his being, of her nearness. He watched her pulse beat at the base of her slim white throat, and the moment was so powerful he found himself wishing it could stretch out and last forever. And then, just when he feared it would, she reached to cup her palm against his cheek. Tipping her head, she brushed her mouth against his, and he felt himself tremble.

He told himself not to be a fool, that it was a kiss of gratitude, that she couldn't be thinking of him as a man—not the kind of man a woman kissed with passion and took into her own body. Then he saw the saucy smile that lifted her lips, and he forgot to breathe.

She took his hand and led him into the room she had made her own. A single candle had been lit against the drab gloom, casting a warm golden glow over the bed's simple counterpane.

He started to say something, but she pressed two fingers to his lips.

"Shhh," she said.

She let go of his hand and took a step back, her gaze locked with his. He watched her arms come up, her fingers working as she loosened the ties of her gown. She let it fall into a puddle on the floor at her feet. Her petticoat followed. She untied her shift, and with exquisite care, clenched her hands in the fine linen. Then she swept her arms up and over her head, stripping it away.

She stood before him naked except for her stockings and garters. She was so finely made, her skin so fair and soft, with a faint sprinkling of cinnamon across the mounds of her small high breasts. Her limbs were long and impossibly slender, her waist and hips narrow, the juncture of her legs a fiery triangle.

"I love you," he said.

"No, you don't. You don't know me."

"I know you."

She shook her head. But she was still smiling.

Reaching out, he fisted his hand in the heavy fall of her hair, drawing her to him.

She pressed her naked body hard against the length of him, her mouth opening beneath his as the kiss became a savage, breathless onslaught that went on and on. She tore at his clothes, working to rid him of his waistcoat, his shirt. He felt her fingertips skim his naked back, and the sensation was so raw that he cried out. Then she moved to the buttons of his flap, her hands brushing the exquisitely sensitive flesh of his groin, and he almost lost control.

He said, "I don't know if I can do this. It's been so long—"

She laughed and pushed him down on his back, his wounded head cradled by her soft pillow, her flesh glowing golden in the candlelight as she straddled him. "Then let me do it."

She bent her head to kiss him again, and touched him tenderly. And when the time was right, she put him inside her.

He felt her envelop him with her warmth and her love, and he surrendered himself to her, to his passion and her gift of herself. Only, it came to him, as her head fell back, her mouth open and her eyes closed, as the rhythmic contractions of her inner body pulled him over into the abyss with her, that what she had really given him was the gift of himself.

Afterward, when they lay cradled in each other's arms, they spoke of many things, of his childhood in Ireland, of her days with the Grand Army in Spain, of her frustration as a physician unable to practice the full range of medicine in England.

"You could go back to Italy," he said, even though the very suggestion tore at his gut and tightened his throat, so that he felt as if he were strangling again. "Or Germany. They have a long tradition of female physicians in Germany too, don't they?"

"They do, yes."

She was silent for a moment. She lay on her side, her elbow bent, her head propped up on one fist as she traced a delicate pattern across his bare chest with her free hand. After a moment, she said, "There's something I haven't told you. Something I believe may help explain what happened to my brother."

He had been lying lost in a pleasant, half-dreamy state of warmth and quiet contentment. Now he found himself instantly alert.

He listened as she told him. Then he said, "You need to take this to Devlin."

She pushed up on both hands so she could stare down at him. "Are you mad? Lord Jarvis is his wife's father!"

"He is, yes. But Devlin is not Jarvis's ally. Far from it, in fact. If anyone can find your brother's killer, it's Devlin. He'll not be letting Jarvis's involvement turn him from his purpose—and he'll not be betraying you to his lordship either, if that's what you're thinking."

Her gaze met his. "I don't trust him."

He caught up the heavy lock of hair that had tumbled forward to half hide her face. "One of these days you're going to be needing to tell me what happened between the two of you, in Portugal. But not now. This isn't about the past. It's about the men and women who are dying here, in London, today. First your brother, then Karmele, now Foucher. If you know anything that can stop it, you must tell Devlin."

"You trust him?"

"With my life."

Her lips parted, trembled with uncertainty and proud stubbornness and an onslaught of memories he could only guess at. Then she nodded, and he found himself both humbled and inspired in a way he could not have defined.

Chapter 43

That evening, Sebastian was in the library reading Augustin Barruel's work on the Revolution when he heard a peal at the front door. Lifting his head, he listened to a woman's soft French voice. A moment later, Morey appeared in the doorway.

"A Madame Sauvage to see you, my lord. She says it is in regards to the murder of her brother, Monsieur Damion Pelletan." The major-domo's expression remained remarkably bland. But then, he had been in Sebastian's employ for more than two years; like Tom and Calhoun, he wasn't easily overset.

"Show her in," said Sebastian, and set aside his book.

He came from behind his desk as Alexi Sauvage entered the room. She drew up just inside the doorway, one hand knotted in the strap of her reticule, the other holding close the worn plaid shawl she had wrapped around her shoulders.

"Please, have a seat," he said, indicating the chairs before the fire.

She shook her head. "What I have to say will not take long. I am only here because of Paul."

Paul.

His reaction to her use of Gibson's given name must have shown on his face, because her chin came up. "He says that I should trust you, that I have been wrong to keep back information that might help you to make sense of what happened to Damion. That Jarvis is your enemy too." She paused, then added, "I hope he is right."

Sebastian was aware of Hero coming down the stairs toward them. But all he said was, "What information?"

"The day before he was killed, Damion told me he had overheard a conversation between Vaundreuil and Charles, Lord Jarvis. He couldn't catch everything that was said, but it was enough to convince him that Vaundreuil is engaged in a double game—that rather than representing France's interests, he is deliberately playing into Jarvis's aims, which are basically to see that these peace overtures go nowhere."

It fit only too well with what Lady Peter had told him. Yet Sebastian found it difficult to accept anything this woman said at face value. He said, "It's my understanding that both André Foucher and Camille Bonderant were included in the delegation specifically to prevent that sort of connivance."

"Yes. And now Foucher is dead too."

Sebastian leaned back against his desk, his arms coming up to cross at his chest. "You're suggesting Foucher might also have discovered Vaundreuil's activities? Or that Damion might have told him?"

"I don't know. But it seems reasonable, does it not?"

"And the attack on Golden Square?"

"Was presumably meant to kill me, on the assumption that Damion must also have told me what he knew."

"And how does any of this explain the macabre mutilation of the bodies? Pelletan's heart and Foucher's eyes?"

"That I do not know."

Sebastian walked over to pour two glasses of burgundy. He held one out to her, and after a moment, she took it.

He said, "Vaundreuil may well be playing a double game; he

would hardly be the first to do so. But I find it difficult to believe him ghoulish enough to desecrate the bodies of his colleagues. To what purpose?"

"I'm not suggesting Vaundreuil is the killer."

Sebastian studied her fine-boned, tightly held face. And he understood why she had withheld such a vital piece of information from him for so long. "I see. Not Vaundreuil, but Jarvis. That's why you didn't tell me before? Because you think Jarvis is the killer, and you feared I would betray you to him because he happens to be my father-in-law? Or is it because you suspected me of being in collusion with him?"

When she remained silent, he said, "I'd be the last person to deny that Jarvis is both ruthless and brutal. He would unblinkingly murder ten thousand men if he thought it would save England—or at least, England as he thinks it should be. But I can't imagine him cutting out the hearts and gouging out the eyes of his victims for amusement."

"I believe that was intended to throw suspicion on someone else."

"Such as?"

"I don't know."

"Not exactly an effective tactic, then."

His words brought a flush of angry color to her cheeks. "I didn't expect you to listen to me." She set aside her wine untasted. But rather than leave, she said, "Have you given more thought to attempting to turn your child in its mother's womb?"

The question took him by surprise. "I told Lady Devlin of your offer."

"And?"

Sebastian looked beyond her, to where Hero now stood in the doorway.

Hero said, "You accuse my father of murdering your brother, then offer to help save my child. Why?"

Alexi Sauvage pivoted to face her. Physically, the two women could not have been more dissimilar. Where the Frenchwoman was small and almost unnaturally thin, Hero stood tall and strong. Yet both possessed a comfortable sense of self combined with a rare willingness to buck the conventions and expectations of their day.

Alexi Sauvage said, "I am a physician. That is what I do."

"Yet you'll understand, surely, if I distrust your motives?"

Something wafted across the Frenchwoman's face. "If you are unwilling to allow me to attempt to turn the child, there are certain positions which sometimes achieve the same objective. You must kneel with your arms folded on the floor or mattress before you and your head resting on your hands. Do this for fifteen or twenty minutes, every two hours. It might be enough to nudge the child into turning itself."

When Hero remained silent, Alexi Sauvage said, "Try it, please. But if the child still refuses to turn . . . Do not wait too long. I promise, I mean you no harm." She glanced over at Sebastian. "Good evening, *monsieur*."

Then she swept from the room.

They listened to her light step descending the front steps. Hero's gaze met his. "Do you trust her?"

"No," he said, and took a long swallow of his wine.

Hero went to the window to watch the Frenchwoman climb into a waiting hackney. After a moment, she said, "Do you think she's right, that Jarvis is behind this?"

"Honestly? I don't know."

She turned to look at him. "I think you need to talk to Hendon."

He knew she was right. Not only was Hendon directly involved in the preliminary peace discussions, but no one knew better than Hendon what Jarvis was capable of.

That didn't make what Sebastian was about to do any easier.

Once, Alistair St. Cyr, the Fifth Earl of Hendon, had been the proud father of one daughter and three strong sons.

The two older boys were his favorites, a reality the youngest child, Sebastian, accepted even as it grieved him more than he ever let anyone know. Over the years, he had sought endless explanations for his father's harshness, for the undisguised mingling of anger and bemusement that so often pinched the Earl's features when his gaze fell on his youngest and least satisfactory son. Was it because Sebastian was so unlike the Earl, in temperament and interests as well as in appearance? Or was it for some other reason entirely? Sebastian could never decide.

And then, one by one, Hendon's sons died, first the eldest, Richard, and then his middle son, Cecil, leaving only the youngest, Sebastian, as the Earl's heir. It wasn't until Sebastian was a man grown that he'd learned the truth: that Hendon's beautiful, laughing, golden-haired Countess had played her husband false. That Sebastian was not, in fact, the Earl's own son, but a bastard sired by one of the Countess's nameless, faceless lovers. As Hendon had always known.

Always.

The Earl was dozing in a chair beside the library fire in his massive Grosvenor Square town house when Sebastian came to pause in the doorway. Hendon was in his late sixties now, his body stocky and slightly stooped with age, his heavily jowled face lined and sagging, his hair almost white and beginning to thin.

Sebastian paused in the doorway, his gaze on the man he'd thought of as his father for twenty-nine years—the man the world still believed to be his father. Sebastian supposed that, in time, he would be able to forgive Hendon for all the lies of his growing-up years. But he wasn't sure he could ever forgive the Earl for allowing those lies to drive Sebastian from the woman he'd once loved with all his heart and soul. The fact that Sebastian had found a new love in no way diminished either his anger or the hurt that fueled it. Yet as his gaze traveled over the old man's familiar, once-well-loved features, he felt an upswelling of powerful, unwanted emotions that he quickly suppressed.

He closed the door behind him with a click and watched Hendon draw in his breath in a half snore, then straighten with a jerk.

"*Devlin.*" The Earl swiped one thick hand over his lower face. "Didn't hear you come in. This is . . . unexpected."

Since the two men had barely exchanged half a dozen painful, polite greetings for many months now, that was something of an understatement. Sebastian said, "I understand you're involved with the delegation sent by Napoléon to explore the possibility of peace negotiations between our two countries."

Hendon cleared his throat. "Heard about that, have you?"

"Yes."

Hendon pushed to his feet and went to where his pipe and tobacco rested on a table near the hearth. "I expected you might, once you started looking into the death of that French physician—what was his name?"

"Pelletan."

"That's right; Pelletan." He fussed with his pipe, filling the bowl with tobacco and tamping it down with the pad of his thumb. Then he cast Sebastian a sideways glance. "You know I can't discuss the progress of the negotiations with you."

"I realize that. What I'm interested in is the attitude of various individuals toward the possibility of peace. I'm told Jarvis favors continuing the war until our troops are in Paris and Napoléon is ousted from the throne."

"I'd say that about sums it up, yes."

"And Liverpool?"

"Ah. Well, the Prime Minister's attitude is slightly different. He'd like to see Boney gone as much as anyone. But he's also sensitive to the economic and political costs of the war. I suspect that if France would agree to withdraw to its original borders, Liverpool could find a way to live with the Corsican upstart. After all, Napoléon is now married to the sister of the Emperor of Austria; there's something to be said for viewing their young child as a living union of the traditional with the modern. A reconciliation, of sorts."

"True," said Sebastian. He knew without being told where Hendon stood on the issue. As much as Hendon hated radicalism and republicanism, he'd been growing increasingly troubled by the toll that twenty years of war was taking on Britain and her people. "In other words, you and Liverpool are receptive to the negotiations, whereas Jarvis wants them to fail."

"You said it; I didn't."

Sebastian watched the Earl light a taper and apply it to his pipe. "In my experience, Jarvis usually achieves what he wants."

Hendon looked up, his cheeks hollowing as he sucked on his pipe, their gazes meeting through the haze of blue smoke. "Yes."

"Any chance Jarvis could be actively working to ensure that the negotiations fail?"

"By literally butchering the members of the delegation, you mean?" Hendon sucked some more on his pipe, his eyes narrowing with thought. "Bit ghoulish, even for Jarvis, wouldn't you say?"

"Perhaps. What about the possibility that Jarvis has suborned Vaundreuil himself?"

"To be honest, I've wondered about that. I've no proof, mind you; it's just a feeling I have."

Sebastian nodded and started to turn away. "Thank you."

"Devlin?"

He glanced back at the Earl.

Hendon's teeth clamped down on the stem of his pipe. "How does Lady Devlin?"

"She is well."

"And my grandson? When is he expected to make his appearance?"

The child would be no true grandchild to Alistair St. Cyr. But if a boy, he would someday become, in turn, Viscount Devlin and eventually Earl of Hendon. "Soon," said Sebastian after only a moment's hesitation.

Hendon nodded, his lips relaxing into a faint smile. And Sebastian knew again the whisper of an old emotion he did not want, a sensation all tangled up with every painful and joyous memory of a childhood he had no desire to revisit.

"You'll let me know?" Hendon asked gruffly.

"Yes."

And then, because there was nothing more to say, Sebastian left.

The night was cold, the fog a thick, foul presence that seemed to press down on the city. Sebastian walked through empty streets, his footsteps echoing hollowly in the moisture-laden air. He was trying to sort through a tangle of evidence and explanations surrounding this baffling series of murders. But his thoughts kept returning, unbidden, to a lonely old man standing beside his hearth, his pipe in his hand, his startlingly blue eyes clouded with a host of contradictory emotions that Sebastian suspected the Earl himself never completely understood.

He was about to turn and climb the steps to his house when he became aware of someone running behind him.

He whirled, his hand going to the dagger in his boot just as a breathless voice exclaimed, "My lord Devlin?"

One of Lovejoy's constables appeared out of the fog, his open mouth sucking air painfully, his somewhat ponderous stomach jiggling with his half trot.

Sebastian relaxed. "Yes; what is it?"

The constable drew up, his full, florid face slick with sweat despite the cold, his hands on his knees as he hunched over and sought to even his breathing. "Begging your lordship's pardon, but there's been a murder. Sir Henry thought you might like to know."

"What's happened?"

"A gentleman's been murdered in Birdcage Walk." The constable straightened, his breath still coming in panting gasps. "Leastways, the lady—er—gentleman with her—er, him—says it's a gentleman. A gentleman dressed up like a lady, it is. Never seen nothing like it in all my born days!"

Chapter 44

*T*he promenade known as Birdcage Walk ran along the south side of St. James's Park. A broad carriageway lined with rows of elm and lime, it was open to commoners traversing it on foot. Only members of the royal family were allowed to drive down Birdcage Walk. It wasn't a privilege they exercised often, but the prerogative remained exclusively theirs, nonetheless.

Over the past fifty or more years, the walk had become notorious as a popular "molly market," or cruising ground. The area's proximity to the nearby barracks meant that handsome young guardsmen eager to earn an extra guinea or two could inevitably be found here. As Sebastian walked beneath the fog-shrouded branches of the winter-bared trees, he wondered if that was why Ambrose LaChapelle had come here.

But as he approached the huddle of greatcoated men near the eastern end of the walk, he was surprised to see the tall, chestnut-haired Serena sitting hunched on a bench off to one side. She had her head down, her hands thrust between her knees in a posture that would have made more sense if she had been wearing breeches. Her green silk gown was torn, the black lace that had once trimmed the neckline ripped so that it dangled off one shoulder.

"Ah, Lord Devlin," called Sir Henry Lovejoy, separating himself from the knot of constables beside what Sebastian could now see was the sprawled body of another woman—or in all probability a man in a woman's red velvet gown, topped by a short white fur cape stained dark with blood. "I thought you might want to see this."

Sebastian glanced again at Serena. The French courtier did not look up.

"What happened?" Sebastian asked the magistrate.

"Her name is Angel Face. Or at least, that's what she called herself when she was wearing skirts. In breeches, he was James Farragut, a jeweler who keeps—kept—a shop in the Haymarket. According to the—" Sir Henry paused, as if trying to settle on an appropriate noun. "—the person who was with her—him, they were simply walking along the carriageway when an unknown man came up behind them, stabbed Farragut in the back, and then ran off."

"Farragut is dead?"

"Oh, yes. I gather he died almost instantly."

Sebastian went to hunker down beside the dead man. Of medium height and slim, he had softly curling dark hair and a delicately boned face ending in a strong jawline. Sebastian had never seen him before. "How did you know I might be interested?"

"The . . . person . . . who was walking with the victim suggested it."

Sebastian pushed to his feet and went to where LaChapelle still sat. The French courtier might have fought bravely against the forces of the Revolution, but the murder of his friend had obviously affected him profoundly. "You all right?"

"Yes." Serena thrust out her jaw and blew a long breath up over her face. "Oh, God; it's my fault. Angel is dead because of me."

Sebastian sat on the bench beside her. "What were you doing here?"

A ghost of a smile touched the courtier's painted lips. "Caterwauling, of course. There are some grand guardsmen to be found along here."

Caterwauling. Sebastian had heard they also called it "picking up trade" or finding someone to "endorse." He said, "Bit chilly, isn't it?"

Serena shrugged. "The cold tends to discourage the bastards working for the Society for the Suppression of Vice."

Sebastian stared off across the fog-shrouded park. "Why do you say you're responsible for Angel Face's death?"

Serena kept her gaze on the sprawled body of her friend. "She was cold. I lent her my fur cape. It's very distinctive—I'm known for it. I think whoever killed her saw it and thought she was me."

Sebastian studied the dead Haymarket jeweler. In the darkness and fog, she could easily have been mistaken for the French courtier. And yet . . .

"You can't know that for certain," said Sebastian.

"What? You think this is a coincidence?"

Sebastian shook his head. "What can you tell me about the man who stabbed her?"

"Not much, I'm afraid. It all happened too fast. At first, I thought he'd simply run up behind us and pushed Angel, to be rude. People do that sometimes, you know. But then she coughed and staggered against me, grabbing my dress to try and stay upright, so that I had to catch her. By the time I realized she'd been stabbed, the man who'd done it was gone."

Sebastian studied the rows of limes along the border of the carriageway. Just to the south of the park lay the Recruit House and, beyond that, the gardens at the rear of the Gifford Arms Hotel. Until now, everyone killed had been either a member of the French delegation or connected to it in some way. So why the hell had LaChapelle been attacked?

Aloud, he said, "Who would want to kill you? Not just any random molly, but you?"

"I honestly don't know."

Sebastian brought his gaze back to the courtier's painted face. "Did you tell the magistrates who you are—I mean who you really are?"

Serena rolled her eyes. "Seriously? Do you truly think I would? There will be an inquest, remember. What would you suggest as my choice of attire for the occasion? Should I go as Serena Fox, or as Ambrose LaChapelle, the gentleman who was cruising Birdcage Walk dressed as a lady? Either way, what do you imagine my reception would be?"

"I wouldn't think you'd care."

"Do you know how many mollies have been beaten to death by London mobs?"

"No. But I would imagine it's a fair number."

"It is."

Sebastian watched the mist drift between the dark trunks of the trees. He could smell the damp grass and the wet stones of the walk and the spilled blood of the murdered man. "If you're not going to tell me who you think did this, then why the bloody hell did you have the magistrates alert me to what happened?"

An unexpected smile flashed across the molly's somber features. "It was amazing the effect your name had on the local constabulary. One minute they were all set to hustle me off to the nearest roundhouse. Then I chanced to utter your name, and it was like a magic talisman. I'd tried asking them to contact Provence, but they seemed to find it difficult to believe that the uncrowned King of France would consort with one of my kind." She paused. "You obviously consort with all kinds."

Sebastian suspected chance had nothing to do with it. But he simply rose and said, "I suggest you avoid dark parks and arcades for a while—or else, if you must, carry a muff gun and keep your wits about you. If you should suddenly think of someone with an interest in doing away with you, you know where to find me."

He was turning toward Sir Henry when he recalled something

Lady Giselle had said to him the previous night, at the Duchess of Claiborne's soiree. He paused. "What can you tell me about the 'Dark Countess'?"

Serena leaned back against the bench's rails. "Good God, what has she to do with anything?"

"I have no idea. Who is she?"

"No one knows, actually. That's one of the reasons why she's called the 'Dark Countess.' She lives in a castle in Thuringia and has never been seen in daylight—only glimpsed in the shadowy interiors of carriages. When she walks the castle's grounds, she is always veiled, and she dresses only in black—black gown, black gloves, black veil. She has a man with her—a count, although they say he is neither her husband nor her lover. Speculation has it that he may be a courtier. Or her keeper."

"Her keeper?"

"Mmm. Those who serve her are kept carefully guarded. But rumors have naturally circulated. They say she's in her mid-thirties and is as blond and blue-eyed as our own dear Marie-Thérèse was as a child. Oh, and she has a fondness for the fleur-de-lis."

The stylized lily or iris had been associated with the royal family of France for a thousand years. Sebastian's eyes narrowed. "What are you suggesting?"

"I'm not suggesting anything. Only that one can understand how certain speculation might have arisen. The journey of Marie-Thérèse from Paris to Vienna in 1795 was cloaked in secrecy, as were her years in the Temple. Some believe she was raped while in prison, that she was pregnant when released by the revolutionaries and had to be hidden away. Others suggest that her experiences overturned the balance of her mind, so that after her release she was either unable or unwilling to take up the kind of prominent role required of the only surviving child of the martyred King and Queen of France."

"The theory being that an imposter was put in her place, while the real Marie-Thérèse lives out her life in seclusion in a castle in Germany?"

"That is the theory, yes. Although anyone with any sense knows that it is pure myth."

"Why is that?"

Ambrose LaChapelle met his gaze. "Because anyone undertaking to arrange such a dangerous substitution would be certain to select an imposter with a strong mental fortitude and unshakable balance. Whereas the Marie-Thérèse the world has seen these past eighteen years . . ." He shrugged and shook his head, as if unwilling to put the rest of his thoughts into words.

"Is she mad?" Sebastian asked quietly.

The courtier thrust the splayed fingers of one hand through his hair in a typically masculine gesture. "She is damaged. No one can deny that. You've noticed her voice? They like to say it is the result of her refusal to speak to her jailors—that she found it difficult to make sounds once she finally began to speak again. Yet she also likes to boast of her proud responses to the revolutionaries' taunts and questions, and she frequently recites her rosary aloud."

"So what did happen to her voice?"

"I have heard that severe emotional trauma can permanently affect one's vocal cords, although there are also those who suggest she screamed so long and so loud that it damaged her voice."

"Was she raped in prison?"

"If she was, she would never admit it. But when one thinks of what was done to her brother . . ." Again, that silent, suggestive lifting of the shoulders. "I've heard her say she used to sit up all night, dressed, in a chair because she was afraid to undress and go to bed. Why do that unless something had happened to make her afraid? Can you really imagine that the men who did such vile things to the boy Prince would spare the Princess? An attractive but despised young woman, alone and utterly in their power?"

Sebastian shifted his gaze to the gravel carriageway. The men from the nearest deadhouse had arrived and were shifting the jeweler's body onto their shell. He watched them lift the burden between them with a grunt.

A new explanation for Damion Pelletan's murder, and for the attempted murder of his sister, was beginning to take shape in his imagination. He said, "The man who killed your friend . . . what did he look like?"

The courtier frowned with the effort of thought. "I didn't see him well—he wore a greatcoat and scarf, with his hat pulled low over his forehead. All I can say with any certainty is that he was dark-haired and roughly your height, only slightly stockier."

The description matched that of the man who had attacked Sebastian at Stoke Mandeville and again in York Street, although he had no doubt it also matched any number of other men in London. "He didn't say anything?"

"No. Nothing."

"Did you notice his eyes?"

"His eyes? No. Why?"

Sebastian shook his head. "I'll ask you one more time: Who would have reason to kill you?"

But Serena simply stared off across the park, as if looking for the answer in the mists that swirled among the winter-bared trees.

Chapter 45

Thursday, 28 January

The next morning, Sebastian was easing on his Hessians when Calhoun said, "You know how you asked me to look further into Sampson Bullock, my lord?"

Sebastian glanced over at his valet. "Discovered something interesting, did you?"

"You were right, my lord: Bullock spent six years in the Ninth Foot. He came back to London when his unit was reduced in 1802, after the Peace of Amiens."

"In other words," said Sebastian, stomping his foot into his boot, "he knows more about gunpowder than your average cabinetmaker."

"Considerably more, I should think. He was in the artillery."

Sampson Bullock was flooding a new tabletop with boiled linseed oil when Sebastian walked up to him. The fog was still so thick that a deep gloom filled the shop, and the cabinetmaker had lit the lantern suspended over his work. The air was heavy with the smell of warm oil and freshly shaved wood and rank male sweat.

Sebastian stood for a moment, arms crossed at his chest, and watched the cabinetmaker turn the pale raw wood a deep, rich brown as the oil soaked into the surface. Bullock glanced up at him, then dipped his cloth into the tin of oil and went back to rubbing the piece.

"Wot ye want from me?" he demanded after a moment. "I got nothin' t' say t' ye."

"I understand you were in the Ninth Foot. The artillery, to be precise."

"Aye. Wot of it?"

"I would imagine you know a fair bit about gunpowder, don't you?"

Bullock kept his gaze on his work, although Sebastian noticed his movements had become slower, more deliberate. "Suppose I do? Wot of it?"

"You heard about the explosion in Golden Square?"

"Ye'd be hard pressed t' find a body hereabouts who hasna heard of it."

"Did you know the charge was set directly beneath Madame Sauvage's rooms?"

"Now, how would I know that?"

"I thought you might have heard. After all, it's not often someone tries to blow up a London house with gunpowder."

The cabinetmaker flung down his cloth with enough force to send thick golden globules of oil flying in all directions. "Wot ye sayin'? That I done it? Is that wot yer sayin'?"

Sebastian subtly shifted his weight, his hands hanging loosely at his sides. "You did threaten to kill her, remember?"

"Yeah? Well, she weren't killed, now, was she? It was that Basque bitch wot bought it."

Sebastian studied the man's small black eyes. The scar across his cheek had darkened to a deep, vicious purple. "A mistake, I wonder? Or a deliberate attempt to hurt Alexi Sauvage by killing someone she loved?"

When the cabinetmaker remained silent, Sebastian said, "She didn't kill your brother; he died of gaol fever, in prison."

"She put him there!"

"You mean, by having the courage to stand up and say what everyone in the neighborhood knew to be true? That your brother was a brutal wife beater?"

"Why, ye—"

His face twisted with raw savagery, Bullock grabbed a long, sharp awl and lunged around the table to come at Sebastian with the tool clutched in his fist like a stiletto.

Sebastian yanked his own knife from the sheath in his boot, the carefully honed blade winking in the lamplight as he settled into a street fighter's crouch.

The cabinetmaker drew up, his lips twitching, his fist still tight around the awl's worn wooden handle.

"What's the matter?" said Sebastian. "Does the idea of a fair fight give you pause? Do you prefer stabbing men in the back and blowing up women in their homes?"

A strange, eerie smile lit up the cabinetmaker's face. "Ye think yer real smart, don't ye? High-and-mighty lord that ye are, livin' in that big fancy house, surrounded by all them other grand nobs. Think ye can come in here and talk t' me like yer still a captain and I'm jest some swadkin? Think I gotta play by yer rules?"

"How do you know I was a captain?"

The man's smile widened. "Think yer the only one can ask questions? I know all about ye—about ye and yer wife, and about the child she's carryin' in her belly. I even know 'bout that black cat you fancy."

Sebastian was careful to keep all trace of his instinctive reaction off his face and out of his voice. All that remained was a cold, lethal purposefulness. "You stay away from my wife."

"Wot's the matter, Captain? Ye scared?"

"I see you anywhere near my wife, my house, or my cat, and you're a dead man. You understand?"

Bullock laughed. "Ye sayin' ye'd risk hangin' fer killin' the likes o' me?"

"Yes."

For a moment, the man's self-satisfied smile slipped. Then it slid wide again. "I reckon maybe ye mean it, after all. But ye gots to see me comin', don't ye, Captain? And I can move real quiet when I wants to. Quiet as a raindrop runnin' down a windowpane, or a dog dyin' somewhere alone in the night."

"I have extraordinarily good hearing," said Sebastian.

And then he left Bullock's workshop before he gave in to the temptation to kill the bastard then and there.

It was only afterward that Sebastian found himself wondering if he'd just made a terrible mistake.

Chapter 46

Sebastian had long ago come to the conclusion that there were two types of madmen in this world. Places like Bedlam were full of those society labeled as insane: men and women who heard voices, who lurched between mania and despair, or who were so tormented by life's vicissitudes or their own demons that they simply disengaged from the world. Many were undoubtedly crazy enough to commit murder. But they seldom got away with it.

More dangerous by far, in Sebastian's estimation, were those like Sampson Bullock: men with a solid grasp of reality who seemed sane, yet whose thought processes were breathtakingly brutal in their single-minded self-interest. Easily enraged and never forgiving of the most insignificant of perceived slights or injuries, they moved through life with an utter disregard for the wants and desires of those around them.

But there were times when Sebastian wondered if he was wrong, if perhaps people like Bullock weren't actually mad, after all. Perhaps they simply lacked a fundamental component of what we like to believe it means to be human. The problem with that theory was that

Sebastian had known dogs and horses capable of the very love and compassion such individuals seemed to lack. Utterly without conscience or empathy, they saw others not as fellow beings but as targets or opportunities. Not all were violent or lethal. But those who were could kill without guilt, convinced that their victims either brought death on themselves or were too inconsequential to merit consideration.

A man like Bullock could easily have killed both Alexi Sauvage's brother and her aging, faithful servant as part of a twisted plan to avenge himself on the woman he held responsible for his own brother's death. For the same reason, Bullock was also more than capable of cutting out a man's heart. Sebastian had no evidence to suggest that Bullock knew about the relationship between the young French doctor and the woman Bullock hated, but it was certainly possible that in the process of following and watching her, Bullock had somehow learned of the connection. And yet . . .

Why would Bullock also kill and mutilate Colonel André Foucher— or try to kill Ambrose LaChapelle? That implied a connection to the Bourbons or an interest in the peace negotiations that Bullock lacked. The connection between LaChapelle and the peace delegation was tenuous, but there.

Still thoughtful, Sebastian turned his steps toward the Gifford Arms.

Monsieur Harmond Vaundreuil was feeding the ducks beside the Ornamental Water in St. James's Park when Sebastian walked up to him.

"There was another murder last night. Just over there, on Birdcage Walk," Sebastian said. "Did you know?"

The Frenchman scattered a handful of bread crumbs, his attention seemingly all for the ducks quacking and jostling around him. "According to what I am hearing, the attack was on one of the mollies who frequent the walk. What could it possibly have to do with me?"

"I don't know. That's what I'm trying to figure out."

"Perhaps you see connections where none exist."

"I don't think so."

The Frenchman smiled faintly and scattered more bread crumbs.

Sebastian said, "I've been listening to some interesting whispers. Whispers that tell me Damion Pelletan discovered you're playing a double game; that while you pretend to serve the interests of France, you're actually cooperating with Lord Jarvis to ensure that the peace negotiations come to naught."

Vaundreuil puffed out his chest and lowered his heavy dark brows with an admirable display of moral outrage. "That's preposterous! Why would I do such a thing?"

"Material reward is the most typical reason. That, and revenge. For some previous slight, perhaps? Then again, there's always the possibility of securing a prestigious position in the restoration government—although if that is your motive, you can't be aware of Marie-Thérèse's scathing opinion of you."

Vaundreuil threw away the last of the bread crumbs in a swift, angry gesture. "What are you suggesting? That I killed Damion Pelletan because he discovered I'm an English agent of influence? What about André Foucher? Am I to have done away with him for the same reason? And why, precisely, would I steal their hearts and eyes? As grisly mementos of their past faithfulness and service?" He swiped one hand through the air before him as if brushing away an annoying fly. "Bah! This is ridiculous!"

Sebastian studied the Frenchman's red face and thrusting jaw. He had no trouble believing Harmond Vaundreuil capable of killing two of his colleagues, if he thought it necessary to protect himself. But the conviction that something else—or at least something more—was going on here remained.

Sebastian said, "Did Damion Pelletan ever speak to you of his father? Specifically, of his father's visits to the Temple Prison in the summer of 1795?"

The Frenchman looked confused, his mouth hanging open, so that he had to swallow before he answered. "What?"

"His father, Dr. Philippe-Jean Pelletan, visited the Temple Prison at least twice in the summer of 1795. He treated the little Dauphin before his death, and he may have seen Marie-Thérèse, as well. Damion Pelletan never said anything about it to you?"

"No. But . . . surely you don't think something that happened so long ago could have anything to do with the murders here in London today?"

"I don't know. How much time did Pelletan spend with Colonel Foucher?"

Vaundreuil frowned. "Some. They would sit together of an evening, drinking brandy. Talking."

"Talking about what?"

"Foucher's time in the army. Women. Their hopes for the future . . ." He shrugged. "What do young men speak of when they drink? I never paid much attention to them."

"So Pelletan might have told Foucher of his father's observations of the Orphans in the Temple?"

"I suppose so, yes. But . . . what are you suggesting?"

Sebastian watched the ducks waddle away across the wet grass, quacking contentedly as their bulbous bodies lurched comically from side to side. What was he suggesting? That Marie-Thérèse had been brutally raped by her jailors in the Temple Prison? That she had been impregnated—or so badly injured that they'd summoned a physician to her? That the possibility of what had happened in the Temple—of what had really happened there—becoming known had so horrified her that she'd dispatched her minions to kill and kill again, in the hopes of keeping the truth quiet? Sebastian had no doubt she was capable of ordering the deaths of any number of men, if she thought it necessary to preserve what she saw as her divine family's honor. But was she mad enough to order her henchmen to steal her first victim's heart and gouge out the eyes of the second?

He wasn't sure.

Vaundreuil said, "Are you suggesting these killings are somehow related to the death of the Dauphin? But . . . that is madness!"

Sebastian met the Frenchman's gaze and held it. "Cutting out a man's heart is madness."

Chapter 47

Claire Bisette came to see Hero shortly before eleven that morning.

The Frenchwoman was pale and wraithlike, with hazel eyes set deep in a gaunt face and dull, dark blond hair drawn back in a severe knot. Her old-fashioned dress was hopelessly faded and darned at the elbows, cuffs, and collar, although she'd obviously tried hard to present a clean, neat appearance. She looked as if she hadn't eaten in a fortnight.

She brought with her the names of "respectable" people who could vouch for her integrity, honesty, and trustworthiness, although she admitted she had never held such a position as the one for which she was applying. Her only qualification was having cared for her own two children, both of whom were now dead.

Hero took the list of names, sent for tea and sandwiches, and slowly coaxed the anxious, stiff woman to talk. They spoke not only of children, but of Voltaire and Rousseau, of the concept of limited monarchy and the recent attempts to launch an expedition to the North Pole. After half an hour, Hero said, "I'll have Morey show you to your room in the nurseries. You can make arrangements with him to have your things brought over."

The woman's eyes widened. "But . . . you can't mean to engage me without checking my references!"

"I will check them, of course. And if they tell me you are a charlatan, I shall let you go. Only, I hope I am not such a poor judge of character."

Claire Bisette was surprised into a soft laugh. It was the first laugh Hero had heard from her. Then the woman cocked her head to one side and said, "The child is due when?"

Hero's hand tightened around her cup, but she said calmly enough, "Soon."

"There is a problem?"

When Hero simply stared at her, Claire Bisette hastened to say, "I beg your pardon, my lady; I should not have asked."

Hero shook her head. "No. As it happens, you are right. The babe is lying breech."

"Ah. My first child, Henri, was stubborn in that way. But a good friend of mine turned him in the womb."

"Do you mean Madame Sauvage?"

"I do, yes."

"And what she did worked?"

"It did, yes. I knew the instant he turned—it felt just like a giant fish flopping inside me."

Hero set aside her teacup. "How long have you known her?"

"Madame Sauvage? We were children together, in Paris."

"So you knew Damion Pelletan, as well?"

"No. My family had moved to Nice by the time Dr. Philippe-Jean brought Damion home."

Hero shook her head, not understanding. "What do you mean, brought him home?"

"Damion Pelletan was Alexi's half brother. She didn't know he existed until she was nearly grown."

"When was this?" Hero asked sharply—more sharply than she had intended.

Claire Bisette frowned with the effort of memory. "I do not recall precisely. It was sometime after the Terror. The summer of 1795, perhaps?"

Chapter 48

The Dowager Duchess of Claiborne was famous for never leaving her bedchamber before noon or one o'clock. She was still sipping her hot chocolate in bed when Sebastian walked into the chamber and tossed his hat and driving coat on a chair.

"Do I take it my useless excuse for a butler has simply abandoned all attempts to exclude you?" demanded Henrietta, sitting up straighter.

"Give the man credit; he tried."

She put up a hand to adjust her bed cap. "What do you want now?"

Sebastian went to warm himself before the fire. "I want to know what you can tell me about Lady Giselle Edmondson."

"Lady Giselle? Good heavens; whatever for?"

"Humor me."

"Well, let's see . . ." She frowned thoughtfully. "Her father was the Third Earl of Bandor. Handsome man, but sadly emotional and far too taken with the works of the French philosophes. He moved to Paris shortly after he came down from Oxford, and refused to return home even when his father died and he inherited the title and estates."

"He married a Frenchwoman?"

"He did. One of Marie Antoinette's ladies. Giselle spent much of her early childhood at Versailles. She and Marie-Thérèse were essentially raised together."

"And then came the Revolution."

Henrietta set down her chocolate cup with a soft *chink*. "Yes. Foolish man. He could have left. So many did. But he was convinced he was witnessing something extraordinary."

"And so he was. Only, not quite what he had anticipated. He and his countess were killed?"

"Yes. Giselle survived, of course, but no trace has ever been found of the two younger children. The boy—who would have been the fourth earl—was declared dead some years ago."

"So who holds the title now?"

"A cousin."

"Since the majority of Bandor's wealth was safe in England, I assume Giselle's portion survived the Revolution?"

"Oh, yes. She could have married at any time, had she wished."

"So why didn't she?"

Henrietta gave him a long, solemn look. "Really, Sebastian; use your imagination. You know what those days were like—the things that were done to gentlewomen. I hear there was even a child, although fortunately it died shortly after birth."

"I see," he said softly. And he thought it probably explained much about both Lady Giselle and Marie-Thérèse.

Henrietta said, "Most of those hanging around the Bourbons are a drain on their resources. But not Giselle. If anything, I suspect she actually helps to support the Princess. They've been together ever since Marie-Thérèse was released from prison."

"What do you think of her?"

Henrietta pushed out an oddly heavy sigh. "Well . . . she's charming, and pretty, and certainly far more likeable than Marie-Thérèse."

"But?" prompted Sebastian.

"Let's just say I would have been very troubled had one of my own sons wished to wed her."

"Meaning what?"

But Henrietta only shook her head, reluctant to put her implications into words.

Ambrose LaChapelle was inspecting a tray of imported laces in a small shop on Bond Street when Hero descended from her carriage and bore down upon him.

"Walk up the street with me a ways, *monsieur,*" she said, smiling. "There's something I'd like to discuss with you."

He cast a quick, apprehensive glance at her swollen belly, then looked away. "*Can* you walk?"

"Of course I can walk. I promise, I've no intention of delivering in the middle of Bond Street, so you needn't look so alarmed."

He raised his chin and twisted it to one side, as if his neckcloth had suddenly become too tight. "Why me?"

"I've just discovered something extraordinary. And in thinking it over, I've decided you're probably the most likely person to be able to explain it to me."

"I don't believe I like the sound of that," said the French courtier.

But Hero simply gave a tight, determined smile and bore him inexorably up the street.

Chapter 49

*A*fter leaving his aunt Henrietta's Mayfair house, Sebastian spent the next several hours in St. Katharine's, talking to the residents of Cat's Hole and Hangman's Court. He was working on a theory that was still missing too many parts to be even remotely feasible, and he was beginning to wonder if he was driven more by his own prejudices and presumptions than anything else.

He finally found a half-blind, gin-soaked ex-soldier who claimed he'd seen a couple of strangers near Hangman's Court the night Pelletan was killed. But his descriptions were vague, and he said the two men didn't seem to be together. The soldier also swore that if there'd been a woman there too, he'd have noticed her and remembered her.

Sebastian wasn't so sure.

He was standing on London Bridge, his elbows on the stone parapet, his gaze on the cold, mist-swirled waters below, when Ambrose LaChapelle walked up to him.

"You're a hard man to find," said the Frenchman.

Sebastian shifted his gaze to the man beside him. "I didn't know you were looking for me."

Today the courtier wore the polished Hessians, buckskin breeches, and elegant greatcoat of a man about town. Only the soft curls peeping out from beneath the brim of his top hat reminded one of Serena Fox.

Sebastian said, "Last night, you told me you didn't know who might want to kill you. Change your mind?"

"Let's just say your wife changed my mind."

"Lady Devlin?"

LaChapelle stood with his gloved hands clasped behind his back, his gaze on the forest of masts that filled the river below the bridge. After a moment, he said, "How much has Madame Sauvage told you of her brother's childhood?"

"You mean on the Île de la Cité?"

"No; before that."

Sebastian studied the courtier's exquisite, fine-boned face. "I didn't know there was a 'before that.'"

The Frenchman nodded, as if Sebastian had only confirmed what he'd already known or at least suspected. "Until the summer of 1795, Philippe-Jean Pelletan had only one child, a girl named Alexandrie. But then one day in early June, he returned to his house on the Île de la Cité bringing with him a small boy. He claimed the lad was his own son—a love child, born of a secret affair some ten years before. He told his curious neighbors that the boy and his mother had been im-prisoned during the Terror. The mother died, so Pelletan was now bringing the child home to raise as his own."

"Are you saying that child was Damion?"

"He was, yes. Needless to say, there were whispers. Philippe-Jean had been a widower for some years. So why had no one ever heard of this boy? Not only that, but the child was quite fair, whereas the elder Pelletan had black hair and dark brown eyes."

A cold gust of wind blew the mist against Sebastian's face. He smelled the river and the dankness of the bridge's ancient wet stones, and the smoke from a hundred thousand coal fires burning unseen in the fog-shrouded city. "What are you suggesting? That Philippe-Jean Pelletan was somehow complicit in a scheme that successfully rescued the Dauphin and substituted a dead or dying child in his place? That Damion Pelletan wasn't his son at all, but the Lost Dauphin of France? You can't be serious."

"Don't get me wrong; I'm not saying I believe it myself. But that doesn't mean the possibility has not been suggested by others."

Sometimes a piece of information was like a solitary candle kindled in a dark, empty room, burning bright but useless. Yet there were times when its light made sense of what had until then remained subtly inexplicable or unseen. Sebastian said, "So that's why both the Comte de Provence and Marie-Thérèse went out of their way to consult with Damion Pelletan. It had nothing to do with their health at all; they wanted to see for themselves how much he resembled the dead Prince. And what was their conclusion?"

The Frenchman shrugged. "In my experience, we tend to find resemblances where we look for them—whether in truth they exist or not. After so many years, who could say with any certainty?"

Sebastian thought about the body he'd seen lying on Gibson's slab, the high, sloping forehead and prominent nose so much like Marie-Thérèse's—or a thousand other people's. If Provence and Marie-Thérèse had gone looking for a resemblance, they would have found it. He said, "How did the Bourbons come to know the details of Damion Pelletan's childhood?"

"You think we have no contacts in Paris?"

"I've no doubt you do—although as I recall, the Comte de Provence would have me believe those 'contacts' somehow failed to tell him the purpose of Harmond Vaundreuil's visit to London."

LaChapelle simply gave a faint smile and shrugged.

The plash of a wherryman's oars carried to them through the fog. When it came to powerful motives for murder, Sebastian suspected that preserving one's position in the line of succession to a throne probably ranked right up there near the top—even when the throne in question was temporarily occupied by a Corsican usurper. The re-appearance of the Lost Dauphin would completely overthrow the claims of the current aspirants to the French crown—and Marie-Thérèse's chances of someday becoming queen.

"Of course," LaChapelle was saying, "there is no real proof, one way or the other."

"To your knowledge."

"To my knowledge," LaChapelle conceded. "However, given what is at stake, the mere possibility might have been enough to put Pelletan's life in danger."

Sebastian watched the courtier shift his gaze to the piers at the base of the bridge, where the river churned and swirled in deadly ed-dies. If the Comte d'Artois had been in London, Sebastian would have suspected him in an instant, for the youngest of the three Bourbon brothers could be as cruel and vicious as he was vain and self-indulgent. But Artois was far away, in Scotland, while if the wheelchair-bound, uncrowned King himself were involved, Sebastian found it difficult to understand why LaChapelle would have believed himself the target of the attack in Birdcage Walk.

Sebastian said, "Why try to kill you? I can understand killing Foucher—and mutilating his body—in the hopes of frightening Vaundreuil into abandoning the peace negotiations. But why you?"

"Perhaps because of what I know—or suspect."

"Someone told me of a child born to Lady Giselle during the Terror—an infant that did not survive. How did that baby die?"

LaChapelle lifted his gaze to meet Sebastian's. He was a man who had witnessed life at its most barbaric, who had no illusions about his fellow men or the depths of depravity of which they were capable. Yet Sebastian caught a glimpse of fear in his eyes—the kind of fear instinctive to all men when confronted with evidence of a certain kind of callous inhumanity that bordered on madness.

"She smothered it."

Chapter 50

*A*lexandrie Sauvage was hunkered down beside the entrance to Gibson's surgery when Sebastian walked up to her. She had her head bent, her attention focused on the bandage she was wrapping around a ragged child's finger. He knew she saw him, for she stiffened. But she didn't look up, saying to the child, "Next time, Felicity, remember: Geese bite."

The little girl giggled, thanked her prettily, and ran off to join the gang of urchins waiting for her in the shadows of the Tower.

Alexandrie Sauvage rose slowly to her feet and turned to face him. "Why are you here?"

"We need to talk."

The wind fluttered the locks of dark red hair framing her face, and she crossed her arms at her chest as if she were cold. She made no move to step into the surgery, but simply stared back at him with wide, unblinking eyes.

He said, "Why didn't you tell me that Damion was only your half brother?"

"'Only'? You say that as if our different mothers should make him somehow less important to me. Is that what you're suggesting?"

"No. I'm suggesting the fact that some people believed him to be the Lost Dauphin of France might have had something to do with his murder. Why the bloody hell didn't you tell me?"

"Mother of God; why would I bring up some ridiculous, decades-old rumor? Damion was my brother—my half brother, if you will. He was no Bourbon."

"Are you so certain?"

"Yes!"

"How old were you when your father brought Damion home?"

Her eyes glittered with animosity. "Fourteen."

"Yet you had never seen him before?"

"No. I did not even know he existed."

"You didn't find that odd?"

"Then? Of course. Now?" She shook her head. "No. His mother was a noblewoman. The birth would have been seen as something shameful, something to be hidden. Her parents cut off all contact between her and my father."

"Did your brother ever talk to you about his mother?"

"Not really. He remembered little of their life before prison. When the trauma of one's life becomes too great to deal with, the mind sometimes ceases remembering it."

"Was his ordeal traumatic?"

"He and his mother spent years in prison, without light or proper food, in conditions considerably worse than those endured by Marie-Thérèse. Then his mother was torn from his arms and killed. He never completely recovered from the experience, either physically or mentally. He had dreadful nightmares, and his legs were always weak—it's why he was never able to serve as a physician in the French army."

"And why he hated the dark?"

"Yes."

The implications of that fear and the knowledge of how he had met his death weighed heavily in the silence between them.

Sebastian kept his gaze on her face. "Your father has never said anything to suggest that he might have been involved in an attempt to save the Dauphin from the Temple Prison?"

"Good God, no! How many times must I tell you? *Damion was my brother.*"

"Did your brother know about the speculation that he might in fact be the Lost Dauphin?"

"Of course he knew. Nothing would make him more furious."

"Sometimes anger is a product of a refusal to believe the truth."

"Not in this case."

She went to stand beside an ancient stone watering trough set in front of the stepped-back facade of the neighboring house. She still had her arms crossed, as if she were hugging herself, and her features had taken on the flatness of those who look into the distant past.

She said, "When my father performed the autopsy on the body of the boy in the Temple, he removed his heart. For nearly twenty years now he has kept that child's heart in a crystal vase in his study. Why would he do that if he knew the boy was an imposter? If he knew that the real Dauphin was alive and masquerading as his own son?"

"Perhaps he feared that he himself might have been deceived. I doubt the plan of substitution was his own. Knowing that he was simply one player in a much larger plot, he may not have known whom to trust. Whom to believe."

"And so he took the heart on the off chance the dead boy might indeed have been the real son of Louis XVI? Is that what you're saying? But if what you're suggesting is true, then why not tell his own children? Why not tell Damion himself?"

"For your protection, perhaps?" said Sebastian. "The very fact that he kept the child's heart suggests to me that your father retains some royalist sympathies. Did Damion?"

"Hardly. He despised the Bourbons."

"As do you."

"As do I."

She stared off down the lane, to where the children were now tossing withered cabbage leaves at a pig in an effort to capture its interest. Her face was set in tight, hard lines. But he could see the telltale tic of a muscle along her jawline.

He said, "In a sense, it doesn't really matter whether your brother was the Lost Dauphin or not. All that matters is that someone believed he was—someone who considered him a potential threat to the current line of succession to the French throne. A threat to be eliminated."

She brought up one hand to press the fingertips against her lips. "You're saying that's why they took his heart? Because they thought he was a Bourbon? What are they planning to do with it? Enshrine it someday in the Val-de-Grâce? As if he were another martyr of the Revolution rather than a man they themselves murdered?"

"I suspect they do consider him a martyr of the Revolution."

"And the colonel with the French delegation? Why kill him? Why gouge out his eyes?"

"To disguise the true motive behind Damion Pelletan's death, perhaps? To frighten Vaundreuil into abandoning peace negotiations that might end with Napoléon still on the throne of France? I'm not sure."

She dropped her hands to her sides. "Who? Which of the Bourbons do you think was behind this?"

"I don't know."

She studied his face, her eyes hard and searching. "I don't believe it."

When he said nothing, she expelled her breath in a harsh rush. "I keep going over and over that dreadful night in my mind. The bitter, numbing cold. The glitter of the ice. The echo of our footsteps in the stillness. I keep trying to remember something—anything—that might help. But I can't."

"You said you thought you heard footsteps behind you, in the lane."

"Yes."

"One set of footsteps or two?"

"Only one. Or at least, only one close at hand. There may have been others, farther in the distance."

"A man's footsteps, or a woman's?"

"A man's. Of that, I am certain. Why do you ask?"

"I found the prints of a woman's shoe in the alley."

She shook her head. "If there had been a woman there, I would have known it—I would have *felt* it."

Another man might have questioned her assurance, but not Sebastian. As acute as his senses of sight and hearing were, he had learned long ago to rely even more on those senses to which language had as yet given no name.

She said, "Surely you're not suggesting that Marie-Thérèse of France or one of her ladies stalked my brother through the wretched alleys of St. Katharine's and thrust a knife into his back?"

Sebastian shook his head. He didn't believe even Lady Giselle would do her own killing. She would leave the dirty work to men like the dark-eyed assassin who had attacked Sebastian outside Stokes Mandeville, a man Sebastian had once assumed was English but whom he now realized could as easily be a Frenchman who had lived the last twenty-odd years in this country, losing all trace of his native inflections.

Yet he found himself coming back, as always, to that bloody imprint of a woman's shoe. And he was aware of a conviction that he was still missing something terribly important.

And that time was running out.

Chapter 51

*T*hat night, a fierce wind blew in from the north, scattering the dense, choking fog that had smothered the city for days and bringing with it a killing cold.

Sebastian could hear the wind even in his sleep, a low, mournful cadence that joined with a chorus of inconsolable grief. He dreamt of sad-eyed women with flailing arms that reached up to the heavens as they cried out with an anguish borne of empty wombs and empty cradles, even when the blood of their murdered infants stained their own hands. Then the wind became the thunder of the surf beating against a rocky shore, and he was a boy again, standing at the precipice of a sheer cliff face, the sun warm on his face as he stared out to sea. Watching, waiting for a golden-haired, laughing woman who would never, ever return.

He jerked awake, his eyes opening on the tucked blue silk of the tester above. He sat on the side of the bed, the breath coming hard in his chest, like a man standing against a gale so strong he had to fight to draw air. The room was filled with dancing shadows, the wind eddying the dying fire and shifting the heavy drapes at the window.

He rose to his feet and went to throw more coal on the fire. The icy air bit his naked flesh, but he ignored it, standing with one hand resting on the mantel, his gaze on the leaping flames. He heard a soft whisper of movement from the bed, and Hero came to drape a blanket around his shoulders.

He had returned home that evening to find her kneeling on the bed with her arms folded on the mattress and her forehead resting on her hands. She might not trust Alexandrie Sauvage to manipulate the child in her womb, but she was desperate enough to spend twenty minutes every two hours in an ungainly posture that thus far had done nothing to encourage his recalcitrant offspring to assume a position best calculated to preserve her and her mother's life.

She said, "You can't solve every murder, unravel every mystery, right every wrong."

"No."

She gave a soft huff of disbelief. "You say that, but you don't really believe it."

He gave a crooked smile. "No."

She snuggled into the chair beside the fire, a quilt held close around her. "Do you seriously think it possible that Marie-Thérèse could be behind all this?"

"When you're brought up to believe that you're descended from a saint and that your family has been anointed by God to fill a position of limitless power and authority, it does tend to have a somewhat warping influence on your thought processes—even without the damage inflicted by three years of hell locked in a tower and guarded by men who hate you."

Hero was silent for a moment, her eyes clouded by a troubling memory.

"What?" he asked, watching her.

"I was just thinking about a dinner party I attended a few years ago. Marie-Thérèse was there, and she told a story about her brother, about a time when Marie Antoinette allowed the children to milk the

cows at the Petit Trianon, and how the little Dauphin squealed with
delight when he was accidentally squirted in the face with the warm,
fresh milk. It's the only time I've ever seen her looking relaxed and
vaguely happy. I think she remembers the days before the Revolution
when her mother and father and brother were all alive as a golden age
in her life, a sacred time of joy and love and serenity. If she genuinely
thought Damion Pelletan was the Lost Dauphin, I can't believe she
would have had him killed. The others? Perhaps. But not a man she
believed to be her beloved little brother."

"You could be right. It's possible she knows nothing about it. But
that doesn't mean it wasn't done to benefit her."

"By whom?"

"I'd put my money on Lady Giselle."

She blinked. "Can you prove it?"

"Prove it? No. To be honest, I'm not even entirely convinced I'm
right." He gave a wry smile. "It isn't as if I haven't been wrong before."

She watched the flames lick at the new load of coal. "How do you
explain the explosion at Golden Square? I mean, why would Lady
Giselle try to kill Alexi Sauvage? Simply because she was there when
Damion Pelletan was killed?"

"It's possible. Although I'm not convinced the Bourbons had anything to do with what happened in Golden Square. That was probably Sampson Bullock's handiwork."

"Then how do you know he didn't kill Damion Pelletan too?"

"I don't. I'd probably think he *did* kill Pelletan, if it weren't for the
removal of Pelletan's heart. That, and the way everything seems to
keep circling back to the Bourbons."

"That doesn't mean they're to blame."

"No. But they are involved. Somehow."

She pushed up from the chair with the slow, stately grace that
had come to characterize her movements of late. The dark fall of her
hair glowed in the firelight, a soft smile curling her lips as she brack-
eted his cheeks with her hands and kissed his mouth. He rested his

hands on her hips, breathed in the familiar heady scent that was all her own. He kissed her again, then leaned his forehead against hers as he felt his heart swell with a flood of love and joy, all tangled up with a fear more terrible than any he had ever known.

Even after they had gone back to bed and she had fallen asleep beside him, he found the night's shadows haunted by dreamlike images of empty arms and silent cradles.

Friday, 29 January

Early the next morning, Sebastian was coming down for breakfast when Morey opened the door to Lady Peter Radcliff.

She carried an overstuffed satchel and had brought with her the child known to the world as her brother. He stood on the top step with his two wooden boats clutched to his chest. There was a pale, pinched look about his face, and he kept shivering as if he were so cold he might never warm up.

Lady Peter wore a cherry red velvet pelisse with a high white fur collar and a silken bonnet whose stiffened velvet brim hid her face. But when she turned her head, Sebastian saw the thin line of blood that trickled from her split lip and the purple bruises that mottled and swelled her once pretty face.

"I'm so sorry," she said, her voice a cracked whisper. "I know I shouldn't have come here. But I didn't know where else to go." And then, as if she had been holding herself upright by a sheer act of will, her eyes rolled back in her head.

Sebastian caught her just before she hit the tiled marble floor.

"I don't think she's sustained any serious internal damage," Gibson said, keeping his voice low. "Although it wasn't for lack of trying on someone's part. Who did this to her?"

"That would be her husband, the younger son of the Third Duke of Linford, and brother to the current Fourth Duke."

They were standing just outside the door to the darkened chamber where Lady Peter lay beneath a pile of warm quilts. Her eyes were closed, although Sebastian didn't think she was sleeping. Hero had carried off the boy, Noël, to the morning room, where she was plying him with milk and cookies and trying to coax the disgruntled black cat into being sociable.

Gibson said, "I tried to get her to take some laudanum, but she refused. Perhaps you can convince her to change her mind."

After Gibson left, Sebastian went to sit beside her. He watched her throat work as she swallowed and opened eyes that were swimming with unshed tears. Then she blinked, and one tear escaped to slip sideways into her hair.

"It's all right," he said. "You're safe now."

She shook her head, although whether it was to refute his statement or to deny her need for safety, he couldn't have said. "Peter . . ." She swallowed. "He never beat me like this before. Not this bad. In the past, he was always careful to hurt me where it wouldn't show. But this time . . . I thought he was going to kill me."

"What set him off? Do you have any idea?"

"He was out drinking most of the night and came home in a rage. He's badly dipped, you see, and his brother is refusing to pay his debts. The last time the Duke rescued him from dun territory, he swore he'd never do it again. I knew he meant it, but Peter refused to believe it. Now he's getting desperate. He ran through everything I brought to the marriage years ago, and he wants to get his hands on what my father left for Noël. I told him I wouldn't help him do it— that I'd rather die. That's when he started hitting me."

She was silent for a moment, then said, "He called me . . . such names. Said he had put up with my bastard all these years, that the least I could do was help him now, when he needed it."

"He knows Noël is your son?"

She nodded, the tears sliding freely down her cheeks. "I never deceived him."

"Did you tell him Damion Pelletan was the boy's father?"

"No. But I think he might have guessed." Her fingers picked at the lace trimming of the sheets. "When Damion first begged me to go away with him, I told him I couldn't do it. I wanted to, but I'd made a vow and I believed I owed it to Peter to honor it. But then . . ."

Her voice faded away. Sebastian waited, and after a moment she swallowed and started up again. "Last Wednesday, Noël left one of his boats lying in the entry hall. Peter tripped over it, and he turned around and backhanded Noël so hard he made his nose bleed. I couldn't believe it. Peter had never hit him before. But that's how it started with me; one day he lost his temper and slapped me across the face. He swore he'd never do it again. But he did. So I knew . . . I knew it would be the same all over again with Noël. That's when I realized I had to leave—with or without Damion."

"So you told Damion you'd go with him when he left for France?"

"Yes."

"Is it possible Lord Peter discovered what you were planning?"

"I don't know." Her face crumpled with the force of her sobs, splitting open the cut on her lip so that it began to bleed again. "He may have. *Oh, God.* Has this all been my fault? Did Damion die because of me?"

Sebastian knew most people in their society would blame her, whether Damion died because of her or not. She had borne a child out of wedlock, then conspired to leave her noble husband for her former lover.

But he could not find it within him to either judge or condemn her for the tangle her life had become. She had been young and vulnerable when she gave in to her passion and the enchantment of love, and unwisely created a child. Torn from the future that might have been hers, she was forced by her parents and the dictates of their society's stern, unforgiving sense of propriety to disown her own child and marry a man who agreed to give her a veneer of respectability in exchange for her father's wealth. It was a contract she entered into in good faith, determined to honor the vows she made to a man whose easy geniality and practiced charm hid an angry, self-indulgent, and ultimately abusive petulance.

He said, "Lord Peter claims he was home with you the night Damion was killed. Was he?"

She shook her head from side to side against the pillow. "No. He was supposed to meet Brummell and Alvanley at White's for dinner that night, but he never showed up. He said he spent the night drinking in some low tavern in Westminster and ended up getting into a brawl there. When he came home early the next morning, his clothes were covered in blood."

"Was he hurt?"

"No. I think his knuckles may have been skinned, but that was all."

"Where is he now?"

"I left him sleeping." She drew in a deep, ragged breath. "I've made such a mess of things. What am I to do?"

Reaching out, Sebastian laid his hand over hers where it rested on the counterpane. "Right now, all you need to do is rest and get better."

"Noël—"

"Is petting our cranky black cat in the drawing room. He'll be fine."

"I should see him—"

"I'll have him come in after you've had some sleep."

Her hand trembled beneath his, then lay still. And it occurred to him as he watched her eyes close and her breathing deepen with sleep that whoever had killed Damion Pelletan hadn't only robbed a caring young physician of his life.

They'd also deprived a little boy of his father and a lonely young woman of the chance to reach again for the gentle love and happiness that had been snatched from her so long ago.

Chapter 52

$\mathcal{B}$efore he rang the bell of Lord Peter Radcliff's town house in Half Moon Street, Sebastian loosened his cravat, tousled his hair, and splashed his face with some of the contents of the brandy bottle he held. Then he leaned one elbow against the doorframe, affected a slightly befuddled smile, and waited.

Radcliff's butler was a small, slim man with a mouthful of large, crooked teeth and a long, sharp nose. He gazed at Sebastian with watery gray eyes and sniffed.

"Ah, there you are," said Sebastian, staggering slightly as he straightened. "I'm here for Radcliff."

The butler sniffed again. "I'm afraid Lord Peter is not presently at home to visitors."

"Still abed, is he?" Smiling cheerfully, Sebastian pushed past the startled butler and crossed the entrance hall toward the stairs. "That's quite all right. He won't mind me waking him."

"But— My lord! You can't do that!"

Sebastian took the steps two at a time. "Not to worry. I can guarantee he'll be delighted to see me." Pausing halfway up the stairs, Sebastian swung around to hold the bottle aloft as if it were a rare prize. "What you see here is some of the best brandy never to pay a penny of tax into the coffers of good ole King George." He pressed one finger to his pursed lips and winked. "But *shhh;* mum's the word, eh?"

"My lord, please!"

"That will be all," called Sebastian gaily, running up the rest of the stairs.

At the top of the second flight, he threw open the doors of two rooms before finding the right one. The chamber lay in darkness, the heavy drapes at the windows closed tight to exclude all light. The space was large and square, furnished with a high tester and delicate Adams chests, its pastel-hued walls accented with beribboned moldings picked out in cream. The air reeked of stale sweat and despair and the alcohol-tinged exhalations of the man who snored loudly from the depths of the bed.

Sebastian closed the door behind him and locked it, then crossed the room to do the same to the door leading to the dressing room.

The man in the bed did not stir.

Radcliff's clothes lay scattered across the floor where he had obviously discarded them on his wobbly path to the bed. First the cravat, then a meticulously tailored coat dropped on the floor with its sleeves inside out. Sebastian saw a waistcoat, its crumpled, white silk front splattered with dried blood, and he felt a surge of rage that was like a hum in his ears.

It was Julia's blood.

The bottle still gripped in one fist, he went to stand beside Lord Peter.

Sprawled on his back in a tangle of sheets, he had one bare leg dangling off the edge of the bed, his nightshirt rucked up around his hips. He lay with his face turned to one side, his golden hair plastered to his forehead with dried sweat, his lips pursed so that his breath whistled softly on its way out.

Sebastian stared down at him for a moment, then crossed to the window and yanked open the drapes.

The cold light of midmorning flooded the room. Lord Peter gave a strangled half snore, then resumed his previous cadence.

Setting aside the bottle, Sebastian fisted both hands in the frilled front of the man's nightshirt. "Come on; up with you, then," he said as he hauled the drunken man's limp body out of the bed and swung him around to slam his back against the carved wooden post of the bed with enough force to rattle the frame.

"Wha—?" Radcliff wavered, his eyes fluttering open, his mouth foolishly agape as his legs crumpled and he slid down against the side of the bed.

Closing one hand around the brandy bottle's neck, Sebastian smashed it against the carved bedpost, raining down brandy and broken glass on the drunken man's head and shoulders.

Radcliff shook his head like a dog coming in out of a storm. "What the devil?"

Crouching low, Sebastian grabbed another fistful of Radcliff's nightshirt with one hand and pressed the sharp edge of the broken bottle up under the man's chin. "Give me one good excuse to slit your throat," he said, enunciating each word with awful clarity, "and believe me, I will. I've just had a surgeon to tend your wife's injuries. It's no thanks to you she's not dead."

"Julia? Wha'd the bitch say? If she told you—"

Radcliff let out a yelp as Sebastian increased the pressure on the sharp edge held against his throat.

"*Don't.* Don't ever let me hear you use a word like that to describe your wife again. Do I make myself understood? I have no mercy for a man like you. There's a special place in hell for a man who uses his fists on his own wife, and I'll be more than happy to send you there."

Lord Peter stared up at him with bulging eyes. He might not be entirely sober, but he was now wide-awake. "You're mad."

"I may well be. I'm beginning to suspect that we all are, each in our own way."

"You can't come in here, threatening me, acting like I'm some—"

Sebastian shifted his weight in a way that made Lord Peter break off and draw a quick, shallow breath.

Sebastian said, "In case you haven't noticed, I am already here. Where you made your mistake was in lying to me. You told me you spent last Thursday night at home with your wife. You didn't. You got into a row with her. You were angry about her renewed acquaintance with an old childhood friend—"

"He wasn't simply some 'old friend'! He was her lover."

"Nine years ago. Not now."

"Is that what she told you?"

"Yes. And I believe her." Sebastian let his gaze drift over the other man's face, slick with sweat and slack now with the aftereffects of too much alcohol and too little sleep. "Is that why you followed Pelletan to St. Katharine's and stuck a knife in his back?"

"I didn't! I swear I didn't. I won't deny I was angry; what man wouldn't be? I even went to the inn where the bastard was staying. I was going to tell him that Julia is my wife and he'd better stay the hell away from her. But I didn't even do that."

"Why not?"

"Because when I got there, he was standing on the footpath outside the inn, talking to Lady Giselle."

Sebastian stared at him. "Are you telling me you saw Damion Pelletan talking with Lady Giselle Edmondson?"

Radcliff looked puzzled by Sebastian's vehemence. "That's right. Why?"

"How do you know the woman you saw was Lady Giselle?"

"Because I recognized her. How do you think? She was wearing a hat with a veil, but she'd pushed back the veil and the light from the oil lamp beside the door was falling full on her face."

"Did you hear anything of what was said?"

"No; of course not. What the bloody hell do you think I am? I don't go around eavesdropping on other people's private conversations."

"Was there a man with her?"

"There was, but I couldn't tell you who. He stayed in the background."

"So then what happened?"

"I don't know. I left."

"You left? Why?"

"At first I'd planned to wait in the shadows until she went away, and then confront him. But the longer I stood there, the more I realized that would be a mistake."

"Oh? Why?"

"Because I'm not a killer, whatever you may think. And I realized that if I approached him then, in the rage I was in, I might very well murder him. So I left. I won't say I'm sorry the bastard is dead because I'm not. But he didn't die at my hand."

"Where did you go after you left York Street?"

"I don't know. I wandered the streets for a while—I couldn't say for how long. I ended up in a low tavern someplace in Westminster. At one point I got into a brawl with a drunk who drew my cork. Then I spent what was left of the night in a back room with a whore I wouldn't even recognize if I saw her again."

Sebastian studied Lord Peter's haggard face. He'd said he had no mercy for men like Radcliff, but that wasn't exactly true. If not mercy, then he at least acknowledged a measure of pity even though he knew it was probably misplaced. In his own way, Lord Peter was a victim. A victim of a society that valued show above substance, birth above real worth. A victim of a hereditary system that brought up younger sons in an indulgent, pampered atmosphere even as it tormented them with the knowledge that the vast estates and palatial homes they'd enjoyed as children would never be theirs. And he was a victim of his own weakness, the recognition of which led him to strike out in anger and frustration at his wife when what he really wanted more than anything else was to be admired and indulged and loved.

Sebastian said, "Listen to me carefully because I'm going to say this only once. Your wife is going to leave you, and you are going to let her."

"*What?* You've no right to—"

Radcliff made a strangling sound as Sebastian subtly shifted the broken edge of the bottle against his throat.

"If your debts are as pressing as I suspect they are, you might consider fleeing the country. I hear America is a good place for people looking to start over."

Radcliff's face contorted with revulsion. *"America?"*

"Frankly, I couldn't care less where you go. But you will make no attempt to contact your wife or her son again. And if I ever hear of you laying a hand on her, I'll kill you. It's that simple. Do I make myself clear?"

"What does it matter to you, what happens to her?"

"It matters," said Sebastian, and let him go.

Sebastian walked back down the stairs and out of the house, only dimly aware of the butler, two housemaids, and a footman peering at him wide-eyed from around the doorframes as he passed.

Outside, the air smelled of coal smoke and the coming rain. He paused on the footpath, his gaze on the jumble of rooftops and chimney stacks that jutted up dark against a gray sky. Was Radcliff lying? Sebastian doubted it. Men like Radcliff were basically cowards; they beat their wives because it gave them a sense of power and control so sorely lacking in other aspects of their lives. Sebastian couldn't see a man like that somehow finding the courage to stalk a rival through the cold, dark alleys of St. Katharine's and then cut out his heart in some twisted ritual of symbolism and revenge.

But what occupied Sebastian's thoughts as he turned toward the home of the Comte d'Artois in South Audley Street was the vital piece of information Lord Peter had unknowingly provided. Sebastian had believed that Marie-Thérèse and Lady Giselle passed the night of Damion Pelletan's murder closeted together in prayer for the martyred King Louis XVI. He'd thought their role in Pelletan's death—if it existed at all—had been limited to directing their minions from afar.

Now he wasn't so sure.

Chapter 53

Sebastian wouldn't have been surprised if Lady Giselle refused to see him. But he underestimated her. She sent word that she would be down in a few moments, although, instead of having him escorted to the drawing room, she met him in a small, book-lined chamber on the ground floor that looked as if it might be devoted to the use of a steward or man of business.

She wore a simple gown of dove gray wool trimmed with black ribbon. Her fair hair fell in gentle curls about her delicate face; a plain band of black velvet encircled her long, delicate neck. Her only jewelry was a small gold watch pinned to her breast, and a dainty pair of pearl earrings.

"Lord Devlin," she said, holding out her hand to him, her smile one of warmth that hinted at a secret shared. "Forgive me for receiving you here, but Marie-Thérèse is in the drawing room. I fear the very mention of your name is still enough to send her into spasms."

"Thank you for agreeing to see me—particularly under such circumstances."

"Please, have a seat. Have you discovered something of interest?"

He took the seat she indicated, a red leather desk chair with worn wooden arms. "I have, actually. I was wondering: Where did you and Marie-Thérèse spend a week ago Thursday? I know you devoted the day to prayer for her father, the King. But were you here, in London, or at Hartwell House?"

A vague shadow passed her face. It was there and then gone so quickly he couldn't identify it. Apprehension, perhaps? Calculation? Or simply remembered sorrow?

"Here," she said. "We had come up to London several days before, so that Marie-Thérèse might consult with Dr. Pelletan. We left for Hartwell House again early Friday morning."

"I should tell you that I now know why Marie-Thérèse was so anxious to consult with Damion Pelletan. It had nothing to do with his reputation as a physician and everything to do with the fact that his father first brought Damion home the very summer the little Dauphin died in the Temple Prison. I think the Princess knew about the rumors that he might be the Lost Dauphin, and she wanted to see him so that she could judge for herself whether or not he was her brother."

There was a long pause, during which Lady Giselle's face showed not a hint of consternation or alarm. She simply gave a small, sad smile and said, "You are right, of course. Marie-Thérèse has never given up hope that her brother might one day be found alive. You've no notion the number of pretenders she has interviewed over the years, each time working herself into a frenzy of anticipation, only to be cast down with disappointment at the realization that she has once more been deceived."

"But Damion Pelletan never claimed to be the Lost Dauphin."

"He did not, no. Which is one of the reasons she was particularly anxious to see him."

"And what was her conclusion?"

"To be frank, she found him so much like her dead mother that she was overcome with emotion. It had been her intention to ask him a series of probing questions about his past, but she was so distraught that she found she could not. I had to take her away."

"Is that why you went back to see Pelletan again on Thursday night?"

He expected her to deny it, but she was too clever for that. And he realized she'd probably guessed from the beginning what his questions were leading up to, and why.

She tilted her head to one side, her gaze intent on his face. "How did you know?"

"You were recognized."

"Ah."

When she remained silent, he said, "You told me you spent the day in prayer with Marie-Thérèse. Why not tell the truth?"

"It seemed best at the time. Now I realize it was a mistake. Forgive me."

"Am I to understand that for the first time in eighteen years you deserted the Princess on the anniversary of her father's death?"

She shook her head. "No. I fear there are times when Marie-Thérèse's grief simply becomes too much for her. When she reaches that point, she is impossible to calm and can make herself ill. In such situations, sleep becomes the only reasonable recourse."

In other words, Lady Giselle had dosed the hysterical Princess with laudanum.

Now she sat with her fingers laced together in her lap, her features composed in an expression of calm beatitude that would have done justice to St. Louis himself. She said, "Marie-Thérèse had asked me to return and see Pelletan—to ask the questions she herself had been unable to broach. And so I did."

"What did you discover?"

"Very little, actually. He became quite angry when he realized why I was there and refused to discuss the subject any further. So we left."

"We?"

A faint note of exasperation crept into her voice. "You don't seriously think I would undertake such a visit alone, do you? My mother's cousin, the Chevalier d'Armitz, was kind enough to accompany me." Again, that charming tilt of the head as her pretty forehead crinkled with a show of confusion. "Why are you asking me these questions?"

"Because you and your cousin were amongst the last people to see Damion Pelletan alive. What was he doing when you left the inn?"

She shrugged. "The last I saw, he was standing on the footpath outside the inn, staring up at the night sky. As I said, the conversation visibly disturbed him. He may have been trying to compose himself before returning inside."

"Did you see anyone else while you were there?"

"We spoke to a servant in the coffee room, if that's what you mean. But I don't recall noticing anyone else."

"What about your cousin, the Chevalier d'Armitz? He might have noticed someone. Would it be possible for me to speak to him?"

"I'm sorry, but I believe he is away from London at the moment."

"A pity," said Sebastian.

"Yes. It is, isn't it?"

"Tell me about him."

She smiled and gave a little shrug. "What is there to tell?"

"Has he been in England long?"

"Most of his life."

"He's young?"

"In his twenties, yes." She glanced at the watch pinned to her bodice. Sebastian had outstayed his welcome, and she was not hesitant to let him know it. She rose to her feet. "And now I fear you must excuse me, my lord. We plan to return to Hartwell House in the morning, and Marie-Thérèse has expressed an interest in making one last expedition to Bond Street."

Sebastian rose with her, his hat in one hand. "Best hurry, then," he said. "It looks as if it is liable to come on to rain."

"Hopefully not until after midnight," she said, smiling sadly. "I've a private service at the chapel to attend this evening."

He studied her delicate, fine-featured face. She was a beautiful woman, still young enough to bear children and well dowered enough to attract suitors, had she wanted them. Instead, she had devoted her life to the support of a fragile, damaged princess regarded by the indulgent as haughty and high-strung, and by the less charitable as half-mad.

Aloud, he said, "Why have you stayed with Marie-Thérèse all these years?"

"Because she needs me," Lady Giselle said simply. "When she was released from prison eighteen years ago, I promised I would stay with her until the Bourbons are restored to their rightful place on the throne of France. I am a woman of my word."

"And if there never is a Bourbon restoration?"

She looked at him with the clear, steady conviction of a Joan of Arc, or the kind of officials who once burned witches at the stake. "There will be. It is God's will."

"Divine right of kings and all that?"

Her jaw tensed. "You can scoff if you like. But the fact remains that God has bestowed earthly sovereignty on the Bourbons, just as He has given spiritual sovereignty to His Pope. That is why no monarch can be subject to earthly authority, for his right to rule derives from God's own will, not from his subjects. Any attempt by those subjects to depose their lawful king or curtail his power in any way is an affront to God and thus cannot long endure."

"The United States of America seem to be enduring just fine."

"Yet the French Revolution endured for how long? Little more than a decade. I doubt Napoléon will last much longer."

"Napoléon's mistake is the same as the Bourbons': He is trying to stand against the tide of history. The age of monarchs is passing.

Even if Napoléon is defeated and the Bourbons restored by the armies of Russia and Britain, they won't last for long."

She held herself stiffly. "I'd no notion you were so radical in your thinking, my lord." Somehow, she managed to turn the 'my lord' into a mockery—which he supposed in a way it was, although she didn't know that. "What do you believe in, then? *The Rights of Man?*"

"Actually, there's very little I believe in."

He had been deliberately trying to provoke her, and he had succeeded far better than he had anticipated. But now she seemed to become aware of the extent to which she had betrayed herself. She blinked, and the steely moral certainty that had inspired the likes of Cotton Mather, Oliver Cromwell, and Maximilien Robespierre slid behind the careful assumption of calm good humor that typically characterized her.

She said, "I think you believe in far more than you give yourself credit for, my lord."

"Perhaps."

She walked with him to the entrance hall, nodding quietly to the butler, who moved to open the front door.

"Tell me, my lord," she said, pausing beside him. "Are you any closer to discovering who is behind these dreadful murders?"

"I believe I may be, yes."

"Indeed? Then hopefully soon we may all sleep better in our beds."

"Have you been afraid?" he asked, his gaze on her face.

"Fear has been our constant companion for many years."

"I don't think you need worry about this."

"Yet you will let us know if you discover anything more?"

"Of course."

A woman's voice floated down from upstairs. "Giselle? *Où es-tu?*"

"You must excuse me, my lord." She gave a slight bow. "And thank you again."

He watched her move away, her tranquil self-possession once more firmly in place. He did not for an instant believe that she was losing sleep due to fear of some brutal murderer prowling the streets of London. But he could believe she was worried.

For a very different reason entirely.

Chapter 54

Sebastian walked the cold, rain-washed streets of Mayfair and tried to think. Would a woman who believed in the divine right of kings plot to kill a young man she thought might be the only surviving son of Louis XVI of France? On the surface, the answer seemed to be no. And yet, this was a woman who had dedicated her life to the restoration of the Bourbon dynasty, not to the restoration of a certain frail young prince who may or may not have died in the Temple Prison. If she considered Damion Pelletan a threat to the eventual accession of Marie-Thérèse and her husband to the throne of France, would Lady Giselle kill him?

Sebastian believed she would.

What had Alexi Sauvage said about her brother? *Damion despised the Bourbons.* Had he expressed those sentiments to Lady Giselle? If he had, it might well have led to his death.

The family trees of Europe's royal houses were littered with kings who had fallen victim to a usurper's hand. Fathers murdered by sons, nephews by uncles, cousins by cousins. How did Lady Giselle explain such irregularities, he wondered? As the divine wisdom of Providence working in mysterious ways? Probably. Those who believed God was on their side all too often found it easy to kill in His name, secure in the comfortable certitude of their own righteousness.

And yet . . . And yet his imagination still balked at the image of Lady Giselle and her cousin the unknown Chevalier stalking Damion Pelletan through the mean streets of St. Katharine's on one of the coldest nights of the year. Sebastian knew he was still missing something. The question was, *What?*

He kept coming back to the image of Damion Pelletan standing before the Gifford Arms, his head thrown back, his gaze on the cold night sky above. How many people knew Damion and Alexi Sauvage intended to visit Hangman's Court that night? Lady Giselle? No; she was gone by the time Alexandrie arrived. Lord Peter? Possibly, if he had lingered longer than he claimed. Jarvis's man? Again, possibly—if he had been close enough to overhear their conversation. Harmond Vaundreuil? Again, possibly.

Sampson Bullock?

Sebastian paused. The wind gusted up, cold and damp against his face and carrying with it all the smells of the city. Could Sampson Bullock have known that Alexi Sauvage and her brother were headed for Hangman's Court that night? Yes. Bullock had been following and watching her for days. What if he learned of not only her plans to visit St. Katharine's, but also her intent to ask her *brother* to accompany her?

Two things about this convoluted string of murders kept tripping Sebastian up: the bloody print left in the alley by a woman's shoe, and the brutal murder of the Frenchman Foucher. Combined with the attack on Serena in Birdcage Walk, the latter seemed to suggest either the Bourbons or some other enemy of Napoléon's peace proposals. Yet how could either be linked to the explosion in Golden Square? If Alexi Sauvage were able to identify her brother's killer, she would have been murdered with him.

Yet an idea was forming in Sebastian's mind, an explanation that accounted for these discrepancies and more.

It was time he had another talk with Mr. Mitt Peeples.

Sebastian arrived at the Gifford Arms to find a dray half-loaded with trunks drawn up outside the inn, its mules standing with legs splayed and heads dipped in the cold wind. Mitt Peebles, wearing his leather apron and at his most officious, was directing two workmen carrying a handsome campaign desk out the inn door.

"Careful there, now," he called as one of the men bumped into the doorframe.

"What's all this?" asked Sebastian, walking up to him.

"They're leaving—what's left of 'em, that is. Guess they figure they'd best get out while the getting is good. You heard another of 'em was found dead? Had his eyes gouged out. Who'd do something like that? Ain't no Englishman, if you ask me."

"Are you saying Harmond Vaundreuil is returning to France?"

"Well, can't say I know for certain *where* he's going. But I can guess, can't I?"

Sebastian watched the workmen maneuver the desk into the back of the dray. "I wonder: Are you familiar with a cabinetmaker by the name of Sampson Bullock?"

"Bullock?" Mitt paused, his saggy-jowled face going blank as he pondered the question. "Don't believe so, no."

"He's a giant of a man, tall and big boned, with curly black hair he wears long. Ever see him hanging around the inn?"

Mitt shook his head. "Not so's I recall, no. Why? You think he may be the one doing all this?"

"At this point, I don't really know."

Mitt grunted, his protuberant eyes watering in the cold wind. "All I hope is that word don't get out, linking these goings-on to the inn. Won't do to have folks thinking the place is hexed. Won't do at all."

Sebastian watched the two porters head back into the hotel. "Is Monsieur Vaundreuil about?"

"Aye. In the coffee room, last I saw him."

Sebastian walked into the coffee room to find Vaundreuil and his clerk, Bondurant, standing beside one of the tables near the front windows. They had a tan leather case open on the tabletop and appeared to be verifying the papers it contained. Bondurant glanced over at Sebastian, then silently thrust the last of the papers into the case, buckled it, and left the room.

"I hear you're leaving," said Sebastian, staring after the clerk.

Vaundreuil swiped one hand across his lower face. His eyes were red rimmed and puffy. "You blame me?"

"No. But what about the negotiations?"

The Frenchman shrugged. "They weren't exactly going anywhere."

Sebastian went to stand with his back to the fire. "When I saw you yesterday morning, you were determined to stay. What changed your mind?"

"My daughter. She insisted I needed some slippery elm for a sore throat I've been complaining of, and walked down to the apothecary's yesterday afternoon to get it. Someone followed her."

"Did she see him?"

"No. The fog was too thick. All she heard was footsteps, and then a man's cough. But she had no doubt he was following her. He stopped when she stopped, then started up again when she moved on. She ran the rest of the way back to the inn."

Sebastian studied the other man's drawn face. "Who do you think is doing this?"

"The Bourbons, perhaps? Some industrialist or financier like that Scotsman, Kilmartin? Who can say? All I know is, I've had enough."

"What about Jarvis? Any chance he could be behind the killings?"

"No."

"So certain?"

Vaundreuil turned toward the window, his gaze on the workmen, who were now loading a pile of bandboxes into the wagon. "Am I certain? No, I suppose not," he said after a moment. "There's no denying that Jarvis plays a deep game—a deep and dangerous game. It's reached the point I don't trust anyone anymore." He gave a humorless huff of laughter. "And pray don't bother to point out the irony of my saying that because, believe me, I see it. The only person with nothing to be ashamed of in all this is Madeline. And I want her safely out of it."

"When does your ship sail?"

"At ten this evening."

"Then if you'll take my advice, you will get your daughter aboard quickly and stay in your cabin until the ship has cleared Greenwich."

The sound of a woman's footsteps on the stairs drew Vaundreuil's gaze to the entrance passage. "But why would anyone want to harm my daughter? Who would do such a thing?"

Madame Madeline Quesnel appeared at the entrance to the coffee room. She wore a black wool carriage gown and carried a traveling reticule in her hand. Her gaze went from her father to Sebastian.

Sebastian said, "When the destinies of nations are at stake, some men will stop at nothing." *Some men, and some women.* He swept her a bow and smiled. "Have a safe voyage, *madame.*"

Chapter 55

*T*he last of the light was leaching from the sky when Charles, Lord Jarvis, crossed the forecourt of Carlton House toward his waiting carriage.

He was feeling mildly pleased with the recent progression of events. There would be no peace negotiations with the impudent upstart, Napoléon; that avaricious little opportunist, Vaundreuil, was at that very moment scurrying toward home with his tail between his legs. The war in Europe would continue to its proper end, with a triumphant host of British troops marching down the Champs-Élysées and the forces of radicalism utterly crushed. Not for a century or more would any nation rise up to threaten Britain's global dominance, nor would any populace again dare to overthrow their betters and proclaim the rights of the vulgar masses.

He paused while a footman hastened to open his carriage door and let down the steps. Settling comfortably on the plush seat, Jarvis was spreading the carriage robe across his lap when the door opened again and Viscount Devlin leapt up to take the seat opposite.

"Mind if I ride along?"

"Actually, yes."

The Viscount smiled. "I won't stay long. I take it you've heard that Monsieur Harmond Vaundreuil is leaving London?"

"I have."

"Was that your doing?"

"Not entirely."

"But you did send someone to follow his daughter."

Jarvis leaned back in his seat and simply raised his eyebrows.

Devlin said, "Vaundreuil thinks you killed Pelletan and Foucher."

"Harmond Vaundreuil is a venal, foolish man. Why would I bother to indulge in such ghoulish theatrics when I already had the head of the delegation on my payroll?"

"Perhaps Pelletan and Foucher threatened to expose Vaundreuil to Paris."

"Ah. In that case they most definitely would have needed to be eliminated. However, to my knowledge, Foucher at least remained blithely ignorant of Vaundreuil's treasonous activities. And as you know, my knowledge is quite extensive."

Devlin stared out the carriage window at a ragged young crossing sweep leaping out of their way. "You told me once that you had a man watching the Gifford Arms the night Pelletan was killed."

"Yes."

"Tell me again what he saw."

Jarvis sighed. "Really, Devlin; this obsession of yours is becoming rather tiresome."

"Humor me."

"Very well. Let's see . . . An unidentified man and a veiled woman arrived by carriage; for reasons doubtless understood better by you than by my informer, Pelletan elected to speak with them outside the inn rather than inside. The exchange was heated, but since my agent unfortunately lacks your acute hearing, the subject of that conversation remains unknown."

"And then what happened?"

"The man and woman returned to their carriage, leaving Pelletan on the pavement in something of a passion. He was still standing there when Alexandrie Sauvage arrived. They also quarreled. Pelletan then returned to the inn and came out again wearing a greatcoat and gloves, after which he and Sauvage went off in a hackney."

Jarvis was aware of Devlin sitting forward, his lips parted.

"What?" asked Jarvis, looking at him with disfavor.

"And the man and first woman? You said they returned to their carriage. When did they drive away?"

"Immediately after Pelletan and his sister left in a hackney."

"You're certain?"

Jarvis was known for his flawless memory. It was one of his greatest assets, for he could recall conversations and reports, verbatim, long after their occurrence had faded from other men's minds. At the Viscount's question, he simply curled his lip in contempt.

Devlin said, "Tell your coachman to pull up."

"Gladly."

The Viscount started to jump down, then paused with his hands braced against the doorframe to look back and ask, "Are you by chance familiar with a young French émigré named the Chevalier d'Armitz?"

"Vaguely. Why?"

"Can you describe him for me?"

"Above medium height. Stocky. Dark hair."

"What do you know of him?"

"Very little. He forms one of that horde of émigrés attached to the Bourbons. He killed a man once—and I don't mean in a duel. Some captain in the Home Guard accused Armitz of cheating, and later that night was found stabbed in the back."

"Interesting. He's tried to kill me twice."

"What a pity that he didn't succeed," said Jarvis.

But Devlin only laughed.

Hero stood at the nursery window, one hand resting on the crest of her belly, her gaze on the dark storm clouds gathering over the city. She had come here often over the past six months, to supervise the workmen preparing the rooms, to indulge in some uncharacteristically maudlin reveries, and, lately, in search of quiet solace.

But tonight she was smiling.

She had spent fifteen to twenty minutes every two hours for the better part of two days on her knees, telling herself she was a gullible fool and yet doing it anyway. And then, when she'd been about to give it up in disgust, she felt a sensation akin to a giant fish doing a somersault in a tight barrel. Over the past several months she'd become familiar with the movements of her child. And so she knew even without being told that Alexi Sauvage's bizarre suggestion had worked; the babe had finally turned, and her chances of surviving the coming birth with a living child had just soared.

Hero knew no one would ever describe her as a humble woman; she was proud, impatient, and opinionated. But she was also not above owning up to an error. And as she watched the last of the daylight fade from the sky, she knew she owed Sauvage both an apology and a heartfelt expression of gratitude.

Intent on ordering her carriage and setting out for Tower Hill, Hero was about to turn from the window when a movement caught her eye. A man stood in the shadow of a cart drawn up across the street. He was a big man, tall and broad shouldered, dressed in the clothes of a tradesman, with a battered hat pulled low over dark curly hair worn too long. In the gathering gloom, his features were indistinct. Yet she could not shake the impression he was staring at the house with a level of malevolence that was almost palpable.

"Claire," she said to the Frenchwoman who was folding clothes into a chest in the small room off the nursery. "Do you see that man—there, near the cart? Do you know who he is?"

Claire Bisette came to stand beside her, a chemise held in her hands. "No. I've never seen him before. Why?"

But Hero simply shook her head, unwilling to admit to a sense of foreboding for which she had no real basis.

Leaving the nursery, she sent word to the stables to have her barouche brought around, then changed into a carriage dress of green gros de Naples with a vandyked shoulder cape trimmed in black. By the time she left the house, an icy wind had kicked up, the lamplighter and his boy hurrying to touch flame to the last of the oil lamps that stretched in a line toward Grosvenor Square.

They caught her eye as the footman was handing her up into her carriage. And for a moment, she saw the man again, tall and dark, with long black hair and a scar across one cheek, standing near the corner of Davies Street.

Then he drew back, the wind fluttering a torn page of newspaper in the gutter and bringing her the scent of the coming rain.

Chapter 56

$\mathscr{B}$y the time Sebastian reached the French chapel on Little George Street, a fine cold rain had begun to fall from out of a heavy black sky.

He paused in the shadows cast by the jutting angle of the nearby stables. The night smelled of wet pavement and fresh horse droppings and hot oil from a distant streetlamp flickering in the wind. A faint light spilled from the church facade's three high windows and from the carriage lanterns of the lone barouche drawn up before the chapel portal; a coachman wearing the livery of the Comte d'Artois dozed on the carriage's high seat. But otherwise, the narrow street lay dark and deserted beneath the coming storm.

Settling his hat low against the rain, Sebastian gently tried the front doors of the chapel. They were locked. He glanced again at the sleeping coachman, then slipped around the side of the chapel to the narrow passage that led to the sacristy door. The rain was falling harder now, sharp, needlelike drops with the sting of sleet. He'd almost reached the short flight of steps when he heard the stealthy footsteps of someone entering the passage behind him.

Sebastian whipped around.

A young man dressed in an unbuttoned greatcoat and a top hat drew up abruptly with a faint, nervous laugh. He looked to be perhaps twenty-five years of age, his features unremarkable except for a pair of large dark eyes as thickly lashed as a girl's.

"The Chevalier d'Armitz, I take it?"

"Yes."

"You were being very quiet," said Sebastian. "You weren't by chance trying to sneak up on me, were you?"

"Now, why would I want to do that?" The Frenchman held his left arm straight down at his side, his hand half-hidden by the folds of his coat. In the deep shadows of the passage, he must have been confident that no man could possibly see the dagger clenched in his fist. "Just thought you ought to know that the church is closed."

"I see candlelight."

The Chevalier advanced one step, then another. "It's a private ceremony."

"Oh? And what sort of ceremony might that be?"

"A funeral."

"Yet there is no hearse."

"The body has already been buried elsewhere." The rain drummed around them. The Chevalier kept coming, the knife held out of sight, his features composed in an affable expression as if they were engaged in a pleasant conversation. "It's the practice amongst certain émigré families to preserve a loved one's heart separate from the body. The urns are kept in a vault here, in the chapel, for the day when they may be returned to France."

"In this case, to the Val-de-Grâce?"

"As it happens, yes." He drew up perhaps four feet from Sebastian, his smile slowly fading into something intense. "You are a difficult man to kill, Monsieur le Vicomte."

"Yet you keep trying."

"The odds are better this time, I think."

"Oh? Because you have a knife in your hand and I don't?"

A faint cloud of surprise followed by uncertainty drifted across the Chevalier's face, then cleared. "I've heard you have the eyes and ears of a cat. I never credited it, myself."

"Your mistake."

He shook his head. "I think it's an image you cultivate."

"I've heard you have a fondness for stabbing men in the back. Literally. Yet my back is not turned."

"I'm adaptable," said the Chevalier. Still smiling, he lunged forward, the knife flashing up toward Sebastian's heart.

Sebastian pivoted to grab the Chevalier's outthrust arm with one hand while grasping his fist with the other. Gritting his teeth, Sebastian twisted the fist hard, the knife handle giving him leverage. He saw the flash of shock in d'Armitz's face as the Frenchman realized just how badly he had miscalculated.

The knife slid from the Chevalier's helplessly limp hand into Sebastian's own. Yanking up the Frenchman's arm, Sebastian drove the blade straight into his heart.

"But . . . ," sputtered the Chevalier, eyes widening as he smacked into a reality he could not finesse, an opponent he could not cheat, a fate he could not elude. Then fury replaced astonishment, an indignant rage made all the more acute by the realization that his luck had finally run out.

"Not quite as adaptable as you thought," said Sebastian, wrenching the blade free.

The rain poured around them, wetting the Frenchman's upturned face and mingling with the blood soaking his white waistcoat. The light of comprehension was already fading from his eyes. Yet the rage remained, like a fiery hot coal doomed to extinction in an unforgiving darkness.

The door to the sacristy opened soundlessly to Sebastian's touch. The space beyond was small and untidy, the air thick with the smell of dampness and stale incense and a musty odor often associated with old men's clothes. A narrow band of flickering candlelight spilled into the dark room through the door to the chapel itself, which stood slightly ajar.

Sebastian paused in the shadows. From here, he could see most of the two rows of empty benches and the wooden west gallery built above the main entrance. The church appeared deserted except for the old priest, clothed in his white alb with the gold-embroidered black stole draped around his neck. He stood before one of the wall-mounted monuments, open now to reveal a shallow niche containing a row of urns. He had his hands raised, the low drone of his voice echoing through the stillness.

"Requiem æternam dona ei, Domine."

Sebastian heard a rustle of cloth, a light step, and Lady Giselle Edmondson moved into his line of vision. She wore a high-waisted gown of black cashmere scalloped and edged with crepe. A black lace veil draped her head, the delicate folds accentuating the fair luster of her hair without hiding her face. In her hands she held a clear rock crystal urn mounted with two silver handles and a silver lid and base. Within lay a red-brown heart he suspected had once belonged to Damion Pelletan.

"Et lux perpetua luceat ei . . ."

She stood with her head bowed, her eyes closed, her beautiful features composed into a study of intense concentration and reverence as the words of the priest washed over her.

"Requiescat in pace . . ."

Sebastian shifted so that his view took in the rest of the chapel. He half expected to find Marie-Thérèse here, as well. But the church was utterly empty except for the aged priest and Lady Giselle.

"Anima ejus, et animæ omnium fidelium defunctorum, per misericordiam . . ." The priest's chanting was reaching a crescendo. Sebastian pushed the door open wider and walked into the chapel.

"Dei requiescant in p—" The priest's head turned, his voice trailing off into a high-pitched squeak as his eyes widened and his jaw sagged.

At first, Giselle must have assumed Sebastian's footsteps belonged to her cousin, for she turned slowly, her head coming up as she opened her eyes. Her reaction was more controlled than the priest's.

She stared at Sebastian for a moment, then said, "I take it that's my cousin's blood?"

It was only then that Sebastian became aware of the spurt of dark blood across the front of his coat and waistcoat, and the bloody knife he still clenched in one hand. "It is."

"He's dead?"

"He is, yes."

He saw the flame of emotion in her eyes, fury mingled with careful calculation rather than grief.

"*Monsieur!*" protested the priest. "You would bring a bloody weapon of murder into the house of the Lord?"

"My apologies, Father." Keeping his gaze on Lady Giselle, Sebastian carefully laid the knife at his feet, the metal hilt clinking against the stone paving.

She said, "I am aware of what you must think, but you are wrong. The Chevalier did not kill Damion Pelletan."

"I know." Sebastian continued walking toward her, his empty hands at his sides. "But you intended to kill him. That's why you followed his hackney when he left the Gifford Arms that night, isn't it?"

"Perhaps. Yet in the end, what we *intended* is immaterial. If all those who wished ill of their fellow beings were held accountable, England would soon be very thin of company."

"So what did happen that night?"

She shrugged. "When the hackney set Pelletan and the woman down at the entrance to Cat's Hole, I told my coachman to pull up and sent the Chevalier to follow them on foot."

"To Hangman's Court?"

"If that is the name of that foul cesspit, then the answer is yes."

"And then what?"

"While Armitz waited, he became aware of another man loitering in the shadows—a large, rather crude ruffian with dark curly hair."

"Sampson Bullock."

"Yes."

Sebastian studied her calm, flawlessly composed features. "How did you know his name?"

"Does it matter? The point is, Armitz watched Bullock follow Pelletan as he left Hangman's Court. At one point, the woman must have heard something because she started to turn. Bullock struck her in the head with a cosh and stabbed Damion Pelletan in the back. Armitz waited until the man left, then came to me."

"And you returned together to where Damion Pelletan and his sister lay?"

She tilted her head to one side. "How did you—"

"How did I know you were there, in the alley? I found the prints left by your shoes."

"But you could not possibly have known the shoe prints were mine."

"No," he agreed, then said, "Why did you return with Armitz to Cat's Hole?"

Her hands moved possessively over the crystal urn in her hands. "I needed the heart."

Sebastian studied the proud lift of her chin, the gleam of self-confident righteousness in those deceptively soft blue eyes. "You cut out his heart yourself, didn't you? That's why you went back with Armitz. He couldn't bring himself to do it. So you did."

"Yes."

He'd known it, and yet, hearing her calmly admit it made the fact seem somehow worse. He could not rid himself of the image of this delicate, ethereally beautiful woman surrounded by the refuse of a dark, foul alley as she savagely hacked Damion Pelletan's heart from his still-warm flesh. He said, "You believed Pelletan the Lost Dauphin, the only surviving son of the martyred King of France; and yet you would have killed him, had someone else not done so first. Why?"

She stared back at him. "He was not fit to rule. He was not raised as a prince, and his mind had been hopelessly corrupted by the influence of the Revolution. When the Bourbons are restored to the throne of France, it will not be through him."

"Yet you would see his heart given a place of honor amongst the royal tombs in Val-de-Grâce?"

"He is still a son of St. Louis."

"Does Marie-Thérèse know? Does she know you would have killed the man she believed might be her brother?"

Rather than answer him, Lady Giselle turned to the priest. "Please continue the service, Father." To Sebastian, she said, "You may leave us now."

Sebastian expelled his breath in a low, humorless huff. "Not without Damion Pelletan's heart. It's up to his sister to decide what's to be done with it."

"No." She shook her head. "His name was not Damion Pelletan, and the woman who accompanied him was not his sister."

"You're wrong," said Sebastian, advancing on her.

He could probably never prove that the Chevalier d'Armitz had killed both Colonel Foucher and the molly, James Farragut, just as there was no way to prove that the Chevalier had acted under this woman's orders. But he'd be damned if he'd let her enshrine Damion Pelletan's heart in a monument dedicated to a dynasty that the man had hated.

"Give me the heart," he said.

"*Monsieur,*" protested the priest, attempting to step between them.

"Father—," Sebastian began, just as Lady Giselle gave the priest a violent shove that sent him staggering into Sebastian.

"Bloody hell," swore Sebastian, reaching out to steady the old man as Giselle whirled and ran for the front of the chapel.

She had the heavy skirts of her gown fisted one hand, the urn clutched tight against her side. She'd almost reached the doors when she obviously remembered they were locked. She hesitated only an instant, then veered off, intent on circling back toward the sacristy. But Sebastian was already setting the bleating priest aside and moving to cut her off. For one intense moment, her furious gaze met his. Then she turned and dashed up the narrow wooden stairs of the west gallery.

He pelted after her, taking the steep steps two at a time. He erupted onto the creaky gallery to find her backed against the wooden balustrade, the urn raised like a weapon.

"Don't come any closer to me," she said with awful calm.

He drew up abruptly. "I won't hurt you. Just give me the heart."

She shook her head. "You asked how I happened to know the identity of the cabinetmaker, Bullock. Well, I'll tell you. I made it my business to know. I realized he might prove a useful distraction, if it looked as if you were becoming more than a nuisance—as you have. Which is why, before he came to meet me here, my cousin stopped by Tichborne Street to make certain Bullock knows about the child. He's very angry with you, you know. He's sworn he'll take his revenge against both you and Alexi Sauvage."

"Damion Pelletan's son is safe." Sebastian took a step closer, then another. "Bullock will never get to him."

She gave a high, ringing laugh that echoed around the small chapel. The rain drummed on the roof and the gusting wind drove the torrent against the windows in waves. "I'm not talking about Noël Durant, you fool. What interest have I in a prince's bastard? I'm talking about *your* child. Your unborn child."

Sebastian drew up abruptly, a cold prickling running across his scalp.

"Bullock is going to kill it," she said with cold triumph. "The child and its mother both."

Sebastian took another step toward her. "I don't believe you."

"Then that is the greatest revenge of all, is it not?" she said, and slammed the heavy urn against his head.

The sharp edge of a silver handle sliced into his scalp, sending hot blood coursing down the side of his face. He put up an arm to fend her off, but she swung the urn at him again, her features distorted with rage and hatred and blind determination.

He flung her off, the blood in his eyes now. She stumbled back, off-balance, careening hard against the gallery's wooden balustrade. Sebastian heard the crack of breaking wood, saw the horror of comprehension flood her face.

The old railing gave way, the banister shattering. She scrabbled one-handed to catch herself. If she had let go of the urn, she might have saved herself. But she held on to it, falling backward into space with a cry of rage, her black skirts billowing around her.

"Mon Dieu!" screamed the priest as she slammed into the pavement with a bone-breaking smack.

The impact knocked the urn from her grasp, the rock crystal shattering against the pavement in a shower of clear, glittering fragments, the torn heart coming to rest just inches from her outflung hand. She stared up at the chapel ceiling with wide, sightless eyes. But Sebastian didn't even pause to make certain she was dead.

He was already running for the door.

Chapter 57

*P*aul Gibson sat with his back propped against the edge of the kitchen table, a smile crinkling his eyes as he watched Alexi fill the teakettle and set it on the trivet.

"I didn't offer you a place to stay to turn you into some one-legged Irishman's cook and housekeeper."

She looked up at him. The firelight gleamed through the glorious cascade of her hair in a way that made him think of misty sunrises and the first turning leaves of autumn. "Mrs. Federico will be back, just as soon as she feels she's made her point." She straightened and came to stand between his spread thighs, her hands on his shoulders, her gaze locked with his as she mimicked his brogue. "And what's wrong with a one-legged Irishman, then? Hmm?"

He rested his hands on her hips, still awed by the realization that she desired him, that she saw something of worth in him. He was desperately afraid she'd eventually realize he wasn't worthy of her, that she was driven more by a combination of gratitude and pity than by a recognition of deep affinity and the kind of loving respect that could endure.

"Alexi—," he began, only to break off at the sound of a knock on the front door.

"Well, go on," she said, moving away with a laugh when he hesitated.

He pushed regretfully to his feet. "That'll be Devlin, come for the results of the autopsy on that Haymarket jeweler."

Snagging a brace of candles, he limped down the passage to open the front door. Only it wasn't Devlin; it was Lord Jarvis's tall, intimidating daughter, a footman at her side holding an umbrella. A fine rain had begun to fall, driven in stinging eddies by a growing wind.

"Good God, Lady Devlin." Gibson took a quick step back. "Come in, please. Is something wrong?"

"Nothing's wrong," she said, giving her wet skirts a shake as she entered the narrow passage. She nodded to the footman, who closed the umbrella and darted back toward the waiting carriage. "I'd like to speak to Alexi Sauvage. Is she here?"

"I am."

Gibson looked over his shoulder to find Alexi standing with her head held high, her arms folded tight against her waist. The two women's gazes met, clashed.

"I won't keep you," said the Viscountess. "I've come to apologize for my rudeness. I accused you of the basest of motives, when your sole intent was to try to save the life of my child, and for that I am sorry."

Alexi came up beside him, her lips parted in surprise. "It worked? The babe turned?"

A strange smile played about the Viscountess's lips, and Gibson thought he'd never seen her look more approachable—or more likeable. "Yes. I don't know how to thank you, except to say . . . I'm sorry."

She turned to leave, but Alexi put out a hand, stopping her. "I was just making tea. Please say you'll join us."

The Viscountess shook her head. "I don't want to intrude."

"At least stay 'til the storm eases up a bit," said Gibson as the rain pelted down harder.

She hesitated, then gave a slow smile. "All right. Thank you."

He led the way to the parlor while Alexi disappeared into the kitchen. "When I heard your knock," he said, setting the candlestick on the chest near the door, "I thought it might be Devlin coming about Farragut's autopsy."

She went to stand before the fire, her hands extended toward the blaze. "Did you discover anything?"

"Just this, which I'll admit has nothing to do with the poor man's murder." He picked up one of the heavy, alcohol-filled specimen jars that lined the mantel. "It's a wee bit hard to see, I'll admit."

"What it is? It looks like a—"

She broke off, the color draining from her face as she stared beyond him, toward the doorway.

Breathing in a sudden stench of wet wool and fresh wood shavings and rank male sweat, Gibson turned, feeling as if he were helplessly caught in a dream spinning into an irrevocable nightmare.

Sampson Bullock filled the doorway, his hat and shoulders dark with rain, his features twisted into a triumphant sneer. He held Alexi before him, a hank of her fiery hair wrapped around his meaty fist, the blade of a butcher knife laid flat against her cheek. Her face was alabaster white, her throat working violently as she fought to swallow.

She was so small the top of her head didn't even come up to the massive cabinetmaker's shoulder, and Gibson felt his heart thump against his ribs, heard a strange roaring in his ears. His gaze locked with Alexi's and he took an unconscious step forward. "What the bloody—"

"Come any closer and the lady doctor here loses an eye," warned Bullock, increasing the pressure on the flat of the blade until it pressed into Alexi's face, distorting her features and drawing a trickle of blood high on her cheek.

Gibson drew up, his hands gripping the specimen jar so hard they hurt. He was suddenly, hideously aware of the rasp of his breath sucking in and out, the violent flickering of the candle flames eddied by a cold draft he realized must be coming from the open kitchen door.

"Who are you?" demanded the Viscountess.

"Don't ye know?" The cabinetmaker gave a jeering laugh that held no real humor. "Ye mean to say your husband, the high and mighty Viscount Devlin, didn't tell ye 'bout me?"

"His name is Sampson Bullock," said Alexi, her voice awe-inspiringly calm, "and he's here because he holds me responsible for his brother's death."

Bullock tightened his hold on her hair hard enough to make her wince as he pulled her head back at an unnatural angle. "Ye are responsible, ye bloody bitch. I told ye I'd make ye sorry ye ever stuck that Frenchie nose of yers where it don't belong. Ye sorry now, hmm? Thanks to you, yer brother's dead, and that woman of yers too. Now it's yer turn." He slid the knife away from her cheek to point it at Hero Devlin. "And hers."

Gibson took a slow, careful step forward, then another, the specimen jar still gripped in his hands. He was shaking so badly he nearly dropped it, his gait an awkward hobble.

"Damn ye; I told ye not to move," swore Bullock. He nodded to the specimen in Gibson's hands. "Wot the bloody hell is that?"

"This?" Gibson held up the jar. "It's a heart." His gaze locked with Alexi's. He tried desperately to convey to her what he intended to do even as he acknowledged that was impossible. He hoped that at least she understood to expect something.

He eased the cork from the jar's wide top. "It's quite oddly shaped. Want to see?" he asked, and dashed the contents in the cabinetmaker's face.

Bullock roared and reared back as the alcohol stung his eyes. He held on to the knife but let go of Alexi to swipe his big hand across his face.

Ducking beneath his arm, she snatched up the brace of candles from the nearby chest and thrust their flames against his coat.

The alcohol-soaked cloth caught with a *whoosh*, the flames leaping up to light his long black hair.

"Alexi!" screamed Gibson, terrified the flames would ignite the alcohol that had inevitably also splashed over her head and shoulders.

Bullock let out another bellow, turning blindly this way and that, sending his battered hat flying as he beat at his head and tried to tear off his flaming coat. "I'll kill ye!" he screamed. "I'll kill ye all."

Devlin's wife whirled toward the fireplace. It wasn't until she seized the poker with both hands that Gibson realized what she was about. Throwing all her weight behind it, she took a step forward and swung the poker at the cabinetmaker's head.

The solid iron bar smashed into the side of Bullock's skull with an ugly, bone-crunching *thwunk*. He went down hard, knocking over the end table as he fell, the flames leaping from his coat and hair to catch the tattered, alcohol-soaked carpet.

"Quick," shouted Gibson, stumbling and almost falling as he lurched toward the windows. "The drapes!"

Alexi got there first, yanking down the worn, heavy cloth in a cloud of dust and cobwebs. Hero Devlin tore off her cape, smoke billowing as she beat at the flames that were already crackling toward the door.

"Here!" shouted Alexi, flinging the drapes at the fire.

Together they beat and stomped until the last of the flames had died and the cabinetmaker lay in the midst of a black, charred carpet, his head a pulpy mess.

"I trust he's dead," said the Viscountess.

"Yes," said Alexi.

Their breath coming hard and fast, their faces flushed with heat and triumph, the three exchanged exultant glances that required no words to clarify their meaning.

Then a distant shout and the crash of the front door brought them around.

Devlin catapulted into the parlor, only to draw up short, his gaze jerking from his wife, to Gibson and Alexi, to the bloody, blackened corpse at their feet.

"What the hell?"

The Viscountess wore a strange, stunned expression that puzzled Gibson until he noticed the wet stain that soaked her skirts and spread across the carpet at her feet—a stain that had nothing to do with the alcohol he had thrown.

"Well," said Gibson with a laugh driven by giddy relief. "You may be a wee bit late to help take care of Mr. Bullock here. But at least you're in time to escort your wife home—quickly, I should think. From the looks of things, your babe has decided that now is a grand time to be putting in its appearance."

Chapter 58

Saturday, 30 January

The babe might have turned, but Hero labored hard all that night and half of the next day. At first, Sebastian helped her walk back and forth before the fire as the storm outside whipped wild gusts of wind and driven rain against the house. Then, when the pains came so hard and fast she could no longer walk, he sat beside her, her hand held fast in his. If he could have taken her pain into his own body, he would have done so. After a few more hours, he thought that if he could give his life to stop this endless, inhuman agony, he'd do that too.

And still the babe refused to come.

"Mother of God, why don't you *do* something?" he raged once at Alexi Sauvage sometime around midafternoon. Gibson had insisted on deferring to the French doctor, saying she'd delivered more babies in the past year alone than he had in his entire career. But as the hours dragged on and on, and Hero labored in grim-faced, silent endurance, Sebastian had to doubt his friend's wisdom.

The Frenchwoman looked at him, her own face flushed and etched with lines of exhaustion. "Your son will come when he is ready, my lord."

"First babes do have a habit of taking their own sweet time," said Gibson softly.

How much time? Sebastian wanted to scream. But somehow he swallowed it and plastered a facade of calm over a cold, soul-destroying terror.

Occasionally he could hear the voices of Hendon, Jarvis, and Lady Jarvis, waiting together in a tense vigil downstairs. Claire Bisette kept bringing food that Gibson and Alexi both ate with a hearty appetite that Sebastian found revolting. And then, just when Sebastian thought Hero could surely endure no more, Alexi said, "It's coming."

He couldn't look. And so he looked instead at Hero's face. And he knew that any man who'd ever arrogantly boasted of the male sex's superior strength, endurance, and courage had never watched a woman give birth.

"You did it, my lady," said Alexi, her voice thick with a rare emotion.

Hero clutched Sebastian's arm, her fingers digging deep into his flesh, her entire body shaking and heaving with exhaustion and triumph. "Is it all right? Please tell me it's all right."

She was answered by a lusty squall that brought a sting of tears to Sebastian's eyes, so that he had to bury his face in the sweat-soaked tangle of Hero's hair.

"You've a fine son," said Alexi, holding up a kicking, screaming infant smeared with a hellish mixture of blood and something white and waxy.

Hero gave a tired, shaky laugh, her arms opening wide to receive her son.

She lay smiling down at the screaming infant for the longest time, an expression Sebastian had never seen before softening her features. Then she looked up, her gaze meeting his, and he fell in love with her all over again.

"Told you it was a boy," she whispered. "The next one can be your girl."

Just the thought of putting her through this again made his legs suddenly feel weak, and he found he had to sit.

"Have you decided on a name?" asked Alexi.

"Simon," said Hero. After months of wrangling, they'd finally reached a compromise: She could name the boys, while he would name the girls. "Simon Alistair St. Cyr."

She shifted the babe to face Sebastian, so that he got his first really good look at his son. He had a head of thick dark hair plastered to his skull, but his eyes were screwed shut, his face contorted and flushed red with his howls.

"What color are his eyes?" asked Gibson.

"I don't know," said Hero. "He's screaming so hard I can't see."

And then, as if aware of the intense scrutiny directed upon him, Simon St. Cyr drew in a shuddering breath, ceased his cries, and opened his eyes.

"The Lord above preserve us," said Gibson.

They were yellow.

Tuesday, 2 February

The day dawned gray and blustery, the clouds heavy with the threat of more rain.

Paul Gibson stood beside the grave of Damion Pelletan. A small hole had been dug down through the grave's soft, recently filled earth. Alexi stood at his side, a small wooden box containing her brother's heart held in her hands. The wind whipped the hair around her head and flapped the black skirts of her mourning gown. Her face was pale but composed, her head held high. He wondered if she was praying, and realized he didn't even know this about her—if she believed in a God, or sought solace in her religion.

He'd asked her last night as they lay in each other's arms if she was truly certain that Damion Pelletan was her father's son and not the Lost Dauphin of the Temple. She'd looked at him quietly for a moment. Then her gaze shifted to someplace far, far away. She shook her head, her breath catching, and said, "No."

He supposed they'd never know the truth. Perhaps some questions were never meant to be answered. He wondered if anyone would ever know or even care how many millions had lost their lives in this endless war that raged from one end of Europe to the other. Some died filled with that oddly altruistic hubris known as patriotism; some died for glory or God or money to buy ale and whores; others for a dimly understood—or misunderstood—principle. But most died simply because they were in the wrong place, or because they were doing what they were told.

He figured arrogant men of overweening ambition and insatiable greed would always manage to convince or coerce others into dying for them.

He watched Alexi nestle the small wooden box containing Damion Pelletan's heart deep into the space that had been dug for it, then take a handful of dirt from the pile beside it and release it in a rush of falling earth.

Gibson nodded to the sexton, who began to fill the hole with heavy shovelfuls that quickly hid the box from their sight.

The heart of an uncrowned king or a simple physician's son; did it matter which they buried? Gibson wondered. He thought not, although he knew that for questions such as this wars were fought and men died, and other men such as he limped through life on mangled limbs.

They stood together side by side until the last of the earth lay heaped upon the grave and the sexton walked away. And still they stood, her hand creeping out to take his, their gazes meeting as the wind snatched at her hair and her lips curved into a trembling smile.

Author's Note

The district of St. Katharine's and the evocatively named Cat's Hole and Hangman's Court were real places that have now disappeared. In 1827, the old church and monastic buildings, along with the surrounding streets, were knocked down to create what is now St. Katharine Docks. More than eleven thousand poor people were rendered homeless by this early urban renewal project. Most were not compensated.

For a look at childbirth practices in England during the regency, see Judith Schneid Lewis's *In the Family Way: Childbearing in the British Aristocracy, 1760–1860.* Lewis's account is slightly skewed in support of her premise that the rise of male accoucheurs was a good thing; thus, she ignores the harmful effects of the abandonment of the birthing stool in favor of more "modest" delivery positions, and downplays the lives lost to heavy bloodletting and the disastrously reduced diet advocated for expectant mothers (particularly deadly for those such as Princess Charlotte, who suffered from porphyria). However, she does an excellent job of showing the extent to which upper-class women continued doing things such as attending the opera and giving dinner parties up to within hours of labor, and explodes many myths and misconceptions. Sebastian's presence at his son's delivery was normal;

Prince Leopold remained at Princess Charlotte's side throughout her fifty-hour ordeal. It was also typical for various family members to await a birth in a nearby room, as Hendon and Lord and Lady Jarvis do here.

Richard Croft was indeed London's most esteemed accoucheur at the time (he became "Sir Richard" in 1816 after the death of his elder brother). He attended Princess Charlotte's botched childbirth and tragically committed suicide after her death.

The English distinction between surgeons and physicians dated back to the Middle Ages, when most physicians were clergymen and the church forbade churchmen from engaging in the kind of activities practiced by surgeons. Interestingly, that distinction was not common on the Continent, where the medieval clergy had never dominated the practice of medicine.

The invasion of Russia in 1812 was a disaster for the French forces, and there was a real coup attempt against Napoléon in December that year. But Vaundreuil's peace delegation to London is my own invention.

The practice of burying the bodies of the French royal family at Saint-Denis and sending their internal organs to various other churches was well established. Most of these cardiotaphs were melted down during the Revolution, and their contents burned. However, some of the hearts were actually sold to artists. For example, the heart of Louis XIV was sold to the landscape painter Pau de Saint-Martin. Some speculate that the red coats of figures in the foreground of his *View of Caen*, now in the museum of Pontoise, owe their unusual pigmentation to the royal heart.

King Louis XVI of France, his Queen, Marie Antoinette, and their two surviving children, Marie-Thérèse and Louis-Charles, were in August of 1792 thrown into a tower of the Temple, a prison that was once the medieval stronghold of the Knights Templar (the building was later destroyed during the Restoration). Also incarcerated with them was Madame Elisabeth, Louis XVI's young sister, although

I have restricted references to her to avoid confusion. The King was sent to the guillotine on 21 January 1793, with the Queen following in October, and the Princess Elisabeth soon after. The summer before the Queen's trial, the little Dauphin was separated from his mother, aunt, and sister and locked in a separate cell beneath theirs.

The Dauphin, Louis-Charles, was just seven years old when first thrown into prison. By all reports he was a happy, healthy boy with chubby cheeks, who enjoyed the family's forced seclusion at the Tuileries because, as he once confided to a courtier, it meant he got to see so much more of his parents than he had at Versailles. His treatment in prison was actually worse than described here.

Interestingly, the physician who first treated the Dauphin, Dr. Joseph Desault, is reported to have said that the child in the Temple did not resemble the prince he had seen before the Revolution. Desault died suddenly on 1 June 1795 after hinting at dark deeds afoot. His wife insisted he had been poisoned.

After Desault's death, Dr. Philippe-Jean Pelletan was brought in to treat the boy. When the child died, Pelletan was brought back to the Temple to perform an autopsy. At the end of the postmortem, Pelletan did indeed wrap the boy's heart in his handkerchief and smuggle it out of the prison in his pocket. He preserved the heart in alcohol and kept it in a rock crystal vase in his study.

The history of the heart after that is long and convoluted. At one point, one of Pelletan's students stole the heart. The student soon died of tuberculosis, so Pelletan was able to retrieve the heart from the student's widow. After the Restoration, Pelletan tried to give the heart to Marie-Thérèse, and then to the newly crowned King Louis XVIII and to several other royals, but no one would accept it.

Finally, nearing death, Pelletan gave the heart to the Archbishop of Paris. The heart was in the Archbishop's Palace when it was looted by rioters during the Revolution of 1830. The crystal vase was smashed, and the heart thrown on the floor.

However, some days after the riots, Philippe-Jean Pelletan's son,

Gabriel, who was also a physician (the real Pelletan had two sons and a daughter; Damion and Alexi, however, are my own inventions), went to the palace with one of the rioters, a man named Lescroat, and is said to have found the heart amongst the debris. The heart was put into a new vessel and ultimately given to the Bourbon claimant to the French throne.

After that, the heart traipsed around Europe, from Spain to Austria and Italy, threatened repeatedly by war and destruction, before finally being entombed in 1975 at the Basilica of Saint-Denis outside of Paris, the traditional burial place of French kings. But controversy over its authenticity continued. Recent DNA tests on the heart have shown that, despite its shaky provenance, the heart did indeed come from a descendent of Marie Antoinette's Hapsburg maternal line.

However, that evidence is not as conclusive as it might seem, for (amongst other possibilities) Louis-Charles had an older brother, Louis-Joseph, who died in 1789. His heart was buried at Val-de-Grâce and lost during the Revolution. The Archbishop of Paris, to whom Philippe-Jean Pelletan gave the heart in his possession, also had in his collection another heart, said to have belonged to Louis-Joseph. So it is possible that during the riots of 1830, the hearts were confused. At any rate, the Dauphin's heart now has its own book: *The Lost King of France: How DNA Solved the Mystery of the Murdered Son of Louis XVI and Marie Antoinette*, by Deborah Cadbury.

Marie-Thérèse's ordeal in the Temple is much as described here. Whether she was raped in prison is not known, although most people at the time suspected or even simply accepted that she was. There are also letters in existence that hint at a resultant pregnancy. The most recent biography of the Princess Royale, as she was called, is Susan Nagel's *Marie-Thérèse: The Fate of Marie Antoinette's Daughter*. Nagel is a professor of humanities rather than a historian, and her book is frustratingly thin on footnotes. She is also extraordinarily sympathetic to her subject, which tends to color her account. But the story of this unhappy princess's life makes fascinating reading.

Napoléon did indeed refer to Marie-Thérèse as "the only man in her family," but the comment was made in 1815.

For years after her release from the Temple, Marie-Thérèse was besieged by pretenders claiming to be the Lost Dauphin. Very real plots had indeed been hatched to smuggle the boy out of prison and replace him with a dying deaf-mute, which naturally gave credence to the persistent belief that one of those plots had actually succeeded.

A gravedigger at the churchyard of Ste. Marguerite in the rue Saint-Bernard in Paris, to which the Dauphin's body was sent, buried the prince's body to one side and marked the grave. Later in the nineteenth century, that grave was twice dug up (in 1846 and 1894) and its contents autopsied. Both autopsies came to the conclusion that the remains were those of a boy who had indeed died of tuberculosis but who was older than ten at the time of his death. Those remains have never been DNA tested.

Hartwell House, owned by the same Lee family as that from which Robert E. Lee was a descendant, was indeed hired by the Bourbons, who essentially trashed the place. It is now a hotel.

Louis Stanislas, the portly Comte de Provence, reigned as King Louis XVIII of France after the Restoration until his death in 1824 (with a minor hiatus for the brief return of Napoléon from Elba). Provence's comment about the "ninety-eight percent," while sounding startlingly modern, was actually a point often made at the time. He was succeeded by his brother, the Comte d'Artois, who reigned as King Charles X. Charles's ultraroyalist, pro-Jesuit policies—encouraged by Marie-Thérèse—helped spark the Revolution of 1830.

Marie-Thérèse died childless in 1851 and is buried at the Franciscan convent of Castagnavizza in what is now Slovenia. She reigned as Queen of France for twenty minutes in 1830.

The small French chapel near Portman Square was real but is no

longer in existence. Originally dedicated to Notre Dame de l'Annon-
ciation, it was later renamed in honor of St. Louis. At one time, there
were some thirty bishops and eight thousand French priests living in
exile in London.

The outstanding authority on homosexuality in Georgian England is Rictor Norton. He has most generously published his material online, at http://rictornorton.co.uk. His articles on the molly
underground in London are fascinating and provided the background
for my portrayal of Serena Fox.

There actually is a legend about a Dark Countess who was re-
puted to be the true Marie-Thérèse. Known in German as the *Dunkel-
grafen* and in French as the Comte et Comtesse des Ténèbres, the
"Dark Counts" were a wealthy, reclusive couple who took refuge in
Thuringia. The man called himself "Count Vavel de Versay," but the
woman's identity was kept a secret. When the "Countess" died in
1837, she was buried with unseemly haste. The doctor who attended
her death reported that she appeared to be about sixty years of age,
which would have put her birth around that of Marie-Thérèse.

The count was eventually shown to be Leonardus Cornelis van der
Valck, a Dutch diplomat at one time attached to the embassy in Paris.
But speculation about the identity of his companion persists. Rumors
linking the Dark Countess to Marie-Thérèse began as far back as the
Princess's 1799 marriage to the Duke of Angoulême. The mysterious pair
are enduringly popular in Germany; there is even a Madame Royale His-
torical Society dedicated to them, complete with lecture symposiums.

A word about titles of nobility: While it might seem strange to
American ears, the wife of a duke's younger son would indeed be
known by "Lady His-First-Name," or Lady Peter. Likewise, although
logically one would expect Hero to be called "Hero St. Cyr," in conversation she would actually be known by her own first name combined with her husband's title, "Hero Devlin." Consider, for instance,
the famous "Sally Jersey," who was the wife of George Villiers, the
Fifth Earl of Jersey.